RECALLED

—

THE ADVENTURES OF
RHONE & STONE,

BOOK 3

BY

STRIDER S.R. KLUSMAN

<u>Recalled</u>

The Adventures of Rhone & Stone

book 3
Edition 1.2

Copyright © 2025 by Strider S.R. Klusman

Published by Duramen Publishing

Contact at: DuramenPublishing@gmail.com

ISBN: 979-8-9851196-8-8 (paperback)

ISBN: 979-8-9851196-7-1 (ebook)

ISBN: 979-8-9851196-9-5 (hardback)

Cover Art by: James T Egan, BookFly Designs

RECALLED

For the Joy

For the Joy of Reading

CHAPTER 1

Precursor

The building was old, so old that its mortar was dissolving, washed away by the more than common rains beating against the walls of the ocean-side retreat. What had once been a magnificent home had become a walled fortress, secure in its isolation and solitude. The tall stonework seemed to grow from the top of the rocky cliff as though it had been carved out of an even taller mountain and only made to look like the castle walls they really were. Leave it to say, they made an impressive statement, though few saw its wonders, for few came, and fewer wanted to—the whispered stories enough to keep strangers at bay.

The large room, tucked deep in the aged structure, had a chill to it that never seemed to leave, possibly the result of the stonework walls of the old mansion, but just as possible from the cold demeanor of its occupants. The very air of the almost vacant room seemed to vibrate with their open hostility as each glared daggers at the others, the backs of their elegant chairs standing as a backdrop to the five now quiet voices.

The five brothers sat glumly in their large and ornately carved chairs, their scowling faces belying the fact that they were brothers. Secure or not, the brothers were neither satisfied nor calm. They had been at this hastily called meeting for two days now, and none felt secure enough to leave. To do so would put their position in jeopardy, at least the jeopardy of losing their position in the ongoing struggle for dominance.

At the moment, Jared, the eldest, befitting his oversized belt and stout stature, waited for the dissent he knew was coming. There was always dissent. It didn't matter if it was simply a call for dinner. Someone would want it delayed, while another would invariably ask why it hadn't been served yet. It had always been this way, but had gotten worse after their father's death. Now it was often a stalemate, even with a vote of five. Sometimes numbers didn't count as much as the strength of the parties involved.

"We must come to some conclusion," Jared stated reasonably, and with less harshness than he actually felt. "We all have important matters to attend to. Now, what say you?"

Leaning forward, he pointed a meaty finger at the youngest, Mathias, a strong, lean figure in blackened leather garb that fit him like a second skin. His other brothers affectionately called him Snake, his slim and sleek profile seeming almost to slide from place to place rather than the average plodding walk of the others. But no one trusted him, nor for that matter their other brothers. They had learned that lesson well.

"You first," Jared announced. "You're youngest, and it's as good a place to start as any."

"Well, it sounds stupid to me," Mathias announced, eyebrow raised in an extravagantly pompous manner.

While still young enough to enjoy playing the game, he was old enough to know it could go sour at any moment. He played his part as they expected and knew it wouldn't be well received. But his words were never received well.

"It's a total batch of made-up data, supporting plans you already invested in, but found worthless. Now, you want our backing, taking our time and funds to cover your mistakes. Really though, it's nothing more than I would expect, and may Father turn over in his grave if I'm wrong."

Byron crossed himself, warding against possible condemnation as he cautioned, "No need to invoke the dead, Mathias. It will bring nothing but ill." Being a couple of years older than Mathias, Byron was number four in the lineup of succession, not that it meant much to anyone other than his brothers. The entire estate had been split between the five, each piece held with fingers of unrelenting iron.

It had seemed a simple and equitable equation. A five-way split of a very sizable estate was still a large sum. The problem was Father's 'charm'. His lucky talisman. The one that helped him create his massive empire that stretched into the very interior of the government itself. Not only was it land, but it was also the intricate machinations of politics that allowed him to realign politicians and, therefore, legislation. It was on that foundation that his own empire was built.

While it may not have been an empire of old, with territories, warriors, and slaves to do his bidding, it wasn't far off the mark, simply more civilized. A behind-the-scenes working of government and institutions, granting very similar powers and wealth.

But to the problem. Whitworth Pedderton, father to five, and unwilling to grant it to his unworthy sons, had smashed his own source of power, his talisman.

Having sworn that no other would have it, his last act had been to wield a heavy iron mallet, smashing the beautiful amulet. The resulting blow had not only shattered the stone; it had taken him too. His over-worn heart and shattered soul couldn't handle the blast of the stone's breaking, and he died instantly, the shattered talisman scattering across the stonework floor.

The resounding blast brought his sons at a run, but he was already gone.

Stunned and not understanding, they stood staring at the body lying heaped before the heavy iron anvil, the stone's shattered pieces glinting irresistibly from where they lay scattered, indiscriminately mixed with the dust and debris of the forge-room floor. The shock of seeing their father's body lying in obvious death only stalled the sons for a moment, until the eldest slowly stooped, picking up a shattered remnant glinting with an eerie light.

Suddenly, every brother dove to the floor, scratching through dirt and dust for the remains of the talisman. In near panic, they scooped dust and dirt through their fingers, looking for any piece that might have been missed.

Since their youth, the boys had been awed by the gemstone. They had seen their father speak to it as though it were alive, answering as though it spoke back. Each had thought their father somewhat dim-witted, supported in their belief by the others until it had become a joke among them. But now, at his final act, the possibility of its truth became a matter of survival, each wanting their share, their inheritance, and each jealous of their piece, tiny as it was.

As the eldest, Jared had years more training from their father, their mother having left long ago, unwilling to take second place to a luck charm. Stepping into his father's shoes, as they say, Jared attempted to recreate the invisible hold of power his father had so capably done.

With their futures bound together, the brothers created rings, settings for the broken pieces of their father's amulet. But even with the rings, they were not so adept. Their first attempt had gone poorly, almost getting them caught as they worked to steal government documents. With time, they had gotten better, taking the name The Brotherhood as a symbol of their bond, if not their love. Eventually, they disappeared from view, just another piece of forgotten history.

It wasn't until several years had passed that they began to understand the connection their father had with his luck charm. They began having dreams, then connections of their own. Truly, they were The Brotherhood, if with only a fraction of the power their father once held.

It was also the cause of the dissension, for as they soon learned, working in conjunction with another brought combined power. Unfortunately, jealousy of their own power kept them apart, keeping the pieces from uniting and giving away the secrets each held.

It was a difficult game, each brother attempting to get the better of the others, yet still needing to work with one another to overcome the influences of the rest.

Such were the games they played, and such were the disappointments.

The years had passed in unrelenting succession, their divisions and groupings coming and going, rearranging themselves at need or whim until no one trusted the other, and none would relent. Age had merely hardened their already hard hearts.

Age, however, seemed to have stayed time's unrelenting corrosion, for the five brothers showed only half the actual passage of time, their ill will and corrosive attitudes seeming to have paid off at least that much. Their luck charms were more than rings for show and profit. They had become bound to their very lives.

CHAPTER 2

First Contact

Rhone slumped tiredly in his saddle, worn out and bone-weary from his long trek. Even Blue's easy pace didn't make up for the ongoing miles that kept adding up, his rump feeling more like hamburger than solid muscle. He considered getting off and walking, but his legs said he'd already done that.

His youth had been spent running around the arid hillsides of Skragmoore, thinking nothing of an afternoon's climb to the top of the escarpment. He had even helped Mom cut the tops from the wild grasses growing in the upper meadow, using the grain for the bread she baked. But this was different. He was headed back to the Capital Stronghold, and if he had to admit it, he was grumpy. He had been recalled, ordered to leave the little harbor town of Corgy as quickly as convenience allowed, which wasn't convenient at all.

Carefully shifting his leg forward, Rhone eased the pressure away from the hot spot that had developed on his inner thigh, but even grumpy, tired, and sore, he knew the saddle was far more comfortable than going bareback. His days of sitting in the saddle made even the hard seat of a wagon sound like heaven, which would at least allow the use of a pillow. He knew. He had done it on his first trip to the city, but that was before becoming part of the workings of the OPR, a far quicker way to say, The Office of Public Recrimination—his employer.

Yep, he was an agent. A seasoned agent, now that he was returning from his very first, and supposedly easy assignment, which it wasn't. It was supposedly so easy that Aundrea, his boss, had sent him off by himself, although that too wasn't quite right since he wasn't really alone. He had Stone, his crystalline friend and collar-mate.

Very few knew of Stone. They saw him set in the hand-carved leather collar Rhone wore, but no one, other than Aundrea, knew what he really was. *Aundrea and Bella*, he thought regretfully.

Rhone drew a resigned breath, knowing that he himself was something most people didn't understand. To the people of Corgy, he was a highfalutin', wealthy aristocrat's son, strutting around in his fancy duds, wearing a jeweled collar only a king could afford. But it was a farce; a cover for the real reason he had been in Corgy.

That was before he uncovered the pirate problem hounding the town's shipping industry, or the mayor making it his personal duty to ensure Rhone was kicked out and sent home.

What the mayor didn't know was that Rhone was an agent, and new agent or not, he had taken it as his job to fix the town's problems.

Now he was being recalled. Why, he hadn't been told. Maybe it was the mayor, and maybe not, but return he would. He had been ordered, and it was his job to respond.

Rhone grumbled quietly to himself, his tired body having just about that much energy. He knew Corgy wouldn't be his station forever, but the unexpected recall had sent his life into a new spin, once again forcing decisions he didn't want to make. Hence the problem. He hadn't actually finished his tasks. Close, but not quite. He had developed a plan, created the method, and finally brought the pieces together, even fighting the grumpy mayor to get it done. Then, without warning, Stone had received the message from Jewel, Aundrea's own crystalline friend and partner. And since Aundrea was his boss, he was now on his way back, recalled without knowing why. It would be enough to make anyone grumpy.

"Have you been able to make contact?" Rhone grumbled, this time speaking to Stone riding snugly in the leather collar around his neck.

You know I have not, Stone replied silently, his words heard in Rhone's mind but not through his ears. *Perhaps you could sing or something? Take your mind away from the problems you have created.*

Stone was nothing if not practical. The beautiful golden-pink stone shone brightly in the light of the morning sun. He was positioned to protrude just slightly from the hand-worked leather of the collar, his location perfect to 'view' all that Rhone saw, adding energy signals from everything they passed, then transferring the data on to Rhone's more mundane sight. It was interesting having two views of the same thing, and had taken time as each learned to interpret the signals, creating a truly empathic relationship. It was one reason Aundrea had trusted sending Rhone out on his own, as she, too, had a partnered We, the name the crystalline entities called each other from their days as space-faring life forms.

But that was long ago. Even Rhone hadn't known about the We until almost two years ago. He sighed as he considered how that had changed his life. His escape from the badlands and his training at the OPR academy, done on his own without Stone's crystalline memory to offer answers. It had been their pact, allowing Rhone to gain the experience he needed. Now he was a full agent, rescued from his rugged and lonely past, which didn't answer his question. Why had he been recalled?

It had been difficult being forced to leave Bella with The Lady Luna, his new airship. He flinched at the memory, realizing he would have to remember to call her Captain Belle now. But Captain Black had been right. She had been the perfect replacement. No one knew the Luna better than she. After all, she had helped with the construction of not only the airship, but Bo, and BoToo, his original balloon creations. Just as importantly, she had helped him learn the skills needed for naval attack, using the playbook sheets drawn up by the very knowledgeable Captain Black.

So much for an easy first assignment.

His mind wandered, the doldrums of rhythmically clopping hooves bringing boredom as the long trek through the now-dark forest became a journey to be survived but not necessarily enjoyed.

Until Blue's unexpected snort, and his abrupt stop in the dusty roadway.

It wasn't all that unusual. Blue did pretty much what he wanted, but when Blue pawed the ground nervously, shaking his head with another sharp snort, it was almost as though he was giving a signal.

"What's up, boy? You need a break?" Rhone asked cheerfully, more than ready to stand on his own two feet for a while. After all, Blue had to be tired too.

Blue tossed his head in response, which obviously wasn't an answer, even if it was timely.

"Alright. I'm tired too," Rhone played along, enjoying the interaction of at least talking to something. Something other than his friend and collar-mate, who was usually grumpy.

As though the thought triggered a response, a sudden vibration from his collar announced Stone's weighted words.

Rhone, we might have a problem.

A chill shiver ran down Rhone's spine. He was a firm believer in Stone's warnings, especially since ignoring them had caused significant trauma, including Stone's theft and his own near-death, at least twice.

Straightening in the saddle, Rhone drew up the reins into a more action-ready position, glancing uneasily into the surrounding brush that crowded between the equally dense foliage of the moss-covered tree trunks.

"What do we have?" he asked aloud, too tense to think his words to Stone.

Blue has alerted to something. Are you prepared for action?

Glancing uneasily at the sword hanging from his side, Rhone mumbled, "Ahh, maybe?" but knowing it was almost useless to him.

With so many other things to worry about, he hadn't spent much time practicing his sword work. In fact, it hadn't been until after he'd fought the pirates that he had even carried one. Nor had flying an airship given him any opportunity, or need, to use it.

At least he had one now, even if the useless weight simply hung from his hip with his sincerest hope it wouldn't be needed.

The virtuous Captain Black, on the other hand, had carried weapons attached all over his body, looking more like a Christmas tree than a ship's captain. Not only did he wear them, he knew how to use them, having successfully fought in many sea battles in his career, even winning enough loot to design and build The Backwater Mistress, the slim-hulled Zebeck-styled vessel Rhone loved almost as much as his own.

Bella's own, he had to admit. The Lady Luna was no longer his.

He couldn't help the feeling of loss that came with the thought. Not only had he left his beautiful airship, he had been forced to leave his girl, though not by choice. Regardless, he was here, alone, facing whatever had caused Blue to alert.

Warily, he drew his sword. He might not use it well, but no one else would know that. Armed and determined, he at least looked like the fighter he wasn't.

One thing Rhone was good at was playing parts. The OPR had trained him for that, and he had successfully proven their belief in him.

Pretty much, except his penchant for continually breaking his cover story. Maybe he wasn't so good at keeping certain kinds of secrets, but when things got tight, he did what he had to and had come out on top.

Again, pretty much.

He was mulling over the issue when Stone's voice again rang through his head.

Rhone! its sound reverberating through his head much like a hammer striking an anvil.

Instantly, Rhone jerked into awareness, but too late. Blue's sudden lunge threw him off balance, his teetering body barely staying connected to the saddle. The sword, so recently drawn, quickly became a lost cause as it twisted from his grip, tumbling gracefully through the air to finally land, tip buried in the dirt bank of the roadway, if you could even call it that. The road had dwindled to slightly more than a trail's width since it entered the woods, maybe foretelling that of the few who entered, fewer continued, rethinking the wisdom of their journey.

But Rhone had no time to think about that particular issue as Blue's continued charge kept him unbalanced and unable to regain his seat. Floundering wildly, arms thrashing to regain his balance, he fought for some sense of order, his 'up' refusing to remain up.

While his valiant attempts may have looked comical, his wild sway was also timely as a crossbow bolt shot past, the shaft mere inches from his chest. Being skewered through-and-through like the proverbial shish-kebab would have put a quick end to his day's concerns.

With his right hand now free of the sword, Rhone grabbed awkwardly at the saddle's cantle and swell, frantically working to pull himself back into place. Swaying like a drunk, he struggled desperately to regain both his seat and his composure. Riding, much like swordplay, wasn't his forte, and while he could ride, he certainly wasn't a lifer. He simply hadn't had enough experience to do much more than loops around the paddock or follow along a good road, as his recent history had ordered. Even Blue was just a loaner from the OPR stables, although they had been together since his assignment and made a pretty good team.

He was just congratulating himself on staying with the saddle when a blow struck his chest, driving the wind from his lungs and tumbling him backward out of the saddle and over Blue's rump. A short moment later he struck the amazingly solid ground, his grunt upon landing expelling whatever air was left in his lungs, mixing it with the flying clods of dirt and leaf litter as he cartwheeled and rolled along the road. When he finally came to a stop, his body lay piled in a limp, undignified heap, covered from head to toe in detritus and dirt. So much for looking like a skilled fighter.

He also found that 'lights out' was more than just a saying.

It could have been minutes, or perhaps days, his slowly growing awareness unable to decide, but the one thing he did know was, this wasn't his best moment, the taste of dirt bringing that much awareness to the forefront. Even his groggy, pain-infused head told him dirt wasn't supposed to be eaten.

As the spinning in his head stilled and his mental darkness slowly turned lighter, Rhone began working his achy body in small disconnected flinches, first drawing an arm from under his piled body parts, then flexing his stiff fingers, happy to find them still attached. He moved gently, his head throbbing at every motion as animal-like sounds escaped unbidden through his gritted teeth.

He knew the sound well. His experience with falling down mountainsides, stone stairways, dying of thirst, and drowning in flash floods had all produced similar sounds, or so his foggy memory told him. Actually, this had become almost normal, which was in itself oddly comforting.

When a booted foot came into focus, he thought maybe this would be different, but then again, it wasn't the first time either.

"Uhhh—hgg," he managed, trying to vocalize a hello.

But the boot didn't offer conversation. It simply launched forward in an accelerated arc, and everything went black—again.

CHAPTER 3

Pandora's Box

The dim light of a small campfire reflected weakly off the surrounding bushes, providing barely enough light to see by. The huddled figure beside it was only viewable as a silhouette, its hunched form close to the flames, gloved hands stretched out to warm them.

Groggily, Rhone opened one eye while the other refused the effort, stubbornly remaining shut. His head throbbed, its staccato beat so intense he thought he would vomit. The taste in his mouth, however, said that was probably a moot point. Regardless, he controlled the feeling as he searched for clues.

The first thing he noticed was his bound hands, then his bound legs, the ache in his back telling him he'd laid there for some time. Not, however, long enough for the rock to have softened as it poked painfully into his ribs. He attempted to scooch into a slightly different position, but only succeeded in increasing the hammering pain in his head.

Needing to know more, he craned his neck for a better look—until a threatening wave of darkness forced him to stop. But no matter how tempting, he couldn't allow the sweet peace of blackness to claim him. He was an agent of the OPR, after all, and this was no way for a government officer to be treated.

Or perhaps it was... if they knew.

Silently, he cursed himself for his lack of awareness. This wasn't Corgy, or even Skragmoore. No. He was headed to the big city, and even he knew what the big city was like. He had been there during his academy years.

He was pondering the information when a thought came to mind. *How did they know I was here?* With no letter, and no warning of his arrival, they had still waylaid him as they would any ordinary traveler.

So much for my training, he thought morosely. Then another thought came to his creaking mind, and he wanted to kick himself for not thinking of it sooner.

Hey Stone, who are these guys?

But there was no answer.

With rising panic, he tried again, his query so strong he could almost feel the thought pulse from his head. But again, nothing. Slumping in despair, he realized Stone, his best friend and collar-mate, was gone, and once again, he hadn't protected him.

Stone couldn't do it for himself. He was a rock, for goodness' sake, not a person. Stone couldn't even move, except for slight vibrations. He wasn't a jumping bean after all. He was a rock . . . thing.

Rhone slowly came to the realization that his mind was rambling, not thinking concisely as Stone had taught him. He had only been a country kid until Stone taught him how the world worked; of science and math, of how to calculate and design. They had built Bo and BoToo, and with Bella's help, they had then built The Lady Luna, their monstrous balloon airship. But none of that helped him now, tied as he was, beaten and waiting for who knew what.

Worse, if that was even a concept here, he couldn't report for his recall.

Finally, the bite of the ropes left his conscious thoughts, as despondent and aching in pain, he again drifted away into darkness.

Minutes, hours, or perhaps days later, he became aware of a warmth like a blanket on a cold night. He knew he was cold. His body told him that much, as it complained in earnest when he attempted to move. But hurting from one end to the other had become almost normal, certainly nothing unusual. Why was it that his excursions never seemed to end the way other people's did? He heard people talk, telling of their exciting travels, of the beautiful things they had seen and done. Of hiking, of trips by boat and carriage. Of great food and unique art. But his trips tended to bring somewhat more painful memories, which didn't seem fair. Then again, who said life was fair?

At least he had gotten out of Skragmoore. That in itself was a win since he hadn't ended up as a dead husk lying forgotten in the middle of the puzzle-work passages of the badlands. No, instead, he was lying almost dead, hidden away somewhere in the dense woods in the middle of nowhere, as though that was much better.

At least the sun was warm, which he cracked open his eye to verify, not the scalding, blanket-heavy heat of his old home. That was indeed something to be thankful for.

Thankful, yes, but it didn't make the pointy rock poking into his ribs any softer.

Rhone squirmed and squiggled, grumbling under his breath as he tried to correct the problem. But in his position, hands tied behind his back, knees bent before him, it was hard to do anything more than squirm. Nor did it help that both hands and feet were swelling, fighting to move blood past their bonds. It also brought recognition that their feeling had long since stopped, making him more worried than grateful.

"Ahh…, hello?" he croaked, his mouth tasting like mud and saliva thoroughly mixed with whatever else had been in his mouth.

"Good. You're awake," came a muffled voice. "I thought the cold and hard ground might have been enough to finish the job for me."

That didn't sound good, and Rhone attempted to turn his head, but pain brought a quick stop to the movement. Then he tried speaking again, spitting futilely to help clear his mouth.

"Ah, should I ask what you want? I don't have much, but maybe I can offer something?"

"Aren't you a funny boy," came the reply, followed by a scornful chuckle. "You say, 'I don't have much', yet your collar has a stone bigger than the one owned by the Prince of Arabia. You don't lie very convincingly, you know. On the other hand, you'd already be dead if it hadn't been for the collar, so let's talk. It might be profitable, or at least entertaining."

A shadowy figure stepped into Rhone's view, its well-worn cloak almost absorbing the fire's dim light, but left just enough to show the leather yoke that held it in place.

"Nice cloak," Rhone muttered, trying to be decent to the scum who had him tied. It felt like the right thing to do.

"Thank you. It is nice, isn't it?" the voice answered. "Took it off a dead man a while back. Didn't think he needed it anymore."

The voice had a strange clarity to it—muffled, yet understandable. A mask, probably. That fit. Bandits always hid their faces, didn't they?

Rhone clawed through the fog of his aching head, searching for answers his mind refused to give. In the academy, they'd taught him to listen for truth beneath the sounds, to catch the lie between the breaths—but his skull throbbed, and the lesson slipped out of reach. Stone would've known.

The thought of Stone sent a fresh spike of pain, sharper than the rest. But this was his fight now. He had to survive it alone. Then he would find Stone. They were a team after all.

"So you have my collar?" he asked, putting as much cheerfulness into the question as he could muster.

He knew it was a stupid question—it didn't just slide off by itself—but he needed information. Every hostage situation hinged on information, and even if he was the hostage this time, the principle was probably the same. What he needed was a plan and a good story to work with. Luckily, he was pretty good at coming up with stories. The hard part was remembering what you had told someone, so you wouldn't expose yourself later when you said something else that didn't fit.

It was harder than it sounded, but with Stone's help, he had managed to keep things in order. Had—since this time he didn't have Stone.

When his tormentor didn't answer, Rhone tried again. "Were you hoping for something in particular? I honestly don't have much. In fact, I don't even own the horse. It's a loaner. I work for a living and was on my way back from a job when I bumped into you."

"That nag? I actually feel better hearing it. A collar like yours, and you choose **that** animal? Why, you should be shot full of holes."

"Hey, Blue's a good horse!" Rhone complained, feeling more than a little jealous for Blue. "He may not be a blue blood, but he has a big heart, and we get along just fine." The horse had indeed done well by him, allowing him to learn to ride, hauling goods back and forth, and even pulling wagons. "He's a good boy," Rhone said defensively.

"But not, as you say, a blue blood. Nothing a person with a collar like yours would have. So that leaves me wondering, who are you, and what might I get as a ransom? No ransom, no life."

It was a cold statement, but one Rhone believed. He wouldn't even be missed, since almost no one knew he was here. Let alone right here, wherever that was. Then his academy training jostled a memory. *When in doubt, change the subject.*

"Ah... If you wouldn't mind. I have a question before you do anything irreparable."

When he received a snort for an answer, he decided to go for it. He wouldn't be any worse off for asking.

"What in the world did you hit me with? I mean, I thought I had gotten away clean. Then, WHAM. I'm on my back and out cold." The mere mention of the staggering blow was enough to make his back cramp.

The cloaked figure chuckled lightly before answering. "I'm almost sorry to say it, but I didn't do a thing. You took off like a bat out of hell. Dodged my crossbow bolt and practically vaulted back into the saddle. Best riding I've seen outside of a circus. Then, unfortunately for you, you ran headlong into a low limb. Knocked yourself right out of the saddle. Shoot, I couldn't have planned it better myself." The chuckle had turned into an all-out laugh, but it was light laughter, not the deep resonance of a man.

Rhone felt like kicking himself as the understanding hit. He'd been beaten by a girl.

Then realization overran his pride, recognizing it didn't make much difference who pulled the trigger. The bolt would still hit wherever it was aimed. In this case, it had been him. Besides, he'd been beaten by females before. MaryEllen had bested him cleanly at his testing, a thought that brought a weary smile to his bruised lips. Female or not, he would have to tread lightly.

"So, you don't like my horse?" he began again, wary now and trying to keep the conversation going, yet without putting too much stress on the situation. The longer he talked, the longer he lived. Besides, knowledge was power, and at the moment, he had no knowledge or power, which didn't bode well for his future.

"Oh, the horse is just fine," she answered in a bored voice—something he didn't like the sound of. "So, thank you. Nice of you to stop by and drop him off. I can always use another horse, even if it's just to eat. You, I'm almost sorry to say, won't be needing him."

"But...I thought we were talking ransom?" Rhone responded cautiously. "Dead, and I'm not good for much more than fertilizer."

"But you just told me you weren't good for much. So why should I disagree?"

Rhone realized this wasn't going well and wished he had paid better attention during Hostage Negotiations class. He had depended on Stone, which worked great, but definitely had its downsides when he wasn't there.

"What I meant was, I'm not a guy to be owning a collar like the one I was wearing. It is mine, yes, but it's all I have."

"Had," his keeper said dryly. "It's mine now."

"Had," Rhone admitted, his sigh long and deep. *And where are you anyway,* he sent, hoping to hear Stone's ever-present voice barge into the conversation. When it didn't, he resigned himself, knowing it was up to him. "I hope you're keeping it safe. People like to wander off with it, I'm afraid." Which was far too true.

"I don't think I'll have that problem. Not many get out this far," came her now obviously bored response.

This far? He already knew they were isolated, but it was knowledge, and more than he had a moment ago. While there might not be anyone to help him, it could also mean there was no one to help her. A one-on-one is almost always better odds than a dozen-to-one, so maybe there was hope.

Buoyed by the thought, he tried again. "Okay, you have my horse and my collar. So what next? You want my pants?"

The words hadn't left his mouth before he knew it had been the wrong thing to say.

"You think pretty highly of yourself, don't you?" she responded, smirking as she eyed him up and down.

"Ahhh...I don't know about that," he said hesitantly, and feeling terribly vulnerable. "I'd just as soon keep my hide, and my pants." He had to find a way out of the situation, but her low snicker made his worries double.

"That's too bad, since I decided I'll take your recommendation and your pants. They're nice leather too, now that I'm looking, and I like the buckles. It's been a long time since I had anything that nice." A moment later, she added, "Strip!" her words forceful, and no longer entertained.

Her tone left no doubt she would enforce the issue, but Rhone wasn't in the mood to agree. At least not right off.

"What? Strip?" he asked guardedly. "Out here? But I don't have anything else to wear." It wasn't exactly true, since he did have a second pair wrapped up in his bedroll behind the saddle, but he wasn't going to tell her that.

The lady bandit slid back the hood on her cloak and bobbed her eyebrows alluringly. "Too bad, isn't it? Just try not to get sunburned. I hear it hurts."

Rhone blinked as her mass of dark hair cascaded from the confines of the hood, tumbling onto her shoulders in a fascinating disarray. *Not half bad, even for her age,* he thought to himself. Then, realizing his thoughts, called himself a fool, knowing Stone would never have let him forget this.

And where was Stone? That was the truly important question.

Coming back to topic, he asked, "Ah, excuse me, but how am I supposed to get my pants off when I'm tied like this?"

He would have waggled his fingers, but they weren't answering at the moment and would probably be useless for a long time even if they were freed.

"Would you mind untying my hands? I lost feeling in them a long time ago. My feet too, actually. I couldn't run away even if I tried."

Which was all too true. Even his rump was numb now that he was sitting up.

"You're too much," she replied with another snicker. "Pretty soon you'll be asking me to cart you to your own house so you can grab another pair."

"Hey. That sounds pretty good. This pair's dirty now anyway," Rhone agreed cheerfully.

He still had some faith in female morality and was beginning to have a little hope. Maybe if he played his cards right, he wouldn't get shot and left in the woods to rot.

Her response, however, wasn't what he had hoped for, nor was it a picture he was interested in viewing.

"And what if I'd rather have you running around without your pants?"

Rhone grimaced, a reaction that was actually his failed attempt to grin. At least she seemed to be having fun with the conversation, which was undoubtedly better than his being dumped into a deep ditch and covered with dirt. Scrunching his skinned nose, he mumbled, "Maybe we should get back to the ransom."

Like hanging and swordplay, this was serious stuff, a fact that reminded him he no longer had his sword.

"Maybe," she offered, "but I thought the other would at least be a diversion. I do get tired of digging all those graves. There must be dozens out there by now. Hardly any open space left."

"Yeah, now there's something we can agree on," he stated, looking for some sign of agreement. While it might, possibly, be a lie, she had indeed been good at the ambush thing. "Besides, not killing me means no grave digging, and I'm thinking, maybe I'm not worth the worry? You already have my horse, my collar, and my sword, and that's a pretty good take as far as I can see."

"And I'll bet you can't see very far with that eye all puffed up like it is."

Her wordplay was contagious, but Rhone knew it could change in a blink, even if he couldn't. He also knew he had to focus.

"You know, if you keep me around, you'll have to feed me too, or I won't be worth anything for a ransom." *If it ever comes*, his mind added, but why tempt fate? "Oh, and the pants stay," he finished.

At least his captor was smiling, humored as she was by her bound prisoner. "Pretty high demands for someone all tied up. Maybe you need to be gagged too, if just so I can take a nap in peace."

Rhone's academy-trained ears heard the signs. She was beginning to tire of the conversation.

Quickly changing tactics, he gave it his best. "Tell you what. Untie me, and I'll see you get that ransom. And . . ." he added, noting the instant change of humor, "You can keep the horse and sword. Unfortunately, I need the collar. Technically, it belongs to the OPR, and I have to return it. You do know of the OPR, don't you? The Office of Public Recrimination? That's who I work for. They're expecting me, and I'm already late."

It was pretty much his last hope.

Unexpectedly, his mention of the OPR brought an instant change to his captor. "Oh, crab-apples," she groaned, dropping wearily to a seat, her soft comment filled with consternation. "You work for the OPR? Shoot, everybody knows about them. They're the only reason this country manages to work."

Even through swollen eyes, Rhone saw her doubt and maybe fear too. There was a question here, and whether or not his life was hanging in the balance, he was an agent, and it was time for answers.

"You know the OPR?" he asked cautiously.

"Of course I do, stupid. I wasn't born yesterday." Her mood had suddenly turned surly, and she began nervously chewing on a strand of loose hair that had come undone.

"Sorry. I didn't suppose you had. But . . . would you mind untying me?" he asked, his grimace more than a put-on. "I really will lose my hands if they don't get some blood soon."

His hands had swollen into what he was sure were puffy white sausages, deep indentations showing where the rope had cut deeply into the swollen tissue.

"Shut up and quit whining," she commanded, jumping up and pulling a shiny double-edged dirk from a leg sheath. "I don't want to hear a peep out of you."

He watched as she stalked toward him, his panic growing with her every step. With a frantic edge to his voice, he croaked, "You know, I think they'll be just fine! I—I can talk less, too, if that's what it takes."

He tried squirming away, but hadn't scooted more than an inch before the seat of his pants caught on something, tipping him onto his side. With his hands and feet tied as they were, he landed on a shoulder, rolling face-first into the dirt. Belly down and totally vulnerable, he wrenched himself sideways, muscles screaming in protest as he swung his head to see her.

"Didn't I say to keep quiet, or aren't you aware of what shut up means?" she demanded, her stance wide as she glared down at his prostrate form.

With no more warning than a smirk, her long knife swept out in a wicked arc.

CHAPTER 4

And Once Again

Tied as he was, Rhone could do no more than flinch as the glinting blade swept through the air, then he felt a momentary tug before the knife completed its arc and slipped smoothly back into its sheath. He blinked twice, afraid to look at where his entrails would be slipping out of his abdomen. He had cleaned enough rabbits and grouse to know what it would look like, and knew the knife must have been incredibly sharp to have cut so cleanly. But he also knew that really sharp knives could cut deep without you even realizing you'd been cut.

Bound as he was, he couldn't do more than lie there.

At least it had been painless, and his surprisingly calm thoughts went to Aundrea, and how she would never know what happened. Then to Bella, and the sinking loss at never seeing her again.

He knew he was drifting into a shocky awareness of his coming death, but the thought of dying brought his mind back into focus, and the recognition that pain would be coming soon. Even cuts from sharp blades would begin to hurt before long.

Steeling himself, Rhone glanced bravely toward his belly.

The view of the severed end of a slim brown snakelike thing slithering to the ground made his stomach react and he almost retched, knowing he was seeing his intestines slipping out of his body. Then confusion took hold. The brown thing hadn't been his entrails. It had been the rope, severed as cleanly as if it had been thread.

He couldn't help but be awed by the blade's sharpness.

Confused, Rhone raised his eyes to the cloaked figure, the slope of her drooping head showing her depression as much as the draping hood that now covered her face.

Then the muffled sound of her stress-filled voice reached him. "Freakin' frog legs and flapjacks," she mumbled, her curse seeming more of self-chastisement than at him. "Why this? It's been nearly two decades, but now it comes back to haunt me. I could have gone anywhere. Done anything. But no. I stayed, stupidly believing it would just go away. Now it's back, and the damnable OPR finally found me."

It wasn't depression. It was defeat. But why? He hadn't done a thing, other than walk into an ambush and talk his way out of being killed. It simply didn't make sense.

Realizing she was no longer paying him any attention, Rhone began wiggling his hands and feet, freeing them from their binding ropes. Then the tingling burn of returning circulation began, unpleasant, but far better than losing them.

Somewhere during the process, his captor had pulled a hip flask from inside her cloak and popped the stopper, downing a generous swallow of whatever was in the little bottle. Then holding it in both hands, she sat staring at it as though it had brought her to this despicable state, but not blaming it.

"Are you all right?" he asked cautiously, feeling a surprising amount of concern. She had planned on killing him, but it hadn't happened, and now she sounded like she could use a friend. "I want to thank you for cutting me loose. I owe you one," and actually meant it.

When his words brought no response, he shrugged and began massaging his still-numb legs with equally numb hands, keeping a furtive watch on her as he worked. When he could finally stand, he tried a stiff hobble, feeling like the man on stilts he'd seen in the big city. With studied effort, he attempted his own—more typical length appendages, his stilted gait taking him in staggering steps toward the log where she sat.

"By the way, my name's Rhone," he managed, grimacing as he eased himself awkwardly onto the log, sitting close, but not too close, to his cloaked captor. "I'd like to thank you again for cutting me free." When she still didn't respond, he tried one last time. "What I'd really like to know is, what's going on?"

"Why don't you make like a tree, and just leave?" she growled, his request rousing her ire once again. "I don't need the OPR snooping around, causing even more problems in my life. I've got plenty of my own."

Having suspected as much, Rhone didn't take offense. "Did you have a run-in with them? Is that why you're upset? I suppose, being an outlaw could bring retribution of some kind, especially if you went against some policy they were trying to fix."

He didn't want to give false hope where none was due, but the OPR weren't police.

"I am an outlaw, I suppose," she answered. "But I only do this to stay alive. Certainly not by choice," which was not the answer he had expected.

"But . . . isn't there something else you could do?

"Like what? Like be an agent?" she snapped. "I *was* an agent, dumbhead, and you had better keep a heads-up or you'll be right where I am."

Rhone stared in total shock. "You were an agent?" he asked dumbly, though it would explain why she was so good at what she did. She was OPR trained.

Still numb with disbelief, he stumbled on. "I don't understand. What happened?"

She paused, then in frustration asked, "Are you just stalling for time, waiting for your legs to limber up so you can run off—or do you really care?"

Rhone held his face immobile knowing it was at least partially true. Some feeling had returned, but it would be a long time before he could actually make plans for a getaway.

Shrugging, he allowed both answers. "Since I am an agent, I would like to know what happened. I figure, if it could happen to you, then as you said, it could happen to me. Honestly, I would prefer to see it coming than to get blindsided."

"First smart thing I've heard you say," she admitted grudgingly. "They aren't after me for something I actually did, although I have gone a bit rogue lately. Still, I doubt I'm worth the trouble."

Now Rhone was more confused than ever. If she hadn't done anything, then why would she be worried? And didn't all crooks say that? But the truth in her voice made his interest grow.

"And no doubt, you're wondering why," she stated, hands on hips as she scowled, brows merging in a knot of frustration. Then, taking a long... deep breath, she let it out in an even longer sigh. "Listen carefully, pup. The better you are, the bigger your enemies become, not that it's planned that way. It's more like, the better you get, the bigger the problems you get put to."

"Sure," Rhone agreed. "We always put our best people on the worst problems. It just makes sense."

"It does. But what happens to those people when things go bad? Ever think of that? It only takes one slip to fall from a mountain."

Rhone flinched, knowing exactly what she meant. He had climbed the cliffs around his home since he was a kid, and had fallen more than once. One missed step, or a hunk of bad rock crumbling underfoot, and you'd be sent tumbling.

"So what happened?" he asked again. "This seems like a long fall from the OPR."

After a moment without an answer, he tried again. "I know this may be a bit personal, but do you have a name? I mean, of course you have a name, but what should I call you?"

Her look said, 'Don't call me,' but she shrugged in annoyance as she changed her mind. "I'm Lev, and it's a long story."

"Lev. That's nice," Rhone said, smiling as he realized he had just won the round.

"You think so? Most people just say, 'Wow, that's a weird name,' and leave it at that."

"It might be, but I wouldn't know," Rhone acknowledged. "I don't know much about the world, and names are just one of those things. I've never met many people. Maybe fifty in my whole life, so it sounds fine to me."

Lev looked at him questioningly but decided he wasn't a threat. Relaxing, she pushing back her hood.

The morning sun sent piercing beams through the surrounding trees, glinting off the jet black of her hair, a perfect complement to her dusky complexion. Her dark brown eyes seemed almost sorrowful in her slightly weathered face, a fact that surprised Rhone.

She must be close to Aundrea's age, he decided, but without the embellishments life in the big city could give. Honestly, she looked more tired than anything else.

Trying not to be caught staring, he changed subjects. "I grew up with my mom outside a very small town called Skragmoore, but I'm sure you've never heard of it. It's a long way from here."

"Skragmoore? Near the badlands?" Lev asked, the mere sound of the name setting new worry lines on her face.

Rhone's startled expression gave her all the answer she needed.

"Few do," she nodded in acknowledgment. "I know something of it, but I've never been there myself."

Rhone had been warned many times not to speak of his past. It could bring consequences he couldn't foresee, and as he had learned, knowledge carried power.

"So you've never been there, but you know of it?"

Lev sighed, realizing he wouldn't let the matter drop.

"It was a good friend of mine," she began, weighing how much to reveal. "He'd been dismissed from his office and sent there as an outcast—defiled and belittled for something he didn't do. My guess is the governing body of The Council decided a scapegoat was better than accepting the blame themselves, so they stripped him of title and rank and exiled him to Skragmoore."

She paused a moment before continuing.

"That was almost twenty years ago, but I remember it well. I was caught up in the same turmoil and dismissed too—though not exiled. Just dumped without retirement, backing, or recommendation for other work. I survived as best I could, and now here I am, brought low by the backhanded, behind-the-scenes control of The Council and the silent Brotherhood."

"The Brotherhood?" Rhone whispered, the name stirring a memory.

Aundrea had mentioned it once. Her search of the archives for references to gems had led her to a story about a brotherhood—never confirmed, only hinted at. Yet here it was again.

"You're saying, The Brotherhood had something to do with Skragmoore? That sounds pretty slim."

"True. Probably not Skragmoore itself," she agreed. "I'm sure it was just a convenient and out-of-the-way place to dump their offal. You know, out of sight, out of mind. And since no one goes there, no one would remember, and soon, no one would care."

It made sense, but it made him wonder. He knew most of the names from Skragmoore. So who could it have been? But actually, it could have been anyone, if they'd even stayed.

Still, the question lingered, and Rhone rubbed his bruised forehead as he considered her story. It was indeed interesting, but it didn't excuse her actions.

"So you just decided to use your OPR training to attack people instead of defending them? Doesn't sound right by me," he said critically, though trying not to sound so. Actually, he was incensed at the thought, but it only took one look at her wretched face to know there must be more to the story. "Sorry, it wasn't very thoughtful of me," he apologized. "I guess I jumped to conclusions."

Her shallow nod said he had guessed right.

"I was married then," she mumbled quietly. "My husband was killed by a band of brigands not long after we left the city, and I swore never to put my faith in someone else again. No one would own me like The Council did, telling me what to do and where to go. I was one of their own, and they didn't take care of me. They were done with me and dumped me like trash!" she said savagely, her words like salt on an open wound, which undoubtedly they were.

Rhone stared at nothing as he tried to get his mind around it. "I don't know, but it still doesn't sound right. The OPR should have taken care of their own, especially the good ones." He had no doubt she had been, and swore to check on it. "Lev, I'm sorry about everything, especially your husband. It must have been hard," he offered, his voice softening as he sided with her.

Lev sniffed, her shoulders slumping as a single tear made its way down her cheek.

"He was a good man. Not OPR, but a good man," she mumbled, pain filling her quiet voice. "He worked with fine metals. Things of bright steel, silver, and brass. Intricate things, like clocks and the newer machining for the gadgets you find everywhere now. Not out here, of course, but in the big city."

Now it was Rhone's turn to nod, remembering the odd items people wore like clothing but were actually tools to do all sorts of tasks. He had even owned one, a calendorium that told the time, season, weather, and moon phases, but he had given it as payment to Captain Black for training him on how to sail. It had been a good trade, and helped his designing The Lady Luna. The Lady Luna that was no longer his, he reminded himself.

"So he worked with machinings?" he asked, intrigued despite knowing it might be a poor subject right now. "Did he design them, or just make the parts?"

Luckily, Lev didn't seem to mind. Maybe being able to talk about her husband, without the hatred it normally brought, was healing. She spoke proudly, allowing her long-held love to show.

"He did the design work too, and he was so good at it. Honestly, the pieces were beautiful and highly prized throughout the Stronghold and beyond. They weren't just functional. They were works of art. Here, let me show you."

Throwing back the draping fold of her cloak, she drew a fine chain from around her neck and held it up for Rhone to see.

Rhone stood open-mouthed as he gazed at the likeness of a tiny dragon clinging to the chain, its wings folded tight against its back, its tail curled along its body. The little creature was exquisitely detailed. Flowing lines of scales lay etched into the metal, the muscles and delicate feathering of the wings worked with astonishing care.

As he leaned in for a closer look he sucked in an astonished breath.

Tiny gears and articulated pieces formed the miniature creature, so cleverly worked into its design that they seemed less like machinery and more like part of the creature itself.

"It's gorgeous," he muttered, hardly able to speak as he gazed at the intricate piece.

Lev beamed at his praise, eyes sparkling with emotion. "Watch. It gets even better," she whispered, and with careful, loving hands, she gently drew the tail away from the body.

Slowly—like a butterfly emerging from its chrysalis—the fairy-like wings unfurled, quivering lightly as they spread from the tiny figure.

"Oh-my-gosh!" Rhone exploded, his face a picture of wonder. "I've never seen anything so perfect. It's a masterpiece!"

Reverently, he held out a finger to touch the dragon, but stopped mid-move, looking to her for permission.

Lev smiled as she nodded, happily lifting the little mechanical sculpture toward him.

Rhone was almost afraid to touch the gossamer wings with their delicate ribbing of fine netting. Instead, he chose the smooth metal of the thin arching neck, finding it as warm as her living body. A moment later, he blushed in embarrassment, realizing it had been inside her blouse, with her heat becoming its own.

Lev's smile took on an almost haunted look as she folded the tiny dragon's tail back against its body, the wings collapsing and tucking smoothly into their resting place. One would never have known the little creature wasn't simply asleep as it hung by the fine silver chain.

Rhone looked up to Lev's proud eyes, blowing out an appreciative whoosh of air.

"Thank you," he said gently, not sure how to give his thanks in a way she would understand. She had already given back his life, and now she had given him a view of what could be.

Bo, BoToo, and Luna had been great creations, truly wonderful, teaching him that he could achieve whatever he could conceive, but now he had something new to work toward.

Creation for perfection.

CHAPTER 5

Not What it Looks Like

Rhone drew back with an audible sigh, his eyes lingering on the tiny metal creature. "Your husband was a true master," he said needlessly, repeating words he'd already said.

"He was, and my world will never be the same," Lev agreed, her sadness marring her dusky complexion. "I'm afraid I went a little mad after that. I fought my way through the brigands, which wasn't all that difficult for someone trained by the OPR. But my husband wasn't. He was a master craftsman, not a swordsman. We fought side by side, but he was no match for them. When he took a sword to the chest, I watched him fall, his last words... 'I'm sorry,' whispered to me as he dropped." Lev's lips quivered as her eyes moistened, the long-past picture rerunning through her mind.

"I went berserk after that. I slashed my way free, doing everything I could to damage them body and soul. I screamed and raved, beating my justice into their bodies. But some freedom it turned out to be. I became as bad as they were." Her breath caught as she reviewed her recent life, wishing it were different. "I have no idea how many men

I've killed. Men who won't go home to their own loved ones. I simply quit caring, then quit counting."

Rhone couldn't help but feel for her. She had been wronged, and admittedly done wrong, but he still felt guilty somehow and didn't know why or how to express it.

"Lev . . . I'm so sorry. It's a horrible story and shouldn't have happened, but . . . maybe I can help, if you'd like," he said hopefully. "Especially if The Council was behind your dismissal. That's another long story, but I do know something about them. Not much, but I know someone who might."

Lev's face wore a look of discouragement and disappointment—but of herself not of him. She had accepted him as a confidant, not a prisoner or enemy.

She hadn't said anything, but Rhone felt her hope, as he asked, "Lev, I have a boon to ask. I'll do what I said, but I'll need my collar back. It's hard to explain, but you could say it's one of the tools I'll need to get it done."

His pleading eyes probably explained it better than his words, and Lev snorted at his audacity. "Might as well ask for all your stuff then. Honestly, I don't need another sword, and I'd just have to feed the horse. Shucks, I can't eat the collar either, and it's too valuable for anybody in the area to trade for. I'll end up going hungry either way." She shrugged, almost like a friend, before sighing in defeat. "Shoot, I've lost so much now, what's a bit more?"

"Wait—You really will?" Rhone asked, totally surprised by her agreement. "Honest, Lev. I promise I'll do everything I can, but I do need the collar," he said, glancing around as though expecting to see it hanging from the nearest branch.

Lev shook her head with a snort. "Yes. Besides, your Blue is eating me out of house and home. He does like his grass, that one." Her voice was still grumbly, but her smile said she was happy with the way things were headed.

Rising, she twitched her head to indicate direction, expecting him to follow.

Rhone followed at an awkward hobble, his hands and feet still stiff and unreliable, far from working to their norm. While he had improved, he was glad it wasn't far.

They'd gone a few hundred feet when the ground dropped away, sloping down to a little creek running through the densely shadowed trees, their massive moss-covered trunks towering over him. These were ancient trees, thick with quiet strength, as if the forest itself breathed through them. They had lived long and healthy lives and seemed to pulse with the vitality of a giving mother earth.

The creek ran along one side of the small clearing where an ancient tree had fallen long ago, its aged trunk now reduced to a dark, weathered log. Where it had once stood, sunlight now warmed the thick grasses that claimed the space, with Blue standing knee-deep in the luxurious growth, a circle of closely cropped grass eaten down around him.

Rhone could have sworn Blue snorted a welcome before dropping his head back down for another greedy mouthful.

"Well, you look happy," he commented, hobbling up to his equine friend. "Did you happen to notice you weren't the only one tied up recently?"

Blue stomped his hoof, a hot blast from his nostrils showing insult at his comment.

"I suppose you did try to warn me," Rhone apologized, receiving a toss of Blue's head in agreement.

Lev laughed at their reunion. "You two are really something. How did you get him to respond like that?" she asked, the stress of her own story melting from her face.

"I didn't do anything," Rhone replied in confusion. "I don't know much about horses and never had one. Blue's just a loaner from the OPR stables."

Lev chuckled as Blue stomped a foot again, shaking his shaggy head at such a ridiculous statement. "Well, I'd say he's a pretty good fella," she remarked. "If you ask me, you two fit each other."

When Blue nickered, head bobbing in agreement, even Rhone had to laugh. His being back with Blue felt almost like family, but the thought brought his mind back to Stone? And where was Stone? He swept the area with eyes searching, but saw nothing suspicious.

"It's right here," Lev said with a sigh, and stooping, she dragged a woven bag from behind the ancient log. "Don't you dare let anyone know I'm such a giving soul. It would totally spoil my reputation, such as it is."

Rhone grinned with relief when she dumped her bedroll from the bag and Stone's voice instantly flooded his mind.

What took you so long? Stone grumbled, his irascible voice sounding like a rock rolled down a corridor. *I hope this is not going to become a pattern.*

Hey, you missed me, Rhone thought back in relief. *And I'm glad you're back too, but let me get this collar on before I forget and start talking out loud.*

They were a team again, reveling in the connection they had missed.

Unaware of the conversation, Lev stooped again, reaching under the big log. "Here's your sword, too," she announced. "I already have one, and it's been with me so long I wouldn't dare try another. You know how jealous blades can be. I'd probably forget how to hold it and would end up slicing off my own leg." She smiled as she handed him the sword, feeling freer with every step they took.

With his sword back, the one Captain Black had given him, Blue quietly munching the thick grass, and Stone around his neck, Rhone had everything he needed. "This sure feels better," he said appreciatively, stretching enough to make his back crack. "I might even get back before Aundrea sends out the entire agency to look for me."

"This Aundrea sounds like a pretty amazing woman, "Lev sighed wistfully. "She must be for you to be so attached."

"Yeah, I guess so," Rhone said, realizing it was true. "She is pretty cool. She even went all the way to the badlands to find me, although she didn't know it was me." Lev's raised eyebrows brought a dismissive shrug from Rhone. "That's a different story, but without her, I'd probably still be there."

His life had been interesting, or maybe boring, if you left out all the times he had almost died. But he hadn't, and now that he had Stone back, what could be better?

A warmth seeped into his body as, *I am here*, whispered softly through his mind.

Rhone realized just how hollow he had been without him. They were indeed collar-mates.

With a relaxed smile, Rhone shifted to a more pertinent topic. "Lev? About your issue—if you could put it down on paper, I'd be happy to deliver it to Aundrea. She's the one I mentioned who might know more about the Brotherhood. She once told me she came across some documents about them, and I know she'd be interested in learning more. She'll also want to hear about your case, and might even be able to help. She's the best."

Lev's lips tightened into a slim line as she squinted, considering his offer—then raised a shoulder as though she wasn't sold.

Without saying more, they returned to camp, the quiet settling around them comfortably.

As the sun rose higher, Lev threw her cloak back over a shoulder, allowing Rhone a stolen glance, noticing how worn her clothing was.

Life hadn't been good to her, but maybe her life's path was changing again, following the throw of the dice and the goodwill of a young man she had tried to kill. It would be enough to make anyone nervous.

"You really think you can make a difference?" she asked, the tension in her voice showing fear that she was making another poor decision.

"I can't promise anything, but I'll do my best," Rhone acknowledged. "I'll explain everything as best I can, but it's up to Aundrea. She's my boss and runs the show. She has things to deal with that are far above my pay grade, but like I said, she's pretty awesome. Honestly, I'm pretty sure she'd be happy to have you."

Lev smiled at the warmth in his words. It had been a long time since she'd felt anything near that kind of conviction.

But Rhone's thoughts began to race as he considered what he was offering and where this might lead. After all, he had been recalled. What if he was dismissed—or sent somewhere in a hurry? And if he had to leave, what if he couldn't return right away? What would happen to Lev? Frustrated, he knew he had to do something.

"Lev, I know I asked you to write a letter of explanation, but I'm not sure it will work. Would you be willing to come with me instead? Remember, I told you I was recalled? Well, I'm not exactly sure what that means, so it might be better if I introduce you personally—before whatever happens, happens. I could even be dismissed. I just don't know."

Lev frowned as uncertainty tugged at her heart. An hour ago she would have scoffed at the thought of returning to the OPR—let alone the Stronghold. It was the last place she ever wanted to see again.

But the last few hours had changed something.

In the darkness, a small glimmer of hope flickered, no more than a spark, but it was a spark.

Then a voice drifted through Rhone's mind like the smoke of a candle. *She needs help,* Stone whispered.

Understanding at once, Rhone made the decision simple.

"Come on," he said, motioning toward the camp. "We've got places to go. Let's get you packed."

His offer was simple, but it took Lev tremendous effort to go against decades of thinking. Finally, her simple nod accepted his offer, the release of worry removing years of stress from her face.

A quarter hour later, camp was broken, and the two mounted, ready for the long ride back.

"It will take a couple of days to get to The Stronghold," Rhone announced. "That will give you time to tell me the rest of your story. I'm a pretty good listener. So is Aundrea," he added, receiving nothing more than a worried smile.

The quiet clip-clop of hooves thudding on the dirt and leaf-strewn roadway was lulling, giving Rhone plenty of time to feel the aches and pains of his thumping the night before. Stone too must have been waiting, as he only made quiet comments now and then.

It was up to Lev to break the silence.

Rhone's timing was justified when Lev cleared her throat, drawing his attention from the ache in his back. "I'm tired of doing what I'm doing," she began without preamble. "Nor am I very proud of it. So, if I can be of service again, it's probably time. When Lady Fortune turns to look in your direction, it's best if you don't look the gift-horse in the mouth. And as they say, beggars can't be choosers. So, while I may not have reached that level quite yet, I understand something of why it can happen. I just hope I don't get hanged for it."

Her words had stopped, but her face held a look as though she were actually trying to decide.

Rhone nodded his acceptance as they rode on in silence, each absorbed in their own thoughts.

Well done, my boy. Well done, Stone said approvingly.

CHAPTER 6

Return We Must

With Lev as a guide, the trip to the big city and the Capital Stronghold was not only faster, it was far less boring. Her memory of the OPR and its dealings may have been a decade or two old, but held as many stories of missions gone awry. It was entertaining as well as instructive, teaching Rhone more of the agency's ways and wiles than he could ever have done sitting in a classroom.

The reach of the OPR was not only expansive, it was legendary, even before Aundrea had taken over. Stone too was intrigued and remained quiet, which allowed Rhone to keep his mind on her words.

"So, why were you dismissed?" Rhone asked apologetically. "I'm sorry I have to ask, but I should probably know."

Lev gave a thoughtful pause before granting him a small nod. "I suppose it is time," she agreed. Her eyes closed, brow drawing into furrows that might have been pain, but when Rhone started to speak, she raised a hand, stalling his words. "No. You're right. You deserve that much," and with a deep breath, she began.

"I was sent on an assignment that went bad. Some do. That's just the way it is. Not every assignment turns out smelling like roses. Some simply stink." She paused, giving a slight frown before starting again. "It was after a particularly crummy assignment. I turned in my report as always, but the next day, I was called to the inner sanctum. Our Super, what we called our supervisor back then, wasn't alone. There were three others in the room, all members of The Council. It was short and brutal. When my Super tried to speak on our behalf, he was put down and threatened with his job. They said that I had done my assignment sloppily, fingering people who were above suspicion. Since my actions had brought disfavor to the agency, I was being released, posthaste—no recourse for pay or appeal. I was done. Finished. My employment ended. One of them actually pointed at the door and waited for me to remove myself. My Super looked conflicted, like he wanted to object, but merely watched as I walked out.

I left and never looked back.

Within a day, my husband and I packed our stuff and left town. Shortly thereafter, and I mean within a few miles, attackers assaulted us, and while I don't have proof, I firmly believe The Council knew about it and planned to eliminate us. No shadows in the hallway meant nothing to worry about later."

Rhone could hardly believe what he was hearing. "But The Council are the good guys," he complained, breaking into her story. "They're the ruling body of the government, not just one man who can potentially go crooked. They're a group, bound by a code and morals. At least, that's what my mom taught me, and what I learned in the academy."

"And you don't believe me," Lev said, shaking her head sadly.

Rhone squared his jaw as he sorted through the new data. *Stone, what do you think? It doesn't fit well with everything else we know, but I think I believe her.*

Stone took a long moment before replying. *Her words ring true, and her body's systems do not show an attempt to hide anything. My best assumption then, is that something we believe we know is false.*

Rhone nodded in thought, which Lev took as an answer.

"I'm sorry, but if you don't believe me, then it's best I leave," she said, disappointment heavy in her voice.

"No, wait," Rhone cried, seeing the flicker of hope dissolve in her eyes. "My nod was agreeing with the problem, not that I didn't believe you. I came from a place where the local government went bad, but the OPR did what they could to fix the problem and it worked. Now I'm here as part of the OPR. I want to fix this problem too, no matter where it goes. It's what we do."

"And you are still so young. How did you get so smart?" Lev asked, her gentle smile showing her appreciation.

She meant it as a rhetorical question, but Rhone answered it in his normal, unquestioning manner. "I guess I have good teachers and good examples. Our motto is, 'If the people are happy, the government is happy'. So if you're not happy, and you are one of the people, then it's my job to see what I can do to fix the problem."

Lev's eyes teared at the honest statement, and she whispered, "Thank you. It's been a long time, but I've had enough training to see honesty when it stares me in the face. You really believe this stuff, don't you?"

Rhone could do nothing more than nod, as in sudden shyness, he answered, "I do. If we don't try, then we fail before we even start."

"Then let's get this fixed," she said, wiping happily at her dark brown eyes.

***

It was days before they reached the big city. They were working their way through the tangled streets, the thronging pedestrians, carts, and buggies slowing their progress as effectively as the looming buildings blocked the sun. As they approached the massive stonework building of the Capital Stronghold, Lev slowed further, staring up at the mammoth structure. Rhone remembered his own first view and understood, giving her time. It may not have been the first time she'd seen it, but it had been years.

Climbing the wide apron-like stairs, they entered the massive structure, then crossed the sprawling foyer before climbing several more sets of stairs. Even Lev was feeling the strain by the time they stopped at a heavy wooden door, its engraved plaque saying, Office of Public Recrimination. Below the plaque, a note, written in quickly scrawled ink, stated, 'Enter at your own risk', but Rhone simply shrugged, giving her an apologetic look.

"You'll like it here. It really is a good team, and Aundrea is the best boss ever."

"So you've said," Lev reminded him, granting him a half-smile and a raised eyebrow. "This Aundrea must be something special to have gained so much of your approval. She wasn't here when I was, but neither was this office, so I'll just have to trust your words and pray for the best."

Relieved, Rhone opened the door and ushered her in.

The noisy rooms were much as he had left them, filled with activity and feeling almost like home. Lev paused as she took in the strange surroundings, feeling less awkward than she had expected. While it wasn't the same building, it held the same air of purpose.

"Come on, I'll take you to the boss," he announced, grinning as he remembered his own introduction to the building. They passed quietly through the rooms, receiving only one comment of, "Hey, Rhone, what are you doing back?" But a quick wave and a finger pointed to the glass-topped door directly ahead was a recognizable reason not to stop and talk.

The hand-painted letters on the door's frosted glass simply said, The Boss, and Rhone knocked quietly.

Moments later, the door swung open, and Bran stepped out, almost running them over in his haste.

"Excuse me," he said automatically, but a quick double-take stopped him in his tracks, realizing who it was. "It's about time. What took you so long?" he asked, his face brightening as he welcomed Rhone. His next look took in Lev. "And I can see you have business," he said, smiling appreciatively. "She'll be glad to see you, so hurry up. She's about having fits waiting." Then he offered his hand to Lev. "Hi, I'm Bran, sort of second fiddle around here."

Lev was a little taken aback by the hand, but returned it in a firm but feminine shake.

Before either could say more, Rhone broke in. "Bran, meet Lev, but we do have business with Aundrea. Make sure to see us after. You'll want to meet her for real."

"I'll look forward to it," Bran said, adding another of his smiles. He was good with his smiles and handed them out whenever he could.

Lev looked ready to make an apology, but Rhone quickly dragged her into the office and shut the door.

"Rhone! You're here," came a surprised cry from Aundrea that caught them both unexpectedly. It wasn't a true cry, with tears and everything, but she did sweep out from behind her desk and engulf him in her arms.

Lev may have been caught off guard, but instantly knew it was the love of a mother figure seeing her prodigal son's return. Trying not to watch the intimate scene too intently, she took the time to survey the office, its wainscoted lower walls of beautiful dark oak topped with decorative flower-wreathed wallpaper above. Together, the room had a look of power and charm, making the office both strong and feminine.

Rhone was more than a little surprised at the enthusiastic homecoming. He had been recalled, after all, and told to show up at his earliest convenience. So why all the hullabaloo? Embarrassed by the close scene, and with his boss, he asked, "I got the recall notice. Weren't you expecting me?"

Aundrea sniffed lightly, then held him at arm's length, looking him over as she had so many times before. "I did, yes—but you've been gone far too long."

Then her expression shifted, brows drawing together in concern as she tilted his chin. "Is that a bruise?"

It certainly wasn't the first time Rhone had been given the head-to-toe check for damage, but this was different.

Embarrassed, he stammered, "Yeah, well . . . I'm fine, and I would like to introduce Lev. We met on the way here."

Aundrea spun as his words sank in, surprise crossing her face. Then it was gone, replaced by composure. "I do apologize. This isn't very professional," she said, her gaze taking in the woman standing with a knowing smile on her dusky face.

Lev raised a hand, stalling anything further. "No apology needed. I'm trained well enough to know a homecoming when I see one."

Aundrea wiped distractedly at her remaining tears and nodded her thanks. "Well, I'll be the first to admit, it's not our normal agent's homecoming, but this guy is something special," she offered.

"That much I already knew," Lev replied, noting Rhone's embarrassment. "I'm afraid we have our own story to tell, but we've made it this far, and I hope the rest will work out too."

Aundrea nodded, sweeping a hand toward the chairs. "Sounds like we could use some refreshment then, so have a seat and I'll have something brought in while you explain."

But as she stepped toward the door, it opened with Bran's head poking through.

"I thought you might like something to drink," he announced, grinning at Aundrea's surprise.

"And your timing is as good as normal," she responded, eyebrow raised in a 'that was pretty well timed' expression. "Put it on the desk, please, and since you're here, you might as well stay. I would simply have to repeat everything as soon as they leave."

Bran's smile looked remarkably like the one molded into the Cheshire cheese Rhone had eaten recently, and he gave an eyebrow bob to Lev as he stepped in, his full six-foot frame slipping through the doorway behind a tray of glasses and a pitcher of sun tea.

"I like being prepared," he stated, deftly setting the tray on Aundrea's desk.

Aundrea cast Lev an apologetic look. "I'm honestly not sure how he does it, but he's good at it, so I can hardly fault him for that."

Bran poured the drinks while Aundrea took a seat in her hand-carved chair, then picked up her glass, sipping appreciatively before settling herself comfortably with a sigh. "Alright, first things first," she announced. "Rhone, welcome back, and none too soon. What took you so long? We sent the missive weeks ago."

Rhone's tea was halfway to his lips, but he lowered the cup, glancing quickly toward Lev before answering. "I came as soon as I could," he said, not sure how much to explain. "Unfortunately, I was on the way when I got waylaid just a bit, which took some time." Another furtive glance saw Lev's forehead wrinkle, but he continued as if it were nothing. "Anyway, I got your message an . . ." but a quiet throat-clearing from Aundrea stopped him again. After a silent acknowledgment passed between them, he started over. "When I got your message, I finished up with my work and headed here as quickly as I could get away. I knew it must be something important, or you wouldn't have sent a recall. At least that's what I figured, since I couldn't think of anything I'd done wrong." He felt a silent chuckling vibration from Stone, but closed off any further distraction from his friend.

Aundrea was quick to note the extra color showing on Lev's cheeks and understood there was something more to their story.

"I assume there is more to the story, but we can leave it for now," she offered, receiving a disappointed look from Bran. "Lev, I love the name," she mentioned invitingly. "And thank you for escorting my errant knight back to the fold. Please know that I appreciate it." Her sincere smile left nothing to doubt.

"It was my pleasure, to be sure," Lev answered politely. "Without him, I most certainly wouldn't be here. But as you said, that is for a different time."

"Unfortunately, yes," Aundrea answered, her face giving a knowing smile. "I have a great need to speak with Rhone, though I would like to take some of your time later today, if that would be all right? Until then, I can offer Bran as an intermediary, for which he will no doubt thank me. He is quite incorrigible most times."

Bran looked stricken by her words, and rose, hand over his heart. "I will take it on my honor to assist the lady in a manner as befits our glorious establishment," he gushed, his genteel elegance not fooling a soul. "Alright, I'll be good and show her around," he conceded, which brought a snort from Rhone.

Shaking her head in disavowal, Aundrea stood, ending the short session. "Thank you, Lev. I'll come gather you as soon as we're done." Then, shrugging in helplessness, she added, "He'll be good. I promise."

Lev gave an appreciative smile, intuitively understanding the camaraderie of the group. "I'm sure I'll be fine, and if not, I've dealt with pups before."

Aundrea strangled a chuckle as Bran groaned, leading Lev from the room.

Once the door had closed, she turned back to Rhone and pointed to a chair. "Sit," she commanded. "We have a lot to talk about, and thank you for not mentioning Jewel's contact."

"I know Jewel is a secret, or at least was," Rhone said, as he again took a seat. "What I don't know is, what happened since."

Aundrea didn't answer, but raised her hand, admiring her beautiful ring, its small golden-pink stone glimmering in the lamplight. "Let's start with, yes. Jewel is still our secret. She has been doing very well and has continued to grow her abilities. I often wonder how I did so well without her."

Rhone felt Stone searching reach for Jewel's interaction, but didn't pry. Stone had a right to his own life, and Jewel was another We, after all.

"So what's with the recall?" he asked. "And by the way, how did she do it?"

"I told you she's been learning," Aundrea said proudly. "Remember when you told me how you and Stone sent out calls for other We? Jewel explained your use of the ground for the energy-wave transmission, so she took that and worked up a system to transmit through air. Isn't she amazing?" she said, gazing at the little jewel centered in the ornate ring.

It was, without a doubt, a beautiful piece, but the fact that it was also Jewel, her crystalline friend and partner, made the placement in a ring the perfect choice. As a ring, Jewel was always front and center, allowing a seamless reading of the energy of others. The information was then passed on to Aundrea, making a truly symbiotic relationship.

"Our Jewel designed an array of metal rods we then placed on top of the Stronghold," Aundrea explained excitedly. "When she's connected, she can send messages, like she did to you. It will make communication between us as simple as sending a letter, only much, much faster."

Rhone was amazed. He and Stone had considered multiple methods for sending their queries, finally choosing the ground as the most optimal medium. Somehow, they had missed this one with its sending array.

Stone, however, wasn't impressed. *We may be able to receive, but we have no way to respond,* he commented archly, quickly bringing up the downside to the process. *Still, it is a great achievement, especially for one so small.*

It may have been an acknowledgment, but it sounded more like a petulant rockslide than a compliment, and while Stone's thoughts were undoubtedly true, Rhone could feel the slight current of jealousy hidden in their depths.

It's okay, my friend. We would have figured it out if we hadn't been running all the time, Rhone replied.

Yes, and we did accomplish messages through other means, did we not?

We did. Or you did, Rhone answered. *As I remember, I had very little to do with it, other than being your pack mule.*

I never called you a mule, Stone answered. *Although there were times when their stubbornness seemed a good fit for your actions.*

When Rhone rolled his eyes, Aundrea understood the action for what it was.

"What's Stone got to say about it?" she asked.

"Ahhh, he wishes he could have been here to help," Rhone answered quickly, covering for his friend.

"She did do good, didn't she?" she agreed. "We didn't want to announce our work yet, so we snuck the array between the tubing and pipework, using them for support as well as a cover."

"Hey, that's cool, but how does she make the connection?" Rhone asked, his interest perking. He remembered needing bare rock for Stone to connect well, but Jewel had obviously discovered a different method.

Aundrea beamed as she explained. "I had a special setting built for her. I wish it could receive too, but we haven't had enough time to work it out yet."

This is all good, but if 'they' can, then 'we' can, Stone said brusquely, his thoughts coursing through Rhone's mind. *Even you know that two-way communication is required to be effective.*

Rhone could only agree. The sending unit was undoubtedly an impressive accomplishment, but he had been frustrated for weeks at not knowing why he had been recalled.

He was still considering the concept when Aundrea's voice took on a solemn tone. "That is all good," she said, repeating what he had just heard from Stone, "but it's not why I called you back. I need your input."

"Mine?" Rhone asked in surprise.

"Yes, yours. It has to do with The Council, and I have no one else to speak to."

CHAPTER 7

Comme ci, Comme ça

The Council? "Have you learned something new?" Rhone asked, his expression guarded. "What can I do?"

"There is something, yes," Aundrea acknowledged. "I have always feared that our being too effective would gather eyes—Eyes I would have preferred weren't watching."

The comment brought a gleam to Rhone's eye. "That shouldn't be a problem. We just have to goof up more," he said with a grin. "They obviously haven't been keeping close track of me, 'cuz I've goofed up dozens of times."

"The word is 'Because,' Aundrea said reprovingly, then smiled, appreciating his optimism. "I suppose that is one way, although I would hate to think of the effect it would have on the people."

"Probably true," Rhone said, shrugging innocently. "So how can we help?"

Aundrea gave him a searching look before answering. "I need someone they don't know."

"Okay . . . but who are 'they' and would the 'someone' be Stone and me?" He wasn't sure he liked where this was going, but he would go, of course. He owed her everything.

"I was considering you, yes, and I know, or at least I think I know who 'they' are. I believe it is The Council, though I doubt it's the entire group. It is far more likely to be one person, or perhaps a small cadre within The Council. What I am asking is for the two of you to find out what you can. I certainly can't go sneaking around. I am far too noticed and have tails following me most places I do go. You, however, are new to the system and won't be under surveillance, at least not yet. Once the knowledge of your airship gets out, that will undoubtedly change. I'm holding that information back for as long as I can, but it will come to the front eventually. Until then, I plan to get as much use of your skills and Stone's as possible. For now, I need your sleuthing. With you and Stone doing some behind-the-scenes surveillance, we may find the information we need to place some leverage of our own. Are you good for the try?"

What do you think? he asked Stone, their silent conversation followed closely by Aundrea's watchful eyes.

We can but try, Stone answered, sounding much like one of the upper-class Rhone had studied to impersonate. *She would not ask if she was not in need, therefore, it is my personal opinion that we agree. Succeed or fail, we will do our best.*

Rhone rolled his eyes at Stone's elaborate answer, but Aundrea had been watching with the awareness of someone who knew We.

"So it's a yes?" she asked, already guessing the answer.

"Yes, it's a yes. Stone just takes a while to say things," Rhone answered, shaking his head to remove himself from the equation. He was, after all, mostly the transportation Stone needed to get things done.

That is not true, Stone responded indignantly. *You may be my transportation, but I also need your view on the human things that I do not yet fully comprehend. We have been through this before, have we not?*

Rhone smiled ruefully, remembering previous discussions. It may be true that Stone did a majority of the thinking, but without himself, Stone would be going nowhere. They were a team after all.

"Thank you," Aundrea said, having just received the buzz of approval from Jewel, confirming it from both. "I've written up a starting agenda, but from that point on, it will be totally up to you. Immerse yourselves in The Stronghold. Learn its ways and the people, then do whatever it is you do. But find the culprits so we can get back to work without looking over our shoulders constantly. Any questions?"

"Uh . . . None at the moment, but I'm sure we'll come up with some before long," Rhone answered, though he had no idea what he would even ask.

How about starting with the agenda she has for us, Stone advised, the feel of an eye roll so real Rhone checked to see if he'd actually done it himself.

Hey, that was pretty cool. Did you just come up with that, *or have you been saving it for the perfect moment?* Rhone asked silently, impressed by Stone's newest mental effect.

You are such a child, Stone responded in his normal, slightly supercilious manner. *I know it will be* difficult, *but try keeping your mind on task.*

Aundrea had watched their mental discussion, waiting until Rhone's expression changed before asking, "Everything okay?"

They are just being boys, Jewel announced, her mental picture of disgust verifying her thoughts.

"Yeah, Stone was just reminding me that I should get the agenda you set up for us," Rhone tried to explain. "Sorry. I should have remembered."

"Thank you, Stone, but I would not have let you leave without it," Aundrea said, addressing the We at Rhone's collar. "It's one of the reasons I love having We around. You never forget."

That is a very wise woman our Jewel chose, Stone said approvingly.

Rhone could only agree. With Aundrea and Jewel's partnering, he had a mentor who truly understood his situation.

Still, he was startled when she said, "Thank you, Rhone. I believe we're done for the moment."

"B . . . Wait. Is that it?" he asked in surprise. "You don't want to debrief me?" He was more than ready to be done, but this wasn't what he'd expected.

"No. We're good for now," she explained. "I'm sure we'll get to the rest later, but right now we need to find Bran and Lev. I have a feeling we girls need to talk."

"You want me to go find them?" Rhone exclaimed, practically leaping from his slouched position.

"Thanks, but I'm pretty sure I know where they are," she said, giving him a wink as she too stood, leading the way from her office.

It didn't take long. Her first stop was the Cantina, where they found the two seated at a table making small talk.

"I'm glad we found you," Aundrea said warmly, grinning as she braced herself against the tabletop, leaning toward Lev. "I think it's time for a girl's chat."

Accepting with a nod, Lev gave Bran a quick wave. "Thank you, Bran. Best brew I've had in ages," she said before sliding to the end of the bench. A moment later, the two ladies headed off, chatting amiably, while Rhone slid into the seat Lev had just vacated.

"How was the debrief?" Bran asked, eyebrows bobbing in expectation of a good story.

"Not so bad. Just long," Rhone said, as he slumped into a relaxed position.

Bran looked almost disappointed by the short answer, but shrugged his acceptance. "Well, you're lucky. I remember my first debriefing. It was long and tedious. Seems I had missed half of what I was supposed to check on. It literally took me h-o-u-r-s to redo the reports," he complained, lengthening the word to make it more dramatic.

Rhone merely shrugged in response. He'd sent his reports, so this was totally different. On the other hand, he had never received a response, so maybe they had never gotten there. Either way, he wasn't too worried.

Finishing his drink, Bran stretched and took a deep breath. "Well, I'd better be getting back," he said reasonably. "I have reports to get in, and they won't get done by my sitting at the cantina."

"Is it okay if I come along?" Rhone asked, sliding to his feet, too. "I'll walk home with Aundrea when she gets done with Lev."

"That's a good plan. Always keep on the upside of the boss." Bran said approvingly, giving Rhone an affectionate slap on the shoulder.

The ladies' chat, as Aundrea had called it, took all afternoon. Rhone spent the time wandering the office, reacquainting himself with his fellow agents and office workers. After that, he found Bran again and they sat waiting outside Aundrea's office, discussing his previous assignment.

"So you have a flying balloon contraption?" Bran asked, amazed at the accomplishments of this, their youngest agent. "Does Aundrea know about it? Although I'd be surprised if she didn't. She knows most everything that goes on in her territory."

Rhone merely shrugged, not knowing how much he should say. Nor did Bran worry about such small considerations.

"I had no idea there were pirates in Corgy, but I doubt Aundrea did either. I'm dead sure she wouldn't have sent you if she had. You know how she is. As protective as an old banty hen."

Rhone knew about mother hens and how protective they were of their brood, and while he didn't think much of being thought of as a chick, Aundrea did fulfill the protective mothering part pretty well.

"From what I heard, you fixed the Corgy problem," Bran continued thoughtfully, not noticing Rhone's disconnect. "That's really good work, first-timer or not, but, you do know Aundrea's going to want a full report, right down to the minute. So, you'd better be prepared to get some blisters on your fingers from all the writing it's going to take."

He seemed almost pleased when Rhone's face took on a worried look.

"But I sent reports. Didn't she get them?" Rhone asked, still undecided on that issue.

Bran gave a theatrical grimace before answering. "Gosh, I don't know, fella. She doesn't tell me everything. You know how it is. She's busy."

Rhone gave a long sigh as he thought of the hours it would take to rewrite the reports.

"Hey, don't look so worried," Bran said consolingly. "She'll probably have you out of here in no more than a week. Shouldn't take any longer than that, I'd guess." Rhone slumped in dejection until Bran snickered, "Dad-gummit, Rhone. You're too easy. I'm sure it won't be nearly that bad. You said you already sent interim reports, so it shouldn't take more than a day or two."

Rhone was both relieved and appalled. He was readying a response when he was rescued by Aundrea's office door opening.

"Rhone, it's your turn," Aundrea called, stepping aside to let Lev out. "And Bran, would you see that Lev gets some dinner? Just put it on the tab."

"Yes, ma'am. Dinner it is!" Bran responded, obviously pleased with his chore.

But glancing at Lev's travel-stained gear, Aundrea changed her directive. "Perhaps she'll want to check in first, so she can get cleaned up a bit. See that she gets settled at The Councilman. It's classy enough, and I'm sure she could use a hot bath and a night's sleep in a soft bed." She pretended not to notice Lev's grateful expression as she added, "We girls may even do some shopping tomorrow."

She studiously ignored the pained glances the guys gave each other, but Bran took over from there. "Sure enough, Aundrea. And don't worry. I'll take care of seeing her settled, and dinner," although he was more than happy he had other things scheduled for his morning's agenda.

That done, Aundrea turned back to Lev. "I want to thank you for coming in. And don't worry. I'll personally see that this gets taken care of."

Lev dipped her head in gratitude, then turned thankful eyes to Rhone. 'Thank you', she mouthed as she passed by, following Bran through the office.

Rhone's eyes followed her until he felt Aundrea's hand on his shoulder.

"Come on in. I need you to explain a few things," she said with a tired sigh.

Rhone grimaced, realizing that rewriting the reports might have been the easier job.

***

Their talk took far more than an hour, and that didn't include his rewriting the reports on the pirate situation in Corgy. All in all, it had been a very long day.

Thankfully, as Aundrea had told him many times, her home was close to the office, making the daily jaunt less time-consuming. He had never moved from her place, having never found the need, and after spending so many hours at the office and the training grounds, he wasn't any more desirous than she to drag himself across town to somewhere else. Then, after successfully completing his agent training, he had been quickly shipped out to Corgy, so again, there had been no need. It may have been strange to some, but to him, it was home.

With an exhausted sigh, Rhone flopped bonelessly into the well-cushioned window seat.

Nothing had changed in the few months he had been gone. The window still overlooked the street below, granting a view of the big city. The bustle of the overcrowded streets flowed by with the endless stream of pedestrians, carts, wagons, and even a few of the strange steam-powered vehicles he'd used as inspiration for his powered airship, although most of that credit belonged to Stone. It had been Stone's lift and stress calculations that allowed the airship to stay in the air, but Rhone could almost hear Stone's, *'Not true'*, although nothing but a faint chuckle came through their mental connection.

But it was true. Without Stone's engineering and calculations, the airship could just as easily have turned turtle, dumping the occupants for a long fall to the ground.

They had definitely been lucky. The only failure had been on the balloon's test without passengers. They had been forced to rebuild the entire contraption, but the outcome had made it both bigger and better. Now the mammoth craft had an actual ship-like hull hanging below the ballooning bubble of gas, not just the simple basket of their earlier days.

It truly was an airship now. The first and only.

Rhone gave a dismal sigh, realizing his daydream had been both real and wistful. The Lady Luna was no longer his. It belonged to Bella now.

Captain Belle, he reminded himself, acknowledging that it did have a nice ring to it. He smiled, remembering her fancy get-up at the town's reception dinner for the homecoming heroes. She had been an eye-catcher for sure.

He was still smiling when Aundrea's gentle voice broke him from his thoughts. "Rhone, I think you did a marvelous job in Corgy.

Then you topped it off by bringing Lev back into the fold. I knew you were special from the very first time we met."

Rhone blushed at her praise, knowing just how lucky he had been. "I could have done better," he said honestly. "I almost got myself killed a dozen times, which reminds me, I need some retraining in sword work. I actually have a sword now, the one Captain Black gave me, but it might as well be a club for all the good I could do with it."

"I noticed the sword," she said, tossing the words over her shoulder as she puttered around the apartment. "I was a little surprised since I didn't know they had much need for swords in Corgy."

Rhone shrugged self-consciously. "Captain Black told me, 'If a captain doesn't act the part, they won't be respected', or something like that."

Aundrea paused at that. "He's right. It is important. But didn't you have sword training at the academy?"

"Yeah, sorta, but I did a lot better with knife throwing than I did with sword swinging. I figure, a little more training might help keep my head on my shoulders," though he didn't mention his poor showing with Lev.

"Then I recommend it," Aundrea said with a nod. "But it will have to wait. Tomorrow, we're going to plan our next step in The Council issue. I have a feeling we have very little time before something happens, and Lev's story only intensified my own feelings. Jewel, by the way, is in total agreement."

As am I, Stone added, throwing in his two cents' worth.

Rhone shrugged again, suddenly feeling picked on. "I don't have a problem with it. It's just that I don't know anything about The

Council, or how things work around here. I'm new at this, remember?"

"You'll do fine," she encouraged. "It will be important for you to know who's who in the zoo, so I've instructed Jewel to transfer all the pertinent data directly to Stone. It will be much faster than having you sit through a month's worth of lectures on how the council works."

Rhone was relieved to hear it. Days of sitting at a desk, listening to an instructor's monotonous lecture, wasn't his idea of fun. Doable, yes, but not necessarily fun.

Stone, were you aware of this? he asked silently.

Why, of course, Stone answered, his immediate response a thing that always caused Rhone to worry. *Jewel and I have discussed the topic on several occasions.*

And when exactly *were you going to share it with me?* Rhone asked, not sure he liked the behind-the-scenes machinations of the two We creatures.

But Stone picked up on the feelings and made a gesture of reconciliation. *There has been no actual data transfer yet, simply the discussion of its need,* he said, easing Rhone's mind. *Do not worry yourself so much, my friend. I would have told you. Remember, your time has been filled since our arrival, and Aundrea has not yet set the schedule. You could ask her* now *if you think it appropriate.*

Sorry. I really am tired," Rhone apologized, realizing his thoughts had been on Bella and The Lady Luna, which brought an instant feeling of loneliness, even here at Aundrea's.

I too miss our recent friends, Stone said quietly.

But Rhone didn't answer, his tired mind turning to the feel of flying, as a gentle breeze blew his giant craft across the sky.

CHAPTER 8

Inspiration and Perspiration

As it turned out, Jewel's sending array wasn't much more than a metal rod projecting from the roof.

Okay, maybe slightly more than that. It was, after all, held in place by clamps securing it to a length of clay piping jutting from the sidewall of the roof access, but if you didn't know what you were looking for, you wouldn't see it, just another element of the changes the Capital Stronghold had been going through for the past several years. The new technologies made life interesting but were often confusing to anyone not in the loop.

Aundrea gave Jewel a motherly pat, then closed the lid on the heavily padded box that looked suspiciously like a jewelry box. "Now it's up to her," she said, turning to face Rhone. "I know the system works, or you wouldn't be here, but let's give her a moment to warm up and she'll give you a demonstration."

Rhone was oddly nervous and sent a silent question to Stone. *Are you getting anything yet?*, a dumb question, since he knew Stone would let him know the moment he received anything.

Regardless, he was relieved when Stone cautiously answered, *Nothing yet. Wait! Yes. I have contact. This is amazing. Well done, Jewel, but of course, she cannot hear me.* It was an unnecessary statement but he kept up his chatter, keeping Rhone informed. *It is only a one-way unit, you realize. Better than none, but too bad it does not go in both directions.*

But you heard her, Rhone reminded him. *Is it like the recall message we received in Corgy? If so, just think, we could cut our communication time in half.*

Aundrea couldn't hear their conversation, but she saw Rhone's expression. "Good. It worked," she said in relief. "I had my worries," her pent-up breath showing more concern than Rhone would have expected.

"Yep, Stone said the message was as clear as if they were actually touching," he said, quickly easing her worries. "Now, if it could just go both ways."

"That would be great, but we haven't got this one figured out just yet," she agreed, visibly relaxing with the news. Then she paused in thought. "I wonder if we could build a smaller version you could take with you."

It might be possible, Stone agreed. *I must admit, even one-way transmission is a tremendous accomplishment, but being able to send from both ends would be marvelous.*

"Stone agrees," Rhone passed on, remembering again how tiring it was to be the middleman in these conversations.

"Excellent. I'll have the lab begin working on it. They're getting very good at these new technologies," Aundrea said cheerfully.

The comment made Rhone think of Lev's tiny dragon, but he kept the secret to himself. It had become his personal desire to develop the intricate systems, designing a working creation for more than just decoration or toys. Time would tell.

With the demonstration a success, Rhone felt a sudden urge to get back to his designing. Excusing himself, he waved his goodbye and headed to his favorite corner of the OPR lab.

M ost of his time was spent learning the twists and turns of the Stronghold, but his remaining hours were devoted to sketching odd designs on rolls of brown paper scavenged from the mercantile. The paper was meant for wrapping packages, not inventions, but it was cheap—and using OPR funds for his own tinkering never sat right with him.

He was deep in his work when a hand suddenly closed around his shoulder.

Jerking back in surprise, Rhone jabbed his finger with the tiny tool he'd been using. "Dad-gummit. Can't you see I'm working here?" he hissed through clenched teeth, glaring up at Bran's broad grin. Then, wisely, shoved the injured finger into his mouth before he could say something he'd regret later.

He'd picked this well-equipped corner of the OPR lab specifically because it was tucked safely out of the way, but apparently, it wasn't as hidden as he'd thought.

Bran stood with arms crossed, his grin turning grim as he shook his head. "Hate to say this, fella, but you're going to have to do better than that if you plan on winning the next in-house agents' tournament." A chuckle took most of the sting out of the jibe, but Rhone's continued scowl brought a finger raised in warning. "You do realize you have to be aware you have an opponent before you can win, don't you? You never even heard me come in."

"Sorry," Rhone said reflexively. "I didn't realize..." but Bran's raised hand cut off his excuse.

"Hey, don't worry about it. Your opponents certainly won't mind. Unfortunately, it's also a good way to end up dead. Remember, you're an agent now. You've gotta keep your mind split in two directions. Always."

"But I was working," Rhone began, astounded that he even had to explain. "I mean, of course, if I were on assignment, or even on the practice field, things could be dangerous, but I'm in the middle of the OPR complex. Why should I get scolded for working?"

Bran shook his head again as he blew out a tired breath. "Listen, kid. I know what you're thinking. Been there myself. But we didn't go to all the time and effort to train you for you to get yourself killed. You have to stay alert. Remember, your enemy might choose the exact time when you feel the most comfortable to attack, specifically because that's when you let your barriers down." He pondered Rhone a moment longer before making up his mind. "Okay, I'm going to do you a favor," he said resignedly. "I'm going to see to it that you are . . . ah, approached, every single day, or maybe more often. If you survive these encounters, you can take the coin they'll have. If you lose, well . . . they get yours. When you have enough coins, you can buy your way free of the exercise. If not, they continue until you can. Good enough? I'd rather see you broke than dead."

Rhone sat with a dumb look on his face, not quite believing what was happening. "But I was working," he tried to explain.

"Yep, and dead is dead, whether you were working or not. Anyway, I've got to go. Aundrea's waiting for me. You have fun, and stay alert."

"But it's just not right," Rhone complained. But his complaint was either unheard or didn't make a difference. Bran never slowed, and a moment later he was gone.

"It's just not right," he complained again, speaking louder now that Bran was gone. But he knew better than to expect Stone to take his side. Stone was a stickler when it came to rules and regulations, and if Bran said it, then it was a rule as far as he was concerned.

You do realize Bran is correct, Stone remarked, neither pushing Bran's punishment nor supporting Rhone's position.

"Whatever. I was doing work for the OPR," Rhone sputtered in indignation. "There's no way I was in the wrong."

And Bran is your superior, Stone summarized. *You must also admit, you were indeed somewhat focused on your project. I might also question if your tinkering is truly for the OPR, or simply your own machinings?*

Rhone slumped in defeat, knowing it was true. But a moment later, he gave a sly grin. "Two can play that game. All I have to do is win a few bouts, then I'm free. I could even win a few extra coins for a trip to the cantina."

With that happy thought, he returned to his work, ignoring Stone's disappointed sigh.

It wasn't a couple of hours later when Rhone felt a sharp jab, causing him to jerk reflexively before spinning around on his stool.

"What the—!" he started to shout, but cut himself off as he nearly collided with MaryEllen, blowing on the tip of her finger as if snuffing out a candle.

"You're dead, and I'll take a coin, please," she said, smiling as she held out her dainty hand with its brightly painted nails.

It was a pretty hand, as far as hands go, but also a very dangerous hand. He knew that only too well, having tested against her at the academy—and lost.

"But I wasn't ready," he protested, already knowing it was a useless defense.

At least it had been MaryEllen, undeniably the best there was at sneaky attacks. In reality, then, even if he had been ready, he'd had no chance, which made it somewhat easier to take. He still grimaced when she waggled the fingers demanding payment.

Reluctantly, Rhone dug a coin from his pocket and held it out. The flash of movement later, the coin was gone, and MaryEllen was giving him an impish grin, her beautifully balanced curtsy a dance all by itself.

"Thank you, good sir. And now that I have a coin, I believe I'll be heading to the cantina after work."

With a bright smile and a quick wave, she spun on the tip of her toe and left, just as Bran had, although Bran's departure had been a mere amble, while MaryEllen seemed nearly to float as she swept from the room, glancing back over her shoulder with another smile.

Frustrated and angry, Rhone slumped in his chair, his face a picture of dismal defeat. Not only was he out a coin, he hadn't finished the project he'd been working on.

Stone, why didn't you warn me? If I had known she was coming, I could have put up at least some kind of defense.

His only answer was a faint chuckle reverberating in his head, which didn't bode well.

"Why are you siding with Bran when you know I'm right?" he asked grumpily. When there was still no answer, he made one last comment before angrily shutting down their contact. "I passed the academy on my own, and I can do this too."

Feeling better at hearing his own statement, Rhone set himself back to his tinkering.

A few hours later, and deep into his work, a voice from across the room dragged him back to awareness. "Hey, Rhone, I almost hate to mention it, but you've just been shot full of holes. I've had my crossbow aimed at you for five minutes. I even snuffed my runny nose once, but you were like dead to the world, dude. Are you always this blind to what's going on? If so, it's no wonder you got recalled. You'd be a real danger in the field, at least to yourself."

Frustrated, Rhone dropped his head to the tabletop, only to connect solidly with the tiny anvil he'd been working on. He managed to stifle the swear word that almost slipped out, but knew he'd be wearing a bruise to go with his chagrin. "Come get your coin," he growled, his clenched teeth muffling both his pain and humiliation.

"Hey, thanks," his assailant whooped. "I hear there's a group going to the cantina tonight. Now I can actually afford to go along now."

Rhone dropped the coin into his attacker's hand as he grumbled, "At this rate, I might as well go along, just to pay the tab."

"Hey, cool. Sounds fine to me," his assailant chimed, then raised an eyebrow in thought. "Would you mind if I signed up to do this again?" But one look at Rhone's basilisk-like stare, and he quickly found his way out.

With his assailant gone, Rhone stared morosely at the tiny pieces he'd been working on. The tangled gears lay scattered across the tabletop, with the little anvil lying on its side reminding Rhone of a ship grounded on the beach. He groaned, knowing it would take an hour just to get them separated again. With a resigned breath, he dove back into his work. It would take more than a couple of near-death experiences to keep him from his task. He'd been there before. Only when his eyes finally became too bleary to see did he pack up for the night. It had been a good day, except for the lost coins and the humiliation of his lost encounters.

"Stone? Are we good?" he asked, not certain how Stone would take his day of silence.

I am here, Stone said quietly, reciting the words of their first encounter.

"Good, it just didn't feel right not having you in my head all afternoon," he replied, the simple joy of hearing Stone's voice easing his tired mind.

But I 'was' in your head, or at least at your neck, Stone said pragmatically. *I also believe you are being too hard on Bran. You know he is only trying to help. You were, after all, just a wee bit preoccupied.*

"I know. I know, but I wasn't just goofing off," Rhone stated in justified frustration. "I thought you would understand."

I do. But that does not change the fact that Bran is right. You need to be more aware of your surroundings. You must admit, you are not doing so well on your own. Therefore, Bran was absolutely correct in placing this burden on you. Particularly as I may not always be available, as we have already found.

Another point on which Rhone couldn't argue. He had been "killed" twice in a single day. If his luck didn't improve soon, he would be out of coins altogether.

"Alright, I'll try to stay more alert," he promised. "But I have a lot of work to do, and it would help if you could keep an eye on things. By the way, I thought you might like what I'm making."

Stone's curiosity flared as he asked, *Is it possible that I might look?*

Their early days together had been filled with discoveries, and over time they had settled into an unspoken agreement not to intrude on the other's private pursuits.

"Sure! Let me tell you about it," Rhone agreed happily. "Remember the little dragon Lev has? The one her husband made?"

Of course I do, came Stone's indignant answer. *The little creature was well fabricated, moving much as a real creature would.*

"Exactly," Rhone agreed. "You and I have made some pretty neat things, don't get me wrong, but I want to try some really intricate machinings. Something like the dragon, but not just for looks."

I see . . . Stone commented, not sounding sure at all. *But for what purpose? You humans are already very resourceful. What possible use would you have for a little machining that would do the same job you already accomplish?*

Rhone's nose wrinkled as he tried to explain. "Like I said, I'm not sure yet, but I want them to actually do things. Something useful. I figured I'll need parts no matter what it is, so I'll start there, creating parts that can be used for different applications. You know, like gears, levers, and rivet pins, things I'll need no matter what I'm going to build."

Oh, I see. Like all the little pieces you are picking up, Stone commented, his tone a bit too pleased to be considered understanding.

"Yeah, like those," Rhone answered disappointedly. "I didn't realize how difficult it would be to make such tiny gears. It's a lot of work cutting all those little teeth into the rings. That's bad enough, but there are different sizes, too, and different tooth counts on different gears for different purposes. Some even have teeth on the inside. Some with both. I'm almost going blind trying to work with them."

I can see why you were a bit touchy, Stone admitted, granting his friend a warm feeling of accomplishment. *Could I perhaps assist with the calculations? You know that I am good at such things, and it would leave you one less task to do. But only if it would help*, he offered quickly, not wanting to offend his friend and collar-mate.

"Honestly, it would be a big help," Rhone said with relief. "I'm not so good with gear calculations, let alone the rotation ratios and addendum coefficients." He smiled as his collar warmed, showing Stone's acceptance of the lightly veiled compliment.

I do love calculations, Stone said excitedly. *I will, however, need some direction as to their use. I would be working blind, as the saying goes, and I have come to enjoy our vision. As soon as you have determined the direction of our efforts, please let me know.*

Rhone grinned at Stone's sudden enthusiasm and began explaining his project. "I thought I'd build something like the little dragon, but since I don't know anything about dragons, I was thinking about using things that I do know. Not big things like vehicles and balloons, but something small, like bugs. I would at least have a pattern to work from."

I am actually pleased with the idea, Stone murmured, sounding almost surprised by his own admission. *If Mother Nature can, then why not us? We will duplicate her efforts, using the genuine item for patterning our endeavors. Well done, Rhone. I am feeling quite enthusiastic about this project of yours. Where shall we begin?*

Rhone began to blush at Stone's high praise and had to apologize. "Ahhh, I haven't gotten to the design part yet, so it may take a while. I've been stuck trying to get gears that work."

Yes, a good plan. Gear-driven machinings, Stone said approvingly. *And what is your power source?*

"Power source?" Rhone echoed, his shoulders sagging. "Rats! I haven't gotten that far either."

Unexpectedly, his mind filled with intermeshed gears spinning in perfect unison as a belt-driven track rolled endlessly beneath them. Along its length marched a line of determined rodents, tiny legs pumping furiously as they drove the mechanism forward.

Rats? Stone said in astonishment. *They would be a unique source of power, but they do seem to have endless energy. It just might work.*

"No! Not rats as a power source," Rhone sputtered in disbelief. "Rats, as in, drat it all anyway! But honestly, I hadn't thought as far as a power source. I'm still stuck in the movement of things, like rotation elements causing movement and action."

A rational concern, Stone replied in his usual stoic manner. *Unfortunately, it does leave one rather significant problem. No power. No action.*

"Wow, thanks, Stone. I could have figured that out by myself," Rhone muttered.

But you just said . . .

"I know what I said. I said, I haven't gotten that far," Rhone growled.

It was a moment before he felt Stone sigh in resignation. *Then we are back to, Where shall we begin?*

Rhone slapped a palm to his forehead, but only lightly, as the knot from his earlier action was still sore.

Is that enjoyable? Stone asked in interest. *It does not seem as though it would be, yet you continue doing it. I was just wond...*

"No, it doesn't feel good!" Rhone snapped.

But... Are you certain you feel all right? I am becoming a bit concerned, Stone asked carefully, not wanting to vex his friend further.

Dejected, Rhone released a deep breath as he settled to the ground. "I'm sorry," he whispered quietly. "There are just so many things I want to do, but I don't know how." After a moment's silence, he asked, "Stone, how long did it take for you to learn all the stuff you know?"

He felt Stone's chuckle as the words, *Eons, I'm afraid,* quietly drifted through his mind.

"And, ahhh . . . How long is an eon? Is it like a couple of years?" Rhone asked worriedly.

Perhaps a couple more than that, Stone replied evasively.

Rhone paused before answering. "Okay, I guess I can wait. I was just hoping it wouldn't take quite that long."

Perhaps I should rephrase my question, Stone said quietly. *If you wish to create a small creature-like machining device, what creature would you use as a pattern? Is that more clearly stated?*

"Yeah, it's good," Rhone said with relief. "The problem is, I really don't know. I guess I got a little carried away with the idea, and now I'm afraid to look much further. What if I can't do it? As you said, there has to be a power source, or it's just a toy, so I guess I'm stuck." A moment later, he felt motion like a slow river flow through his veins, its awesome power turning great and ponderous gears.

It is said that what the mind can conceive, it can achieve, Stone said, his casual words flowing along with the river's current. *So, while your creations may not be possible at the moment, they may, in the future. The only certainty is, if you do not work toward your goal, you will never accomplish it.*

Rhone felt the river's energy course through his veins and wondered how it all moved. Then he considered Stone's remark, finally accepting the words as wisdom. "So you think I should try?" he asked before answering his own question. "It does make sense, and if we don't try, we'll never know."

Exactly, my friend.

Accepting Stone's words, Rhone turned to the next phase. "So, I was thinking, the simplest creations might be bugs. They're tiny, so maybe they wouldn't need a lot of parts."

Sounds like a very practical application, Stone answered graciously. *Do you have a preference? There are many kinds of bugs and insects to choose from.*

"Not really," Rhone answered. "But what got me thinking was the sending device Jewel designed. I've got to admit, I was a little jealous, but that's not fair. She's good at her job too."

I agree on both accounts, Stone commented. *I too felt the . . . jealousy, as you call it. A terrible reaction to a wonderful idea. And yes, she did well. It is also quite probable that we would have come up with the* concept, *but were simply pulled in other directions at the time. So where were you going with this? I am intrigued.*

Rhone settled himself more comfortably before answering. "Since Jewel designed a sending unit, maybe we should go ahead and build a receiver. Do you think we can?"

It does seem reasonable, Stone agreed, taking a moment to run some calculations.

"What are you doing in there?" Rhone laughed, feeling the tickle of mental gears whirling in his head.

Oh, just a few simple calculations, Stone answered vaguely, but a moment later he began to vibrate. *I believe you have something. I told you we make a good team.*

CHAPTER 9

To Be, or Not

Having spent the morning reacquainting himself with the town, Rhone took the rest of the day off, deciding to do a little tinkering to fill the time. A large magnifying lens helped as he squinted at the tiny pieces, but after hours of work his eyes burned, and he hoped he wouldn't go blind before he finished.

"What time is it?" he asked, rubbing wearily at his tired eyes.

Time for you to get some sleep.

It seemed more an order than a simple comment, but Rhone was too tired to even mind when Stone continued his harangue.

If you continue to waste your rest period with your tinkerings, I can only see a diminishing of your other skills. I will also take it upon myself to warn you that the time you spend playing in the workroom keeps you from doing your real tasks.

"But I need to get these done," Rhone groaned. "We keep changing the design, so I constantly have to rebuild them."

Both were right. Time was an issue, but it was also true that as they learned more, their creation's design would need to be changed to meet the new needs.

And what of Aundrea's request? Stone reminded him. *Did she not ask you to find who in The Council was watching?*

"You know she did," Rhone said, both miffed and relieved that the conversation had shifted. "But it's a gamble. First, I've got to learn my way around the Stronghold, which is a job all by itself. Then I'm supposed to figure out who's paying a little *too* much attention to the OPR—more than they should or need. And even if we find someone like that, what then? We still have to decide whether they're working against the government or just... curious. And curiosity isn't a crime, last I checked."

He paused, searching for a better way to explain it, then shook his head. "It's just a lot, Stone. I know she hauled us all the way back from Corgy for this, but I'm not sure there's actually anything we can do to help."

The discussion made him less than happy, but he put his tools and bugs aside for the night. They were, after all, just toys, and he did have more important issues to deal with. After locking up, he wandered back to Aundrea's apartment, considering what he knew about The Council. Stone, of course, had gotten data directly from Jewel, but it wasn't as though that helped him. He had to wait until Stone determined the information was useful before he divulged his knowledge. It was probably just as well, since he wasn't sure he even wanted to know. Sometimes ignorance was bliss.

"Got any ideas?" he finally asked his friend and collar-mate.

Stone didn't answer immediately, seeming to consider the idea. *I am not certain,* he finally acknowledged, which was no better an answer than Rhone's.

"That sounds like a no," Rhone answered gloomily. He didn't blame his friend. He had simply hoped for a better answer. "No problem. I understand. We'll just have to try something simple and work from there. Tomorrow, I'm scheduled to go to the committee gallery. That's as close to the actual council chamber as we can get without an invitation. Maybe we'll get lucky and learn something."

A good plan, my friend. Jewel has already informed me of our scheduled itinerary, and if nothing else, it will assist us in finding our way around the Stronghold.

"And hopefully, another way out," Rhone said with a sigh. "I should have thought of that too."

Morning brought an early start with Rhone making his way to the corner café and a cup of coffee. Aundrea always had some brewing, but he liked the feeling of being an adult, ordering his cup as though still playing the part developed from his first assignment. His front had been to act the part of a nobleman's son, which had its privileges. Sometimes he missed those days, if you left out the parts of being dragged across the road on his face, or blown off his feet by a rupturing envelope. Maybe just being himself wasn't so bad, even if it was boring.

The Capital Stronghold was nothing like Corgy. He had learned every street of the small coastal town within a day. But The Stronghold itself was bigger than ten Corgys, with more levels, rooms, and stairways than he could count. Luckily, Aundrea had given him a map showing the main routes through the gigantic complex.

Unfortunately, even though the OPR office was in the outer section of the place, the remainder was worse than he had expected, its myriad hallways as baffling as the jigsaw-puzzled passages of the badlands.

To Stone, of course, it was simply a matter of triangulating forward motion and inertia, translating it into distance and direction. Anywhere he had been, he would be able to find his way back. But Rhone wasn't so sure he could do the same. He tried to keep an eye on the map, talk to Stone, and keep a pleasant expression on his already stressed face, but he noticed more than one person's look as they passed, seeing him talking to himself. He wasn't overly worried. The halls were so busy he could barely hear himself think, let alone his conversation with Stone.

"The map says the chambers should be two corners ahead and to the right," Rhone murmured, talking to Stone as he gave cautious glances at the map.

Yes, I believe that is what the sign says, Stone commented helpfully.

"Sign?" Rhone asked in surprise, then sighed, blinking his tired eyes as he focused on the signboard directly in front of him. The next few minutes he spent scolding himself for his lack of awareness and foresight, particularly as he was supposed to be an agent. What kind of agent couldn't find his way around his own building, especially in the area used by the general population? They, of course, would need directions. He simply hadn't thought about it, being far more used to the backcountry trails where you could see where you were going. Oddly, he was buoyed by the thought. He honestly didn't want to be back in the dry desert valley of his home. This was his life now, Capital Stronghold or not.

Rhone, are we going to enter? Stone asked patiently.

Startled by the comment, Rhone realized he was indeed standing at the entry to the committee gallery. Blushing at his lack of awareness, he gave a mental, *Thanks, Stone. I'd be totally lost without you,* his silent comment showing he hadn't totally lost his senses.

Stepping determinedly toward the door, he nodded to the man standing watch, who nodded back, acknowledging his right to be there. This viewing area was for the general public, allowing them to overhear the proceedings, if not actually to take part. Rhone took a seat toward the front where he could overlook the large room. The place had an official look with its massive podium standing on a raised dais at the room's end, the rows of heavy chairs lined before it mostly filled already. Rhone hadn't taken the time to read the board announcing the day's proceedings, but the topic didn't really matter. His job was simply to absorb the workings of government. Interestingly, the place had the feel of immense heaviness, as though the entire weight of government centered on one building. He had never considered how government came about, but below were some of the people who made it all happen. He, too, was a part of it now. A teeny-weeny part to be sure, but like a tiny gear in his machinings, it helped the other parts work.

Rhone gave a snort at the thought of himself as a gear in a world-sized mechanical machine, but when the man standing watch at the doorway scowled, Rhone ducked his head in embarrassment, surprised at the feeling of pride he had in knowing he was an agent, and part of this government.

The sharp clack of a gavel sent echoes through the hall, and Rhone settled back to listen. He had a lot to learn.

The government proceedings had been long, but far more interesting than Rhone had expected. He left feeling his day had been well used, even if he hadn't found anything new about who was digging into the OPR's affairs. But he hadn't expected to. He knew the process would be similar to their original search for other We—trial and error. It may be time-consuming, but it did work. Already he had learned his way to the gallery, or at least Stone knew, and once there, Stone could find his way back. His own directional sense was pretty good when out in the wilds, but inside the confines of the massive building, he found himself continually turned around, unable to see further than the next corner.

He was carefully working his way past a distinguished-looking older gentleman shuffling slowly along the corridor when Stone broke into his rambling thoughts. *Excuse me, but I believe we would make better progress by going in the other direction.*

Rhone rolled his eyes and spun on the ball of his foot. The gentleman behind him checked his stride so abruptly his hands shot up in self-defense. The effect traveled down the corridor like a dropped line of dominoes, each person stopping just a fraction too late. Moments later the hallway was hopelessly jammed, and an impressive number of people had already decided the whole affair was Rhone's fault.

Blushing, Rhone blurted an apology to the man he'd just cut off. "Sorry, sir. I . . . I guess I got turned around."

"So it seems," the gentleman said graciously. "Do not worry yourself. I understand entirely. It took me quite a while to get my directions straight. Now, if you're headed out, stay to the left. It may be a bit more circuitous, but it will get you there, and far more simply." Tapping a finger to the brim of his hat, the gentleman gave a dignified tip of his head and passed a thankful Rhone.

"Thank you, sir. I appreciate it," Rhone called as the man quickly disappeared in the throng. Unfortunately, those following didn't seem as understanding, as several glowered as they made their way around his still-stalled form.

This will not be the way we took on our way in, but it would be good to see another route, Stone commented helpfully.

Rhone didn't bother to answer, as his attempt to stay out of the way still got his booted toe stepped on twice before the backup had cleared. Only then was he able to wander his way through the office-lined corridors, eventually making his way to the fresh air of the streets. Free at last, he breathed deeply, quickly rethinking the concept of 'fresh air' as smoke from the surrounding chimneys, the pungent aroma of the gutter's filth, and rotting vegetables from behind a small grocery, brought the closeness of the city into sharp focus. The cloying air was anything but fresh.

Blinking at the eye-watering heaviness, Rhone fanned the air before his face, as though that would clear the stinking miasma. Even the fishing fleet of Corgy hadn't been this bad, though his memory of the whale cutter's warehouse had been close. For the moment, though, this was his assignment, and with his duties done for the day, he had some tinkering to do.

Unfortunately, his arrival at the hallowed halls of the OPR's office caught Aundrea's attention, and she waved him down. "Rhone, good timing. How did your day go?"

With a noncommittal shrug, Rhone gave what he hoped would be a quick rundown. "It went okay. I learned a lot about the government, but nothing about whoever's sticking their nose into our business."

"I would prefer you not make open comments of our concerns," Aundrea said quietly.

"Sorry. I guess I wasn't thinking," Rhone said, somewhat surprised by her comment.

"I'm not overly worried, but I would like to keep it to ourselves. It's probably a moot point, but for the moment let's consider it hush-hush."

Rhone's color began to rise as he nodded his understanding.

Noting his embarrassment, Aundrea motioned him toward her office. "Come on in and tell me what you learned. You've been gone all day."

Rhone sighed, realizing his day wasn't over. Seating himself in the cozy, overstuffed chair across from her desk, he gave her his abbreviated rundown. "It was a bit scary at first," he admitted. "The speakers talked for hours. Honestly, I didn't understand most of it, but it was actually pretty interesting. I never thought about all the work it took to run things. Do you go to those meetings too?"

"Not very often," she admitted. "Occasionally, when I need to explain something or verify some bit of information we recommended or disagree with, but most often they leave us alone. I think they recognize that most of our work is best done without too much notoriety or surveillance. Or maybe they simply don't want to know. It's okay. I like it that way. But now, to you. Are you planning to go back tomorrow, or do you have something else in mind?"

Rhone blushed again, realizing he hadn't planned at all.

Luckily, Stone dropped a helpful hint. *Let us sit in on The Council's committees again,* Stone murmured in silence, *but this time I will attempt to reach out for a connection. I do not expect anything, but we must start somewhere.*

Rhone nodded, as much to his own relief as to answer Stone. "Stone thinks we should go back. He wants to try reaching out for a connection while we're there."

"That sounds fine. One step at a time makes forward progress," Aundrea said appreciatively. "Now, shall we head home, or were you planning to do more of your tool tinkerings?" His instant flush made her smile. "You honestly thought I wouldn't know of your new obsession? It's practically the news of the day around here," she said mischievously. "Everyone is waiting to see what your newest creation will be. You do realize that news of your airship has practically made you a standard in the office gossip column, don't you?"

He honestly hadn't, his further embarrassment showing clear to his earlobes. With a shrug, he tried to make little of it. "I thought I might spend some time down there, yeah. I'm not sure where it's going yet, but I did manage to make a bug."

"A bug? I'm not sure I understand," Aundrea said cautiously. She was a practical woman, and quite tolerant of her agent's peculiarities, but a bug?

When her concentration seemed to drift for a moment, Rhone understood she was talking with Jewel, and waited until she snapped back to reality, brow lifted in a smile of interest.

"What do you think? Will it be worth anything?" he asked, realizing Stone must have passed Jewel a picture, or at least data.

Aundrea tipped her head as she gave careful consideration to the question. "Actually, I can think of several applications where a bug might be useful. But weren't you supposed to be taking lessons in your sword work? You mentioned it when you returned, so I told the sword master to expect you."

Rhone blew out a deep sigh, knowing she was right. He had intended to see Master Crank, but the work on his creations had been so exciting that it had unintentionally kept him from finding the time. The other fact was, Master Crank had the misfortune of being the epitome of his namesake. He was not only cranky; he was a true stickler for form and presence. Worse, since Aundrea had announced his need, Master Crank would be forewarned, and would drive Rhone even harder to make his presentations and parries perfect.

"Okay. I'll go see Master Crank after tomorrow," Rhone replied, but his words brought a look of skepticism from Aundrea. "After the committee sessions," he added quickly. "I really was going. I just haven't gotten there yet."

"Good plan," she said pleasantly, "and have fun playing with your bugs. But don't stay out too late. I'll be expecting you."

With an absent nod, Rhone got up from the chair, wondering what ideas she could possibly have for his little creations.

⚜

Tiny gears rotated in almost unseen motions, spinning on their minuscule axles and housings that supported them. The entire creation shifted and moved, re-creating the original creature that was now pinned to a board for close inspection.

With the aid of a magnifying lens, Rhone carefully measured the tiny joints and pivot points, then designed suitable replacements until an almost exact mechanical copy of the original sat patiently awaiting its activation. The only difference was, one had been a living creature, while the new duplicate was an imitation of nature's wonders, delicately constructed from tiny metal parts.

The tiny beetle skittered across the tabletop, almost falling to the floor before Rhone jumped forward to capture it.

"I think we got it this time," he said proudly, releasing the creation to once again scurry across the scarred work surface.

It does move with greater dexterity than the first version, Stone agreed. *But I must ask, what is its use? You previously* said *you wished to design things that did a task. But what task will this creation accomplish?*

Rhone took a weary breath, needing the time to come up with an answer. Finally, he simply shrugged. "I don't know. I get carried away with the mechanism and forget the reason. I guess it doesn't do anything but run around."

And . . . Stone questioned, the rumble of his voice cascading through Rhone's mind like an ocean wave.

"And . . . I'll come up with something," Rhone mimicked, trying to evade the issue. Then, in a show of frustration, he moaned, "I don't know! It crawls, so maybe we could use it to hunt down other bugs. There are plenty of those around."

That is a possibility, Stone admitted, but seemed unimpressed by the idea. *It would, however, require a way to capture them, or at least do away with them. Do not despair, my friend. I am sure you will make something useful one of these days.*

"Gee, thanks, Stone," Rhone said in annoyance. "At least we got it working." But he knew Stone was right, and chose the high road. "Hey. It was your idea for the power source that really made the difference."

It is good to see that you are paying attention, Stone allowed, the mild compliment coming with a warm vibration, almost like a purr, against Rhone's neck. *But remember, there are many options.*

Smiling, Rhone picked up the key and used it to tighten the unit's spring tension before setting the tiny creature back on the floor. When the enclosed coiled spring began to unwind, its rotational motion spun tiny enmeshed gears on their axles, affecting the fulcrumed levers that connected with other arms. The culmination of the tiny mechanical actions brought motion, mimicking life's true movement. He watched the little creation run back and forth for while, but knew Aundrea had scheduled him to meet with Master Crank for his much-needed training, so, gathering his bugs and tools, he dumped them into a box in the corner, knowing he was going to be late, a thing the grouchy instructor took as a personal affront.

With a sigh, he closed the door and headed to the training fields.

CHAPTER 10

Disquiet

The session on sword-work had been fruitless, the only thing gained being bruises and a limp. Hobbling back to his little lab, virtually a large closet he had secretly made his own, Rhone painfully dragged out his box of mechanical bugs, planning to spend the remainder of his day tucked away where he could hide the marks of his ineffective sword work. Stifling a groan, he bent to rewind the mechanism, watching as the clicks of tiny feet skittered across the floor, almost drowned out by the quiet whir of the spring mechanism powering it. The bug may not be accomplishing anything useful, but it did run fast, and he was having fun just winding it up and watching as it rapidly skittered back and forth.

Mmmhmmm!

Rhone gave a start at Stone's throat-clearing, knowing he was going to get a lecture.

I do not see the gain in watching a machined creation maneuver itself around the room when there are other, more productive things we could be achieving.

Rhone held back his 'party pooper' comment, knowing Stone had never understood the term. Besides, it would merely delay the inevitable. "I'm just making sure it will work without breaking," Rhone explained guiltily. "The parts are so tiny, it's hard to keep them consistent."

It seems to be working just fine, so can we now move on? There must be other things we can do.

Rhone slumped in response, but had a question. "Stone, you mentioned something about this thing possibly doing away with other bugs. But what were you thinking? How would that happen?"

Is it not obvious? Stone asked in surprise. *You spoke of creating creature-beings that did a task, and this one does not. It merely scurries around, hither and yon. Therefore, if you wish for it to have a task, such as dealing with other bugs, you must have a method to detain or kill the little vermin that cause so much distress to you humans. I myself have no such problem, but that only proves the superiority of the We.*

Rhone chose to ignore the statement, knowing it just might be true. Instead, he considered how he might go about creating an auto-motion bug-remover creature. "Do you really think we could do it?"

A silly question, is it not? You built an airship, as well as this little bug thing. Why not a mechanical bug-catching creation? It would only take a minor redesign of the one you have to allow it to track and attack.

"Cool," Rhone said, his grin almost diabolical as he considered the possibilities.

And what of your job here? Have you given up on assisting Aundrea?

"Of course not. You know I wouldn't, but you've got to admit, this sounds a lot more fun."

Personally, I suggest you quit playing and start working. And remember, you will be meeting with that Master Crank person tomorrow.

Rhone grimaced at the reminder, but knew he needed the sessions. Then a thought crossed his mind. "Stone? I figure you have a pretty good idea for a workable bug-catcher design, or you wouldn't have mentioned it. You also know how much work I have to do for Aundrea. So, wouldn't this get done a lot faster if you just told me what to do. We might even get home before midnight."

They didn't, but even his bleary eyes found it thrilling to watch the tiny, scorpion-like mechanism skitter across the floor, nosing into one corner, then another, before going still—nothing more than a child's toy at rest.

Then, with a spin, its pinchers snapped forward, snatching a shiny, black-shelled beetle from the shadows. With mechanical precision, the tail arched up and over, only to stab down with blinding speed, its tiny pin-tailed stinger impaling the beetle from back to belly.

Unexpectedly, the motion slowed. . . then s l o w e d   f u r t h e r... until it stopped altogether, the tail half-raised. With its spring-wound power totally used up, the beetle dangled obscenely from the pinchers, twitching for several long seconds before finally, it too went still.

"Yaahooo!" Rhone shouted excitedly. "Did you see that? I think we have a winner."

I am glad you appreciate good design, Stone said silently, his words more bored than excited. *Now, are we done?*

"What a great idea. I would never have come up with the sensor idea by myself, Rhone replied, too happy to notice. "Thanks, Stone."

At last Stone brightened, giving off a warm glow at Rhone's praise. *I appreciate the comment, but remember, we are a team,* Stone reminded him. *We do work well together.*

"That we do. Except when it comes to cleaning up," Rhone teased. "That part I get to do on my own." He grinned, knowing he had won at least one point for the night. He didn't often win. Not with Stone's crystalline intellect giving him the upper hand. Satisfied with the day's work, he began gathering his tools. "I won't have time to work in here for a while, not with the committee session and sword drills. I've got to get some sleep, too. It wouldn't look good for an agent to fall asleep in the committee gallery."

Stone's rumbling chortle sounded like distant thunder on a summer day, giving Rhone a flashback memory of the old homestead as he closed up for the night.

Byron had always had difficulty understanding the small thinking of his siblings. Even age hadn't seemed to grant the wisdom professed in the stories. All the old books said the ancients had been wise, their favoritism from the gods granting them additional years. But by his reasoning, it was just as possible that anyone reaching that age had simply seen so many changes, failures, and births that they came to understand the patterns of things. For him, things hadn't gotten better. Different, yes, yet far too much the same. Nothing really changed. The poor were poor. The rich were rich, at least for a while, and it didn't matter how much a person had, they always wanted more.

As fourth son, his placement in the lineage didn't grant him sufficient position for any real future. His duty had been to study clerical canons. The doctrine of leadership. Religious leadership, true, but leadership was leadership, and it was up to him to make use of those teachings.

His brothers, however, thought only of themselves, forever scheming to outmaneuver one another as they clawed toward the pinnacle of their small, ruthless world. Each craved dominance—control of the Brotherhood and, through it, the inner workings of the government that shaped laws for everyone else.

It was a worthy dream, but his brothers were far too self-centered to fit into the leadership position, not without caving under the requirements of that kind of control.

He alone recognized the truth in that awareness. The only disquiet to the plan was his tiny fragment of the talisman, which often gave waking dreams. What would it have been like to hold the entire piece, as Father had? It was no wonder Father had turned inward toward the end, groveling in his own despotic ruin before seizing the courage to end his torment.

Byron smiled, knowing his father's act had also ruined his eldest brother's plans for a takeover. No, he was the only one with patience and training. It had taken far more years than expected, but it had come. Now, he planned for the day when he would step into the position of control, wresting the reins from his undeserving brothers. Even Father had destroyed his own talisman rather than put it into his first son's hands. The rest were simply too young to consider, and in no position to take up the responsibility.

Now it was up to him. He would see to the changes that needed done. It was his fate, God-given or not.

With a mild shift, Byron's right hand slid to cover the ring on his other, its slight pulse of power hidden from any observant eyes. While tiny, it was enough. He also knew that as long as his brothers had their own, there was danger. But he had a plan. In one fell swoop, he would master the group and take their precious rings. He would not wear them. Even the thought of having that much connection to the strange power made his skin crawl, wondering again how Father had done it for all those years.

Gathering his drifting thoughts, Byron made a clerical gesture, shuttering away the strange power, sealing it once more into its oblivion. Waking thoughts he could master. It was the dreams—thick with promise and warning—that slipped beyond his grasp. Still, he would learn their hidden routes in time. All paths led somewhere, and his would end exactly where it should—in power.

He understood what the future required. The Brotherhood had failed—greedy, short-sighted men churning chaos in a system already buckling under incompetence. They thought themselves rulers, but they had only proven how badly the world needed guidance.

He would provide it. He would rule as a benevolent hand, steady and patient, helping the people rise from the muck of their small, struggling lives. Without direction and oversight, it was remarkable that they endured at all. But he would give them the purpose and push they needed to work harder, to become more than they were. Together, they would build a great government. They would enjoy the fruits of their labor, while he oversaw it all.

Deep into his thoughts, he almost missed the discussion of his brothers, not recognizing his own lie for what it was.

Paxton ground his teeth before spitefully accosting the small group. "I'm sure you've heard the rumors, and if I've heard them,

I know you have. Something is going on, and we need to know what. How can we make informed decisions if we don't have all the information?" He wanted to strike the heavily carved arm of his chair but decided the show would only bring smiles from his feckless brothers, knowing he was losing what little control he held.

Paxton was the firebrand, number two and hothead of the group. Strong, balding, and built like a bull, he was ready to run amuck at whatever whim he set his mind to. He had the power, and probably the greatest piece of his father's talisman.

In his eyes, the stone had been stupidly destroyed, a fact that could never be forgiven. He himself had been ready to make his move, only waiting for the moment father passed before doing so, but his father's sudden death had caught them all flat-footed. It was only by chance that he had grabbed the largest piece as they scrambled about, searching frantically for what they could find. Interestingly, his irrational panic had settled as his fingers touched the stone, tiny compared to the original, but the largest that survived. Large or not, it hadn't granted him any better standing in the list of succession that held him. Certainly, none of the others would allow his stepping past them. Bodily over, perhaps, but grouped, they worked to hold him at bay, bonding in a loose and ever-changing alliance as they wielded their minuscule power to keep him in line. For decades, he had been unable to make forward progress, until now, he merely paced in place, waiting his chance.

The day would come. This time he would be ready.

"Settle yourselves, brothers," Warren intervened, his placating gesture attempting to soothe both Byron's overzealous demands and Paxton's simmering anger. He was used to his brothers' fits, and found them unworthy. "There's no need to steam your collars. We've all heard the rumors. But at this point, we have nothing definitive to go on. The OPR has simply been lucky for a change. You know how scattered they are. Occasionally, even they are bound to have things work in their favor. It's just natural. Wait and see. Before you know it, they'll be back in the gutter, right alongside the people they try to help."

There were snickers, but he was enjoying his moment in the limelight and challenged any to make comment.

"There is no evidence of any real situation, and rumors are simply rumors," he continued. "I find it almost disgusting how much effort you put into making sure the OPR doesn't succeed. Besides, no matter what they do for the people, the people don't care. So, I ask you, why does it matter? Go through the streets and look. The people simply aren't worth the effort the OPR puts into them. The masses are simply a waste of time and energy." Finished, he relinquished the floor, shaking his head as though cleansing himself of the scene.

Surprisingly, Jared supported the statement. Standing, he shook his great bull of a head. "My concern is why there is concern at all," he said, looking each of his brothers in the eye. "We have done more than our share in keeping The Council from destroying itself. Our work has proven itself, maintaining the politics and politicians that would crumble the entire structure without our efforts. Why, without our oversight and years of experience, the entire government would fail. They should name holidays after us, not set the OPR on our tails. But whether or not, we cannot allow a query that may tangle our lines. We must keep ourselves above the horde, seeing to our needs and not follow theirs."

Paxton, however, wasn't so easily put off. Jared's council may have put a dent in his own announcement, but he too stood, feigning affront at his older brother's concern. "As our dear eldest brother so equitably stated, I can hardly wait to have a holiday in my name, but I'm not wasting time waiting with bated breath. And as to the evidence, Warren, how would you even know? You haven't left these grounds for so long, I'm not sure you could find the front door." He chuckled at his own words, but got no response from the others and tried again. "Do you remember the line, 'Where there is smoke, there is fire?' In this case, it may merely be smoke, but even smoke can be tracked to its origin. At that point, as you so correctly mentioned, we will have further data." Having completed his oration, he squared his shoulders and stared boldly at Jared, then Warren, before sitting down.

As Paxton relinquished the floor, Jared took the incentive by slapping the arm of his chair, the jarring sound loud enough to gather their wandering attention. "We have heard the comments," he stated. "I say that we put Snake to it. He squirms around the big city often enough not to get lost. Do I hear any objections?"

"No objection," Paxton agreed, his loud announcement pouncing on the opportunity to win the first bite.

Byron followed suit with a knowing smile. "I have to admit, it sounds sensible. If we don't know, then we need to find out. Who could possibly object to that?" He scanned his brother's faces, looking for the dissent that always came.

"Snake? You seem quiet," Jared said, his eyes taking in Mathias, the youngest of the five. "Since you're the one singled to do the checking, what say you? Are you up to it?"

It was a simple question, and one he had been waiting for, but Mathias posed as though pondering the issue, recognizing the grease of slimy fingers all over the question. If he said no, they would think him unwilling or afraid. On the other hand, if he said yes, he would be working directly into their hands, acting as a contractor, something they would consider below their own lofty position. What he didn't show was his desire. It was good being the one with the answers. He could then place the information wherever it would do the most good — for himself, of course.

Mathias rose, keenly aware of every eye fixed on him. "It would be my honor, dear brothers," he said warmly, punctuating his consent with a graceful bow. "Allow me to look into the matter and uncover the truth. Who knows? I might even enjoy myself. After all, what could be so extraordinary as to unsettle the Brotherhood?"

They'd gotten what they wanted, yet not in the way they'd expected. As the other four erupted into a fresh, heated argument, Mathias slipped away through the heavy wooden door, its mother-of-pearl inlay catching the soft glow of the lamps.

He smiled as the door closed behind him, muffling their voices. *Snake*, they called him, and snake he could be. Snakes could bite after all.

CHAPTER 11

One Step at a Time

The speaker's droning monologue was undoubtedly worthy, but Rhone's attention had all but drifted away, his subtle stretch effectively covering his yawn without distracting others in the gallery.

I hope your sword defense proves more effective than your attempts to stay awake, Stone commented dryly.

Rhone sighed and rolled his eyes, then stifled another yawn when he noticed the speaker stepping down from the podium and being congratulated by his colleagues. Glad the session was over, he quickly rose, then waited patiently while the others exited before him.

The day hadn't been a total waste. Stone had reached out, but had received nothing. Rhone had even offered to remove the cravat he had worn to cover the eye-catching collar, but Stone had said no.

I thank you, but there is no need. I can see through the material just fine, Stone had reminded him.

"I just don't know what else I can do," Rhone muttered. "This all seems pretty worthless."

It may seem that way, but over time, little steps will get us far, Stone advised. *Just be patient.*

Rhone followed the others from the gallery, slowly integrating himself into the crowded halls. He tried not to look like a tourist, but couldn't help scrutinizing every new piece of artwork and sculpture he passed. Luckily, most everyone was hurriedly leaving, so all he had to do was move along with them without actually stopping.

Still drowsy from the long session, he inched his way with the crowd until Stone's excited vibration brought him fully awake.

Rhone, did you see it? Are you awake?

"I am now," Rhone mumbled, though even that small distraction caused him to bump elbows with the man beside him.

It was there. Stone said excitedly. *I felt it. Now we have undeniable proof there are other We in The Stronghold.*

Other We? But where? Rhone asked, this time remembering to keep his voice silent.

How am I to know? That is why I called you, Stone reminded him. *Now, quickly. Before they get away!*

Where? Rhone asked again. *Could you at least give me an idea of which way to go?* The crowded corridors were simply too full to get a good view, and even the stairs were jam-packed.

"Just go!" Stone demanded, punctuating the order with a mild zap.

Rhone's leg jerked violently at the stimulus, and he nearly stumbled, but he didn't complain. There would be time for that later. Shoving his way through the crowd, he angled toward the stairwell, then craned his neck to scan the faces of those descending. No one stood out—but why would they? These people belonged here. He was the outsider. Fortunately, no one paid him much attention.

Rhone, you must hurry, Stone lamented. *He is getting away.*

Again, Rhone fought his way forward, then changed tactics and tried jumping to see over the heads of those in front of him. But it produced no better results, other than gaining a handful of unsympathetic looks from those around him.

There! Stone cried again, making Rhone wince at the sudden volume in his head. This time, however, Stone had activated a flashing mental directive Rhone could follow.

Doing his best, Rhone followed Stone's directions, pivoting sharply in the crush of bodies, just in time to see a door swinging shut. With a trail of "Sorry, sir," and "Excuse me," he again forced his way across the crowded hallway, feeling like a salmon fighting its way upstream.

Finally reaching the door, he adopted his most inconspicuous posture and lounged against the wall as if he belonged there—no small feat for someone who had just battled through a human maelstrom. As his breathing steadied, he reached out with deliberate calm and turned the knob.

It was locked.

With a sigh of frustration, Rhone leaned forward, resting his head against the cool surface of the door's polished wood. "Sorry, Stone. I missed him," he said in apology.

But that is not good enough. There must be another way in, Stone complained.

"But . . ."

But nothing. We must find them. It is important.

With a groan, Rhone did as ordered. Turning to the nearest man, he attempted to ask, "Ahh, sir?" But the man shouldered his way past, glancing back but without bothering to respond or slow.

Then pick the lock, Stone said in annoyance. *You are trained in such things? Are you not?*

Which was true. Not only had he done well on the various entry procedures required to pass the academy, he made it a point to carry the little kit whenever he went out. The problem was, he was standing in a hallway of the Capital Stronghold with masses of people trundling past.

Rhone, please. You must not delay, Stone reminded him. *It was one of my kind. Quickly now!*

Forcing his breath to slow, Rhone slipped the kit from his pocket, choosing a slender tool slightly larger than the ones he used for his tinkering. With nerves on edge, he first glanced over his shoulder, then angled his body to shield his work from those passing by.

He'd barely settled into his pose when a hard bump from behind sent his forehead thudding into the door. Rhone's heart leapt straight into his throat, knowing he was caught.

He spun around with a strangled protest—only to see a woman with a red parasol drifting serenely past, completely unaware she'd just turned his skull into a battering ram.

Almost faint with relief, it took a moment for Rhone to gather his nerve and again bend to his task. He had just stooped, tool poised, when he felt the handle twist in his grip. Only his wild flinch of panic allowed him to evade the door's swing, but left him awkwardly crouched before an older lady of some girth, glaring down at him with unfeigned distaste.

"Ah, sorry, ma'am," Rhone mumbled, hastily rising from his crouch. Unfortunately, his embarrassed withdrawal miscalculated the distance, and with an eye-watering crack, his already sore head struck the knob.

At least his look of pain must have helped his case, as the lady unconsciously reached out to steady him. "Are you all right, young man, and whatever are you doing?"

The sentence didn't leave much room for avoidance, but in exceptionally good luck, Rhone had dropped his lock tool and now used it as an excuse. "I ahhh . . . Sorry, ma'am. I dropped my stuff and wasn't expecting the door to open. I was just bending to pick it up when, you know. . ."

His grimace and glance at the door must have sufficed, as the woman continued her glare a few more seconds, but finally drew up her dignity and turned to leave.

Having gotten this far, Rhone went for gold. "Ma'am? Did you happen to see a man just enter?"

"A man? In here? I think not!" she said with disgust. "And I suggest you leave immediately. I will not have people snooping around where they are not to be."

"No, ma'am. Of course not," Rhone agreed, eyes going wide at the realization of what that might mean. "I was just trying to follow . . . and ah, got separated." Which was true enough, although not quite the way she might think.

"I will say again, there is no man inside," the woman huffed, her nose raised in disdain. "Now excuse me, but I must be going, and I suggest that you not run into any more doors. Now, good day," which, of course, meant it was not good at all, but only that she was indeed leaving.

Red-faced, Rhone backed from the door, giving her room to maneuver her more than adequate bulk past and into the throng. Only once did she glance back, probably to make sure he was leaving, or maybe to get a better look at his face for reporting to the authorities. Either way, Rhone took it as a good sign that he too should leave.

"Sorry, Stone," he murmured as he maneuvered into the flow of people.

At least you tried, Stone responded, his wistful voice echoing softly through the halls of Rhone's mind.

With an unceremonious plop, Rhone dropped into his favorite overstuffed chair, the rich dark burgundy of the soft velveteen material seeming to soothe the worries of his day. He savored the calm moment before facing Aundrea, his boss and mentor.

"There's another We in The Stronghold," he announced.

Aundrea raised her brow, then stood abruptly and began pacing the office. "It fits," she said, turning to face him. "We've already discussed the possibility, so I guess, now we know."

"Yeah, and it does make sense," Rhone agreed. "I have Stone, and you have Jewel, so there are bound to be others out there somewhere."

"It also supports my concerns about our friends, and I use the term loosely," Aundrea said, stopping to rest against the edge of her desk, hands folded before her. "My worry has always been that if the OPR is too successful, someone will pay attention. Our having a rogue We out there only makes it worse, as they may make connections a human wouldn't." She shook her head in annoyance before continuing. "I just don't like having that much attention on our office. It makes it difficult for our agents to get their work done. On the other hand, just because there is a We doesn't mean it's working against us."

"I suppose," Rhone said thoughtfully. "It wouldn't have to be The Council either. Maybe someone just picked it up, like I did, and doesn't even know what it is."

"True, although that would be quite a coincidence," Aundrea said skeptically. "It is possible, of course, but it's hard to believe, and I don't like coincidences. They're a good way of getting a big surprise you should have seen coming."

Rhone shrugged, not knowing how to answer that. "So, what do we do?"

Aundrea bobbed her eyebrows as she answered, "We have ourselves a stakeout."

"Really? Cool," Rhone said with a grin.

For the next two days, he and Stone sat in the gallery, listening to speakers drone on about their pieces of legislation or some project they were backing, their long-winded speeches making Rhone wonder how anything got done. The endless hours and long nights had his head so stuffed that he could no longer keep his eyes open. Luckily, Stone was doing a better job as he listened for subtle signals from any We.

My plan is to simply listen in, Stone had announced. *Since our query will not be expecting another We, they might not be concerned about keeping their energies in a tightly confined band.* But Rhone's mind was drifting again, and Stone snapped, *Rhone, are you paying attention?*

Ahhh, I think so, Rhone answered, pulling his thoughts back together. *But what happens if you do make contact?*

Yes, that *could be a problem,* Stone agreed. *But it may be as simple as informing them that they are working for the wrong side.* He fell silent a moment, rethinking his words. *It would be most disheartening to believe my people would fall so far from our ways that they would go against good government, or against the people,* Stone said softly.

Maybe, but as I remember, you all had a pretty good fall just to get here, Rhone chuckled, remembering the story of how the We had arrived so long ago.

We did indeed, Stone agreed, missing the pun entirely.

Rhone knew better than to try explaining, and turned his attention back to the legislative session. It was boring work, but no worse than his class on 'Religious Histories of the Outlying Regions' had been. He had almost fallen asleep in that class, too. By the time the day's gallery sessions ended, Rhone had almost missed his appointment for his extracurricular sword training with Master Crank.

His arrival found the Master tapping his booted foot with the tip of his sword, which didn't bode well for the training session. Not bothering to attempt an excuse, Rhone took his blows as they came, wincing as one after another struck with easy evasion of his ungainly defense.

"I'm glad you chose to show up," the Master commented, delivering yet another punishing blow. "I would hate to disappoint our lady director and have you get yourself killed by your own less-than-favorable sword skills. Have you been practicing at all?"

"Sorry, sir. I haven't had time," Rhone began, quickly realizing the answer had come out wrong. "What I meant was, I should have been here sooner, but got caught up in my work," which only gained him a menacing smile from the Master.

"Indeed, you should have. Where is your pride, Rhone? You are a graduate of this academy. This skill is not only expected, it is required. And of course, you have other tasks. Everyone does. It's why you were hired. But from this point forward, I expect you here at every opportunity. No exceptions! Do I make myself clear?"

"Yes, sir," Rhone muttered, although Stone's rumbled warning gave him enough presence of mind to bow stiffly, accepting the Master's demand.

With the master's slight nod, the practice session began again. The flurry of blows continued, leaving Rhone beaten at almost every move. He was stiff and sore by the time it was over, and limped his way through the already darkening streets, groaning when he saw a flight of steps he'd have to climb. He had just taken the first muscle-aching step when he felt Stone's surface go cold against his neck.

Freezing in place, he asked, *Stone?* remembering at the last moment to keep the words in his mind.

I am not certain, but I believe we are being followed, Stone replied cautiously, making Rhone's blood run as cold as Stone's touch.

Rhone's heart began to race as he considered how he had almost died the last time he heard those words. *Followed? You mean like . . . followed followed?* He couldn't help the fear that rose in him, the thick veil of dread seeming to block his senses.

Be alert, but do not be afraid, Stone offered supportively. *While I am not certain as to our follower, I felt a slight connection with the signature a We would use.*

A We? Rhone answered in relief. *That's not so bad. So, what now?*

Now, you will do as you were trained, Stone directed. *Circle around, but do not lead them to Aundrea's doorstep.*

Rhone started to nod, but was stopped by Stone's warning. *Are you not a graduate of the Agency's Academy?*

Of course I am. Why would you even ask? Rhone thought in surprise.

And were you not taught to act naturally? Stone lectured. *And by all means, do not take too devious a* route, *or they will become suspicious. Now get on with it. I should not need to keep reminding you.*

Rhone barely kept himself from nodding again as he sheepishly continued up the steps.

Stone was right. It was time he used his training, but it was difficult to walk naturally when he felt like every step might betray him. Block after block, he walked down the darkening streets, his mind almost numb in worry. Stressed as he was, he barely recognized the various landmarks and storefronts.

He was ready to cross the intersection when a fancy two-horse buggy came high-stepping along the dark streets, its carriage lights illuminating the darkening cobbles in long, slanting shafts that glinted off the damp roadway.

The added stimulus was enough to catch Rhone's attention. Glancing around nervously, he asked, *Stone, are we going the right way?*

It is, if you are headed to the cantina, Stone answered, though Rhone felt the sad shake of Stone's non-existent head.

Sorry, Stone, but I'm just not sure what else to do, Rhone tried to apologize.

His worry mostly evaporated when Stone chuckled, *Rhone, the contact was only faint to begin with and is now gone entirely. Nor am I certain it was actually following us. It may have simply been in the same vicinity.*

"What? I went through all that for nothing?" Rhone protested, speaking aloud for the first time in a quarter of an hour.

Not at all. You did as you were trained to do, Stone reminded him. *When in a situation where you believe you are being followed, you are expected to evade. I do not understand your reticence.*

I get it, he said silently, knowing he hadn't done well. *But can we go home now?* Defeated and sore, he leaned against the post of a newfangled gaslight street lamp, his energy draining away like water from a broken bucket.

I believe it is safe to return now, and I will remain on alert, Stone replied. *They will not sneak up on us again.*

Thanks, Stone. I'm about worn out, Rhone acknowledged, beginning a circuitous route back to Aundrea's apartment. A few blocks later he glanced up to see the dark outline of the Capital Stronghold dominating the cloudy skyline.

Maybe the big city isn't so bad after all, he thought, recognizing the welcome silhouette. It also brought a welcome and reassuring warmth from his friend.

CHAPTER 12

The Pain of it All

Snake wandered the streets, staying in the shadows as he slid from one corner to the next. It was after-hours, a time he found most effective to do what he did so well. Some might call it skulking, but that was a low-life term meant for others. He didn't skulk. He surveyed and pursued, and he was on a task. His slim smile proved his enjoyment of knowing what others would prefer he didn't and granted him power in the knowledge of where their future was headed. His brothers might wield their own gauntlets, but he preferred working from backstage, the real power of The Brotherhood.

He was considering the unique balance they were held in when the hairs on the back of his neck rose. It was an odd feeling, something like the old saying of 'someone walking over your grave'. A moment later, he stepped quietly into the shadows, virtually disappearing from view of any casual eyes.

Unlike his brothers, Mathias liked the dark and had an affinity for it. Dark clothes, dark streets, dark beer, and dark secrets. His brothers didn't mind, as they enjoyed using him to do their dark tasks, not wanting to dirty their own shoes wandering the city's streets. He smiled, knowing he had them in his palm. Any information he gave them would be at his discretion, and any other contacts they might use would only verify his own data. He would see to it.

His dark eyebrows gathered as the odd feeling dissipated, but he maintained his awareness. He was a master at his game, and if he was being followed, which was possible considering his brothers, he would simply evade the tail, or deal with it.

Sheltered by the deeper shadows, he slid from one place of concealment to the next, his passage no more visible than his namesake's shadow.

The odd feeling had been uniquely familiar, but its very familiarity made him wary. He had long ago categorized the feel of those he associated with, and while this was similar in many ways, it was definitely not one of his brothers. It felt cleaner somehow. Cleaner than the slimy, thin feel they carried. Regardless, he had no other way to categorize it. It was what it was.

It had been decades since he had been so intrigued by anything. Decades of boredom, dealing with his brothers and the business of The Brotherhood. It gained them nothing but money and the ability to manipulate politics, but what good were those when he already had everything he wanted? In fact, it was the main reason he had taken up the skill set he wielded so well, delving into the questionable ways of others, and most often coming out on top.

U nknown to Mathias, his brothers had waited for his absence and were meeting to discuss him.

Paxton growled a warning as he faced his remaining brothers. He'd spent all morning arguing, but it hadn't gotten him more than a half-cold cup of mulled wine. "I just don't like it. We've put our entire trust in one man, and you know perfectly well how much we trust him."

"About as much as we trust you," Warren grunted, granting his brother a bored smile. "But I'll admit, I worry any time I put all my eggs in one basket. But remember, it's just as easy to lose by being overzealous as it is to do nothing. Lean a bit too far and you topple, losing the entire lot." He made his point by slowly tipping his cup until a small amount of the mead spilled onto the stone floor.

Paxton slammed his hand down on the table, disgusted at the waste, and nearly spilling his own. "Then what would you have us do?" he demanded, glaring at his younger brother. "You're the one who brought this to us in the first place? So why change your mind now?"

"It wasn't me. I merely brought up the issue of the rumor," Warren stated brusquely, shaking his head in denial. "It was Jared who tasked our dear, slimy-skinned brother to do the search."

There were smirks from the others, but none said further, as even Jared accepted his part with a shrug.

"I don't care if it was Jared or the devil himself," Paxton fumed in aggravation. "It's you who seems to have a problem with our method, and now you want it changed." When Warren's head tipped in acknowledgment, Paxton continued with a vengeance. "And what great plan do you have in mind? Should we plant a banner in the middle of the market, or something else just as futile?"

Jared began massaging his temple as another of his famous headaches began to grow, groaning at both it and the uselessness of the discussion. "This is nothing but tomfoolery," he griped, wanting nothing more than a darkened corner where he could nurse his cup of mead. His headache would be there regardless, but at least the mead would grant some solace. His brother's complaints certainly wouldn't.

"Oh, nothing as grand as all that, Bro," Paxton answered lightly, seeing its effect on his elder brother. "But I would like to make a motion. Why not fix this by sending out another to track the whereabouts of our youngest? Why should we place our lives in his singular hands? Do you trust him that much?"

"That I do not," Paxton admitted.

Warren raised his hand, flinching as it attracted their attention. "I do not like the thought of throwing good money after bad. It is wasteful, and a poor choice with little gain. We have, as you have acknowledged, accepted Mathias's word on untold actions. I do not see the need to doubt him now, let alone the cost. As long as we stand together, there is nothing he can do to thwart our plans."

"You always were a prissy do-gooder," Paxton grumbled, but allowed a slight shrug to show his acceptance.

"All in favor?" Jared announced, catching the moment's fervor before it dissipated. The display of raised arms was total, and satisfied, he smiled behind his mask of indifference. With another problem overcome and his seat unchallenged, the day could have gone worse.

"I 'll expect you to be more careful," Aundrea warned, her brows drawn in a severe line.

Rhone had reported his evening's jaunt and was now considering what to do next. "Yes, ma'am," he mumbled, stepping out and closing the door behind him. He had found a We. Well, Stone had, but that was almost the same thing. But just knowing there was one didn't help if they couldn't find it. Then there was the 'not getting caught' part, a thing he had some acquaintance with. "Any ideas?" he asked Stone, hoping he would come up with something great.

I believe we are back to the original problem, Stone rumbled silently. *And while we did accomplish part of the task, it was only by accident.*

"So it wasn't a great plan," Rhone summarized, dropping heavily into the wooden seat at his worktable. "But Aundrea is depending on us. Come on, Stone. You're the one with all the knowledge. I'm new at this."

Hush, and let me think, Stone answered absently, leaving Rhone with no more than he'd had before.

Frustrated by his lack of a plan, Rhone decided to accept Master Crank's recommendation.

Taking the day off from his governmental watchdog duty, he chose to spend the time on the training grounds instead.

Only an hour in, and he wished he hadn't. His arms were already aching, and his left leg throbbed where the point of the master's practice sword had struck. The new pain only added to the already sore back muscles as once again he attempted his initial attack ploy. Thrust and parry, counterattack, block, extend, and thrust again . . . but his mind was too slow to keep up. Even Stone's ongoing commentary on poor form and missed opportunities was no longer helping. He was terrible at this, and he was tired, his muscles no longer responding to his requests, making his lunges nonexistent.

You are not terrible, Stone contradicted. *You simply need more practice.*

Master Crank, however, was not so understanding. "Alright, you're done for now," he stated, his harsh drawl only making his statement more poignant. "Can't have you falling on your face before I even hit you. It wouldn't be dignified." The Master's bushy eyebrows bunched in disgust, punctuating his statement.

Rhone was exhausted and had never even gotten close to a touch. His abilities seemed to be more in league with the stuffed practice dummy hanging from the eaves than of a swordsman.

"Thank you, sir. I appreciate the refresher," Rhone mumbled, attempting to put a smile on his face.

"Refresher, is it? Doesn't seem like you've ever picked up a stick before. Have you been practicing at all?" Master Crank grumbled, eyebrows once again bunched in disapproval. "Listen, Rhone, I don't train you to send you out to get pin-cushioned at your first encounter. Or are you trying to make me look bad?"

"No, sir. Of course not! I just, well . . . it's been a while, and I never seem to have the time."

"A while?" the master asked in disbelief. "Here's the deal, Rhone. I expect you here every day, same time, or I'll take it you simply want out." His words struck as seriously as a gravedigger's shovel. "I will not have my graduates dying because they aren't trained. So if you plan on dying, do it on your own time, not as an agent."

Rhone watched as Master Crank stalked away, his receding back making it a statement he couldn't refuse. Not only did he ache from one end to the other, he was disappointed with himself—the obvious dismissal only deepening his failure.

You tried, Stone interjected cautiously. *Perhaps it will go better tomorrow.*

"Not likely. He hates me," Rhone groaned.

Nonsense. Dislike, perhaps, but certainly not hatred.

"Like that makes me feel better," Rhone grumbled, although surprisingly, it did.

Actually, you do have an aptitude for the sport. As I remember, you did amazingly well with the knife work. Perhaps if you try thinking of the sword as a very large knife, it might work better for your balance.

Rhone thought about it and shrugged. "Maybe. I guess I can try. I can't get much worse."

That is the way, Stone said supportively. *A straight back and a stiff upper lip will take you far. I heard Master Crank say so to one of the new recruits. I am certain that it will work for you.*

Rhone managed not to roll his eyes, but mostly because it would hurt. He would try. He didn't have many other options.

I may, possibly, have an option, Stone offered, sounding as though he wasn't quite so sure.

"Like what? Getting a different job?" Rhone groused, already unhappy with his situation.

Nothing quite so dramatic. I was considering your training, Stone replied. *I understand your issue with Master Crank. He is a bit diffi-cult to deal with at times.*

"Like, all the time," Rhone complained.

He is only attempting to make you the best you can be, which at this point can use some bettering. Was it not Lev who bested you without your even returning her attack?

"But she ambushed me! How was I supposed to fight her?" Rhone groaned, knowing it would not have made much difference.

She was a brigand and a former agent, well versed in swordplay, and he was not.

Exactly, Stone agreed. *Which brings me to my original concept. Why do you not train under Lev? She not only knows the OPR and its training regimen, but she also knows the other side of the fighting world and their methods. If you are to be attacked, why not understand their methods also? Does this not answer several questions at once?*

Rhone was too sore and tired to think about it right now. Besides, he wasn't sure Lev was a good choice, let alone how to ask. "I don't know. What if she says no?" he tried, feeling as low as he was sore. "I don't even know where she is anymore," which was an equally poor excuse since Aundrea obviously did. "I'd just feel dumb asking her to train me."

That much I hear, Stone said, leaking a little understanding into his feeling. *Could I suggest that you ask? Did you ever consider that she may have found being back in the OPR a bit difficult, and that things have changed over the years? Perhaps you would be her savior, offering her a way to be included, yet in her own place. We simply do not know, and will not until you ask. Can you do that?*

Rhone paused, caught between his guilt at persuading her into coming back and his worry over asking for her help, but he didn't know what else to do. "Do you think it will help? I mean, her training me. Do you think she can help with my sword work? I may not be horrible, but I'm not very good either. I'm not sure we can even work together."

You will not know until you ask, Stone repeated. *Can you do that?*

Rhone took a deep breath, nodding, more to give himself an answer than to acknowledge Stone. "Okay. I'll see if I can find her. If I do, then . . . Then I'll ask."

He almost expected a bolt of lightning to strike the ground next to him, but nothing happened, and while still sore and tired, he did feel better. He had made a decision, and maybe things would work out.

It was a week of unrelenting work. After putting in hours at the grueling sword sessions, he and Stone would scour the city searching for We. They even managed a few hours at his lab, tinkering with his tiny creations, but ended up falling asleep with his head resting on the table.

At least the hours of sword work were becoming slightly less embarrassing. He honestly had to admit he wasn't terrible. His parries and ripostes were getting better. He had even managed a touch on Master Crank's left arm, before getting thoroughly trounced when Master Crank merely switched to his other arm, the one he normally used for sword fighting. It hardly seemed fair.

Limping his way home, Rhone grimaced as he placed a cool wrap over his ear, the one flattened by Master Crank's off-handed sword strike.

Of course he is good! He is a Master, after all, Stone commented, giving his very objective counsel. *But you must also remember, you did get a touch on him. Keep at it, my boy. Someday you might actually get in a good blow.*

Which didn't make Rhone's ear feel any better.

The five brothers were again gathered, with Mathias giving his rundown of the current events.

"My investigation was to mitigate your concerns regarding the OPR," he stated, his even voice almost hypnotic in its perceived boredom. "Let me start by saying it is true; they have become somewhat more effective of late. While I haven't discovered the exact cause, it may simply be that, at times, things go right. It is even possible they had something to do with our recent losses on the coastal run, although I have not made the determination as yet. I can also assume they will soon be back to their far more normal, unimpressive selves." He gave them a rudimentary version rather than giving away too much information, and he certainly wasn't going to tell them he had felt something. That would only give them undeserved knowledge, and knowledge was power. "Now, as my task is done, I have places to be. I give you a farewell and good day," and with a mocking bow he gifted them an almost cherubic smile before slipping quietly from the room.

Murmuring rippled through the room, and it took several long minutes before—one by one, they realized he was gone. Most hid behind their practiced indifference, but Byron didn't bother. With a righteous sneer, he slapped the arm of his chair. "Forget him. But remember this—I warned you about the OPR. If Paxton could stand letting someone else make a point for once, we'd have finished this stupidity a long time ago."

"So what is the problem?" Warren asked, his voice adopting the calm, clerical cadence he used whenever tempers threatened to boil over. "This is exactly why we sent Snake out there in the first place. He only confirmed what you were already saying. We should be thanking our youngest for taking the time to verify our concerns."

With a tired shake of his head, Warren eased himself back into his heavily padded chair. It was a familiar role. As the middle son, he was often the peacemaker. Not always by choice—but often by necessity.

Byron raised a placating hand, addressing his brothers. "I, for one, thank you, my dear Warren. It wouldn't do any good if we ended up strangling one another, now would it?"

The resulting chorus of sly smiles may have been less than reassuring, but was entirely expected, even when Warren lifted his glass toward Byron and nodded. The game had been enjoyable—maintaining the tension while quietly shaping the outcome. Control was everything, and he had been trained for it. The church had seen to that.

Jared looked exhausted as he blew out a heavy breath. "Enough of this. We have the information. Now, what should we do with it? I say, if the OPR isn't any more problem than normal, we continue as we have. We've dealt with everything they've come up with, and I don't expect anything new. My vote is that we move on. Raise a hand if you agree and down if you don't."

"What about Mathias?" Warren asked, not looking as concerned as he sounded. But when three hands went into the air, he merely shrugged, realizing his own vote didn't matter either. "Good enough, so what's next?" he added, attempting not to be bothered by their votes.

Paxton was ready, and blurted, "I do have a matter," his instant action cutting off anyone else's attempt. "Mathias mentioned our coastal run, of which I already had concerns. It seems our goods have been repeatedly intercepted of late, and we need to organize a checkpoint. One of our own may be playing their hand against us, or it may be the OPR, although that I doubt. They simply aren't in that kind of scheme, even if our dear brother would have us believe so."

"The coast run? I thought we had that down pat," Jared questioned. "We have contracts with the captains and secure landside transport from the ports. How could it go wrong?"

"How? They are pirates," Byron answered. "You say we have contracts and secure transport, but when was the last time you checked? A year ago?" He shrugged as though that answered all.

It had indeed been a burgeoning business, shuffling goods from one hand to another. But if the goods were being intercepted, it would cut heavily into their profits.

Warren raised a hand but didn't wait for acknowledgment. "A checkpoint?" he asked, already wondering at the smooth insertion of the fix. "You obviously have something in mind."

"I do. If someone is breaking our contract or leaking information, it should be dealt with, and in the harshest terms," Paxton answered, keeping his voice reasonable, though the rest knew he didn't go in for halfway measures.

Warren again raised a hand. "I suggest that we not give this task to Mathias. He might consider it as us making him our whipping boy and turn tail to bite when we aren't looking. I'm just saying, we call him Snake for a reason."

"Never mind. I'll deal with this myself," Jared interrupted. "There may be a few heads that need cracking, and I've been stuck in this place all winter. It's past time I get out. Questions?" He stared at the others expectantly, but they were bored and ready to leave. "Then, next meeting, next month, unless something comes up."

Raising his ringed fist in salute, he chanted, "For The Brotherhood," instantly chorused by the other three, "For The Brotherhood," raising their own ring-adorned fists.

Four rings glowed a long moment, their dull golden-pink light holding the few beats before slowly returning to the beautiful glint of polished gems.

CHAPTER 13

Bug Bites

Forty-three, Rhone noted in his journal. That was a lot of dead bugs. His little mechanical bug-catcher creation had actually worked, and his clay jar was now brimming with the husks of once-living trophies. Maybe an auto-motion bug-killer machine wasn't such a bad idea. They would probably sell by the dozens. Of course, he would have to make that many first, which sounded like a lot of boring work. He preferred the designing part to doing the same things over and over.

Are you done playing, Stone asked, his bored voice sounding like a lead ball tossed down an empty pipe as it rolled through Rhone's mind.

"Hey, I'm not playing. This is science," Rhone responded distractedly.

Really? And to what purpose?

"What purpose? I'm taking notes," Rhone grumbled, tossing his quill to the table. "And it's called data-keeping. The part I am supposed to do to prove our efforts? It's a process, remember?"

Of course, it is a process. What I do not see is progress. It has been a week since you built the bug killer, but I do not see any further advancement. It has simply turned into play.

And he was right. Rhone had slacked off in his designing. "I guess I'm stuck. I don't know what else to try," he admitted. "The bug killer is cool and all, but what do I do with it?" When Stone's vibration grew to that of a cat's purr, Rhone began to worry.

As I am certain you know, our rudimentary receiver system uses triangulation to find and attack the innocent bugs you have a penchant for collecting.

"Yeah, sorta," Rhone acknowledged.

And was it not a grand project?

"I'm not sure I'd say grand," Rhone conceded, not sure where this was going.

Good enough, Stone acknowledged, and within moments, a string of data began dropping into Rhone's mind like stars falling from the sky. *We must begin our thinking from Jewel's sending device, and while you are at it, consider the possibility of creating longer-range receivers to gather the signals.*

"The what?" Rhone asked, distracted now by an odd feeling of bugs creeping into his mind. With an involuntary shudder, he demanded, "Stone, what's going on in there? Did you just plant bugs in my mind?"

Now, *why would I do such a thing?* Stone replied, his very cheerfulness making Rhone's worry double. *And why are you becoming defensive so quickly?*

"Stone!" Rhone demanded, fists on hips in one of Bella's favorite actions. But the very memory of Bella left him feeling miserable and lonely, which, interestingly, made the sensation of bugs drop away.

I miss her also, Stone confessed.

Blowing out a doleful breath, Rhone pondered his feelings. "I don't know. I was just wondering if we did the right thing, leaving her at Corgy."

There was no other option. We were recalled, Stone answered with regret. *She then took command of The Lady Luna. No, you did correctly, even if we wish it were different.*

"I suppose, but I wish I could talk to her," Rhone mumbled, slumping into his far-to-ready depression.

Chin up, *my boy. I am sure she is fine. We left her in good hands, remember, and you know Captain Black will keep a watchful eye on her.*

"Yeah, I hope so."

After a moment's silence, Stone brought up a question. *Rhone, our discussion of Bella gives me a thought. I was wondering . . .*

"*Alright.* What's going on in that devious mind of yours?" Rhone cut in sarcastically. "And yes, I did say devious."

That is just a bit harsh, Stone replied, *though I am willing to overlook the infraction as I understand you are upset at the moment.* When he received a glower for an answer, Stone tried to help his friend. *Please listen, Rhone. If we manage to build these receiver things, it may be possible to place one in Bella's possession. Would that not be a good outcome?*

"We could do that?" Rhone asked, his interest suddenly perking. Then, throwing caution to the wind, he reached for paper and quill. "What do we do first?"

Slow down, my boy. I will need to make a connection with Jewel first. She has yet to give me access to the plans, and though I am certain we could develop similar, she does have some proprietary rights. Besides, we could use her assistance to better understand it. At that point, we may be able to make an effective extension of her system.

Rhone grinned at Stone's subtle mention of Jewel. He was pretty sure there was more to it than that, but left it alone. Some things were indeed private. "Sure. That makes sense," he admitted, "and I'm supposed to meet with Aundrea, so maybe we can do it then."

Then why are you still sitting there? I am sure Aundrea is ready by now.

A few minutes later, Rhone halted in front of a glass-topped door, its gold script boldly declaring **THE BOSS**. He knocked almost timidly.

"Come in," Aundrea called, her voice sounding strained.

Stepping inside, he eased into his favorite chair before asking, "Is everything okay?"

"Oh, I'm sure it will be," she replied, sidestepping the question.

Rhone didn't buy it. "Want to tell me about it?" he asked, trying to be helpful. "I am an agent."

"Yes, you are—and a very good one. But I'm afraid this might be above your pay grade."

"Probably," Rhone admitted with a shrug. "I'm at the bottom of the list. But I also have Stone. Maybe we can help. Besides, Stone says he needs to connect with Jewel, so we've got some time."

Aundrea exhaled and slipped off her ring. "I could honestly use another set of ears," she said, shoulders easing just a fraction.

Rhone grinned and removed his collar, laying the two We side by side on her desktop. "Okay, you two. Do your thing," he ordered, briefly wondering how they would take being ordered around. With a mental shrug, he turned to Aundrea. "Sorry I intruded earlier. I should have been more aware. But who were those guys?"

Aundrea took a deep breath before releasing it and the remainder of her tension. "I will not tell you their names, but they were from The Council."

"They were your bosses?" Rhone asked in surprise.

"I suppose you could say that," she agreed. "As a group, they give our office the power of government to do what we do."

"Did we do something wrong?"

His first thought wondered if some of his previous actions had come to their attention, and not in a good way. He had, after all, created The Lady Luna and destroyed other people's property, even if they were pirates. He had also gotten on Mayor Dugan's bad side and had left in a hurry. It may not have been his fault, probably not anyway, but having The Council showing up just might be connected.

Aundrea could almost read his thoughts and tried to ease his concerns. "This has nothing to do with you, at least not directly. It seems the OPR is under observation, and there are some who are not happy with what we're doing."

"So it's The Luna," Rhone answered fearfully. "I thought we were doing good when we fixed the pirate problem, but maybe they had plans of their own and we got in the way. Even Captain Black mentioned that perhaps some in the upper echelon were connected to the pirate problem."

Though perhaps in a more gainful application than your *own destructive method*, Stone added quietly.

Aundrea didn't notice the exchange as she replied, "Not that I'm aware of," her mind still on the recent meeting. "The Lady Luna was not mentioned at all. From all accounts, the OPR is simply being too efficient and is under observation to determine if our methods are above board. There is some concern that we are in cahoots with the underground and are manipulating their actions to our benefit."

"But that's stupid," Rhone blurted. "How could we even do that? We're the ones fixing the problems."

Aundrea's light laughter eased the worry lines on her forehead as she admitted, "Actually, I can understand their concern. We are doing well. Better than ever. Which means someone on The Council is paying attention. Whether they are for us, or against us, is still to be seen."

"So, why are you worried?" he asked suspiciously.

Aundrea frowned and clasped her hands before she answered. "Jewel alerted me. She felt resentment and fear from the two. That is not a good condition from those we work for."

"I suppose not, but isn't there anything we can do?" he asked thoughtfully.

"Certainly. We keep doing our job the best we can, and maybe this will all go away, or maybe they'll see we aren't a threat. Either way, we can't stop what we're doing. It's our job."

Rhone nodded, but wasn't satisfied. "But if we're doing The Council's work, and if we're doing good, why would they want anything else?"

"It's silly, but there is often jealousy in a command structure," Aundrea said, shaking her head sadly. "Power doesn't like someone getting too close. It threatens their security."

"At least it wasn't because of The Lady Luna," he said quietly, then felt guilty for his relief.

"No, it wasn't The Lady Luna, nor have I mentioned her in my reports. I'm a bit worried The Council might hear of her and want to take it over 'for the good of the state', as they would say. I'm also aware that if they haven't heard yet, they will." She stewed on that for a moment before shaking it off. "Now, I'd like to change topics."

But Rhone was stuck at her announcement. The Lady Luna was his airship, or had been. It wasn't for The Council to take over. "But it still doesn't make sense. If it wasn't The Lady Luna, and we've been doing good, then . . ." he hesitated as a new thought came to him. "If someone in The Council is working with a We, would they feel ours? What I'm saying is . . . Stone felt one, so would they feel threatened?"

"That is a possibility," Aundrea said, staring thoughtfully at the wood-grain pattern of her wainscoted walls.

"I guess that means we're back to our surveillance situation," Rhone said in frustration. "Even knowing there's another We doesn't do us any good if we can't find it."

"Then that's what we need to do," Aundrea stated decisively. "If the OPR is being targeted and feels threatened, then we need more information. Do you two have a plan?"

"Maybe," he answered evasively, the thought of the wave receiver coming to mind. "Let me work on it." Then he turned his thoughts toward Stone. *Are you two about done?*

Well timed, Stone answered. *Jewel and I have just completed our data transfer.*

"Stone says they're done," Rhone announced, although Aundrea would have heard the same through Jewel. "Maybe they've come up with something."

With Stone tucked snugly into the thick velvety padding, Rhone had to admit, it did look like a fancy jewelry box.

Beautiful, but ostentatious. Stone had shown more than a little reluctance. It had been designed for Jewel, after all, a thing Rhone understood all too well. On his first assignment, he'd been persuaded to parade around in one set of new-fangled clothing after another until the ladies were satisfied with his get-up. But even those hadn't been someone else's clothes.

"Ready?" he asked as he closed the lid.

I am, but I am not expecting much, Stone muttered, his connection sounding like he was talking into a pillow.

You'll do fine. Besides, you said this technology would change everything. It undoubtedly would, but he knew the real reason for Stone's pique. So far, everything they had done had been their own creation, but this was Jewel's, and like it or not, Stone was jealous. *At least you're safely tucked in a box. As I remember, when I tried something new, I was hanging upside down from a bubble a hundred feet off the ground.*

Whatever, Stone mumbled, the box making him sound like he had a stuffy nose.

Life hadn't been all fun and games. Rhone had been lucky when Bo Too's envelope had ruptured. They hadn't been airborne yet, or he wouldn't be here working on yet another project. As it was, they had been forced to redesign, the new creation becoming the ship-like features of The Lady Luna. But the memory brought a heaviness to Rhone's heart.

Luckily, Stone came to his rescue, sounding more cheerful than he had a moment ago. *Do not be so maudlin, Rhone, and I am not worried. While this box may be somewhat showy, it will suffice. This is only a* test, *after all.*

"Yeah, it is pretty showy," Rhone agreed, "but do you remember the fancy duds they made me wear? This can't be any worse." His playing the part of a wealthy young heir definitely had its upside, but it had its problems too.

I suppose, though I thought you looked very nice, Stone acknowledged. *We will undoubtedly be able to change the* design *of this containment medium to a more practical* version *once we get it figured out. Something less* ostentatious, perhaps.

"I'm sure we can," Rhone agreed.

Jumping to his feet, he found a handy corner to settle into and had barely gotten seated before Stone's voice rumbled through his mind.

I am done. You may replace me in my collar setting.

"What? Already? That didn't take long," Rhone sputtered in surprise, and with a drawn-out sigh, climbed back to his feet. "Well, how'd it go?" he asked as he removed Stone from the velvet padding.

We will undoubtedly need to refine the method, but it does work, Stone admitted almost regretfully.

"Cool. Any idea how far it can transmit?" Rhone said, adjusting Stone's placement in his collar. Merely the thought of long-distance transmission was staggering, especially while on assignment.

I am not certain as to the distance, but far beyond our normal range. I have already considered a redesign to allow for receiving, *and a much-diminished size. One does not require an elephant's ear when even a mouse can hear.*

"I never thought of it that way, but how small are you thinking?" He could think of a dozen ways he could use the device. Then his step faltered as a mental diagram ran past his mind's eye. "Wait, we could do that?" he asked in amazement.

I believe so. But you must understand, it is merely a graphic display. It is also possible that if several are used, they could triangulate the position of the We that we were tasked to find.

"Of course! If they can track bugs, they should be able to track a We," Rhone said excitedly, his mind swarming over the idea like flies on a dead fish.

Thank you, my friend. I am somewhat proud of the concept. But first things first. Is the workshop available this evening?

R hone watched proudly as the little mechanized creatures skittered across the floor. Unfortunately, keeping them moving proved almost as challenging as building them, as he dashed about the room, dodging their erratic paths while scooping up those that were frozen mid-stride, waiting to be rewound. He was working his way to the next stalled unit when a sickening scrunch made him yelp in pain, sending him crashing shoulder-first into the wall, barely missing a good head-banging. Groaning, he slumped to the floor, rubbing his bruised shoulder as he looked at the semi-flattened creation protruding from his foot and the other crushed pieces scattered about the room.

The sore shoulder was no more than most days after sword practice. It was his foot he was worried about.

Gathering himself, he ignored the rest of the mechanical monsters still searching the room and bent to pull a broken stinger from the side of his leather boot. Gingerly, he removed the boot itself, then his sock, massaging the sore spot with its tiny drop of blood. Luckily, he had missed landing on any of the other creations, or he might have had more than one puncture wound to deal with.

That was not very agile, Stone rumbled. *Now you will have to create another to replace it.* His tone was something less than understanding, but it was the truth.

"It was an accident. I didn't plan on squishing the thing," Rhone grumped back. "You could at least pretend to be a bit more concerned. It does hurt, you know." Broodingly he watched as the other creations slowly came to a stop, their odd poses holding whatever action they were doing when their spring power wound down. With a resigned breath, Rhone mumbled, "They just don't last long enough. I can't keep up with winding them all." When Stone didn't respond, he backed up his gripe with reasoning. "Okay. I suppose I could use a bigger spring. It would make them last longer, but it would also make them larger. I was hoping to keep them small, so they wouldn't be so noticeable." When Stone still didn't respond, Rhone's head drooped in frustration. "Alright, I'm sorry I stepped on your fascinating design work, but as I just mentioned, I was trying to keep them wound."

Thank you for your apology, Stone offered. *It was, after all, your own handiwork that you managed to destroy. But I also agree, the coiled spring does not lend itself to long-term energy release.*

There was silence as the two reflected on their problem, Rhone feeling Stone's thoughts along with his own. A moment later Stone's rumbling voice broke into Rhone's thoughts.

It is possible, a miniature reflective boiler unit may work. Consider it a recycled-steam propulsion system. It is undoubtedly *more complicated than a simple spring* mechanism, *but will produce continuous power whenever there is sunlight.*

Rhone's mind filled with the picture of a dished reflector covered with a tiny piece of domed glass. Inside the reflector, a single droplet of water was being heated to the boiling point, producing steam that rotated enclosed impellers. As the steam cooled, it returned to a droplet, to be recirculated to do it all over again.

Oh . . . My . . . Gosh, Rhone mouthed, totally absorbed in the mechanics of the concept. "Will it work?" He instantly felt stupid for asking, because of course it would work. It was Stone's design. All he had to do was figure out a way to create the tiny parts. Unfortunately, he had no idea how to get such minuscule pieces of glass and tubing, let alone the tiny impeller blades. Regardless, his mind was already working on several concepts, only to discard them one after another.

"I might be able to carve the blades from brass," he said thoughtfully. "It's soft enough that I could work it easily, but steel is just too hard. I would still have to work out the design so I don't waste my time doing it over and over before I get it right." His thoughts flitted from one aspect to another as he delegated tasks into categories.

Perhaps you should clean up this mess before you begin another, Stone said tactfully. It wasn't a command or a reproach, simply a quiet reminder from one friend to another. *As to your concerns regarding your impeller design. You do realize, I am very good at calculations, do you not?*

"Hey, that's right," Rhone said, smiling for the first time in ages. "What was I thinking?"

Obviously, you were not. Now, are you going to clean up this mess? Stone commented dryly.

"I suppose I have to since I haven't gotten you trained to do it," Rhone said with a grin. *Like that will ever happen,* he added silently.

Stone was a rock-thing, after all. His job was to think.

Aundrea watched in amazement as Rhone placed the little mechanical creatures on the floor. "What do you call them?" She asked quizzically.

"They don't really have a name. I just call them bugs," he replied, shrugging apologetically.

She wrinkled her nose at the name. "They do look like bugs, but don't we have enough bugs already?"

"Yeah," he admitted. "I started out playing with the idea, just to see if I could. Then Stone came up with the idea of bug trackers that hunt down other bugs. So I changed the design. They actually work pretty well." He waited for her response, but only got a raised eyebrow that didn't look all that impressed. "You know—trackers?" he said, drawing out the word for emphasis.

It took another moment before Aundrea's expression changed. "Ahh, and who would notice a few more bugs," she said appreciatively as she began to follow the logic.

"Exactly! If we scatter them around The Stronghold, they can transmit back to us when they pick up a signal. Then Stone and I can follow the signals and discover who it is." Rhone beamed as if he had just won a race.

Aundrea nodded thoughtfully. "I like it. Simple and neat, and no one needs to know."

"Wait, there's more." He moved to activate the tiny creations, and in no time, bugs were skittering across the floor, each finding a nook or corner to settle into. Within moments the entire batch was gone, tucked into crannies or behind items, practically invisible, with hardly a leg or pincer showing.

"They do it on their own?" Aundrea asked in awe.

"Yes and no," Rhone answered. "Stone developed the patterns they use to do things, and truthfully, I'm not exactly sure how he does it, but once they're in position, they start tracking for energy sources. It has to do with the frequency of the . . ."

Aundrea waved a hand, stopping him mid-sentence. "No need to say more. Here I thought I was the boss, but this is obviously above my pay grade." She grinned as Rhone blanched. "No problem," she reassured him. "We'll just consider this a compartmentalized, 'need to know', and I do not need to know. I'm sure that if it comes to needing more information, Jewel will be able to fill me in, or at least enough to understand. If not, then it is what it is. I simply do not have the time to study up on your research."

But a thoughtful look crossed her face, and she raised a finger. "I just had a great thought. I believe we need a new department in the OPR. We'll call it Developmental Operations, which will really mean Research and Development, but boring enough that no one will wonder or look further." Then she gave Rhone a long, speculative look. "I know you're young and fairly new to the scene, but you've already been instrumental in several new concepts. Not only have you fulfilled your position requirements, you have far exceeded all expectations." Her smile softened into proud approval as she said, "I believe in granting favor to those who prove valuable. So, what do you think? Are you interested? It will need a department head."

"Head of an entire department?" he asked skeptically. "But I just started, and I'm too young. No one in their right mind would follow me." It was intriguing, though. Then another thought came to him. "Would I have my own workspace?"

"Whatever you want . . . within reason," Aundrea replied, carefully watching his ever-changing expression. "You'll have an office, of course, but I also know you'll require a workroom. Whether that is a laboratory or a blacksmith shop, I have no idea. Also, to give fair warning, I will expect continuous updates on your activity. I can not simply give you carte blanche to do what you wish, but close enough for you to do your research as you will. The things you are doing are on the very frontier of technology, so who is to say what you can or cannot do."

"Ah, probably you," Rhone answered with a sardonic smile. "You are the boss around here."

"I suppose I am," she agreed, releasing a long sigh. "But I would never have considered what you are doing, so I leave it up to you. As I said, keep me informed, mostly so I don't get broadsided by someone coming to complain, but I believe in you, and Stone."

A moment later, she spoke directly to the crystalline entity. "Stone, I expect you to keep Jewel appraised as best you can. I know there are trade secrets and such, but she does need to stay up on your information, and I expect her to be able to feed me what I need when it becomes necessary."

Well, what do you think? Rhone asked silently, taking the moment to connect with Stone. *Any problems with her idea?*

None whatsoever, Stone answered immediately. *Aundrea merely recognizes the importance of our work.* But a moment later, Rhone cringed as a mind-rattling pulse reverberated from Stone. *Now, we can really get things done.*

With a warm inward smile, Rhone refocused on Aundrea. "Stone likes the idea, but you should probably re-say the part about keeping Jewel in the loop."

There is no need. I heard perfectly well, Stone replied curtly.

"Jewel just acknowledged your right to release a limited version of your activities, and I trust that will not become a problem," Aundrea added, looking deeply into Rhone's eyes to verify his acceptance.

"No problem at all," he acknowledged. "I can think of plenty reasons of why we would want you to know what's going on." He was thinking back to his days in Corgy when he had felt so isolated, then his recall where he had barely survived Lev's attack. The more he thought about it, the more he liked the idea of someone keeping an eye on them.

"Good enough. I'll do the paperwork while you make a list of what you'll need. I'll have Bran find a location for your workspace. It won't be in The Stronghold, but I want you close, and under some surveillance. As I said, what you're doing is on the very edge of technology, and a lot of people will want what you have. I'll put Bran on that too and have him work up security so you won't need to worry about it."

Rhone was about to say that it wasn't necessary when Stone cut in.

You do remember how easily others reached you in Bran's little game, do you not?

Rhone groaned, which Aundrea took for hesitation. "They will be more than discreet, and all but invisible," she offered, which was more answer than he deserved.

The whole situation was going places he had never considered, though maybe it was just the next step of what the OPR already did.

He would think about that later. With a nod and a light smile, he mentally told Stone to recall the bugs, then set about gathering up the little creations.

Once again, things were changing.

CHAPTER 14

The New Digs

"Aundrea, could I have a word with you?"

Rhone was seated at his favorite coffee shop, waving for Aundrea's attention. He had been waiting half an hour, knowing she would probably stop by before heading to her office. He should have talked to her at breakfast but had chickened out at the last minute, saying he had to leave early to get a project done. He had only changed his mind when Stone refused to talk to him.

"Why, good morning. I thought you had to head in early," Aundrea greeted, slipping into the seat across from him. "This is nice. We should do it more often."

"Yeah. No. Actually, I needed to talk to you, and didn't, then changed my mind," he said, rambling as he tried to drag his mind into some semblance of order. "Anyway, yeah, it would be good."

"That's a lot of talk for someone who wanted to say something but isn't," she said, smiling at the young man who was almost a son to her.

Rhone blushed, but was at least getting closer to the subject. "It's just that I need a favor and I'm not sure I should even ask." Aundrea's raised eyebrows told him a lot, both that she was amused, and that he should have known better than to question her willingness to answer. So, with a light shrug, he asked, "Is it okay if I ask where Lev is? I sorta lost track of her since we got here, and I was wondering..." Seeing Aundrea's look at the mention of Lev, he quickly added, "It's okay if you can't say."

"No, it's just fine, and I'm sorry. I should have thought of keeping you informed. You did bring her in after all, so I would be surprised if you didn't."

"Okay, thanks," he mumbled in relief.

"In fact, I was just speaking to Bran about her yesterday, and it had to do with you."

"With me? What did I do?" he asked in surprise, wondering about the timeliness of the connection.

But Aundrea's smile eased his concern. "I asked Bran to contact her to see if she would be interested in heading the security team for your new department. Would that be a problem?"

"No problem at all," Rhone exclaimed. "That would be perfect ... if she agrees," he added. "I wouldn't want to drag her away from something else if she liked what she was doing."

"I think we're okay with that. She seemed quite pleased to accept the position," Aundrea answered. "I was planning to mention it this evening after work, but this is better. I'm glad you asked."

Rhone sat back and took a sip of his coffee, thinking about how it had all worked out. It was perfect. They could take time to do some extra training, and it wouldn't be noticed by anyone. Maybe his luck was changing.

Aundrea noticed his thinking and sipped from her own cup, enjoying the scent as well as the unique blend, where every sip seemed to bring on a slightly different hint of flavor, from dark fruits to dusky chocolate, each merely a hint, surrounded by the depth of the coffee itself. She closed her eyes, appreciating the scent as she held the cup close to her nose.

"It's good, isn't it?" Rhone commented, noticing her enjoyment. This is my favorite place. I've tried several, but I like the blend here the best. These baristas really know their business."

"I agree. We'll make this a special treat, not every day, but at least a couple times a week," she said with a smile.

"I like the stuff at home too, don't get me wrong, but this is even better, and thanks for the information about Lev. I think it's a great plan. When does she start?"

"I gave her a couple of days to finish up what she was doing, but very soon I would think. I'm glad you're happy with the idea, and it makes me feel more secure too. I like her, and I can't think of a better place for her now that she's back."

Rhone nodded absently, already planning his own request to Lev.

Noticing his distraction, Aundrea announced, "Well, I've got to go. The office won't come to me." Rising, she cupped his cheek in her hand. "You have a great day, and I'll see you at home if not before."

Rhone flashed her a smile and finished his own cup before scooting his chair back. With a quick wave to the barista, he headed to the council chamber.

It would be another long day, but things were looking up.

An odd sensation brought Mathias to an abrupt stop. It wasn't odd to get a feeling from the gemstone, or even to have it glow on occasion, but this was different. Certainly not the soft pulse of energy he often received in response to something he pondered. No, this was a hollowness. Something . . . empty, like loneliness. A memory from so long ago that he barely recognized it. The ring's hollow pang slowly faded, reverting to the far more subtle sensation he considered normal, the slight pressure in his mind which wasn't uncomfortable, simply there.

It had taken a long time to become comfortable with the feel of the ring. He had often thought of it as his own guilt, having grabbed as greedily as his brothers for the small, shattered pieces of his father's talisman. They had fought for the fragments, scrounging in the dirt like beggars in search of a tossed crust, each searching in frantic haste for any piece, knowing without thought of the power that drew them. The tiny pieces now haunted each brother, not in understanding, but intuitively hoarding their birthright. Was it a simple coincidence that each had found only a single piece?

The perfection of the division had never been spoken of, but he didn't doubt the others had also considered the fact. Five broken pieces for the five brothers. He couldn't imagine what it had been like for his father to have carried the entire stone, but it had undoubtedly broken him, as surely as he had broken it. Power comes at a cost.

Once again, he stretched his senses, searching, but he found nothing. Nothing but empty hallways and equally empty rooms. A feeling of foreboding followed him as he silently slipped outside and made his way through the not-so-quiet streets. Anyone who happened to notice his slight shadow quickly chose another direction, intuitively knowing that the nights were not safe in the big city. He could prove it.

Irritated by the feeling, and needing distraction, he stalked the shadows with gritted teeth, nerves on edge. When a sudden skittering in the alley's refuse startled him, he struck reflexively. With a flick of his wrist, he skewered the offending rodent, his aim as sure as his well-earned namesake. In almost morbid curiosity, Mathias watched as the wretched rodent struggled feebly against the long knife embedded in its flesh, then with a sneer of disgust, he flicked the body from the blade, the now lifeless form flopping almost bonelessly against the brick wall before dropping to the grime-covered street, just another pile of offal.

Glancing at his surroundings, Snake headed deeper into the slums. It wasn't his favorite place, but it did require a measure of awareness. Something to keep his senses honed.

***

"Is this what you had in mind?" Bran asked, tipping his head in the direction of an old slab-sided warehouse. "It's a little further out than Aundrea wanted, but it's still within walking distance of The Stronghold. It also allows sufficient room for observation by your security team. Aundrea told me to see that Lev is heading it. I hope that's all right with you. I know you two had a little tussle on your way back from Corgy, but she's good at her job, and I thought you might enjoy working with her."

"No, it sounds fine," Rhone said enthusiastically, impressed both by the building and that they had even considered his feelings on the matter. "We had a bit of a bump, but it turned out okay. Actually, I haven't heard from her since we arrived, so I'm glad to hear she stayed. I honestly expected her to be sent out into the field where her skills could really be useful, not as my guardian. But it's good," he added, instantly worried that they would rethink the issue.

The last he had seen of Lev was her leaving Aundrea's office the day he'd returned, so her previous separation from the OPR must have been worked out. He already knew she was good. He had fought her, or rather, he hadn't so much as gotten his sword raised, and she had totally annihilated him.

"She is good," Bran acknowledged, "but I wouldn't consider her your guardian. Nor is it what Aundrea would call it, though our good boss is a bit protective of her flock." He grinned at Rhone's facial expression, but waved it off. "She'll work out great. I worked with her a bit, but just to bring her up to date. She's got tons of experience, and I felt more than a little redundant after the first day. She's a good one, and we're lucky to have her back."

Rhone could only agree and felt better about the entire situation. He liked Lev and was sure he could use her experience. "So what now?" he asked, staring at the building.

Bran gave a shrug and an evil grin. "Make your magic, I guess. The boss wouldn't say much, other than you're the head of a new division called 'Developmental Operations', whatever that is." His eyebrows bobbed, hoping for information.

"Sorry, but if the boss wanted you to know, she would have told you," Rhone said apologetically, adding a 'what can I say' shrug of helplessness.

Bran nodded in understanding. "Well, it must be something special, 'cause I'm number two around here, and she won't tell me. So, you do your stuff, and do it well, but I wouldn't expect less," his easy smile letting Rhone know everything was fine. "Besides, I know where you came from and how you got here. Beyond that, I know you both designed and built that giant bubble you flew fighting pirates. And you won. So if our good boss lady decided to put you in charge of a brand new division, there must be a really good reason." He grinned again as Rhone's brow gathered in a worried frown. "Hey, I'm not quite as dumb as I may look, and even I can put one and one together. So yes, I expect great things from your department. Don't let Aundrea down, and you won't let me down." With another grin, he reached out, slapping Rhone's shoulder appreciatively. He was one of the team.

"Thanks, Bran, and just so you know, Aundrea wouldn't have you as her number two if you weren't absolutely top-notch."

Bran shrugged innocently and got on with business." Anyway, this place is yours. Let me know what you're going to need, and I'll see it's gotten. But you'd better take a look inside. You may change your mind."

Drawing back the enormous sliding doors, he ushered Rhone inside with a flourishing wave. "After you."

The building was vacant, just a packed dirt floor and open trusses reaching the high vaulted roofline. Old dust and cobwebs made a musty smell in the cool darkness, but it didn't feel oppressive, just unused. An old brick forge stood in a corner with pegs set into the wall at various heights, placed to hold long-forgotten items. The interior was large enough to hold an entire airship, although the doors were nowhere near big enough to fly Luna through.

Rhone wandered around the interior, pacing off the dimensions and even sticking his head into the old chimney. Grinning happily, he turned to Bran, who was patiently watching the assessment. "It's great, and it already has a forge!"

"I figured, if you're working with metal, it'll be handy," Bran said with a nod.

Rhone saw the glint in Bran's eye, knowing he had just gained some of their secret. "Could be," he said evasively, "or we could be smelting ore for the gold."

"Hey, works for me," Bran agreed, chuckling at the evasion. "Nothing like a gold nugget to catch people's attention. Which reminds me, Lev will be by in a few. She wants to look over the new digs and see what she'll be protecting."

They had hardly stepped out the doors before Lev rode up on Blue, waving as Rhone's eyes widened, recognizing his old mount.

Blue obviously recognized Rhone as he tossed his head with a snort and whinnying his approval.

"Hey, fella. How are you?" Rhone asked, reaching out to pat Blue's neck. "Hope you've been good while I was gone."

Blue tossed his head again, nickering softly as though understanding what Rhone said.

"He doesn't do that when I ride him," Lev commented, sliding to the ground. "He does just fine, but not like he knows what I'm saying."

Bran merely raised his shoulders in a shrug, not sure what to say.

Rhone ignored them both as he continued to pat Blue, talking sweet nothings to his old ride. They had spent a lot of time together on his assignment, and it was good to see him again, but Lev was here to see the building. With one last pat, he turned to Lev, addressing the dusky-skinned woman with warmth. "I'm sorry I lost track of you.

I hadn't heard a thing until I asked Aundrea the other day. She told me, you were going to head our security team."

"I want to thank you for that," Lev said, giving a shallow bow of acknowledgment. "It was great stepping back into the fold, but I'd been gone for so long it was difficult to just start over. I did okay, but this is better." She looked almost guilty for acknowledging her difficulty, but Rhone couldn't have cared less.

"So you got things worked out?" he asked, then grimaced. "Of course you did, or you wouldn't be here. Dumb question, I guess."

Lev chuckled, then became more serious. "Not a dumb question, and you were right. Aundrea did listen, then took action. I was signed back aboard before I could even say no. With all your words of praise about the woman, I could hardly have turned her down."

Rhone grinned and nodded his agreement. "I told you she was good. She knows when things are right. So what do you think of this place?" he asked, sweeping an arm toward the warehouse.

Lev turned slowly, giving the building a cursory once-over, then walked around the exterior with the two guys following. "It should work," she said thoughtfully. "There's enough space to keep the riffraff away, and it gives a clear visual from all angles. Can't ask for much more than that. Honestly though, you won't see much of us. We'll have our ways of concealment, and our being 'out of sight, out of mind' will make it easier for you to get your work done. We'll be here though, so no need to worry."

"Hey, I'm good," he said appreciatively, meaning every word.

Bran gave a satisfied nod. "Alrighty then. You two look like you've got this under control. I'll head back and let the boss know. Let me know what you want for the place, and I'll see it done." Then, turning to Rhone, he asked, "Are you going to stay awhile, or do you want to head back with me?" But seeing Rhone already deep in planning, he turned to Lev. "You okay staying with him? I do need to get back."

"I've got it, and thanks, Bran. I appreciate your good words to the boss lady, too."

"Nothing to it. I say what I see. Besides, this only made sense. Now Rhone won't have to take time getting to know someone else." He gave her one of his special Bran smiles, then almost blushed. "Ahh, there's one more thing," he offered. "I wanted to say, welcome back. Not everything from the past can be fixed, but sometimes it works out." Relieved it was said, he flashed her another grin and tapped his forehead with a two-fingered salute. "Gotta be going," he announced, giving a nod as he headed back to the office.

Without a doubt, the next few days were some of the busiest Rhone had ever experienced. His list of wants quickly became things he had to account for, as he checked the incoming goods, signed documents, and found places to put everything. He knew he should be keeping a journal, documenting his reception of the items, but who had the time?

I am quite capable of keeping track, Stone commented, noting his friend's growing frustration.

"You can?" Rhone blurted, instantly realizing it was a dumb question. "Of course, you can. Sorry. It's just, I've never been in charge of anything before."

You are indeed new to this, but do not worry yourself, Stone answered amiably. *You simply need to learn to delegate. Not everything requires your personal touch, you know. Perhaps you should ask for additional personnel, or are you determined to wear yourself to the bone?*

"No," Rhone sputtered, embarrassed that it would even be considered. "It's just that . . . You know. We've always done our own work."

That is not true, Stone interjected smoothly. *Captain Belle was a great deal of help, first with Bo, then Bo Too, and finally, The Lady Luna. She is undoubtedly still doing so, even without our help.*

It was true, but Rhone wasn't in the mood to be reminded, at least not every tiny sliver of information tucked away in Stone's crystalline memory.

"It wasn't my fault," he frumped. "I didn't have a choice."

Why, of course you did. Although I am certain it would have caused its own set of problems.

"Yeah, like getting fired. Then where would we be?" Rhone reminded him.

It was a moment before he felt the tension in his mind lessen. Stone's tension, he realized. Sometimes it was difficult to remember whose feelings he was feeling.

I too worry about her, Stone sighed, *and The Lady Luna. I recognize our actions may have been necessary, but it was not very genteel to leave her alone like that.*

Rhone felt much the same way but was shocked to hear Stone's admission. "Stone, I . . . we,—we have a job. We can't just up and leave whenever we want."

Yes, and that too is an odd thing. The We do not have such strictures on our actions, although I suppose you moving beings do have different needs to consider.

Rhone considered the statement and how odd that must have been. "It must have been weird not having jobs," he said thoughtfully.

Different, at least. But without motion, there is little to do other than think. We do not have property *or acquisitions to accrue, and nowhere to go since we do not move about. We have no needs, so we think. We are very good thinkers.*

Rhone tried to imagine such a society, but it simply sounded boring. Who would want to sit in one place for all of eternity and do nothing? Of course, they weren't actually sitting, but it was as good as sitting if they didn't have movement.

They both considered the ramifications of such a system, but soon, even Stone was bored with the thought.

So, I was wondering, Stone mentioned, his voice almost a purr as he eased into his request. *When might we be free to take a little trip, just to check on them?*

Rhone was about to answer, but paused, trying to consider the problem as a department head might. Finally, he just shrugged, too new to the system to even know what that might be. "I honestly don't know, but we can't just pick up and leave. That much I do know. We have obligations, and Aundrea gave us a problem to solve."

He glanced around the building's interior at what had become somewhat of a cross between a blacksmith shop and a science lab. The whole concept was exciting, but he had no real idea what they were doing. Aundrea said it was research, whatever that meant. Now, they had hardly settled in, and already Stone wanted to leave.

"Tell you what," he said thoughtfully. "If we can get this transmitter-receiver thing developed and on our bugs, I'll ask Aundrea if we can go to Corgy and place one on the Lady Luna. How does that sound?" The sudden warmth at his throat was answer enough. "You're a good guy, Stone, even if you are a grump."

He was saved from Stone's caustic response as Lev walked in.

"How's it going?" she asked merrily. "Ready to start work?" But Rhone's woeful expression brought an understanding smile to her face. "It's a lot of work, isn't it? Is there anything I can do to help? I'm pretty good with a broom."

"Honestly, a broom wouldn't hurt," Rhone admitted. "I've been so busy I haven't had time to keep up with the housecleaning."

"Well, I wield a pretty mean stick, whether there's thatch on the end or not." Grinning, she walked to the rack on the wall.

Rhone sighed deeply and let his shoulders relax, appreciating her humor. "Please make yourself at home, and thanks. I probably wouldn't have gotten to it for days."

The rest of the afternoon went smoothly, even if the flying dust made breathing somewhat difficult. The broom worked almost by itself as Lev kept her eyes moving, scanning the area around the building and the people passing by. The site was a good location, not too close to the home office, but not too far for backup if needed. She had already begun the recruiting process, looking for those with the right skills. She knew what she was doing. She would protect Rhone and his newly created Research Department, even if it meant giving her life to do it.

While she swept, her eyes sought locations for observation and defense, although rationally, she knew the most dangerous threats would be those behind the scenes, or those working within the government's organizations themselves. She knew. She had been there.

With a final aggressive stroke, she swept the billowing pile of dust and debris out the big shop doors. Glancing up, she noticed a support bracket just inside and above head height. With a practiced scan of the area, she again studied the bracket, wondering if it could be reinforced enough to support a small stand. It would be a great location, above the normal visual plane and out of sight from the exterior. Satisfied, she continued her sweeping, feeling confident in her abilities.

Rhone was signing for another wagonload of supplies when she finally went searching for him. He looked tired but was handling the tasks as though he had been born to it. Hearing her approach, Rhone turned, puffing out a tired sigh as he blew hair from his eyes. "That should be the last load today," he mumbled tiredly. "I'm beat."

"Good timing. It's almost dinnertime."

"Dinner? Already?" Rhone sputtered, honestly amazed that the day was gone.

"Time does fly when you're busy," she said knowingly. "And yes, it is dinnertime. Have you got somewhere to go, or can I offer dinner as my treat?"

"I . . . I think Aundrea is expecting me," he said hesitantly, not wanting to appear ungrateful.

"Then you had better head out or you'll have her waiting, and it's not good to make the boss wait," she said, intuitively understanding what the choice cost him. He was a cute kid. She would enjoy working with him and would happily give whatever knowledge she could.

Embarrassed, Rhone glanced around the nearly empty building. "Thanks for the invite, but I guess I'd better go," he said as a blush began to grow.

"Okay. See you tomorrow then, and don't worry, I'll lock up. I just want to check a few things before I leave."

With a quick nod of thanks, Rhone headed up the street.

Lev loved her new job. Being head of the department's safety, and Rhone's new guardian, was a perfect fit. And while she wasn't proud of her days as a brigand, she had survived and could now use her knowledge in ways she wouldn't have recognized before. There were more villains in the world than just the poor and lowly outcasts of society. She would keep a close watch on her new department head. He had, after all, lifted her from the low point of her life and dragged her back into a being of worth. She would happily pay her debts.

History Mustn't Repeat Itself

"Nice outfit," Lev said, as she eyed the cut of Rhone's uptown clothes.

Rhone grinned self-consciously, his face taking on a hue that almost matched the rose-colored cravat tied around his neck. He liked the fancy duds, and had worn similar on his first assignment, but, like almost everything else, his clothing had been one of the many issues and a constant head-banging between him and Bella. While he had worn one fancy get-up after another, as befitted his supposed position, she wore a simple pinafore over her almost threadbare dress. It really wasn't his fault. His front had been as one of the gentry, and he had to act the part, including his clothing. She, on the other hand, was a simple waitress, serving the needs and wants of The Common House clients, which didn't make her common in any way. Quite the contrary. She was pretty much fabulous no matter what she wore.

Realizing his thoughts, Rhone glanced self-consciously at Lev, standing in quiet contemplation of his pause.

"So, how did you end up here?" she asked, grinning at his obvious embarrassment.

"Let's just say . . . it's a long story," he answered evasively, shrugging as though it was nothing.

But she wasn't going to be put off that easily. "Of course it is. Every good story is a long story. I also know the boss lady is pretty proud of you, almost like you were her own son." When Rhone started to object, Lev raised a hand, forestalling his denial. "I know you're not, but that doesn't keep her from feeling like it." Her face took on an almost wistful smile that, moments later, evolved into a quirky grin. "You know, I should just adopt you myself. Nothing wrong with having two moms, now is there?" she said, staring him down with mock severity.

"Ah, I suppose it would be alright," Rhone mumbled, not sure how to take it. "But I'm not sure why you would want to," then felt almost guilty at the admission.

Lev's brows tightened as she tried to express her feelings. "Because I need someone. Someone I can connect with. I've been alone for so long, I sometimes worry that even my shadow will lose me."

Rhone started to chuckle, but stopped abruptly as a wash of emotion swept over him.

Stone? he whispered silently, not understanding what he was feeling.

Lev is serious, my friend. Do not make light of her offer.

"Wait. You're serious?" Rhone blurted, staring at Lev open-mouthed as he processed everything. "I mean . . . I guess it's okay, but . . ." His voice dropped, uncertain, as he said, "Would it be okay if I just called you Lev?"

Sudden tears sprang into Lev's eyes as she gave a nod. "It's a deal," she whispered, her voice choked by her suddenly tightening throat. "And just between us, I couldn't ask for a better son. I really couldn't."

Rhone didn't know what to say. The moment was strange, especially considering she'd tried to kill him not that long ago. Life had a way of doing that. One minute you were flat on your back. The next you were up and flying. Where he had been down, he now ran an entire department and had two moms to replace the one he'd lost.

I have you too, he whispered silently, his need sending him groping for Stone's connection.

You do, Stone answered in a soft, thrumming vibration, warm against Rhone's throat.

Lev wiped at her dark eyes, a subdued smile on her face. "See what wearing the right clothes can do for your day?" she said with a light laugh. "A woman intuitively knows these things, but men seem to have missed that particular class."

Rhone shrugged but appreciated her humor. "They were probably just playing hooky," he added, which sent Lev into another mood-cleansing laugh.

"So, what's the plan for today?" she asked, her system finally clear of the lingering emotion. "Do I need to set up perimeter surveillance, or are you heading somewhere interesting?"

"I have to head out soon," Rhone said, "but if you've got a minute, there's something I wanted to ask you. Before I forget, again," he added, " bringing a questioning look from her.

"Sure. I've got a minute. What's up?"

Rhone chewed on his lip, searching for a way to make it sound sensible. When nothing better came, he went with his usual fallback—a quick shrug. "Would you be willing to give me some personalized sword training? I'm working with Master Crank, but he beats me so badly I'm pretty sure I've already lost before he even starts."

Lev's eyes drifted from his head to his feet, scrutinizing him with bunched brows. "I've noticed you limping from time to time, but is it that bad?" Seeing the answer even before his embarrassed nod, she said, "Of course I will. I'm your head of security, aren't I? How can you feel secure if you don't believe in your fighting skills?"

"Thank you," Rhone mumbled in relief. "I'm not truly terrible, just barely capable," but his wan smile said more than his words. With a start, he glanced quickly at his new calendorium, a replacement for the one he had traded to Captain Black, and realized how much time had slipped by. "Rats. I'm going to be late," he groaned apologetically. "I'm supposed to be at the Capital Stronghold in ten minutes."

"You'd best run then," she recommended. "I'd saddle Blue, but it's only a couple of blocks. It would take longer for you to wait."

Rhone nodded his agreement, and with a wave, headed out the door.

Lev gazed appreciatively at Rhone's fit form as it disappeared through the partially open doors and felt joy at being where she was wanted. Her thoughts drifted to a comment Rhone had mentioned earlier, of his coming from the little town of Skragmoore. Hardly anyone had even heard of the place. Even the word 'small' was almost too big to describe the town, although worn-out, or run-down, would work pretty well. The problem was, she had heard of it. Her previous partner had been exiled there, while she had been kicked out of the OPR, and all because someone in power had felt threatened.

At least, that was her theory. Her talk with Aundrea had filled in a few of the salient points, but Rhone's talk had stirred both her fear and her hatred. She wouldn't allow that kind of power to take another person she loved, whether an actual son or not.

Rhone pulled up before reaching the Capital Stronghold's massive entrance, taking the moment to brush off his clothes and catch his breath. Young noblemen were not prone to run at any point, let alone in the almost sacred halls of The Stronghold. Finally ready, he stood tall and stepped around the corner, almost bumping into a heavyset gentleman leading an equally massive dog.

The lumbering beast strained at its leash, causing the gentleman's tirade to falter as he berated, not the dog, but the door guard to The Stronghold proper.

"Get out of my way!" the man sputtered, drawing himself up to what he must have considered a daunting posture. "I do not have time for your obstinate bureaucracy."

But the guard held his position, turning a blind eye to the man's posturing. "I am sorry, sir, but animals are not allowed inside."

Fisting his hands at his sides, the not-so-gentle gentleman growled with barely contained ire. "I am not asking your permission, for I do not ask. Now get out of my way, or I will have you fired. Do you have any idea who I am?"

But as the saying goes, his demand fell on deaf ears. With only a raised eyebrow, the guard lowered his head a smidge, showing deference if not agreement. "Sir, the rules are the rules. If I were to allow your dog in, I would indeed be fired."

As the gentleman sputtered in puffed-up rage, his dog, unfazed by the goings-on, turned its attention to Rhone, who drew back warily, recognizing his danger. But as Rhone retreated, the beast swung its bulky form to follow, effectively delivering an abundant spray of spittle from its drooping jowls.

"Oh, no you don't," Rhone squawked in disgust, using both hands to catch the big animal's head, and very aware of the sharp points protruding from the beast's collar. But his complaint had little effect on the dog, other than acting as an invitation to play. As the dog lunged forward, Rhone stepped to the side, leveraging the beast's head away from his body. Unfortunately, the motion dislodged additional amounts of slimy drool, sending it in a skyward arc that landed unerringly on his thigh.

"Yuck!" Rhone bellowed in disgust as he wrestled the bulky beast to a standstill. "Sir, will you see to your dog?" but instantly regretted his words as the dog's owner turned, his face mottled red with indignation.

"You there! Get away from my dog! He does not need you distracting him from his duties." Then the man took one look at Rhone's pants, decorated with strings of slimy drool, and snorted in disgust.

"Hey, it's not my fault," Rhone protested, still working to extricate himself from the beast's enthusiastic attention. It was only when the creature's bulk had forced him against the wall that Rhone clenched his teeth and called for help. *Stone!*

Are you requesting assistance? Stone asked, his voice suspiciously calm.

Stone! Get this guy off me! Rhone pleaded, but even that was cut short as the beast rose on its hind feet, placing his front paws on Rhone's shoulders. *Stone...!*

Oh, alright, Stone rumbled, not seeming the least bit worried. *Just a moment.*

Rhone was fighting to stay on his feet when, an instant later, the dog stopped, ears raised as though hearing the dinner bell. Dropping his bulk with a thud, the beast spun around and buried its drool-soaked muzzle squarely into the portly man's unsuspecting backside.

"WHAA!" the man yelped, arms windmilling as he lurched forward, foot snagging on the bottom step. With a desperate grab, his flailing arms caught the doorman's shoulder, sending both tumbling to the ground in a flurry of coats and curses.

Delighted by the chaos, the big dog joined the fray, jowls flapping like a wet flag in a storm as the cries of, "Watch it!" and "Get him off me!" rose to a full-blown symphony. The stalwart doorman, being on the bottom, took the worst of the fray, his "Oooofffff," all too audible as the air was driven from his lungs.

Oh my, Stone gasped, his silent comment bringing a crooked smile to Rhone's face.

"Well... thanks, I guess." And with his afternoon plans thwarted, Rhone quietly disengaged from the ruckus.

Not wanting to be around when the two men extricated themselves, and no longer in a condition to enter, he left the way he had come. Pride wounded but body intact, Rhone pretended not to notice the looks and jibes he received from the gutter-born scamps that were even quicker than his backhand.

It could be worse, Stone commented apologetically. *At least he didn't bite.*

"Which one? The dog or the man?" Rhone mumbled, not quite as happy as Stone appeared to be. "I should probably find that doorman later and give him my apology. It honestly wasn't his fault. He was just doing his job, after all."

And if he got a good look at you, he may never let you through the door again, Stone reminded him.

He had missed the meeting, but it was only another of the unproductive sorties they had planned, and little had come of them. But as Stone had once said, a one-in-a-million chance was still a chance. Besides, he may not make it to the council chamber, but there was always work to do.

"Drop the tip, now push your hand forward, levering my sword away. Good. Elbow up and over your head, carrying my blade as you go, then disengage, dropping your pommel toward your belt buckle, blade following. Now, snap your wrist and... NO! Don't look down! You'll give away your shot," she hollered.

Rhone cringed, eyes darting back up from his almost perfect swing.

And it had been perfect. Even knowing it was coming, Lev had barely blocked the blow. But stepping back, she read his follow-through and surged forward, free hand slamming into his chest hard enough to knock him off balance.

It was close-in work, the exchanges too fast, giving almost no time. You were either ready, or you were too late.

Rhone felt the sweat running down his back as he kept his distance tight. Knife fighting range, but with swords. He knew better than to give her room to swing. That would only make things worse and her blows more powerful.

Parrying with his dagger, he brought his sword back into position, ready for her next move.

They had been at this for almost an hour, and he already knew he was better. Not great, but undoubtedly better. Her style was just different enough from Master Crank's that it seemed a better fit. That, and Stone's ongoing comments, made for improvement.

"Okay, let's call it a day," she announced, smiling as she stepped back, sword tip swinging up in a salute. "You learn quickly. I'm not sure why you've had so many problems, but everyone is different. Sometimes it doesn't take much, just a different way to say it, or a new way to cock your wrist. It all makes a difference." She wiped a stray strand of hair from her face before reaching for a towel.

Rhone could only nod as, hands on knees, sweat dripped from his face as he gulped lungfuls of air. He thought he was in good shape, but Lev was merely patting her face dry, barely showing a sweat.

"How do you do that?" he asked, gesturing vaguely in her direction as he struggled for breath.

"When it means your life, you learn to stay in shape. You do remember what I was doing for a living, don't you?" her wry smile apologizing for her previous lifestyle.

Rhone stretched, feeling the ache in his back, but it wasn't from multiple bruises as his practice bouts with Master Crank produced. This was from working less-used muscles as he struggled to stay in close contact instead of relying on distance for safety. He could see the difference between the two styles, and both were good, but this one seemed a better fit.

"Thanks, Lev. I might actually have learned something," he said with appreciation. "Now I've got to get myself cleaned up before I head to another session at the council gallery. I've learned a lot, but it seems almost worthless since I'm just sitting around."

Lev folded her towel and set it on the counter before addressing him. "It all takes time," she offered. "Time and planning. By the way, how is your work going? You don't seem to be spending much time here?"

Rhone stopped to make a face. "I know. I'm spending all my time running around, which doesn't leave much time for here. But I'm planning to," he added, seeing her lips purse. "I just have to get things set up in the lab, then I can get to my tinker . . . ah, work," he corrected, realizing tinkering didn't sound very professional.

"I agree. It does sound more impressive, or at least productive," Lev approved. "So, will you be back later, or shall I lock up when I leave?"

"Better lock up. I'm pretty sure I won't have time today, and tomorrow morning, I've got another appointment with Master Crank."

His scowl made her fight back a smile as she answered, "Well, you'd better get going if you plan on cleaning up first. The council won't wait for you." She tossed him a towel before waving him off. "Get going. I, at least, have things to do."

Rhone grabbed the flying towel just before it hit him, giving a quick wipe of his face and neck before returning it to the counter. He thought of tossing it back, but knew he would only get the worst end of the deal. With a final wave, he headed home for a change of clothes.

Lev worked her way around the empty warehouse, pausing now and then to study the walls and ceiling. If trouble came, she wanted to be ready. As she traced Rhone's likely approaches and habits, a realization surfaced—how often she'd heard him talking to himself.

She'd never thought it a flaw and had always made a point not to listen, but when she caught the whispered words *"The Brotherhood"* on one of her passes, she froze. Her new mother's instinct collided with old, buried knowledge.

A chill ran through her as she scolded herself. "Come on, you silly old girl—you're jumping to conclusions," she murmured, forcing a slow breath, pushing back the darkness. It had been nothing more than a stray comment, not a warning of things to come... and yet her pulse refused to slow, praying the road ahead wasn't bending toward a place she knew too well.

Growing agitation brought the memory of her 'release', as The Council had put it. What it really meant was her partner's exile to the far reaches, while she and her husband had simply been kicked out, then attacked shortly after leaving town. It was an old story now, but she was OPR trained and knew when things fit too well. But a minute later, she felt stupid and changed her mind, worried that she was stressing over nothing. The whole idea was totally farfetched.

The feeling didn't leave, however. It began to haunt her, bringing a fear that turned her perfect job into a nightmare of worry. After an afternoon of unrelenting stress, she made her decision. It was possible she was worrying over nothing, but she would protect Rhone, regardless. It may be the last thing she did, as it may get her fired, but hopefully, it wouldn't come to that.

CHAPTER 16

Perfect Practice Makes Perfect

Have you considered the use of our sound receiver for targeting other energy sources? Stone asked quietly.

It was an innocent enough question, but the picture Stone flashed, of triangulating energy waves and the little receivers, sent Rhone's mind into a wild scramble. Bits and pieces of data whirled in his mind's eye before finally coalescing to a conclusion. It also brought a comment from Stone.

I am impressed. You could not have accomplished that last year. You, my boy, are improving your mind.

"But I was just thinking," Rhone replied, surprised by the unexpected compliment.

And that is an imprecise statement. You were not, just thinking. You were, in fact, thinking, Stone corrected.

"I suppose. It is getting easier," Rhone acknowledged. "Too bad it doesn't help with my sword work. Master Crank still leaves bruises every time we train. I'm getting better at my attacks, but he gets past my parries like they're not even there." He rubbed thoughtfully at a sore spot from his last bout, as he said, "I don't know why I can't seem to block a blow I know is coming?"

Stone chuckled in amusement. *Yes, I noticed that. I thought you were simply blocking with your leg rather than your head.*

"Whatever," Rhone replied irritably. "Honestly though, he must be double-jointed or something, the way he reaches around my blocks. I just don't know how to block any better." It was an honest assessment. He really didn't know how, or he would. Getting bruised every day made for sore arms and legs, as his constant limp proved.

After a thoughtful pause, Stone commented, *If you wish, I could review your technique and assist in your motion refinement.*

"Wait—You could do that? Why haven't you already?" Rhone asked in astonishment. "You know how many bruises I have."

I thought you wished to train on your own, as you did during your initial testing. I do not desire to invade your personal space.

Rhone sighed but recognized Stone's effort. "Thanks, I guess. I appreciate that you were concerned with my wishes, but I really could use some help. My own attempts don't seem to be working very well."

But you have improved, Stone reminded him. *Master Crank actually seems to enjoy the practice time now.*

Rhone's snort wasn't quite a laugh but was close enough to get the point across. "Probably because he gets to beat me to a pulp whenever he wants. I haven't won a single bout in all the weeks we've been training."

That is true, but it does leave a great deal of room for improvement, Stone answered helpfully.

Rhone rolled his eyes, but after a moment's contemplation, brought up the training again. "So, if you could do that refinement thing, how would it work? Would I still get pummeled?"

Not necessarily, Stone answered cautiously. *But remember, I can only assess what is taking place. So, if you do get beaten, and I am referring to the issue of winning or losing, not the actual acceptance of blows, then I will observe what occurs and can make a plan of action against it happening again.*

Rhone had hoped for a better answer, but knew his own method hadn't produced much more than bruises. "Okay, let's give it a try. I have a training session tomorrow, and we'll see how it goes."

Very good. I will prepare a pictorial blow-by-blow overview showing loss of contact, weapon alignment, defensive posture, and attack stratagem. Will that be sufficient? Stone gushed enthusiastically.

"Can't you just tell me what to do?" Rhone groaned.

Yes, as soon as I have isolated your losing methodology.

"And how long will it take?" he asked with a sigh.

You do realize *you have a way to go,* Stone replied. *So, undoubtedly, several weeks.*

"Weeks? You want me to keep getting mauled for weeks? I could do that on my own," Rhone blurted, as his hope faded.

And you undoubtedly will, unless we come up with a better plan than the one you are presently using. We know how well that works.

Unfortunately, he couldn't disagree. Even his work with Lev hadn't fixed all his sword fighting issues. "Okay. Let's do it," he replied, already feeling the weeks' worth of bruises he hadn't received yet.

But bruised was better than dead, if he could last that long.

Flat-block, spin, counter left, parry, thrust, watch your overhead. Now crowd his sword arm . . .

Stone's continuous monologue carried Rhone forward, crowding Master Crank's sword arm against his side. Then with a tight spin, he rolled along the blocked weapon, bringing his own sword up and around to the sword master's neck.

Rhone was so surprised he simply stopped, not even knowing how to claim a victory. Breathing hard, he glanced nervously at his instructor's face but saw a huge grin from the normally taciturn man.

"Superbly done, Rhone. I must say, I have never had a pupil advance so far in such a short period of time. You made definite improvements in the last few weeks, but this was an amazing jump. I don't know what you did to change your method, but to be honest, I don't really care. It works."

Rhone practically glowed, more relieved he hadn't received a reprimand than for his win. His very first win. For weeks he had been beaten and bruised, thumped, battered, and bashed, but he'd gradually learned, especially with Lev's help. Now he had Stone's ongoing critiques and direct mental contact to warn him of incoming attacks, which, if nothing else, gave him breathing space to make his own attacks.

Their most recent advancement came when Stone suggested adding a red warning flash to alert where the next threat was coming from. Rhone still had to react before it hit, but it was miles ahead of where his own awareness had been. They discussed the process and took it one step further, adding a green alert to show an opening in his opponent's defense.

At first, Rhone felt like it was cheating, until Stone reminded him of Captain Black's words on the subject. 'It's not cheating if you're the one being attacked,' Captain Black had advised. 'It's just good common sense and a way to stay alive. Dang it, boy. It's survival'. He had then given Rhone a final bit of insight. 'Are you just wantin' a fight, or are you fightin' to win? There's a big difference.'

Realizing he still had his sword held to Master Crank's neck, Rhone lowered the blade, giving a short bow in acknowledgment of a good fight. "Thank you, sir. It was an honor," he said, honestly humbled by the experience. "You are a splendid teacher, and I can't say it enough." Then, raising blade to brow, he swept it down in a hissing swipe before bowing humbly to his master.

"Ha, well done, Rhone. Very well done indeed," Master Crank chortled. "I see that our good lady boss has done her part in your training too." He didn't look at all so cranky as he flung his free arm around Rhone's shoulder. "How about a stop at the cantina? I could use a sip or two after that workout."

"Really? I'd love to," Rhone stuttered in stunned disbelief.

But a throat-clearing rattle from Stone brought disappointment. *I am sorry to mention it, but I believe you already have an appointment,* Stone reminded him.

Rhone grimaced before sheepishly correcting his error. "Sorry, Master. I would love to, but I'm supposed to meet with Aundrea."

"Good enough, then. Gotta keep on the good side of The Boss," Master Crank said approvingly. "Just let me know when you'll allow me a rematch. I'm not used to losing." He chortled again, acknowledging a good fight, and waved off Rhone's concern.

"Certainly, sir. I got lucky tonight, but I know there's a ton more for me to learn," and with a hand raised in parting, Rhone headed across the courtyard, feet barely touching the ground.

"I actually won!" he sputtered, still shocked at having done so. "Of course, I couldn't have done it without you, and it's not the first time I've said that."

I am glad I could assist, Stone offered, *but it was nothing more than an adaptation of the principles learned while on The Lady Luna. That, and your work with Lev. It was she who started your fighting improvement, teaching you to move more effectively. I merely connected the training, allowing you to use what they had already taught you.*

"Yeah, right," Rhone tossed back. "But whatever. It was great. I could see every move he was making. Did you see me do the crowd and spin? It was perfect." Then he felt perfectly stupid, slapping a hand to his forehead. "Of course you saw it. You're the one who showed me. Sorry. I'm just not used to winning."

It was with an energetic step that Rhone bounced his way up to Aundrea's office door, giving only a quick tap before swinging it inward. "Guess what?" he called excitedly, then stopped abruptly, grimacing as he automatically whispered, "Sorry!" Ducking back the way he had so recently come in, Rhone gritted his teeth, both at his error and from the expression he'd seen on Aundrea's face. It had been pained, but not aimed at him. She had been in a meeting with two distinguished-looking gentlemen, and they did not look happy. *Guess that was a bad move,* he mumbled in silence, embarrassment at having barged in uninvited. *When am I going to learn?*

His self-chastisement was enough, and Stone wisely stayed silent.

Rhone felt like a new man. He had slept well, and his early morning session with Master Crank had produced fewer bruises than usual. Whistling to himself, he swung open the warehouse door, thoroughly convinced it was going to be a great day.

"Good morning, Lev. Great day, isn't . . ." but stalled his greeting as Lev turned his direction.

Lev had aged overnight, her forced smile shrouded with lines of worry and eyes puffy from an apparent lack of sleep.

"Are you all right?" he asked hesitantly, not sure how to speak to a woman about something like this.

"Is that you, Rhone?" she asked, squinting, hand shielding her eyes from the bright sunlight. "Sorry. It's hard to tell with the sun behind you like that. And I'm fine. It was just a rough night, that's all."

"You sure? I can give you the day off if you need. I don't plan on doing anything dangerous."

He had barely finished before Stone broke into his thoughts. *You are correct, Rhone. Her system shows she is under great stress. You should do something. She is your second mother, after all.*

Technically, that would be my third, and I'm working on it, Rhone grumbled silently. *Just give me a moment, then, if I've missed something, you can offer advice.*

Splitting his attention was as frustrating as it was exhausting, but turning it back to Lev, he again offered assistance.

"I'm serious, Lev. If you need the day off, then take it. Rough nights can get to us all."

He was just congratulating himself on successfully dealing with her situation when Lev burst into tears.

And now look what you have done, Stone scolded, although Rhone had done nothing more than say good morning and offer her the day off.

I didn't do anything, and if you would get out of my head for a minute, maybe I could find out what's wrong, Rhone shot back, sighing as he again refocused his attention on Lev. "Obviously something is wrong," he tried. "Is there anything I can do to help?"

"No, nothing. I'm sorry." Lev mumbled, absently wiping at her nose. "I haven't had this happen in ages. Just give me a moment. Like I said, it was a rough night, but it will pass."

Rhone nodded, painfully aware of his lack of knowledge when it came to women. With no better option, he did exactly as she'd suggested: nothing. Fortunately, a minute later, her hitching breath evened out.

Drawing a delicate handkerchief from her pocket, Lev blew her nose, then offered a small, embarrassed smile over the frilly lace. "I'm sorry you had to see that," she said in embarrassment, then blushed, realizing he would think she meant blowing her nose, not her crying. Her brows furrowed as she considered correcting him, but in the end, she slumped in defeat.

"Sometimes I forget that I'm back in civilized company," she said sadly, "but that comes from doing the things I did to survive. And no. I realize I could have chosen differently, but I was pretty crazy for a while. Nor is it a good excuse, but it is what it is, and this is the outcome." Her eyes took on a far-away look, as though evaluating her words and thoughts. "Sometimes it's almost too much to bear," she whispered, looking like she would break out into tears again.

Rhone could only nod. Not only had he accepted her for his department's security, but he had also accepted her as his second, or more accurately, his third mom. They were connected now.

"It's no problem, but how can I help?" he asked helpfully. "You said it doesn't happen often, which means it's happened before. So, is there a trigger that sets it off, or did you feel threatened by something? I need to know. I mean, you're not only my mom person, you work for me."

She nodded dully as his words sank in. "Yes. You are the boss," she agreed, though reluctantly.

"No... I didn't mean it like that. I mean, well... if it helps, then I guess it's good, but I really would like to know." Glancing around the newly swept and mostly bare warehouse, he realized there were no chairs where they could sit and talk. "Remind me that I need to order some chairs," he said with a grimace, making Lev chuckle softly through a nose gone stuffy. "Tell you what, clean up your tears and I'll buy you a cup of coffee at the shop down the street. They have some great pastries too. I should know. I've almost eaten the shelves clean more than once."

With a sheepish grin, Lev nodded before taking another wipe at her nose. "That sounds like fun. Just give me a minute or two, although it may take three if I look as bad as I think I do."

Rhone grinned, already seeing her improvement. "Take your time. We have plenty," he said, thankful when she headed to the back of the warehouse and the sink for cleaning up after a day's work.

That was well done. Very well indeed, Stone commented, making Rhone blush, embarrassed at his uneducated dealing with a woman.

Lev looked healthier when she returned, her dusky skin all but glowing and her smile back in place. "That does feel better. Thank you," she said, striding confidently across the room. "Coffee sounds good too."

It was only two blocks to the coffee shop, which wasn't a grand place like the Common House in Corgy—more a street-side vendor with a few tables and chairs out front and pull-down shutter to close up the hole-in-the-wall establishment at night.

"Two, please," Rhone ordered, "and a couple of your pastries."

"It'll be right up," the young lady said, her smile bright enough to challenge the morning sun. She gave Lev a cursory glance but didn't look worried. Lev was obviously not a threat to her own quiet infatuation with Rhone.

"A very nice young lady," Lev remarked as they seated themselves to wait.

Rhone glanced back and shrugged slightly. "Yeah, I suppose she is," but his brows gathered as though he hadn't considered it before. "She serves me almost every day, so I should probably get her name. It's just that I'm always so busy I forget."

"That is not very genteel," Lev commented, her hidden smile bringing dimples to her cheeks. "I would think your training would have taught you better than that."

Rhone sipped at his coffee, using the motion to give the barista another subtle glance. But he knew the real reason for his dismissal, and it was beyond his ability to fix. Besides, he was busy, and that was enough. "There just isn't much time for those kinds of things," he mumbled, covering his hesitancy by blowing at the hot liquid.

"All right, we'll leave it for now, but remember to always be a gentleman," Lev offered, "unless, of course, it's the part you're playing at the moment. The rest is all you."

Rhone understood her oblique reference to playing parts, and some of the consequences that went with it. "Okay, I get it," he said, chuckling uncomfortably. "It's sort of like the sneaking assault game Bran set on me." At Lev's interested look, he had to explain. "Bran has the other agents try to kill me when I'm not aware. Well, not really kill me," he said quickly, seeing her eyes go wide. "It's like a game. Then I have to pay them when they do, at least until I get good enough to buy myself free."

"And how is that going?" she asked, the question bringing an instant blush to Rhone's cheeks.

"Let's just say there's been a lot of partying at the cantina lately."

A shallow grin lightened her features. "And it comes out of your pocket," she surmised.

"Yeah. I caught a couple attacks, but most get through," he said, grimacing at the admission.

Her lips pursed as she surveyed him critically. "And are you getting better—or do you not care? I can see why Bran set this on you. You have to be aware, Rhone. Always." She sipped from her cup, her brows knitting with concern. "It might even be why they added me to your department. It's not only you who needs defending now. It's also the work you're doing."

Rhone stiffened and glanced at her cautiously, unsure how much others had told her—and how much she'd deduced on her own. He wasn't even certain it mattered anymore.

Lev was experienced enough to recognize his concern and let him off the hook with a smile. "I may not know exactly what you're doing, or why, but they obviously don't want it getting into the wrong hands. You're too valuable an asset to let go, particularly if they can fix the problem."

"I hadn't actually thought about it like that," Rhone acknowledged. "It isn't just me anymore, is it? I've been doing things alone for so long, I guess I didn't really realize what it means to be a team."

Lev's smile was as gentle as her nod. "Don't be too hard on yourself. I know about doing things alone. I've been there," she said softly. "There is some security in knowing everything from your own point of view, without needing to consider the entire world, or in this case, the organization, but it also has its downsides."

They sat quietly sipping their coffee as they absorbed the warm morning sun. The little shop was in an excellent location, backed as it was by buildings blocking the light breeze but not the sun. After a moment, Lev brought up another subject.

"I want to apologize about earlier," she offered. "I thought it might help if you understood a bit more about why I ended up where you found me."

Rhone nodded thoughtfully before taking another sip, the warmth of the brew infusing itself through his body. He chose not to say anything, leaving it up to her to explain what she would.

Taking that as an affirmative, Lev cradled her cup in both hands as she stared off into nothing, seeing a vision of her past. "You basically know the story," she said contemplatively, "but you can't know what it did to me, losing the love of my life as he fought to save us both. I literally went crazy. Not the kind where you lose your mental knowledge and brain function, but it was a madness nonetheless. I simply didn't care. I didn't care what happened to me or anyone else. I was angry and bloodthirsty, taking whatever I could from any I could reach. Maybe not everyone," she said, giving him a sideways glance. "Even I had enough 'self' not to prey on the poor, hopeless souls I found deep in the woods, those attempting to survive on what they could find and grow from the land. Those I left to themselves, but the others, the merchants, traders, and their guards, those willing to put their lives at risk for money. I was more than willing to prey on them. I truly had gone crazy, and I'm sorry."

Rhone inhaled the fresh aroma of his coffee as he thought over her explanation. "And that led to this morning?

"It did," Lev said, her eyes asking for his understanding. "Nowadays, I have to be careful how deeply I think about things. It can sneak up on me before I know it." Her lips tightened as she analyzed the problem, then shook her head to dispel it. "I was worried last night, and it got to me, but I'm fine now."

"Something got you worried?" he asked, his question honest but naïve. "If we can fix it, maybe we can keep it from happening again."

Lev gave a joking smirk as she said, "I could tell you, but it's probably above your pay grade."

"Which means it's important," he concluded. "Is it a security issue, or something more personal?"

That was well asked, Stone said approvingly, but at Rhone at silent growl, quickly backed out of the conversation. *I know. You will ask when you need help,* he whispered, before sealing the connection.

Rhone couldn't help his smile as he waited for Lev's answer.

"You are head of your own department now," she added, rethinking her statement, "so, both actually. I accidentally overheard you talking to yourself, and your mention of The Brotherhood. I really wasn't listening in, but I couldn't help hearing it. Unfortunately, it brought back memories I would rather not remember and couldn't put away. I stayed up all night worrying." She looked at him apologetically before sighing. "I told you part of what I did, but not all. On our final assignment, my partner and I went looking for the supposed coastal mansion of The Brotherhood. We even found what we were looking for, but a lot of good it did for us. Remember, I told you he was exiled while I was merely fired. It was only the beginning of a hard time that brought on more hard times."

"So my talking to myself set off your memories," Rhone concluded for her. "I'm sorry, Lev. I guess I do talk to myself a lot. It probably comes from being alone so much of my life." It was far more probable it was his talking with Stone, but he wasn't going to mention that. A thoughtful expression crossed his face as he asked, "So you think The Brotherhood are real? Aundrea said she wasn't sure, but thought it was likely since the name carries so much fear behind it." He attempted to sound casual, just a friend asking a question, not the heart-thumping excitement it really carried.

Without a doubt, it was exciting information, and maybe something Aundrea could use.

"Of course they're real," Lev sputtered. "We weren't just out chasing a wild goose. We were OPR-trained agents."

"I didn't mean it like that," Rhone apologized. "It's just that when Aundrea mentioned them to me, she said she wasn't sure they even existed. That's all. I've never had dealings with them, so I wouldn't know either way." Which was almost true, or at least true enough. He hadn't had any connection with The Brotherhood. With a We, yes, but who knew if that had anything to do with The Brotherhood.

Lev nodded her understanding as she talked on in friendly chatter, but Rhone's attention had wandered. By the time his attention returned, his coffee had cooled, and he realized Lev had stopped talking, merely observing him with her soft motherly smile that accepted all.

Embarrassed by his lapse, Rhone shrugged and drew himself into a more upright position. "I guess I'd better be going. I've got a session with Master Crank this morning and need to get moving, but I should be back before noon. Maybe I'll even get some work done in the lab today."

Lev smiled as she stood, her heart swelling. "Good enough. Have a good practice, and I'll make sure the lab is ready," she said, picking up both cups, happy for the young man she had adopted into her life.

Rhone smiled his acceptance and turned to leave, but glanced back at the pretty young barista, conflicted by her as much as the other thoughts running through his head. His mind kept returning to The Brotherhood and the way they had dealt with Lev. It just wasn't right. And if they did have We, like Aundrea suspected, then something needed to be done.

Things had suddenly gotten closer.

CHAPTER 17

The Citadel

Lev glanced back at her second mount, ponied behind her on a long lead. She had been riding hard, towing her spare, which was definitely challenging, but the ability to trade mounts with a mere change of saddle meant she could continue longer. Horses are great travelers, but even they can't run all day with the weight of a rider on their backs. All in all, it had been a long day.

Her ability to stay unseen had been a lifesaving skill from her former profession, so ingrained it hadn't taken a thought when she carefully chose her camp, knowing the copse of trees would hide her reasonably well. While her camp was important, it was of less concern than her horses. As any good rider knew, the horse always comes first. Her rest would come when it did.

Sliding tiredly out of the saddle, Lev caught herself with a quick grip on the stirrup leathers, saving herself an embarrassing fall as her legs nearly buckled, her abused muscles rebelling outright from the long ride. With a few muttered groans, she gathered herself and began unsaddling, dropping the dusty tack into a loose heap.

Only after the two horses had been cared for did she take time to sit, the less-than-soft ground causing her to groan again as a flare of pain shot up her backside and down her legs. "I'm getting too old for this," she muttered, shifting into a slightly more comfortable position. When she finally settled herself, she dug through her saddlebags, coming out with a stick of smoked meat. With a sigh, she ripped off a hunk with her teeth and closed her eyes, chewing slowly as the tough, savory bite began refortifying her aching body. When it was finally gone, she took a sip from her canvas-sided canteen, her body beginning to relax. It was with a start that she remembered the hoarded treasure waiting in her pack, but it was worth the effort as she dug further, finding the chunk of chocolate wrapped in waxed paper, the only indulgence she had accepted from Aundrea.

With a silent thanks to her new boss and mentor, she savored the taste, swooshing the thick, mouth-melted liquid from one side to the other before it too slid down her thankful throat.

Life didn't offer many things that could surpass chocolate, making the simple extravagance the treasure it was.

With dinner done, she wrapped the thick blanket around her weary body and propped herself against the tree. Moments later, she was in a dreamless sleep, lulled by the snuffling sounds of the grazing horses.

Morning came far too soon as Lev found herself slumped over a gnarly root like an entwined lover. Cursing under her breath, she rose stiffly and began saddling the none-too-eager steeds, preparing for another day's ride. Again ponying her second horse, she leaned forward, whispering into her mount's ear, "Let's go, boy. We won't get there any sooner by being slow," and with a prancing step to show his readiness, they were back on the road, drawing ever closer to where she hoped to find Rhone.

The dense trees of the coastal interior had given way to wind-twisted brush, its tangled foliage and intertwining branches forming an almost impenetrable barricade that even her long-legged horses didn't want to attempt.

Even after so many years, she remembered the area. Not wanting to broadcast her presence, she left the roadway on a twisted game trail she knew, eventually leading to a small glade. Even the almost two decades hadn't changed things overly much.

Hobbling the horses near the almost dry stream, she back-tracked and brushed out their tracks, knowing the horses would be safe. They were simply too tired to wander far, not with enough of the stiff grasses growing between the brush to keep them. They wouldn't stray far.

She rested just long enough to take a bite or two from her foodstuffs and a drink from the stream, but being this close to The Brotherhood made her restless. Every step brought her closer to danger, and hopefully to Rhone. There was no other reason she would be here, and many good reasons not.

Twenty minutes of working her way through the scraggly trees and tangled brush brought her to a ridge of scarred rock. Carefully scanning the area, she belly-crawled to a convenient notch and lay gazing at the uniquely beautiful, yet equally monstrous, citadel of stone that fit remarkably well into the desolate hollow in the landscape. Half of the structure had been carved into the stony escarpment, while the other half was built of massive blocks weighing thousands of pounds, if not multiple tons each. Whether you loved its design or not, it was undoubtedly a magnificent structure, a creation of times long past and of a different heritage.

Lev's vantage point gave her a distant view of people working at their tasks, some caring for the gardens tucked gracefully into the designed courtyard, as others carted goods from outer buildings to the inner keep. The citadel wasn't a true castle—more of a manor house, its perimeter walls too low for proper fortification, but enough to contain the daily functions of life while giving a modicum of protection from the outside world. Hidden or not, the citadel would draw the attention of any viewer, its tall tower dominating the isolated skyline, yet part of the cliffs it topped.

A shiver ran down Lev's back, not from cold but from a knowledge of the danger she was in. Only the belief that Rhone had also come here kept her going.

On her last trip, she had come with a partner. This trip, she hoped to leave with one.

Backing quietly from her observation point, she spent the remainder of the day in the cool shade by the creek, wracking her brain for a plan. She had been so sure Rhone was headed here, but she hadn't passed him. Doubts began to gnaw at her. Had she been in a hurry and passed him, or perhaps he had taken a different road, or met up with a friend? Maybe he had stopped for supplies, or had a change of heart. The options were endless. But it was just as possible he had gotten here before her. At least her camp was near enough to the seldom-used road that she would hear anyone approaching. Perhaps even Rhone.

She was still pondering the options when she heard not one, but several horses approaching. Feeling doom's hand closing around her, she crept closer.

She peered cautiously through the scraggly brush, gaining a view of a magnificent steed caparisoned in silver and brocade trappings. He was high-stepping his way down the rough road, a gentleman sitting pompously in the embroidered saddle. The man's dark, curly hair was kept long, his salt and pepper beard trimmed closely, as befitted a gentleman of status. Behind him rode four others, garbed as soldiers, their attitude announcing them as men of some worth, though undoubtedly in their own eyes. Soldiers tended to look like soldiers no matter what era or weapon they used. These carried swords at their side and other, less traditional weapons, strapped about their persons and saddles. The saving grace from Lev's previous work was in noting everything: man, weapon, and ability. While her original training may have been from the OPR's academy, it was the other side of the law that had truly refined her skills.

She knew trouble when she saw it, and soundlessly slid deeper into the scrub, melting into the cover as she waited for them to pass. She had no doubt it was one of The Brotherhood. Who else would travel so far from civilization and still be as haughty as a church lord or king? His lackey guardsmen followed with little thought for surveillance, obviously more for prestige than to guard. Besides, his countenance alone set him apart, saying, 'Touch not, lest ye be touched, and to a far greater extent than thou hast any consideration of.' She almost snickered at the thought, but her cold and more practical inner voice kept her hidden.

When the men had passed, she gathered herself and carefully followed. Information was always of value.

She kept well off the road, holding them at the edge of her vision as she followed their progress, tracking more by the sound of the men's voices and their horses' hoofbeats than sight. When the citadel's dark mass loomed over the brush, she slowed, easing closer until she could see the group halted before the gate. Drawing his sword, one of the guards kicked his horse forward, rapping its pommel against the heavy panel. "Open for Master Paxton!" he shouted, his voice as harsh and bold as a challenge on a battlefield.

Almost instantly, a head popped up above the gate, and with one look, bobbed acknowledgment before disappearing again. A moment later, the gate began its inward swing, the sounds of scurrying feet telling of the chaos inside.

The watch had not been alert nor watchful for their lord's imminent arrival.

Lev took that as a promising sign, proving the manor wasn't often, if ever, under threat. Only when the gates had closed did she creep away. Half an hour later, she was again tucked into the crevice in the rock she had used previously. By the time she was in place, the men had disappeared, but their horses were still being looked after by stable hands.

It was a scene of quiet domesticity, but it wasn't getting her any closer to finding Rhone. Pulling a stick of meat from her coat pocket, she settled in for the duration. Her years of training had ingrained the premise of, 'Eat when you have the chance, for you never know what the day will hold'. Holding to her training, she hungrily tore a bite from the meat. An army may move on its stomach, but as everyone knows, it's mostly hurry up and wait.

Lev blinked her tired, dry eyes, trying to stay awake as the warm sun settled over the distant hills. She had spent the entire day watching the citadel, vainly hoping to spot Rhone, but she had no more information than when she had arrived. It had been her responsibility to protect him, and she had failed, again.

With that specter looming over her, the old adage: *Fool me once, shame on you. Fool me twice, shame on me,* kept repeating in Lev's mind.

It struck far too close to home.

Her previous partner had paid the price for one mistake. Now Rhone—her newest charge—had gone off alone to confront the Brotherhood. Even people who knew nothing of the organization knew enough to fear its name.

It had become the boogeyman whispered about in children's tales, and Rhone had gone looking for them.

"I'll find you. Just give me a chance," she whispered into the void.

It would be another long ride, but it was time to report in.

L ev was still new to the establishment, but need dictated her action. Tapping lightly at Aundrea's glass-topped door, she pushed it open without waiting. "Aundrea, I'm sorry to intru—" she began, but was cut off by Aundrea's immediate welcome.

"Lev, hello. What can I do for you?" she answered, scooting back the papers she had been working on.

Lev smiled, thankful for the warm invitation, but the smile didn't quite reach her eyes. "I was hoping you had a moment to talk," she said, repeating the words as though she had rehearsed them, which she had.

"Of course. That's my job, and honestly, I wouldn't mind a few minutes away from these reports," Aundrea said, sweeping a hand over the stacked paperwork covering her desk. "The paperwork thing is never-ending."

Lev's embarrassment eased with the warmth in Aundrea's greeting, and she settled herself in the cozy wing-backed chair set conveniently across from the desk. "Thank you for your time. I'm not sure of the exact protocols yet, but I need to get this off my chest."

Aundrea sat forward, elbows resting on the desktop. "I'm listening," she said, tipping her head with interest. "You have a history with the OPR, and not just from the inside. If there's something you need to say, then it's probably something I need to hear." Glancing quickly at the door, she verified it was closed and focused back on Lev. "Please, feel free to talk."

"Rhone is gone," Lev stated flatly. "Worse, I believe he's in trouble."

Aundrea's expression froze as she absorbed the data. She didn't doubt Lev's assessment, not knowing Rhone as she did. "When," she asked quietly, "and where?"

Lev shrugged guiltily, knowing there was no way around it. "He didn't tell me he was going, and it's my job to keep an eye on him. I'm sorry. So, when I found him gone, I reviewed his recent questions and came up with a possible, or probable, answer. When I figured it out, I followed him, at least where I thought he was going."

Aundrea took a moment to question Jewel. *Did you know* about *this?* she asked silently, wondering if she had been kept out of the loop on purpose.

I most certainly did not, Jewel replied irritably. *I will have something to say to that Stone creature when he returns. He is always so hoity-toity about being bigger than I am, as though I'm just a child. It is not right, Aundrea. It is not my fault I'm small.*

It was an old story, and Aundrea contained her rueful smile, knowing that Lev was watching her every expression. *That will be for another time, Dearest,* she consoled her little crystalline companion. *Besides, I think you are perfect just the way you are.*

With that question solved, she had another question for Lev. "Did you find him?" she asked, a dangerous question, since Lev wouldn't be here if things were good.

"Possibly," Lev mumbled, her eyes lowered with regret.

"Possibly? Possibly you found him?" which didn't make sense. Either she had, or she hadn't.

"I hope I'm wrong, but I recently mentioned something about my last assignment, so it's possible, and maybe more than possible."

Things weren't adding up, and Aundrea's eyebrows rose questioningly, especially remembering Lev's past—a significant event in OPR history. While she knew some of the ramifications, even she didn't know the full extent. If this incident had anything to do with the previous, then there might indeed be a problem. "Let's cut to the quick," she said, taking the problem by the horns. "I doubt you would be here if you weren't concerned, so to save time, how about you tell me exactly why you've come to this conclusion." Her heart raced as the implications became more real. Rhone might indeed be in trouble.

Lev gave a thoughtful nod before explaining. "First off, I didn't find him, but I'll have to start with the background information to give credence as to why I'm concerned."

The mere implication set Aundrea's body abuzz, her refined and well-honed sense of doom coming to a peak.

"As you might remember, my partner and I were kicked out of the OPR," Lev continued. "I didn't truly explain why, and in truth, I was never told. Nor was I given the opportunity to ask. We were simply and summarily dumped. I was fired and told not to come back. My partner and his wife were bodily removed, deported to some place in the wilds I had never heard of. It took some doing, but I finally managed to gather a few wisps of information that said it was a place called Skragmoore."

Lev dropped the name casually while watching for telltale signs of recognition. It wouldn't have taken the experience she had to notice the change any school kid would have recognized.

"Skragmoore?" Aundrea whispered, her face blanching at the mere mention of the name. Old data flowed through her mind, partially supported by Jewel's connection. Then, with sudden gestalt, waves of understanding collided, fed a moment later by Jewel's agreement.

They do not know, Jewel cried in silent panic. *We must contact them.*

Aundrea simply nodded, answering both Jewel's demand and Lev's look. "Before we do anything, let me get this straight," she said, pleased by her own calmness. "Are you speaking of The Brotherhood?" At Lev's slight nod, she continued, her mind racing as she plowed on. "Alright. I'm going to run a scenario by you, but I want you to fill in where needed, or correct me where I go wrong." Again, a slight nod. "Your past assignment went sour when you found information on The Brotherhood, pointing to a, then recent, situation. Unfortunately, The Brotherhood was connected high enough in The Council to have gotten wind of the find, and doing what they do best, subverted the data and removed those who knew anything about it. Subsequently, you were fired, and your partner exiled to the far reaches of Skragmoore, never to be heard from again.

Once again, Lev nodded her agreement.

"It's no wonder things changed so rapidly," Aundrea murmured, more to herself than to Lev. "It was before my time, but I've read enough reports from the period that it makes sense. Almost instantly, the OPR's efficiency rating dropped by double digits enough so, The Council almost closed the entire organization as a fraudulent expense and embarrassment to the government. It wasn't until a decade later that we began to reassert ourselves as a true and efficient power for the people. I've always wondered what had happened, but now it's beginning to make sense."

Lev solemnly watched as Aundrea's thoughts spun. "There's one more thing," Lev offered, her tone causing Aundrea to glance up in sudden wariness. "It may sound odd, but it's possible that my partner was Rhone's father."

Aundrea's expression was almost comical as she took it in. "No wonder his mother never spoke of his father," she whispered, the parts coming together with what she already knew. "She was hiding, and what Rhone didn't know wouldn't haunt him."

"And I'm part of the reason his father is gone," Lev finished. "First his father, and now Rhone is gone, and that's my fault too." She looked stricken as she whispered, "Why am I here, Aundrea? Everything I do seems to end in tragedy."

Like a mother bear protecting her cub, Aundrea responded, "That is not true! You're back with the OPR, and I don't believe in chance, so there must be a reason. Have you considered that you may very well be the only person who might actually know where Rhone ran off to, or how to find him? Let's get this figured out and get him the help you say he needs."

Lev looked cowed, but nodded, accepting the challenge. "I can be gone in an hour. And don't worry. I'll get him back."

"That's the action I would expect from an agent," Aundrea said approvingly. "What will you need, and how long will you be gone? I don't want to lose both of you."

Lev's cheeks dimpled at the warmth in the comment, understanding what that meant from Aundrea. "I've got what I need, and it will be safer if I go alone. I've learned to move quickly and quietly."

"And where is 'there'?" Aundrea asked, her need making the question more emotional than intended.

"There's a castle-like structure along the cliffs of the ocean bluffs. We called it the citadel, but with the walls surrounding it, it's more of a manor house." She forced a smile, hoping it would lessen Aundrea's worry. "It's a day's ride south of the river's confluence with the great sea. I wasn't even aware of it before that last assignment. I simply followed my partner, but it can be accessed by a small road along the cliffs. The wind is so strong it's seldom used by anyone, so a newer road was cut that bypasses the cliff route. Most travelers take that, the smoother and safer road."

Aundrea nodded thoughtfully as she followed the route on her mental map. "Two days' travel?" she asked speculatively.

"Depends a lot on the weather, but yes, and I'll travel fast, so a bit less. Once I get close, I'll have to go quietly, just to be safe."

"Good enough," Aundrea replied. "Better safe than sorry."

Her thoughts coursed over the map and the difficulties of getting to where Lev had mentioned, then frustrated at her lack of knowledge, she turned back to Lev. "I need more information. Can you tell me anything about what Rhone has been doing in his new lab? I know it's asking you to go out on a limb, but you're the closest person to him that I have, and I've got to learn all I can."

The request brought a tightening of Lev's brows, but she gave a quick nod. "He's very quiet about his work, but he does mumble a bit," she offered. "There's also a storeroom he uses to keep the things he's working on. I've been in it a time or two to clean up, so I have a key. I'm not sure what the stuff is other than strange bug-looking things." She suddenly looked guilty. "I think those are my fault," she said awkwardly. "He began developing them after I showed him the necklace my late husband made for me," and with a self-conscious frown, she reached for a delicate chain around her neck, pulling a little dragon from the neckline of her blouse. Hesitantly, she held out the tiny mechanical creature, coiled amidst the piled chain in the palm of her hand, wings and tail tucked tightly around itself as though asleep.

"It's beautiful," Aundrea gasped, leaning in to study the beautiful creation. "So this is why Rhone became so focused on his tinkerings. He chose to create beauty, not just function." After a long, admiring look, she stepped back and smiled up at Lev. "He has a way to go before he reaches this perfection, but he's headed in the right direction."

Lev grinned with embarrassed pleasure as she replaced her necklace. "I remember hearing him mumble something about needing his creations to do a task, but I'm not sure if these are part of that idea, or even what that might be. They look more like toys than tools."

A moment later, Aundrea had come to a decision. "As to the citadel. I'm going to send you back. Find out what you can, but be careful, and remember, you are by yourself. Find him or find where he is. After all, as you said, he may not be there. But in either case, don't get caught. You'll be our link. But before you go, bring me everything Rhone's been working on. I'll go through it and see if he left anything we can use."

"Yes, ma'am," Lev replied.

Ordered or not, she had already planned to go, and nodding her understanding, took it as her cue to leave.

As soon as the door closed, Aundrea connected with Jewel. "What's your take on this?" she asked her little companion. "Lev is obviously worried, and with her history, she has the right to be. But is it as dire as she thinks?"

If you consider Lev's knowledge *and Rhone's reckless attempts to do what he feels is right, then there is exactly a 93.57% chance things will go wrong,* Jewel answered, her skepticism making her words hardly necessary. *I might, possibly, consider that dire.*

It wasn't what Aundrea wanted to hear, but it did confirm her own feelings. "That doesn't make me feel any better," she scolded.

Is there not some way we can help? Jewel asked, attempting to make amends. *I could send them a message, but what good would it do if other We pick it up?*

"Good thinking on both accounts," Aundrea said wearily. "We know there are other We, but we don't know if they are with The Brotherhood. For us to send an open message saying we're aware would be a fool's errand, giving away our hand before we even sit down to the game."

There was a moment's silence before Jewel's frustration showed itself. *Aundrea, I know I spoke harshly of Stone, but he is so infuriating at times that it almost cracks my core. On the other hand, he is truly impressive. If it was not for him, I would still be in the commissioner's vault, totally broken in mind from living in isolated darkness. We must help them, Aundrea. We simply must.*

"And we will," Aundrea soothed. "We simply have to figure out the best way. I considered the sending unit too, but they already know there's trouble. What other resources do we have?"

Very few, Jewel agreed. *This citadel place is not in an area of commerce, and has few people, so the OPR has little reason to place resources there. It may even be why The Brotherhood chose that area to set up residency. They are out of the* way, *and anyone new to the area would stand out.*

"That makes sense, but it doesn't find us an answer," Aundrea summarized, pushing Jewel to her best effort.

Then, the first thing we must do is find them, Jewel stated fiercely. *Then we can deal with their rescue, if it is needed.*

"Well done. That was fine work," Aundrea said approvingly. "I believe you've picked up some of Stone's good points. Now, as far as I can think, Lev will be our only resource in the area, but let's brainstorm a bit more and see what we come up with."

I am very good at thinking, Jewel said proudly.

"Yes, you are, and we need a list of options and resources."

Then I will work on it, Jewel declared, vibrating with confidence.

Aundrea knew her next action would require careful consideration. If she got it right, there would undoubtedly be a shift in the balance of power. A shift that would affect more than just The Council. But if she got it wrong, she and many wonderful employees would be out of a job, with the distinct probability of the OPR being closed for good. She could see no middle ground.

An hour later, Lev returned, bumping the door with an elbow.

"Ready already?" Aundrea asked, swinging the door wide, then backed up as Lev inched through carrying a large wooden box.

"And I'm off as soon as I set this stuff down," Lev replied, straining with the effort of setting the heavy box on the desktop without scratching its surface. "This is all there was, other than a few pieces that were unfinished and looked like stock. Really, there wasn't much," she offered in explanation, "which surprised me with all the work I saw him doing. He must have been rebuilding the same pieces over and over."

Aundrea squinted disapprovingly at the box before poking an inquiring finger into its midst, but noticing several sharp points in the jumbled mass, quickly decided against random rummaging. "Thank you, Lev. I'll go through this stuff and see what I come up with. I have a few plans of my own, but it will take a few days to see if it comes together. If we're lucky, we'll meet up. If not, do what you can. I'll get there one way or another."

CHAPTER 18

Where to From Here?

Rhone was in no particular hurry. His journey was more of an outing than a quest. His many side detours had delayed their journey, but with no staff to oversee, other than Lev, of course, he wasn't too concerned.

"So, what do you think?" he remarked, drawing his head into the warmth of his thickly furred collar. The chill coastal winds whipped at his coat as though trying to drag it from his body, but he enjoyed the feel, reminding him of his time aboard The Backwater Mistress with the tang of salt water and seaweed sharp on the air. It was invigorating, but he had come for a task, maybe not as well planned as it could have been, but it was better than being stuck in the office, wishing he were elsewhere. "Isn't this better than being cooped up in the office?" he asked Stone.

The office? Do you mean the laboratory you were given to fur-ther develop your mechanical creations? Stone's cryptic observation showed an entirely different view from his partner's. *You know per-fectly well we were not 'cooped up' as you say. It is obvious that you have yet to learn the value of contemplative and determined research. Instead, you continue to crave the life-threatening stress and physical damage which, as I remember, you achieve in most of your efforts.*

Rhone grimaced, remembering his falls down cliffs and stairways, being blown from his feet by a rupturing containment bladder, and his almost dying from both dehydration and drowning in the desert. In fact, it had happened often enough that simply being knocked unconscious had become almost commonplace.

"Okay, you're probably right," he agreed, but grinned nonetheless, savoring his feeling of freedom.

I see that your mind is set, Stone said in resignation. *Therefore, since you have not found it worthwhile to ask for my assistance, I must ask: what is your plan for this venture?*

Rhone's shoulders drooped, his freedom dissipating like fog in the sun. "But we worked out a plan, remember?"

Is that what you call it? I thought it more an exercise in futility, deciding which venue led to greater death-defying acts of stupidity.

"Hey, that's not fair," Rhone grumbled. "You know why we're heading to the coast. It's where Lev said she went on her last assignment, so it must be important."

You are, of course, speaking of the assignment that ended up getting her husband killed, herself fired, and her partner exiled. Perhaps that is your plan for getting out of this mess. Get yourself killed or fired before you need to finish your projects for Aundrea. If so, it just might work.

Frustrated at not getting the support he expected, Rhone drew his coat tighter and scowled at the cloud-filled sky which had quickly become a mirror for his mood. But it was no different from most of their discussions. One had a concept, and the other came up with every good, and not-so-good, reason to grumble about it. They had perfected the art until they hardly noticed it anymore.

Deciding they hadn't come all this way for nothing, Rhone tried again. "Anyway, Lev said they came this way," quickly adding, "and I know she didn't say exactly where, but with the coast just ahead, I figure we'll find it."

That is possibly true, but I do not see why that makes it better, Stone rumbled as though proving his argument. *And what are your intentions once you get there? Do you expect someone to wave you down and say, 'Oh, there you are. We have been expecting you?'*

Rhone groaned, squeezing his eyes shut in frustration. "No. I expect to find something we'll recognize as important."

And why did you not simply ask Lev where it was? Stone asked. *It would have been much simpler than traipsing across several counties in search of something she already knew.*

"I tried . . ." Rhone answered evasively.

But . . . ?

"She wouldn't say."

Rhone decided he'd won when Stone didn't respond, but the moment he relaxed his guard, Stone's words again filled his mind. *Does that not tell you something? If Lev felt it was not information you should have, then I, for one, believe she should be listened to.*

Rhone felt trapped by the simple question, but neither could he disagree. "Stone, we're good at this stuff. We did all kinds of things without anyone's help."

Yes, we did accomplish many things, but you continue to forget that we had lots of help. Did Bella not help us? And Captain Black? And how did we manage to get away from the badlands? It was not you, nor I. It was Aundrea. Where do you come up with these strange notions?

Stone asked, his growing frustration feeling as though Rhone was standing in the smoke of an acrid campfire.

"I don't know. I guess we did get a lot of help," Rhone agreed, his anger draining away, leaving him empty. "I just thought we could do this on our own. Just you and me. Like we used to."

Sensing Rhone's mood, Stone gently supported his young friend. *It was enjoyable, and we did do a great many things. After all, it was you who thought up our balloon concept. I simply found ways to effectively use your ideas. Neither of us did it alone, and together we will accomplish this, or if not exactly this, then other equally grand things.*

"So you think we can find The Brotherhood?" Rhone asked, feeling his spark of hope reignite. "If we do, maybe we can find out if they actually have We. Then Aundrea can . . ."

Can what? Stone interrupted, his sharp words stopping Rhone mid-sentence. *If they have We, which we already considered a possibility, then what are you hoping to accomplish?* The question hung in the air before Stone finished his sentence. *If we find the data to be valid, then perhaps we can come up with a practical method of establishing a connection with them. This is not to be done lightly, nor without thought to possible consequences. You do understand this, do you not?*

Rhone chewed a lip as he rethought Stone's question. "I guess I hadn't really thought it over. After all, the We could like what they're doing, or consider us the bad guys. All kinds of things could go wrong, couldn't they?" He thought a long moment before making his decision. "With your help, we'll make it work. I just know it."

Perhaps so, Stone replied, a feeling of warmth passing through their connection. *It may not be exactly what you were planning, but it will undoubtedly be more practical than simply heading down the road at a dead run.*

Rhone grinned and wiped his nose absently, his widening eyes taking on a sparkle. "Hey, I can smell the ocean," he said enthusiastically. "We must be really close."

I believe you are correct. Perhaps you should climb a tree and see what you can see, Stone advised, sounding like a favorite uncle cheering on the antics of his nephew.

Choosing the biggest tree he could find, a wind-whipped evergreen of some type, Rhone dismounted and used the tree's rough and deeply scored bark to crawl his way to the lowest branches. Then, using them like a ladder, he clambered upwards until he felt the tree swaying dangerously in the wind. Deciding not to chance the slimmer branches, Rhone pushed his way through the prickly foliage until he could see better.

An entire forest of low-growing trees spread out before him, their wind-whipped branches dancing in rhythmic patterns that surged much like the ocean's waves. "I don't see anything," he admitted disappointedly. "Just more trees and brush. It all looks pretty much the same."

Perhaps you should try turning more to the west, Stone offered.

With a sigh, Rhone carefully repositioned himself, forced to squint as he stared into the brilliance of the setting sun. Sure enough, far in the distance, the top of a stone tower-like edifice poked its crown above the thinning trees and rocky steps around it. "I think we found it," he mumbled, the sudden knowledge that he was about to confront The Brotherhood bringing a tingle of goosebumps that just might have been fear.

Having stashed Blue and most of his gear, Rhone started up the rough roadway toward the tower he'd seen from a distance. He'd barely gone a quarter of the way when Stone's warning rang in his head.

Rhone!

Skidding to a halt, Rhone scanned the road just as the rhythmic thunder of fast-riding horses rose behind him. Without hesitation, he dove off the path, crashing into a dense copse of brush wedged between the tightly packed trees. Clawing his way through, he gave a stifled yelp as the ground dropped away, the unseen incline sending him tumbling down the gulley, limbs flailing as he careened through the tall ferns and stiff-branched huckleberries that did little to slow him. His uncontrolled tumble ended with a breathless *oooff*, his aching body tangled in the limbs of a young cedar that finally stopped his unplanned exit.

That was quite a tumble. Are you alright, Stone asked, once his own spinning had slowed.

"Yeah, I think so," Rhone replied, though still orienting himself to which way was up. "Let me get my footing. I'd just as soon not do that again."

Digging his heels into the loose soil, he secured his position, berating himself for not paying more attention. At least his tumble had done what he'd needed, getting him out of view of the road he had so recently been on. It wouldn't pay to be seen this close to his objective.

It took an hour to climb out of the gully and find the quiet meadow where he had left Blue and most of his gear, then another half hour to brush off and pluck the assorted foliage and debris from his hair and clothes. By then, he needed a break.

"I think we should wait until dusk," he told Stone. "There should be fewer people around, and we'll need to get inside the main building."

Are you certain you want to do this? Stone asked.

"What's the matter? Are you afraid? I mean, sure, there's no telling what we'll find inside, but we've got this."

I was merely asking, Stone mumbled, the comment as heavy as a wet blanket in Rhone's mind.

"Whatever. If you want, I can just leave you here," Rhone replied grumpily. "But I've got to go, and you know that."

Receiving no further comment, Rhone set his steps toward the still-distant tower.

He kept off the road this time, and before long was staring at the surprisingly low, one-story wall of mortar-set rock surrounding the tower's grounds.

With darkness close at his heels, Rhone stealthily began his climb, skillfully inching his way up the rock-faced wall, then over and down, but the moment his feet touched the courtyard, Stone began a very constant and fretful commentary.

Rhone, I have a very uncomfortable feeling about this.

Rhone gritted his teeth at the interruption and began working his way across the interior courtyard, sliding silently from shadow to shadow, inching his way ever closer to the towering citadel. He had chosen his entry carefully, the trees and bushes of the almost park-like garden making his stealth an almost unnecessary skill. It was the vibration of Stone's continuous warnings, adding to the nervous sweat already running down his back and underarms, that made his neck itch. While his academy-required skills of snooping sleuth work had been fun to learn, this was no longer a game played with the other students. This was for real, with real opponents and real consequences—opponents who would kill if they found him here. And if Stone was right, which he admitted, was most of the time, then tonight's incursion was into The Brotherhood's base of operations, an unimaginably dangerous thing to do. Even so, they needed proof. Proof that this was indeed The Brotherhood's **headquarters**, and proof of their misdoings. With proof, he could take the information to Aundrea, and she could use it to help Lev's case against the council.

Rhone clung to the cold logic until it felt like ice water coursing through his veins. Interestingly though, it did nothing to stop the nervous sweat that slicked his skin.

Rhone, are you paying attention at all, or is your mind somewhere else, Stone complained again, this time disregarding the block Rhone had thrown up against the almost constant complaints.

Rhone rolled his eyes but stayed silent, not wanting to say something he might regret later—or worse, something another We might pick up. He trusted Stone's contact, but wasn't so sure his own was We-proof, as Stone had just demonstrated. And with at least one We inside the Capital Stronghold, were there more here, and if there were, could they sense him—especially if he couldn't fully shield his energy from their awareness? Maybe it was all conjecture, as Stone liked to say, but without proof, silence felt like the safest choice.

On he went, fear and need fighting to take over as he slipped from one shadow to the next.

The evening's shadows gave plenty of cover as he worked his way through the lavish gardens, their winding pathways, fountains, and gates laid out in an almost tangled array. He had also seen the more traditional kitchen gardens further on, their raised boxes and fine soil probably brought in from elsewhere to support their growth. He had scanned the area before dropping over the wall and had a vague layout of the space, of the stone-paved courtyard where sounds of blustering wind and hollow booming waves let him know the ocean lay somewhere below. In the center of the compound stood the towering citadel, its bulk dominating the low structures and walls that surrounded it.

Rhone scanned the darkness, searching for some clue of where to start. There had to be an office somewhere in the large compound. Where, he had no idea, but that was where the papers would be, papers he hoped he could rifle for information. Unfortunately, without knowledge of where to look, it was turning into a fool's errand. But fool or not, he was determined.

Once again, Stone's warning rattled his mind, but this time far more urgently. *Rhone, I feel a presence.*

Instantly, Rhone stopped, one foot held awkwardly off the ground, caught between steps. *Where?* he asked silently, his query held to a tight mental whisper.

I am not certain, but it was here. Now it is gone, Stone admitted sheepishly. *It is possible that someone is shielding their thoughts, much as you do,* which made Rhone cringe, knowing he did, on occasion, block his thoughts from Stone. *Yes, I believe someone is doing a very good job of blocking their thoughts,* Stone whispered, as though even he was worried about being overheard. *We must therefore assume it is intentional, and that we are being watched.*

But how? We've been really quiet, Rhone asked, still balancing on one foot.

Again, I am not certain, but they are near. Not in this particular courtyard, perhaps, but I believe it would be most prudent for us to leave, and as soon as possible.

Rhone had many skills, including stealth and swordplay, now that he had improved his fighting. And with Stone's tactical assistance, he might actually have a chance. But while the thought was tempting, he also knew his tendency to tempt fate, and exactly how well that had gone. Besides, if someone already knew they were here, then his stealth had proven worthless. It would be down to fighting, which was a poor option at best.

With their chance gone, getting out alive had quickly become the priority.

Rhone gave a quick scan of the darkened courtyard before taking a tentative step back the way they had come.

And why are we not leaving? Stone asked, his urgent whisper as quiet as a moth's flight.

"That's what I'm doing," Rhone whispered, teeth gritted in a somewhat dangerous, and totally unnecessary outburst since he was already thinking the words.

Then you are going the wrong way.

What? Are you sure? Rhone asked, instantly embarrassed and remembering to think his words this time. *I'm pretty sure we just came past that tree.*

Obviously, you have confused that tree with the one to your left, Stone corrected. *It, however, is the wrong one.*

Rhone rolled his eyes but turned in the indicated direction. *Is this better?*

Why do you ask when you know my calculations are always correct? Stone muttered in frustration.

Rhone was considering a suitable response when Stone again broke the silence. *Ahh, there is the gate we came through.*

You sound like you weren't expecting it? Rhone replied, smiling as he sent the silent jibe to his friend. He continued smiling as he slunk toward the intricately detailed gate, its wrought iron bars an elaborately worked pattern Rhone wished he had time to examine.

Yes, it is nice, but perhaps some other time would be better, Stone suggested, urging Rhone forward with a mental push.

Rhone ignored Stone as he reached out, gently turning the gate's animal-head-shaped handle. When it didn't move, he tried again, turning the stubborn handle with a little more effort. He had been very careful on his way in, taking almost a full minute to slowly work the knob, making sure it wouldn't squeal in protest. This time, however, the handle refused to move.

Frustrated by the delay, he added more strength but got no better response. *It's stuck,* he grumbled in silence.

Well, unstuck it, Stone admonished. *We can't allow a simple gate to keep us from our exit.*

Once again, Rhone attempted the handle, but again, it wouldn't move. *I think it's locked,* he mumbled in silence. *But we came through just a few minutes ago, so maybe it's a* one-way *latch* or something.

That is a possibility, Stone admitted, *but it is just as possible, it was locked after our entry.*

Do you really think so? Rhone asked, the comment making his blood run cold.

Unfortunately, I do. I told you we were being watched. It is therefore the most straightforward hypothesis and the most probable.

Rhone felt the hairs on his neck raise as he replied, *Okay, shouldn't be a problem. I'll just pick it.* Luckily, his class on 'Locks and their Mechanisms' had been one of his favorites and had helped tremendously with his tinkerings.

Quickly pulling off his belt, he unzipped the hidden inside pocket and removed the tiny tools of the trade. *This may take some time without a light*, he warned silently.

I would most fervently not recommend one, Stone advised, *but I am confident in your ability. Perhaps closing your eyes will help you visualize the mechanism.*

Rhone nodded as he concentrated on his work, and a few moments later, the slight click of tumblers announced his victory.

What are you waiting for? Stone demanded. *Go!*

Rhone sighed as he stepped through the gate, but stopped abruptly when his eye caught a shadow disappearing around a distant corner. *Did you see that?* he squeaked, fear spiking at the unexpected motion.

Of course, I did. People do live here, you know. Now get a move on. I might also suggest that you take a different route than the one we came in by.

Without bothering to answer, Rhone turned away from the shadow and began creeping along the flagstone path. The further they went, the more relieved he felt, until, shadow or not, they were almost back to the wall.

Abruptly, Stone ordered, *Left*, the silent demand bringing Rhone to a lurching, undignified stop.

What was that for? he demanded as his heart raced in panic.

Shhhh! Can you not feel them? Stone scolded. *Be quick, but move quietly. If I can feel them, they may be able to feel you.*

It was definitely more of an order than a request, and Rhone's sweat-slicked body chilled at the thought.

Working to keep his mind blank, he continued his way towards the outer wall, careful steps moving from one smooth paving stone to the next, until the ground dropped from under his feet.

CHAPTER 19

Brotherhood Central

As soon as Lev had gone, Aundrea moved the box to the floor and began removing the strange pieces. It didn't take long to place them into groupings with others of their kind, but it was interesting how each group showed a definite progression in Rhone's creations. The first was not much more than a simple moving unit, but the final creation was nothing less than a dramatically detailed mechanized monster, its long stinger-tipped tail similar to a scorpion, but the small bulbous dome on its back and ear-like cups on its head making a surreal departure from its nature-made cousin.

It definitely looks dangerous—but what is it for? she wondered, staring at the unique object with curiosity.

"I believe the dome is a boiler-adapted power system," Jewel answered, sounding intrigued. "Stone mentioned something like it recently. The ear cups, I presume, are receivers—though I wouldn't have known that if he hadn't gone on endlessly about my sending unit. At the time, I thought he was just jealous, but I can't think of any other explanation that makes sense. Do you think it works?"

"That is the question," Aundrea reminded her, rubbing a finger lightly over the stone-like gem in her ring. "What do you think? Are you able to work it?"

I will try, Jewel answered grudgingly, *but Stone guards their secrets as though I were an outsider. I am not. Nor am I a child, even if I am small,* she complained.

Aundrea felt Jewel's pout even if she couldn't see it. It was also something she didn't have time for. "Can you do it?" she demanded, knowing she would have to apologize later.

It is possible, Jewel admitted warily. *I overheard some of their discussion and might even have a fairly good idea of how it is done. The exact coding, however, will undoubtedly take time.*

"Good enough," Aundrea approved. "I hate to do this, but I'll be in and out for the rest of the day, so I'm going to leave you here while I work. Your job is to catalog and verify the functionality of these machinings. I need to know our options." She paused as she turned to leave. "I'm sorry I got huffy. It's just that I'm so worried I can't think straight," she apologized, feeling terrible about scolding her little Jewel.

Aundrea had chosen her apartment specifically because it was close to work. It was a mere matter of minutes for her to walk to her residence, gather what she needed, and stuff everything into a carpet bag kept handy for just such ventures. She was back at the office within the hour. She had even spoken to Bran, asking him to procure a buggy from the OPR stables. He would also oversee the office situation while she was gone. It would be good practice for him to have a say on whatever issues came up.

Her next stop was to check on Jewel.

"How are you doing? About ready to leave?" she asked as she popped her head into the office.

Oh, hello, Aundrea, Jewel greeted, sounding surprised as though she had been deep in thought. *I have completed my scan. It seems that six of the units are complete, with two others missing parts. Another looks as though it has taken substantial damage, flattened in a way that has twisted the casing beyond what its own mechanism could have accomplished. I simply do not understand these boys. Can they not take more care? They act as though their projects are mere toys.*

Aundrea almost laughed at Jewel's pout, but caught herself, turning it into a clearing of her throat. "Remember, darling, the boys were not certain what they were developing. They were merely advancing their knowledge as they went. It is altogether amazing that they've accomplished what they have." Feeling Jewel's acknowledgement, she went for gold. "Now, back to the projects. Are there any we can use?"

I believe so. Three have receivers, though one is an older model with an earlier version. It will suffice for tracking, but not much more.

"That is the best news I've had all day, but only three?" Aundrea said, slipping Jewel back on her finger. "It will have to do, though I was hoping there were more."

I am sorry, but I have not had time to activate them, Jewel warned. *It is quite possible they will not work at all.*

"But that won't do," Aundrea stated, disappointment making her voice harsh. After a moment's thought, she made a decision. "Alright. Tonight, I will place you with the three complete units. Your job is to assess their abilities. Tomorrow we will attempt to activate them."

I suppose I could do that, Jewel said, her voice sounding less than confident. *Still, I do not see how more bugs running around will improve anything.*

"You let me worry about that. Your job is to verify their readiness," Aundrea chided, wishing she had more than the three. But three was better than none. Quickly gathering her ring, she sent a thank you to her little friend and partner. "Thank you, my little one. I'm sure they will work out just fine."

With that decided, she turned to the mechanical creations. The majority she returned to the box, while the selected three went into her large carpet bag. "Time to go," she said, slinging it over her shoulder. Then, giving the office a quick once-over, closed the door behind her.

The buggy was waiting at the Stronghold's steps with Bran standing beside an impatient Pasha pawing at the dusty cobblestone street. Handing Bran her bag, Aundrea gave a self-conscious smile as his eyebrow raised, noting its weight. She shrugged and gave Pasha a loving pat. "It's time to get going. Are you ready?" she asked, speaking in loving tones to her beautiful bay gelding. Turning back to Bran, she gave her final words of command. "If there are problems while I'm gone, deal with them, or hold them off until I get back. It shouldn't be more than a few days. But if it's longer than a week . . ." She paused, wondering what could possibly take more time than that. "If I'm not back in a week, and Lev returns, send someone to look for me. I'm headed to Corgy and The Lady Luna. But please keep that under your hat."

Bran took it as she knew he would, merely dipping his head in acknowledgment. "Don't worry. I've got it covered," he said. "Now get done whatever it is you need to do. I know you wouldn't be going if it wasn't vital."

When Bran offered his hand, Aundrea looked thankful, accepting it and stepping up into the driver's seat. "Okay, gotta go," she said, steadying the tremor of excitement she always got when she was headed to a new assignment. And assignment it was, whether she had sent herself or not. "I'll be back as soon as I can," she reminded him once more, but he just waved her off, stepping back as she flicked the reins, setting the buggy on its way.

With Lev gone, her hourglass timer was already emptying.

L ev felt drowsy as she watched workers doing their jobs around the citadel's grounds. The gardens came in two types: those the kitchen used to bolster the foods that had to be shipped in, and those with elegant plants for relaxation and entertainment. Well-laid paths wound between ponds and archways, along short fences, and around the flagstone courtyard in a tangled extravagance. Their mere existence belied the fact that they were perched on the edge of a shoreline cliff, several days' travel from any reasonable form of civilization. But perhaps that was their reason for being, to supplement the rigors of the vast solitude.

Lev tried to justify the setting, but her heart hardened at the memory of her husband reaching for her as he died, hand stretched out as though asking forgiveness for his leaving. Her breath shuddered as her heart broke all over again. She worked to release the pain and emotion that had eased over the years, but never truly left. Only the flickering thought of Rhone's plight allowed her to regain her focus on the present and not anchor to the distant past.

When a dominant figure stepped from the tall building, her senses sharpened, the man's posture alerting her to a disagreement of some type. When he pointed arrogantly at the closest worker, the poor man's negative headshake gave nothing away, but intriguingly, the worker then lowered himself to his knees, not in supplication, as she half expected, but merely to sweep uncertainly at the flagstone path with his hands. At least the gentleman appeared satisfied. Turning abruptly, he left the way he had come, his departure visibly easing the mood of the remaining workers.

Without further thought, Lev slipped silently from her position, beginning a long and circuitous route to the citadel's outer wall. She had chosen the location earlier, her memory of the sloppy watchman at the gate giving her the information she needed. Her careful approach may have been a negligible concern, but she knew there may be other, less obvious methods of surveillance.

The wind had lessened as dusk approached until the gentle breeze barely rustled the stiff leaves. It made for a pleasant evening, but unfortunately wasn't favorable for a stealthy entry. Regardless, Lev grasped the wall's rough stonework and raised her lithe form upward, soon lying prone along the flat-topped wall. She was hidden from ground level, but anyone watching from one of the citadel's windows would have little difficulty spotting her. Feeling exposed, she rolled to the inner lip, and with a cursory check for anyone in the area, flipped over the edge, her calculated move and one-handed grip directing her drop into the park-like yard below. With years of practice, she agilely straightened, then absorbed the impact with a well-schooled tuck and roll, swiftly sliding into the growing shadows, unarmed but for the small dagger tucked in her boot-top.

She waited quietly in the gathering darkness, carefully surveying the courtyard before making her way to where the men's interaction had taken place earlier. Stooping to a knee, she noted the marks in the dust where the worker had brushed at the paving stone. *But why would anyone worry about a flagstone?* It was just one of many in the stone-paved pathway, larger than its neighbors, sure, but with all of different sizes, it hardly made a difference. Yet this particular stone had been the focus of the man's irate attention, and if not irate, then at least concerned. Maybe the stone had been off-kilter and had rocked under his feet? It would have been an annoyance for the pristine garden, but the stone hadn't been raised and reset, merely brushed as if dusting away the light covering of dirt. Most odd, to say the least.

Inquisitive, as her training dictated, Lev lowered herself to within inches of the stone paver, studying its layout and setting before blowing across it in a long, drawn-out breath. Almost like magic, a metal seam began to show around the stone's edge, its metal surface gleaming dully in the quickly lowering light. Glancing uneasily at the building towering over her, she decided she'd seen enough and again scanned for watchers before making her way back to the wall. An uneasy chill coursed through her bones as she began her climb.

R hone woke with a moan, quickly coming to the realization that he was cold. Cold and sore. Or more correctly, cold, sore, and with a headache that seemed to split his head in two, or maybe he had.

"Why do I always get hurt?" he groaned, a reasonable question, but one he didn't expect to have answered. The pain brought back fleeting memories of being lost in the badlands, but that had been in his childhood, over two years past. He quickly put it aside as useless data. His slowly coalescing thoughts brought him to the awareness that he was lying in the pitch dark, again, not a first. His sigh converted to another groan as he stirred his muscles, checking that everything worked, but having aching muscles and creaking bones was almost standard issue. Then, a gentle test-move of his head brought the awareness of a particularly painful spot, and he reached a stiff-fingered hand to check. His searching touch found a lump with semi-dried blood matted into his hair, the tangled crust making itself into an almost solid bandage. Grimacing at the pain, he tried to bring up a coherent thought, and suddenly panicked. "Stone? Are you okay?" he called, wincing as his head responded to the panicked volume.

I must say, I was a bit worried, Stone replied, his irascible voice ringing gong-like in the confines of Rhone's aching head. *I have done a scan of your body and do not believe anything is broken. Are you able to rise? Or perhaps you should wait a bit longer,* he offered as Rhone's feeble attempt brought another groan.

"Yeah. I think I'll just lie here," Rhone agreed, speaking softly as his head throbbed to the beat of Stone's words. "What happened?" he asked, slumping back on the hard rock. "I remember we were almost to the wall. Then . . ."

Then you fell, Stone summarized.

"I fell? Oh yeah. I think I remember," but it came out more as a question than agreement.

I must say, you were sneaking rather well, Stone said supportively. *I almost believed we would make it. Then, you apparently triggered a* trapdoor, *and we dropped into this containment cell.*

"Wait. A trap door? Are you sure?" Rhone asked in surprise.

Of course, I am sure. I was watching, Stone grumbled. *I will admit, however, that I did not notice it prior to your activating the trigger.*

Relieved, Rhone replied, "Then it's not my fault."

I suppose not, technically, but you did trigger it.

"Whatever. If you didn't notice it, then how would I?" Feeling justified, he changed subjects. "So, have you found a way out yet?"

Oh, well, no. It seems we are thoroughly trapped, Stone said, careful not to disturb his friend more than necessary. *Once you dropped through the trapdoor, it swung back into place and is now re-secured. We will have to find another way out.*

While the trapdoor was definitely a problem, it would have to wait. His headache was his main worry. Any movement made him want to vomit, and he tried to blank his thoughts, as though simply not thinking would help. Regardless, he couldn't just sit there.

Rolling over, he attempted to rise, which wasn't a particularly difficult move, but with nothing to orient on in the darkness, he was unbalanced and almost fell. Stifling groan, he attempted several more times before giving up, settling for a fairly comfortable sitting position, arms wrapped around his knees for warmth as much as stability. There he sat, huddled on the cold stone of the cell's floor, forehead to knees as he tried not to think.

When warmth began to radiate from Stone's collar, Rhone's body greedily absorbed the blessed heat, relaxing his tense muscles and easing the stress of his throbbing head. Without thought, he drifted into sleep.

When he woke, it felt as though he had been lying there for hours, or maybe even days. Who could tell in the total blackness?

Are you feeling better? Stone asked, worried for his young friend. *I wish to say that I am sorry. I did not notice the trap, and it was my fault, not yours. How could you have known? It was, after all, a trap.*

It was odd hearing Stone apologize, and Rhone shrugged, instantly wishing he hadn't as his muscles complained at even that slight movement. "Thanks, but don't worry," he mumbled. "It's not exactly how I planned to get in, but at least we're here."

That is a very positive attitude, Stone chuckled appreciatively, *and I am glad to see you awake. You have slept for a very long time.*

"If you say so, but I feel like I could sleep for at least another week."

You are joking, I hope, Stone answered peevishly, which brought a light snort from Rhone.

"Nope, really I'm not. I would also appreciate a little less volume, if you please."

Of course. I will speak in the softest rustle of sound, Stone replied apologetically.

"Thanks, and don't worry. We'll find a way out, but not until we find what we came for." Then, a small trickle of thought brought a ray of hope. "Hey, Stone. Aren't cells meant to keep people from getting out?"

Yes. . . Of course they are, Stone said worriedly, wondering if Rhone had truly damaged his head.

"And weren't we trying to find a way in?"

We were.

"So we're here. Now, we just have to go further in."

Ah. That is very good, Stone answered in understanding. *Do you still have your lock-picking tools?*

"Probably, but I'm still pretty woozy from the fall. It's probably better if we wait just a bit longer."

No problem. I will be ready when you are, Stone announced grandly.

Rhone would have grinned, but quickly decided not to.

A quarter-hour later, he groaned out a resigned breath and again attempted to move. "Could I have a light, please?" he requested, and within a heartbeat the room lit with a soft glow.

I assumed your eyes would prefer a gentle light, Stone offered, *but if you would prefer some other, I could certainly accommodate.*

Rhone painfully levered himself up to a standing position before answering. "No, this is great, and thanks, Stone."

With Stone's light, he could see the cell walls carved from the very mountain it stood on. Only the trapdoor above and the steel-strapped cell door broke the monotony of the stone surface.

"Well, there's no way I'll be able to climb out," he stated, staring dejectedly at the trapdoor high above. "It looks like we either chip our way through the rock or use the door."

Then it is best that you get to it, Stone said, his concern backed with a sense of urgency from their overly-long incarceration. *If you can work the lock, I will warn of any intruders' approach. I must, however, warn you that my sensitivity to life forms is quite limited, surrounded as we are by solid rock.*

Rhone frowned, but had no better options. Easing his aching body to the cell door, he removed his belt, accessing the tiny tools it hid, and with Stone's light to help, bent to inspect the lock.

A light film of rust covered the mechanism, meaning it wasn't well-oiled, but also that it hadn't been used often. With that knowledge, he worked carefully so as not to make noise. A few minutes later he paused, his aching mind not allowing him to focus. He worked in spurts and drizzles, taking far longer than he wanted to admit, but after a while he got the hang of it, allowing his thoughts to drift while his hearing and touch took over. Finally, he felt the tumblers shift and was ready to congratulate himself when Stone's warning rattled his pain-infused brain.

Rhone! Someone is coming!

Rhone blanched as the overly loud warning rang in his head, his hands squeezing uselessly at his throbbing temples. Then recognition of the situation set in, and in near panic, relocked the door before dropping painfully to the floor.

Quickly now. Remove my collar! Stone directed as his light went out.

With his mind too numb to think, Rhone fumbled with the collar's buckle, then stuffed it beneath his shirt just as muffled footsteps stopped outside the door.

Rhone, your belt! Stone shouted silently.

With his head rattled from the force of the warning, Rhone made a frantic search for the wayward belt.

A heartbeat later, the rasp of a key in the lock and the groan of old hinges split the silence as a piercing beam of lamplight swept into the cell, illuminating the dank room.

Rhone didn't need to feign his pain or the groan. Propping himself on an elbow, belt tucked beneath him, he peered inquisitively at the barely visible figure behind the lamp's light. He caught just enough of the man to see tight-fitting leathers and closely trimmed beard, his dark curly hair close-cut at the sides, giving him a rather regal look. Definitely a figure to remember, but it was the soft glow from the man's ring that gave Rhone's heart a startled beat.

"Nice of you to drop in," came the cultured drawl. "It's not often we receive visitors, though we usually prefer they come through the front doors. I suggest you try using that method next time, though unfortunately, there won't be a next time since you won't be leaving." The man snickered when Rhone didn't answer. "What's the matter? Cat got your tongue?"

Be careful. He is aware of much, Stone whispered, his carefully controlled thought sending a chill down Rhone's spine.

When Rhone didn't reply, the man gave a humorless snort and turned on his heel, slamming the heavy door closed. With a grating sound from the lock, his footsteps receded down the hall.

Rhone took a weary breath and sank back to the floor, the sight of the glowing ring enough to make his mind spin.

Yes, I too noticed the We, Stone remarked, concern flooding Rhone's raw senses. *I shielded myself, but I am not certain if it was entirely effective. Still, there was no response, so whether it is aware or not, I do not know. We will simply have to wait and see.*

At least we know they have one, Rhone thought numbly, his mind too tired and sore to do much more than think the thought. *Do you mind if I take a nap?*

Another nap? Now? But we must be on the move, Stone complained. *We cannot free ourselves if we just lie here.*

"Alright. I was just hoping," Rhone mumbled, his head beating with a debilitating throb. Using the pain to power his movements, he clambered unsteadily to his feet, remembering all too vividly the total darkness of the small room in the Commissioner's vault. He also remembered that he had been rescuing Stone on that occasion, while this time, they both needed rescuing. "What now?" he asked as he pulled Stone's collar from inside his shirt.

I suggest you try the lock again. I'm certain it will be simpler this time, since you already accomplished the task once.

With a noncommittal shrug, Rhone shuffled his way to the door, his bruised body complaining with every motion. "What do we do once we're past the door?" he asked, not sure he wanted to know.

Why, we follow the gentleman. He obviously knows the way out.

"Yeah, okay. I guess that makes sense," Rhone replied, too tired to think much beyond that.

Having done so once already, it only took a few attempts before he managed to open the lock mechanism. The light squeal of hinges brought fresh sweat to his brow, and not wanting any more noise than necessary, he slid through the narrow gap, closing it behind him.

Very well done, Rhone. Very well indeed, Stone praised. *Now, down the hall. Come on. You can do it.*

With a sigh, Rhone quietly headed in the direction the footsteps had taken. There seemed little else to do.

Half an hour later, Rhone was still stumbling along the dismal hallways, his tired footsteps dragging as his energy flagged. "How far does this go?" he groaned, stopping for the umpteenth time to sag wearily against the stone wall.

I am quite certain we are almost there, Stone encouraged. *Go quietly though. We must be close.*

Rhone's headache had worsened with the effort of creeping through the hallways, and even with Stone's light at its lowest glow, he was forced to squint just to keep things in focus.

I'm almost done in, Stone, so whatever you've got planned, it had better happen soon.

Do not stop now. You are doing a wonderful job, Stone said approvingly. *Not only did we get past the manor's perimeter, we have made it into its very core. Is that not a significant accomplishment?*

Yeah, maybe, but it looks more like we broke into a dungeon, Rhone mumbled, *too tired to speak.*

And have you not noticed, the hallways are cleaner here, therefore more in use. Now, do be quiet, please. *You are whimpering.*

Rhone frowned, realizing he had indeed been whimpering. *Sorry,* he thought to his friend.

Chapter 20

Perspiration

Aundrea rocked and swayed as the little buggy bounced its way in unmerciful shudders, seeming to aim for every rock and rut in the road. This wasn't new to her, and she took it stoically, knowing it was a price she was willing to pay. She had been on many excursions, and whether by buggy, boat, wagon, or horseback, it was part of her job, undoubtedly the most enjoyable part.

The landscape had changed over the last hour. The road now followed the river as it wound its way through the coastal hills, finally spilling into the marshlands edging the bay. The current slowed as it cut its way through the brown, muddy flats, leaving a dark trail edged in rustling reeds. Above, a patchwork of puffy clouds brought memories of her childhood, where she and her playmates discovered creature-lookalikes in the ever-changing forms.

Aundrea was drawn from her almost dreamlike trance when an enormous whale-shaped cloud drifted free from the others.

"Oh, my," she breathed, her heart catching at the sight. Even knowing what she was seeing didn't lessen the wonder of it. "You must be *The Lady Luna*," she whispered in awe. "No wonder Rhone wanted to return."

For the first time in days, anticipation outweighed apprehension, and with a cluck to Pasha, she flipped the reins, eager to finish her quest.

Her excitement grew as she saw the rooftops of the town sprout up against the backdrop of a cozy harbor, its ship's masts standing like bare-limbed trees ready for winter.

The little town of Corgy lay tucked between the coastal hills and the harbor, its clean streets and buildings well-kept for a harbor town. The largest building was, of course, the town hall, sitting grandly next to the small park adjoining it. Further along the road, a little church with its stately bell tower sat patiently awaiting its parishioners. Close beside it sat The Common House, its gold-leafed signage proudly displaying its existence to the town's folk and guests alike. It was also a name she remembered from Rhone's reports and the bills she had paid for his residency.

It looked as though trade was good, as several ships lay docked at the quay, their stevedores hustling goods back and forth from the ships to the warehouses lining the shore. From her understanding, things had been worse when pirates were still plying their trade, their attacks having made significant inroads into the region's shipping industry.

As Aundrea guided Pasha through the small town, its story unfolded before her like the pages of a book. Corgy had been Rhone's first assignment, and his first victory as an agent. She had recently reviewed his reports with a fine-toothed comb, looking for information on his contacts and problem spots to avoid.

Her first stop would normally have been the mayor, but she turned to the docks, looking for the Port Office.

When the soft tinkling of the little doorbell announced her entry, the surprised eyes of the harried clerk clearly showed that a woman entering his office was not a normal part of his day.

Choosing to ease his discomfort, Aundrea merely asked, "Could you assist me in finding Captain Black of The Backwater Mistress?" batting her eyelashes only once.

"Captain Black?" the poor clerk stammered, his Adam's apple bobbing erratically in his agitation. But gathering his composure, he confronted the issue with studied aplomb. "Why certainly, ma'am. No problem at all. If you could give me but a moment, I'll take you there myself."

Normal or not, Aundrea's dress and manner showed her as a woman of wealth, and one who should be catered to. He could hardly do less.

"Thank you. That would be lovely," she replied, demurely lowering her eyelids in a way that was more for fun than necessity.

It was indeed 'but a moment' before the clerk was back, all grins now that he was better prepared. "You're in luck, Ma'am, The Mistress just got in this morning, but she'll be ready to head back out tomorrow."

"Tomorrow?" Aundrea gasped in surprise. "I was under the impression that this was her home port. I would have been mortified to find she was gone."

"Oh, no, ma'am. Or rather, yes, ma'am," her guide stated worriedly. "She does dock here, but she's on a tight schedule nowadays, with her running down them dang pirates, and following that ghostly flyin' thing as she does." Then, with a guilty look, he added, "Glad she's at it though. Things have been a bunch better since."

Aundrea relaxed when the clerk kept up a stream of banter as he led her to the docks. He strutted his way along the board-walk, swaggering about proud as a peacock, making certain the dockhands took notice. She almost chuckled at the awed looks of sailors and workers, staring in obvious disbelief that a woman would be walking their docks. "Out of the way there," her guide shouted, waving officiously at a stevedore stepping from a ramp, almost colliding with them. "Mind yourselves, gentlemen. This here is a lady. Now make room."

Many ships had once refused to allow a woman on board, believing it would bring bad luck—but that was simply a super-stition from another era. Today's woman could do whatever she was capable of. She herself had started like any new entrant and worked her way to the top. Now, as head of the Office of Public Recriminations, she had proven that anything was possible.

"Here we are, ma'am, The Backwater Mistress," the clerk an-nounced, drawing up before a unique little ship, very unlike most of the massive square-riggers she shared the docks with.

Ready to board, Aundrea turned to thank the clerk when he raised a hand, stalling her advance. "Allow me to call for the captain," he advised apologetically, then barked out a demand for the ship's attention. "Yo, The Mistress. A word with the captain!"

Flinching at the unexpected volume, Aundrea recovered quickly before taking charge. "Sir, I appreciate your assistance, and thank you, but I'm certain I can take it from here." She stood tall, her posi-tion as a gentlewoman requiring an austere demeanor, unfazed by the small things of daily life. "I will, of course, pass on my appreciation to your superior."

The clerk looked disappointed, but her rank and privilege made the requested dismissal obligatory. "Certainly, ma'am. If you need anything further, simply send a runner. I can be here in no time."

Thanking him again, Aundrea was relieved when a voice from the ship broke the tension of the moment.

"Who's calling?" came the abrupt challenge, breaking the morning's stillness as easily as it would have smashed through a gale. A moment later, a shaggy head popped over the rail, the face carrying the harried look of someone whose day had been disturbed. His entire demeanor changed, however, when he saw Aundrea staring up inquisitively from the bottom of his ramp, an instant grin replacing his glower as he placed a hand over his heart and gave a slight bow. "I beg your pardon, ma'am. We ain't used to seein' fine women out here on the docks. Might I be of assistance?"

"You can if you are Captain Black. I would have words with you," Aundrea replied, catching and holding his gaze.

The captain's expression became almost comical as he digested her words, eyebrows raising in wonder. Then, with a flourishing wave as large as his own self-worth, he invited her aboard. "I am indeed, ma'am. Do come aboard. I'll have a glass brought out while we discuss your business. Might I offer you a hand?"

In a fraction of the time Aundrea would have expected, Captain Black had bounded down the ramp, boards squealing in complaint at his every step. "Now, don't you mind the ramp," he chuckled disarmingly. "It complains almost as much as the crew. But it'll hold. Don't you worry none about that." Then, with another grand gesture, held out his arm to escort her aboard.

Not sure what to expect, Aundrea took the proffered arm and her first step up the ramp. She shuddered at the board's instant complaint and took a steadying breath. With one hand securely holding the captain's arm, they made their way up to the hopeful solidity of the ship's deck.

"Thank you, Captain. I must say, I'm not practiced at ramp dancing," she admitted shakily. "You, on the other hand, seem quite light-footed."

"Well, thank'ee, ma'am," he said, grinning like a kid in a candy store. "I may not be a proper dancer, but I've held my own a time or two." In fact, he looked absolutely befuddled as he led the way to the quarterdeck.

Once she was securely on board, Aundrea had taken quick note of the cleanliness of the little ship, as well as the apt service of the crew. She also noted the rapt attention of her guide as they made their way to the quarterdeck. Chairs and refreshments were being laid out by a few lucky crewmen while the remainder gaped from semi-concealment, not to be denied the pleasure of having a female onboard. She knew good management when she saw it and was pleased to see that Rhone had chosen wisely.

Only when she was seated did Captain Black take his own chair, barely managing to fit his large frame between its arms. "Now, ma'am. How can I be of assistance?" he began, dipping his head in deference to her. "As I said, it's not often a lady, such as yourself, comes to visit us lowly types. Therefore, I'm guessin', it must be business." Then, throwing up a hand to forestall any comment, he carried on as though worried she would see his comment as questionable. "Now I'm good for it, mind you. Don't you worry none about that.

It's just that, well . . . Let's just say, we like to stay flexible, takin' on things that need rapid transit."

"And you're a good salesman, Captain," Aundrea answered, purposefully taking the discussion into her own hands. "I must say, you do sound capable. Unfortunately, I am not here to discuss shipping. I am here to discuss Rhone."

The name dropped like a brick into deep water, instantly draining the color from the captain's face. "Who, ma'am? I don't quite recollect a name like that," he stammered, working to regain his composure.

"And I thank you for your discretion, Captain," Aundrea acknowledged with a tip of her head, "but I am Aundrea, Rhone's boss, and we need your assistance." Then, going for gold, she held back nothing. "Captain, Rhone works for me at the OPR, which I'm certain you already know since I have his report stating you were informed."

Looking embarrassed, Captain Black nodded glumly, not knowing what to say. "Where's Rhone?" he finally managed. "That kid means a lot to me."

"To both of us, or I wouldn't be here. My second point is, I need to contact Bella, or should I say, Captain Belle, of The Lady Luna. And yes, I know the story and most of the history, although I will be the first to admit not everything makes it into the reports."

The captain absorbed her news with a bowed head, wondering what was, and wasn't, in the reports. After a moment's pause, he looked up with questioning eyes. "What can I do for you, ma'am? I'm just a ship's captain, not the navy, and if you're here lookin' for me, then it means he's in trouble, or I'll eat my hat."

"You are quite discerning, Captain, but first, is Captain Belle reachable?"

There was a moment's pause before he gave an affirmative nod. "She is, although it may take a bit. She keeps an eye out for us when we're at sea, and I do the same for her, as I can, seein' to her needs for men and equipment. She's a good girl and does us proud."

"I have no doubts, Captain. Secretly, I know Rhone thinks the world of her too. Enough that he gave her the airship. Unfortunately, that is also my need, and I'm afraid, his. Rhone, it seems, has gone after The Brotherhood, by himself."

"He what!" Captain Black sputtered, the arm of his chair squealing in complaint as his grip tightened. Then, with a flash of ire, he rose so fast his chair clung to his hips, his fist dropping to the offending chair with a blow hard enough, the unlucky piece of furniture shattered, pieces skidding across the deck. Gone was his humor and his crusty attempts at gentility. He was all captain, rounding on her with teeth clenched in an angry scowl. Aundrea felt like she was looking down the barrels of a broadside as he snarled, "You let him go after that low-down scum by himself?"

His anger was so intense that she flinched, even as she held her ground.

"What kind of operation do you run?" he growled accusingly. "That kid trusted you. He got your summons, and lit outta here so fast he nearly broke his neck. A recall is a recall, he says, and he obeyed, as blind as a ship in the fog. Turns out it was just as dangerous, too, with you sendin' a kid out where no man has any right bein'." The captain tried to settle himself, but it only held a few seconds before his tirade again found release. "Oh, that kid went, he did, blind and proud, or I'm a clam dug up an' left in the sun to bake." The knuckles on his fists were white with tension, gripped so tightly she heard his knuckles pop.

Aundrea flinched again but didn't stop the rant. She knew he was only blowing off steam and wished she could do the same. But she was the boss, and it had been her recall.

Deciding her best option was to divert his heat, she changed subjects. "Captain, the tide has changed. If we're to make contact with The Lady Luna, we need to sail."

The comment took him totally by surprise. "You know 'bout the tides?"

"Not as well as you, I'm sure, but yes. I have at least some knowledge. And if I am not mistaken, the tide has turned."

"Well, I'll be," he mused, giving her a curious look. "Maybe Rhone wasn't so far off the mark. He said you were top-notch."

Aundrea felt a blush rise on her cheeks, and taking the moment to sweep her gaze over the ship, absently brushed a stray lock of hair from her face. "This is a handy little vessel, Captain. I don't believe I've ever seen her style before. Is she from around here?"

Her comment had its desired effect, drawing his attention away from her.

"She's a beauty, an' that's for sure," he praised lovingly. "Designed her up myself, from similar ships in the far ocean. She's fast, as Rhone could tell ya."

"She is beautiful, Captain. Would you be interested in showing me what she can do?"

Her charm warmed the air between them, but was unneeded as Captain Black was already swinging about, his well-practiced voice bellowing orders to his crew. "Alright, you lazy lubbers. The lady wants to sail. Cast off and up the mizzen. We've got some wind to catch!"

⚜

Aundrea squinted into the blustery wind, hair flaring out behind like the mane of a running horse. But when the bow suddenly dipped, dropping into another of the massive trenches between the towering waves, it was only her stranglehold grip on the railing that allowed her to keep to her feet. She felt silly, allowing herself to be that vulnerable, especially when a tumble would mean a bruising roll across the deck, if not a fatal dump into the grey, churning ocean.

Then the ship gave another shuddering groan as it took up the strain, only to launch itself skyward again as it met the next wave. Captain Black looked like a maniacal god as he stood behind the wheel, teeth gleaming through his spume-soaked beard. "Coming about! Drop the fore and main! We'll spin her on the next peak," came his bellowed command, sending the hardworking crew scattering across the pitching deck as though it was solid ground.

Aundrea caught the quick look between two of the men, but they didn't question the order, simply shrugging it off as they headed to their tasks. Almost unbelievably, the sails dropped, the ship slowing as it reached the frothy crest, bow pointed to the sky.

"Hang on, Missy!" came the captain's gleeful shout. A moment later, The Backwater Mistress pirouetted into a stomach-dropping spin, angling her back down the same wave it had just come up.

Aundrea had been on many a ship in her life, but had never seen, nor even heard of such a feat. Awed by what she had just witnessed, she still wasn't ready when the captain bellowed, "Raise the sails," his storm-honed voice easily cutting through the sounds of the churning waves and grinding creaks of the ship itself. Almost instantly, as though the men had been waiting, the triangular lateen-rigged sails were drawn back into position, catching the wind and increasing their momentum as they slid effortlessly along and down the sloping wave.

Aundrea could only hold on and watch, thankful there were no men in the rigging as on other ships. Her knuckles were bone white as she squeezed the quarterdeck's railing, gulping lungfuls of fresh ocean air as she fought the urge her stomach demanded she vacate. As a woman of means, and always aware of appearance, Aundrea worked to smile, appearing undisturbed by the antics of the man she knew was showing off.

"Men," she mumbled through her forced smile, even if it was a spectacular show.

The turning of the boat brought some ease to the journey, and a few breaths later Aundrea allowed herself to relax, her grip easing enough to release the railing. After a few testing moments, she ventured the few paces to Captain Black's side. "That was incredible, Captain. Do you sail like this often, or is it for my benefit? Either way, it was magnificent."

"That she is, isn't she," he beamed, stroking the ship's wheel like a lover caressing their mate. "Glad you enjoyed it. We don't often get the chance to play, as it were, but it's good experience for the men. You never know when you might need every trick in the book to skedaddle, regardless of the conditions."

"I hadn't thought of it that way," she admitted, realizing it would indeed be a valuable asset. The seas were a dangerous game at any time, but having a quick-acting ship with a well-trained crew could make all the difference in getting home safely.

Captain Black gave a playful wink before turning his attention to the sky. "Ah, there she is. That's my other girl," he said proudly, pointing into the distance. "Just don't tell her I said so. She gets mighty uptight over some things." His grin made it obvious he was proud of her, which covered both The Lady Luna and her infamous Captain Belle.

Aundrea used a hand to shade her eyes, peered into the sun-filled sky as she followed Captain Black's gaze. "I see her!" she exclaimed excitedly. "She truly is amazing. Did Rhone really build it?" then cringed in embarrassment at the silliness of the question.

"That he did. Well, the two of them, I suppose," he stated, giving an innocent shrug. "He and Bella. Rhone didn't give her captaincy until he was recalled by you." He grimaced a bit, sliding a sideways look toward Aundrea, checking her response.

"I know, on both accounts. But it is still unbelievable," Aundrea said, giving a brief shrug and a knowing smile.

The giant airship was becoming more distinct as the distance closed, the blue-grey and white coloring of the odd-looking balloon making it almost disappear against the hazy sky. It was altogether intriguing having the ship-like hull appearing as though it was flying, which, she supposed, it was.

Captain Black absently nodded his agreement, then excused himself. "S'cuze me, ma'am, but I'm needed." Then, swinging around, he bellowed an order. "Raise signal pennants: 'Meeting' and 'Home'.

"Aye, Captain. Meeting, and Home pennants," came the repeated command, echoing the words he'd given.

Within scant minutes the flags were raised, and a responding flag from The Lady Luna said they understood.

Aundrea watched with an administrator's eye as she took note of the happenings, understanding the complexity of running such an operation.

Rhone had indeed chosen a good mentor.

CHAPTER 21

Timing is Everything

Captain Belle stared quizzically at the strange metal creature cradled in the palm of her hand. Carefully turning the little creation to better see the intricate pieces, she asked, "You honestly think these will make a difference? I understand Rhone built them, but I also remember how often his projects went wrong."

"I only read the reports, so I'll have to take your word for it," Aundrea said, shaking her head in frustration. "But since we are standing on the deck of the most technically innovative device I have ever heard of, I'd say that at least some of his plans worked." Her voice was low and neutral, not wanting to tear down the bridge she was trying to build with Bella, nor did she blame her for not seeing the whole picture. Bella wasn't OPR, after all, so how could she understand the complexities?

Bella turned to face Aundrea, hand on hip in what seemed a very natural posture for her. She didn't answer, but her 'How little you know' look was loud enough to make a statement on its own.

Trying again, Aundrea allowed at least some of her impatience to seep through. "Can you get me there? That's all I ask. I had hoped you cared enough for him that you would be willing to take the chance, but I understand that some things go beyond the heart." She had nothing else. Rhone's time was now or never. While unfair and nearly hopeless, this plan was up to Bella.

"I didn't say I wouldn't go," Bella said sharply, flinching as her words came out harder than she had intended. "I would like nothing better than to go, if only so I could kick his skinny heinie into to-morrow." Unexpectedly, her scowl turned into a light chuckle as the picturesque words broke her mask of indifference.

"He can be frustrating," Aundrea admitted, relief like a fresh breeze washing through her. "I've had a few head-bumping moments with him myself, but this is different. I'm afraid he's taken a bite far bigger than he can chew, and if he doesn't get some help, and soon, he may not be coming home." Her jaw clenched as the emotion hit her, her eyes moistening until she gasped to catch her breath. It wasn't very professional, especially for the head of the OPR, but Rhone was something special to her. A son who wasn't.

At least her plea seemed to have struck pay dirt. "Of course, I'll go," Captain Belle answered, chin dropping in memory. "I owe him far more than that. It's just that . . . we have an old story. We're close, not as close as either of us might have wished, but old wounds have a hard time healing." Then she straightened, releasing a deep breath as she took up her role as captain once again.

Turning to the lower deck, she shouted, "Prepare for departure," her command instantly activating her crew. "Number Two. Are we stocked and ready?"

"Aye, Captain! Fuel, water, and foodstuffs arrived this morning."

"Good work, Number Two. We will be making our way south to the mouth of the big river, then along the coast. Cast off when we're ready, fan-sails at full. It appears we have a deadline to meet."

"Aye, Cap," came the return shout. Then, turning to the lower deck, he passed on the command. "Man the lines and prepare for immediate cast-off."

Instantly, the deck reverberated with the slap of bare feet as men ran to their duties, their thrumming beat filled with energy. Aundrea could feel the uptake when the boiler's engine kicked in, its power magnifying the wheezing-whine of the impellers as they increased their spin. She may not know how to fly The Luna, but she had followed the cast-off procedure from Rhone's explanations. Within two minutes, the mooring lines were hauled aboard and the side sails deployed. Soon the airship was rising in a majestic turn, headed for the open ocean and the cloud-filled sky.

"Drop the keel-sail," came Captain Belle's order. "We're going to let this girl fly!"

Aundrea had never been off the ground before, and held her breath at the wonder of it. The sensation of floating, or perhaps forcefully floating, if that was a thing, was almost overwhelming.

And Rhone had designed this wondrous machine? He should have received a title, or medal at the very least, Aundrea muttered silently, although that would have meant acknowledging The Luna's presence to The Council, and she wasn't certain they were ready for that just yet. That wouldn't last long, however, not with what she was hoping to do.

Her grip tightened on the railing as she watched the earth drop away, almost relieved when Captain Belle called her from the view.

"So, how do these things work?" Bella asked, grimacing as she walked up, holding the mechanical bug up between two fingers.

"I believe it uses some kind of miniaturized boiler system," Aundrea answered. "Beyond that, I don't know. Rhone showed them to me as part of an experiment he was working on, but I can't tell you much more, both because I don't know, and because it's classified as, Need to Know."

"Which I don't," Bella clarified with a shrug. "It is a cute toy, and I can see its value in moving around basically unnoticed, but I have no idea what all its little gadgets are for—and I won't ask," she added quickly. "If you think it will save Rhone, then I'm in." Glancing quickly at the sky, she judged the wind and their heading before commenting, "It should take us a day to get to the river. Beyond that, I have some pretty good maps of the coastal areas from the local captains. That will help, but it may take a while to find the exact location. Do we have the time?"

"I hope so," Aundrea answered, her brow creasing in thought. "I'll have an agent in the area, and I hope to make contact. But if we can't, it's up to us. It's the best I can offer."

Bella inspected the metal bug, gently moving its delicate legs before shaking her head. "And you think this little bug thing is going to save the day? I don't see how, but I'm game if you are."

"I hope these will tell us if he's still there," Aundrea explained, then turned to scan the ship's length and height. "How precisely can you maneuver this thing?"

Bella pursed her lips, adding a few facial contortions as she considered the question. "It depends on the wind. We can hold our own in a typical breeze, but it's hard to fight our way upstream. In a real blow, we try to outrun it, or be tied off on the ground with multiple anchors."

"And what about stealth?" Aundrea asked as a plan began to form.

The facial contortions and head tipping made it evident, there could be an issue.

"She's as quiet as a church mouse on a still day," Bella answered proudly. "But if we're making steam to fight a wind, we have the boiler's beat and the whine of the impellers as background noise. We tend not to hear it after a day or two onboard, but others say it's pretty noticeable. It's simply not a sound people hear in their normal day, especially from the sky, so we get some pretty interesting looks when we fly over a farm or ship that hasn't seen us before."

Aundrea nodded thoughtfully, considering her options. "Let's hope we arrive on a windless day then, or better yet, at night."

The prospect of action made Captain Belle grin, the sudden interest bringing a sparkle to her eyes.

It was a good sign. Aundrea returned the look, taking time to appraise the captain's unique attire. No wonder Rhone was so captivated by this young lady. Any man would be. Not only did she captain an airship, the only airship in existence, she was beautiful in a way only those unaware of their beauty could. Her long skirt had been clipped short in front, showing swaths of stocking-clad legs, which made sense considering the freedom it gave for climbing stairs to and from the quarterdeck. No tripping on the hem meant no falling overboard from a misstep. This was, after all, an airship where a fall would be fatal. The crew didn't seem to mind either as they worked feverishly to keep their ship holding its course in the stiff ocean breeze. They were proud of their captain, and their ship, and were willing to fight to protect them both.

While Aundrea planned, Captain Belle studied the maps, using her astrolabe to configure timing and placement. Only then did she lay out their final course, knowing it had to be perfect.

A day and a half later, Aundrea stood at the prow in her self-proclaimed position, unwilling to leave for anything less than a potty break every few hours. She shivered as she stood watch, practically frozen by the damp ocean wind that buffeted her. They had been paralleling the rugged coastal cliffs for some hours when she heard the tinkling of the alert bell from the upper lookout. Unable to stop herself, she quickly made her way to the quarterdeck.

"What is it?" she asked, not waiting for Captain Belle's invitation.

Bella smirked at Aundrea's intrusion but remembered what it had been like as Rhone's lieutenant. "We'll know in a minute," she said, raising a shoulder. "I've already sent a runner for the news." Then, with a curious look, she asked, "Are you cold? I should have warned you about that."

Andrea shrugged, not wanting to be distracted from the moment. "It is a bit chillier than I expected," she acknowledged, unable to stop the shiver that raced down her body. "I hadn't realized how cold it would be, flying through the clouds, and didn't think to bring my winter coat."

She was relieved of further embarrassment when a young lad clambered down the balloon's whale-hide side, startling her with his unexpected appearance. *How did he....* but quickly realizing he was using securing lines cross-tied every few feet like netting. Glancing up, she could barely make out the almost invisible lines that allowed hand and footholds to access the balloon's envelope. She should have known, but then the boy dropped to the deck, saluting sharply, the white of his teeth showing his grin.

"The Citadel's been spotted, Cap. South by Southeast, half a league."

His grin was infectious as Captain Belle and Aundrea both reached for the lensed spyglass.

"Sorry, Captain," Aundrea apologized, reluctantly withdrawing her hand from the brass tube.

Captain Belle gave her an almost wicked grin before placing the long tube to her eye, her mischievous smile holding as she grunted happily. After a long moment, she handed the lensed tube to Aundrea without a word.

Unexpected tension raced through Aundrea as she accepted the glass, putting it to her eye as Bella had. It took a moment for her to train the heavy instrument on the rugged shoreline, then another before she focused the spyglass's lens, bringing the distant picture of crashing surf and rugged cliffs into focus. She took nearly another minute to drag the lens back and forth along the cliff before spotting the vague shadow on the hillside. Only its shadow had given away the tower, hidden as it was by being built of the rock that surrounded it. Without Captain Belle's knowledge and the maps from the sea captains, they could have crisscrossed the area for days without noticing it. With a satisfied smile, she handed the glass back to Captain Belle.

Bella nodded knowingly before glancing up at the leprous mottling of clouds, then at the sliver of moon. "I'd say we're pretty well hidden as long as we keep our distance until we're ready."

The silver and blue of Luna's whale-hide envelope melded seamlessly into her surroundings, making her virtually disappear into the twilight sky.

It was hours before Captain Belle finally gave the order.

"Cut the boiler," she called, then gave Aundrea a nod.

At the signal, Aundrea left to assume her position, while Number Two passed on the command, quietly repeated down the length of the airship. Approaching from near ocean level, they now rose, side-sails and tail fin silently controlling their position and ascent.

Aundrea was mesmerized by the approaching cliffs, only breaking from her reverie to question Jewel. "Are the units ready to go?" she whispered, fearing the crew would overhear being so close.

It is accomplished, but it was more difficult than I had hoped, Jewel answered, feeling of near exhaustion. *I had significant difficulty deciphering the encryption method needed to get the* mechanisms *working.*

"Good is good, but that was cutting it close," Aundrea replied, watching worriedly as the cliff's rocky wall crept ever closer. She couldn't decide which worried her more: the looming cliff, the sounds of crashing surf hidden in the darkness below, or the massive bulk of The Lady Luna hanging over her head. But they were here, and that's what mattered.

As silent as a moth, the mammoth airship turned into the wind, effectively stalling their forward progress. With no need for a signal, Aundrea stepped off the rope and wood-staved ladder where she had hung waiting and turned to catch hold of the basket being lowered to her.

Captain Belle had argued against it, saying, "You are far too valuable to lose," but finally gave in when Aundrea explained that only she had the necessary skills to activate Rhone's creations.

It was actually Jewel who would do the activation, but with Bella not knowing of Jewel, the truth was inconsequential, and if Aundrea didn't go, neither would Jewel.

Carefully removing the mechanized creations, she placed them on the stone-paved courtyard and gave Jewel the go-ahead as she signaled for the basket to be rewound. Moments after, she climbed back onto the rope ladder, with The Lady Luna silently turning seaward, pulling away from the cliff face before dropping back toward the ocean waves far below. Once they were clear of the cliffs and the curious eyes of any that might be awake, they leveled off, the turn and the swaying motion of the ladder pulling Aundrea off-balance. Step by step, she climbed up the unsteady ladder, hands aching from the fierceness of her grip. Each handhold was an effort of will to release as she unclasped her grip from the wooden stave, only to grab frantically for the next. It was only when she reached the security of the deck that she allowed herself a free breath, though in truth, she wanted to kiss the deck itself.

When she was far enough from the working airmen not to be overheard, she whispered, "Are they away?"

They are, Jewel responded. *They are scattering.*

"I hope it's enough," she breathed.

With nothing more she could do, Aundrea closed her eyes in a silent prayer, then headed aft to find Captain Belle.

Waking with a pounding headache, Rhone seriously considered banging it against the wall, but that only reminded him of his time in the Badlands and how he had barely survived that endeavor. At least these walls weren't the convoluted rock walls and open sky of the Badland's corrugated passageways. No, these were smoothed rock walls, without a sky. Other than that, being lost and in pain were indeed common denominators.

Rhone, I believe you have a concussion, Stone warned, the low thrum of his voice enough to bring tears to Rhone's bloodshot eyes.

Does it matter? Rhone asked in a dull thought. *I mean, really? We're still trapped whether I have a concussion or not.* But the mere act of thinking made his headache worsen, so he tried not to.

Keeping his attention dedicated to taking another slow step, he inched his way along the wall, using its touch to guide his footsteps.

Look. There is a stairway ahead, Stone coxed, attempting to support his friend as best he could. *Most likely, there will be a door beyond. Perhaps it will lead us out of this lower level. Tell you what, make it that far and we can take a few minutes for you to rest. Just a few more steps, my boy.*

Rhone was barely listening as he inched his bruised body forward, only stopping when his boot bumped against the foot of the stairs. "I've got it," he mumbled, eyes closed as he began to crawl up the roughly cut stairs. But when his head banged painfully into an extremely solid door, he whined, "Owww, that hurts," and squinted through bleary eyes at the heavy planking. Even through his pain, he recognized the fine craftsmanship, and when Stone's light slid across its elaborately inlaid mother-of-pearl design, he muttered, "Pretty door, but what now?"

That would be the door out, Stone encouraged. *Come on now. You can do it.*

"Are you sure?" Rhone asked, staring at the simple latch securing the door. "I mean, there's not even a lock," which was a good thing since he didn't have the energy or awareness to pick one. Then a more pertinent thought came to his halting mind. "Wait. Is anyone inside?"

Ah, very good, Stone commented, pleased by Rhone's statement. *I am glad to see that you are still with us. But no, I sense nothing. There is, however, a small possibility that they are shielding their presence.*

I'm not sure I even care, Rhone thought, too tired to worry about possibilities.

Stone's light vanished as Rhone put a hand on the simple latch and leaned forward, worked the lever while using his weight to inch open the door. But it was only more darkness, if perhaps a shade less black. Opening it just enough to crawl through, he entered, closing it quietly behind him.

"A little more light, please?"

Why, of course, Stone agreed, and within moments, the growing light revealed a grand room with a circle of throne-like chairs sitting before a regal-looking fireplace. Another door, a duplicate of the one he had just come through, pierced the wall across from him, while a heavy tapestry covered the last, the rugged mountain scene woven into its fabric showing a glimmering waterfall cascading into a deep pool. The silvery fibers used to create the water scene reflected Stone's light in a way that made it shimmer as though it was flowing, but as intriguing as it was, Rhone's interest centered on the nearest chair.

Lurching his way forward, he dropped bonelessly into its depths. "Don't wake me unless it's an emergency," he mumbled, sinking into its thickly padded expanse with a groan of ecstasy.

Though somewhat less-than-happy with their situation, Stone knew Rhone could go no further. *Sleep well, my young friend. You undoubtedly need it.*

Turning his thoughts to their plight, Stone felt for the energy of the We creature set in the man's ring, and keeping himself well shielded, now that they were out of the solid rock of the lower levels, his awareness stretched out, searching for other connections. People were easy to find, their noisy energy sending echoes up and down the halls, but there were also the weaker signatures of We, barely recognizable as their energy flared and dissipated, fluctuating uncharacteristically in a way that disturbed him. Oddly, it took little effort to stay shielded. Even Jewel's small energy profile had been greater.

Feeling secure, his thoughts flowed through his crystalline matrix, confirming the data with possibilities. Satisfied, he stored the data and began mapping the building and the best way out. Once completed, he tuned his nervous energy to warming Rhone's chilled body.

⚜

"We have an unexpected visitor," Mathias stated, his grim visage magnifying the announcement to that of a threat. A swirl of surprised looks passed between the two brothers who were present. There hadn't been guests at the citadel for decades, and their instant suspicions went to those not in the room.

"And where are our dear brothers?" Warren asked sharply.

Mathias answered by raising a placating hand. "I'm quite sure they are not the culprits," he offered. "I have been aware of this intruder for some time, even playing with him a bit before leading him to our . . . surprisingly effective reception area. Do not worry yourselves. It is under control."

Warren and Byron glanced suspiciously at each other, wondering exactly what that meant.

"Still, our brothers should be summoned," Byron commented. "I believe they would find this of interest."

"Oh, I agree, and I expect them momentarily," Mathias answered, his calm reply confident in his ability. "It is breakfast after all, and our dear eldest has a high regard for filling his stomach. As for Paxton, the citadel may be large, but not so large that we cannot find him at need."

Warren, as the middle brother, nodded his agreement, knowing both statements were accurate.

Byron, on the other hand, found direct conflict unseemly, and turned aside, choosing to wait for the conflict he knew was coming.

Jared arrived less than a minute later, his heavy stride announcing him before his bulk filled the hall. Taking the seat at the table's end, as if it were his by decree, he barked for a cup, scowling at his brothers as he waited its arrival. Only after swallowing a long draught of the steaming brew, did he fixed his brothers with a hard stare. "Can't a man dine in peace?" he growled, not enjoying their overt scrutiny.

"We've had a visitor," Warren said, offering nothing more as he let the words settle like ash.

Jared stiffened before slamming his cup to the table. "What? A visitor here?"

Mathias lifted a hand, palm out. "Easy, brother. It has been taken care of. I have been aware of his coming for some time and prepared for it. It is of no matter."

Further explanation was forestalled as Paxton entered the hall, and with the last brother present, the atmosphere thickened almost visibly.

"Good morrow, Paxton," Warren greeted mildly. "You're just in time. Snake was recounting the arrival of an unexpected guest. Do you know who might be bold enough to seek us out?"

"A guest?" Paxton repeated, his surprise genuine. His eyes were already searching the hall, but finding nothing but knowing smiles, his jaw tightened. "Who would even know where to find the citadel?" he demanded. "Its existence is kept from common knowledge, and the staff understands the price of loose tongues." Then realization crept in, souring his expression. "Unless one of you invited trouble." His voice sharpened as he followed the thought, temper rising faster than reason.

Jared gave a snort of derision. "Sit down, Paxton. Mathias was just speaking before you stormed in. If you can restrain yourself for half a breath, you'll get your answers."

With all four of his brothers glaring at him, Paxton found his place and sat, calling for a cup before giving them his attention. "So, Snake," he said derisively. "What's this about a visitor? Did you slip up and allow someone to follow you? You're the only one that consistently has dealings with The Stronghold, which, I presume, is where this guest, as you say, comes from."

Mathias was well used to his moniker of Snake, and enjoyed the subtle power it gave. Amiably, he addressed his brothers. "Believe it or not, I too believe he is from The Stronghold, though not The Council. It seems the OPR has once again found its way to our habitation, which has been a long time in coming. I'm actually surprised it took them this long."

"And it was your job to see that it didn't happen," Paxton shot back. "Are you telling us you failed? And we had such faith in you." His words dripped with malice only a loving brother could manage.

"Knock it off, you two. We haven't heard the story yet," Jared snapped. "I, for one, am interested to hear it." His position as the eldest gave him at least that much say.

As the other two nodded, Mathias took it as his cue.

"Thank you," he said casually, sliding his chair back to stand. "This is but a small situation, and though unasked for, can be used to our advantage. At present, we have no actual proof that our guest is from the OPR, though it is my experienced guess."

When his glance flicked briefly toward his eldest brother, acknowledging the possibility, Jared frowned, as expected.

"I was alerted to the intrusion by my ring, and as you know, they give as they will, not by choice. With that foreknowledge, I was able to draw our guest in. He is at this moment confined in the lower level of our great citadel, awaiting your pleasure." With that said, Mathias inclined his head in a courtly bow, then resumed his seat, calmly awaiting the inevitable response.

"Why haven't we heard of this before now?" Jared demanded, his booming voice causing more than one brother to flinch.

"That's an excellent question," Paxton agreed.

Mathias, however, wasn't concerned. "I considered it, but chose to wait until we broke our fast this morning. Would you have preferred that I wake you in the middle of the night?"

Warren raised a calming hand to settle the dispute. "Of course not. It is not an accusation, merely a question as to time and place. It is still early, after all, and Paxton is irritable at not yet having dined." Which was true. It was also a non-aggressive method of putting his older brother in his place.

Not to be left out, Byron asked, "Do we know our guest?"

"Not to my knowledge," Mathias answered. "I have had no dealing with him as yet, but I believe he is young and has not yet learned better than to step into the adder's nest."

"The Snake's pit is more accurate," Paxton muttered, still irritable and smarting from the earlier rebuke.

"Or that," Mathias allowed. "But whatever your interest, he is below. I had intended to devote at least part of the day to the matter, but he may not last that long." He glanced around the table. "So, if you're curious, now is your opportunity." He almost smiled as their eyes brightened, knowing it was like handing sweets to children.

"But first, we eat," he said mildly. "Questioning tends to upset my stomach."

The lie slipped from his lips so easily that even he failed to notice.

CHAPTER 22

Who Would Have Guessed?

A re you able to wake? Stone asked gently, sending a mild warmth to Rhone's tired muscles.

Rhone's breathing changed as he stirred, working his way to the surface of awareness. "Ahhhrrgggg . . ." he groaned, not quite capable of actual speech.

I believe we are out of time, Stone said quietly. *I feel disturbing emanations, and I believe it would be most expedient that we get on with our escape. Can you move?*

"Maybe," Rhone muttered, working his way to an upright position before rubbing his eyes. "How long did I sleep?"

Long enough. It is time that we go.

Rhone pushed stiffly to his feet, rubbing the tender lump at the back of his head. Switching to their shared mental link, he asked, *Okay —which way?* He already felt marginally better for the rest.

Very good, Rhone. I'm pleased to see you improving, Stone replied. *While you slept, I mapped the building and our route to freedom—but we must hurry. There are people moving in our direction.*

People? The thought snapped Rhone to full alert, and he lurched upright, staggering a step before his legs remembered their purpose. While his movements were clumsy, he was mobile enough to reach the far door without problems.

His fingers were inches from the handle when he froze, as voices drifted in from the other side. Panicked, he spun on one foot, desperately searching for another escape. There was none. The other door was the one he had entered through. The one leading back to the lower levels.

Then he saw the tapestry.

Acting on instinct, he slipped behind the laughably poor concealment, pressing himself flat in hope that whoever entered would be too distracted to notice the unnatural bulge in the heavy drape.

Shhhh, Stone whispered fiercely, the silence only making it that much more terrifying.

Rhone stilled, barely daring to breathe as he waited for whatever came next.

A smooth and vaguely recognizable voice accompanied the muffled sound of the door opening. "Yes, we have a history with the OPR. And I am not saying that it should not be dealt with. I am merely asking if you have learned anything from those same decades of history? Should we not question him before making a verdict? After all, information is power, and the more we have, the bigger the bite we can take."

The comment went unanswered as several people entered the room and proceeded to their allocated positions.

Then, an unfamiliar voice offered a neutral comment. "I closed off all access from the general quarters, so feel free to speak. There will be no possibility of our being disturbed."

"Good thinking, Byron, but I wouldn't have worried about it," came a third, much deeper voice. "Our workers are well-trained, and none would consider coming into this area. They know the penalty."

The sounds of movement were barely discernible beyond the heavy tapestry, yet Rhone could picture the scene with brutal clarity. He stood frozen, fear locking his limbs as the words *Don't panic! Don't panic!* looped endlessly through his stalled mind. He may have come seeking The Brotherhood, but nothing in his academy training had prepared him to stand within arm's reach of them.

His focus snapped back when a voice rang out, loud and commanding. "To The Brotherhood!"

"To The Brotherhood!" came the echoing cry as the other brothers followed suit. Then, chairs creaked as they took up the weight of their occupants.

Never had anyone been so close to The Brotherhood yet so utterly powerless. He might as well have been bound in chains for all the good he could do, but he instantly smothered the thought, afraid even that might be heard by the We that were undoubtedly present.

As silence descended, the voice that had started the proceedings took charge. "To the task at hand," he began. "It is apparent that we have been found. Is that not right, Mathias?"

"In a way, yes. But I do not believe it to be more than a search for answers," Mathias answered.

Rhone stiffened at the familiar voice from his cell, but a faint vibration from his collar coaxed out his pent-up breath. Closing his eyes, he worked to conquer his fear.

"Perhaps a snippet of lost information was found in some ancient dispatch or other," the voice continued, "but we've had no notice from our sources in The Council, so nothing is truly amiss. Therefore, it is only the OPR, which we know is constantly questing for things to stick their noses in. It could even be a ploy to improve their own status. It has always been so, and they have failed repeatedly."

Rhone clenched his jaw at hearing the insult to his agency, but another vibration from Stone, and his silent *Shhh!* warned him to silence.

There was a light chuckle before another voice said, "So, you do not fear our being found?"

Even Rhone knew the question was trickier than it sounded. Answering no would anger his brothers, saying he didn't care. But a yes would say he had failed in keeping them hidden. Either could have consequences.

"I do not see how this is anything more than a stab in the dark," Mathias answered, calmly, yet casually evasive. "It is my job to know, and we have good informants." Standing his ground, he forced them to acknowledge his words.

"We've left security issues in Mathias's hands for decades, and I see no reason to change it now," came the deep voice, most probably the oldest brother and head of the clan. "OPR or not, one errant person is not a major threat. We can deal with it. Now let us get on with our day."

Rhone could feel their tension release, and vaguely wondered how much of it he was receiving from Stone.

It is not me, Stone whispered, his voice so faint Rhone could barely sense the words. *Perhaps you are becoming more sensitive to energy fields.*

The intriguing thought was cut short when the deep voice asked, "Is there anything further to discuss? Warren—how about you?"

"Nothing, except the wish to have this done," Warren grunted, his thinning patience coming to the front.

"Good enough, then. Mathias, we leave it to you—unless, as you suggest, others might wish to observe your skills."

The smile behind the deep voice was anything but holy, raising the fine hairs along Rhone's neck.

When the cry of "To the Brotherhood!" rang out once more—quickly echoed by the others—a sudden prickling sensation flowed along Rhone's body. With sudden surety, he knew there was more than one We in the room. He didn't dare to follow the energy, but he knew Stone had already taken note.

Chairs creaked as the men rose, most moving toward the door they had entered. But one crossed the room and exited through the lower-level door—the same passage Rhone and Stone had used.

Knowing it would be only minutes before the empty cell was discovered, Rhone took it as his signal and began edging along the wall, carefully moving toward freedom.

"I wondered how long I would have to wait."

Rhone froze in his tracks, and with wide eyes, turned his head.

A middle-aged man sat in the shadows of the room, his nearly white hair and neatly clipped beard lending him a veneer of refinement. His eyes, however, stripped away that illusion. They fixed on Rhone with such intensity that he almost couldn't breathe.

"A bit younger than I would have expected," the man chuckled, though with no mirth in it. "The OPR must be getting the dregs if this is all they can come up with. Still, you managed to get away from Mathias. That says something, though I doubt you'll enjoy the outcome." Then his eyes noticed the collar around Rhone's neck, and he rose swiftly for a better look. "What is this?" he asked in amazement.

Instinctively, Rhone stepped back, but found himself against the wall. He was ready to dodge for the door when a golden-pink flash erupted from his collar, instantly blinding both of them.

Why didn't you warn me, Rhone moaned in silence, his vision going red as tears formed in his stinging eyes.

What? And warn our adversary? That is not much of a plan if you ask me, Stone admonished. *Follow my* directions, *and we may have a chance.*

But I can't see where I'm going!

Nonsense. Now turn left, and hurry.

With no choice, other than to stand there and get caught, Rhone sighed and followed Stone's directions.

Go slowly, but continue until I say, Stone ordered.

Taking one unsteady step forward, then another, Rhone worked his way past the whimpering man, hands out to ward off any unseen objects.

Very good. Now, a little additional speed would be helpful, Stone advised.

It was only a few more steps before Rhone got the hang of it and picked up his pace.

A little more to your left and then the door, Stone urged. *Careful now,* which came just in time for Rhone to avoid running headfirst into the door. A moment's fumbling for the handle and he slipped through, free, headed . . . well, somewhere. Where, he didn't know, but he knew enough to trust Stone. With two brothers behind him and no alarm yet, Rhone made good speed, using his hand to guide himself down the hallway. When a sliver of memory crossed his mind, he asked, "Hey, Stone. Remember the training format we used for sword fighting? Do you think it would work here?"

That is a wonderful idea., Stone replied in *amazement. I am sorry I did not think of it myself. Now . . . Let me see . . .*

A moment later, Rhone's mind lit up like candles on a Christmas tree. "Wow, that's perfect!" he said approvingly. "I'll never need a light again." A colorful map now overlaid his mind's eye, showing hallways, doors, and various hazards he would have to negotiate.

I am glad you approve, but we aren't out yet, Stone warned as he unveiled the rest of the citadel's floor plan.

"Okay, but it's still cool," Rhone replied happily.

With the map firmly centered in his mind, he picked up speed. He was almost jogging now, aiming for a door labeled OUT in bright green letters. Innocently, he asked, "This wouldn't be the way out, would it?" snickering under his breath as he crashed headlong into the door, severely bruising an already sore shoulder and battered head. "Owww," he whimpered, gripping his newly bruised and aching shoulder.

You might try pulling, Stone advised in frustration. *Now, please hurry!*

Feeling stupid, Rhone groaned and rolled his eyes as he pulled the door open and stepped through.

Can you lock it? Stone asked, his voice sounding oddly weak.

"Good idea. Just give me a sec," Rhone said quietly, and still not seeing well, swept a hand over the door, quickly finding a keyhole but no way to lock it. Continuing his search, he found a broom beside the door, but still no key. "No luck. It takes a key," he advised. "But wait. There is a broom." Then, laughing at his own ingenuity, he jammed

it through the door's looping handle, securing it from anything less than a truly determined effort.

I believe that will work, Stone agreed, his voice hollow but approving. *Now, the gardens. They are* on *the right, so go left. They won't expect that.*

Doing his best to follow Stone's command, Rhone turned and ran, though his groans and limping gait made it anything but graceful.

Do you see that short wall ahead, the one broad enough to sit on while overlooking the cliff? *Perhaps you should slow down a bit. We do not wish to make a wrong step here, now do we?*

Rhone remembered seeing the cliff when he surveyed the grounds, and could only agree. It would indeed be a dramatic fall. He might even make it to the waves if he didn't hit the cliff first. With that in mind, he was more than happy when his knee bumped into the short wall. Just then, a powerful gust whipped up from below, catching at his clothes as though it would tear them from his body. Shuddering involuntarily, he cautiously stepped back.

"Where to now?" he whispered. He might be out of earshot, but who knew?

A very good question, Stone answered. *I am afraid the stonework of the citadel's walls restricted my view enough that I could not see beyond this point, but consider this: if you could climb over the wall, you should be able to hang onto the other side and be out of sight. I am certain I will have an answer in no time.*

"You want what?" Rhone sputtered in surprise.

Look on the bright side. No one would think to look for you there, Stone encouraged.

"But . . . but I can't even see where I'm going!" Rhone exploded, appalled at the mere thought of the long drop.

Hush, my friend. Remember, we are not alone, Stone soothed. *I am quite certain you will be able to find a hold. I trust you.*

Like that's going to be much help! Rhone thought, a chill running down his back.

It wasn't just the wind blowing up the cliff face. It was his memory of hanging upside down from Bo, a hundred feet off the ground. But with a teeth-clenched groan, he stepped carefully toward the short stone wall and bent to feel its surface. *Here goes nothing,* he thought, making very sure Stone heard. With suddenly clammy fingers, he gripped the rocky edge and slid his legs over. "It's probably better that I can't see," he muttered, grabbing the top edge of the stonework bench and lowering himself over.

Hanging on with already sore hands, he used the toes of his boots to scrape at the rocky bank, desperately trying to find footing. But there was nothing. Nothing he wanted to place his life on. His efforts grew frantic as he felt his hands slipping, then Stone's calm voice flowed into his mind.

I believe there is a foothold just to your right and three inches below, Stone directed. *Careful now. This is no time to slip.*

I love you too, Rhone thought derisively, but stretched to find the toehold in the cliff's rocky face.

There, see. You are doing just fine. Now, can you hold at this location? You are below the top, *so unless they actually look over the edge, we should be safe.*

That's because nobody in their right mind would climb over, Rhone thought in disgust.

Exactly right. I told you it was a good idea.

Rhone was far from jubilant, but they had gotten away, and they weren't falling—yet—so good was good. *Okay, I think I've got a hold,* he advised, *as long as it doesn't take too long. By the way, could you shut off the projection now? I'm pretty sure I don't want to see how far it is to the bottom.* A moment later the projection was gone, leaving his vision with a dark red haze he could almost see through. *Thanks, Stone. That's a lot better.*

Not only were they friends and partners, they were collar-mates.

T he mechanical bug creations did what they were designed for, spreading quietly through the building, searching with their ear-like sensors for the energy emanations of the We. Once found, they homed in on the signals, sending out a silent stream of data for Jewel's receiving unit to pick up.

It is all very simple if one considers the requirements, then finds a way to answer them, Stone had lectured.

Jewel could almost hear his somewhat satirical voice as he had explained the procedure, but as frustrating as he was, she had accepted the challenge. Now she lay in her padded box, velvet-lined to dampen vibrations. A jury-rigged contraption connected her to the heavy metal rods suspended throughout the cabin. The entire array had been quickly assembled, now allowing her to receive as well as send.

Gathering the incoming data, she transcribed, then stored it, and with the data at hand, had just started triangulating the whereabouts of the We units, when a new signature cut through the stream, sharp and unmistakable, halting the process mid-calculation.

Stone? she gasped, the action very human-like in her surprise. There was no hesitation in her knowledge. Stone's signature was as singular as a human fingerprint, and well imprinted into her crystalline memory. But that aside, it was also many times stronger than the other weak signals she had just transcribed.

Aundrea was pacing her cabin, considering her next move. She well remembered Rhone telling of his earlier days of working with Stone, and how he had sat around while Stone sent out messages, trying to find other We. Now she understood how useless he must have felt, playing the part of a pack mule as he toted Stone from one location to another. The humorous memory was shattered when Jewel's excited thought blasted her mind.

Aundrea! We have them!

"Easy, girl," Aundrea said, grimacing as she shook her head. Then grabbing the little box, she flipped back the lid. "You found them? Rhone and Stone, or the other We?" Both were important, but one was much closer to her heart.

Both, came Jewel's equally excited response. *Rhone's bug creations have tracked five We. I was calculating their triangulation when I heard Stone's signature.*

"Five?" Aundrea asked cautiously. "That's more than I expected. Does that include Stone?"

"No. According to my scans, there are five exceedingly weak signals. Their strength was so slight that I was forced to repeat the scan several times before confirming them. Then Stone appeared, orders of magnitude stronger than the others. I cannot explain why he failed to register earlier, but I am confident the signals are authentic."

Aundrea could hardly breathe as she removed Jewel from the box and put it back on her finger. "Can you map it out?" she asked thoughtfully. "I'll need to show Captain Belle exactly where they are so we can make plans."

A minute later she had a quill in hand, following the directions Jewel was piping into her head. Five minutes after that, she was at the captain's cabin, pausing for a breath before she knocked.

"Captain Belle, if you have a moment?"

The wickerwork walls of the airship gave some privacy but weren't the solid wood of the ships she'd been on. Her understanding was that wooden walls were simply too heavy and had been discarded for a woven structure. Only the lowest section of the hull was made of wood, a safety measure in case of an emergency water landing.

When the creak of rope hinges announced the door's opening, Aundrea turned to see Bella's head filling the narrow space. "May I help you?" Bella asked, eyes caught in that bleary look of someone interrupted from a nap. But one look at Aundrea and she swung the door wide, a smile transforming her tired face. "I would ask if it was good news, but I guess I don't need to," she said, as she waved Aundrea in.

"It is good, and we have the coordinates," Aundrea announced. "It's time to plan. Are you up for it, or should we put it off until your nap is done? I'm sorry I intruded."

"Nonsense. A captain never sleeps," Bella said with a chuckle. "We just rest with our eyes closed while we plot proper tortures for the villains that disturb us."

Aundrea couldn't help but laugh, but wondered just how much was true. "If you have a quill and paper, I can draw out their location." She wasn't about to give up her own copy.

Bella gave Aundrea a curious look, but turned to a small table and pulled open a drawer. "No worries. My room is yours, for a short time at least. A girl does need her beauty sleep."

They both laughed as Aundrea took up the quill and removed the stopper from the ink.

O ne glance and Mathias slammed the cell door, the resounding echoes crashing down the dark halls like echoing thunder. He didn't waste time on the how. The fact that his guest was gone was enough. With lantern in hand, and anger gathered around him like a cloak, he returned the way he had come.

Someone would pay.

But his anger spiked when he stepped into the meeting room and found Warren, hands covering his face, red eyes tearing, as he screamed insults into the dark.

"Don't tell me you let him get past?" Mathias demanded, more accusation than question.

"Mathias? Is that you? I—I can't see," Warren pleaded, arms outstretched as he grasped blindly at the air. "I'm blind. You have to help me."

Mathias brushed past his brother's outstretched arms with a snort of disgust. "Unfortunately, I've got work to do, but I'll send someone if I can," he hedged. "For now, sit down before you fall down." He paused before leaving the room, but only to shake his head in disbelief before drawing the ornate door closed behind him.

It wasn't long before near pandemonium reigned in the citadel. House servants ran to and fro, trying to follow the commands of one brother after another, but all to no avail. Their quarry had vanished. Their first rush had been to the gardens and walls, then beyond, but they found nothing. Next came an organized room-by-room search, including the lower levels, but again nothing.

With nothing found, Mathias instantly became the underdog, while Warren, blind or not, was simply scoffed at for losing their prey. With no good explanation as to their guest's whereabouts, they picked each other as opponents.

"He couldn't have simply vanished," Jared griped. "He got in, and back out, so the question is, which one of you helped him?"

These were serious words, instantly dividing the already wary brothers.

Mathias countered with the only explanation he had. "I wouldn't have caught him if I was going to let him go again. It would have been much easier to simply let him in, and none of you the wiser."

"I hate to admit it, but he does make sense," Paxton growled, swinging his gaze toward Jared and Byron. "That leaves you two."

"But what about Warren? Maybe the guy double-crossed him," Byron croaked in panic.

Warren felt the weight of judgment shift against him. "Me?" he shrieked. "But I'm the one that's blinded."

"Yes, you are, but it does make sense," Jared agreed. "Why else would you have stayed in the room after we left?"

As if that settled the argument, the remaining brothers advanced on the blinded Warren, quickly pinning him to the ground. Within moments, his ring was forcefully torn from his finger, his mostly skinned digit held now close to his body as he whimpered in fear and pain.

Jared stood from the ruckus and raised the ring, inspecting the tiny glint of stone. "I'll just keep this," he stated with satisfaction. "As the eldest, I will see that it is kept safe."

But Byron stepped forward. "That would not be right," he said cautiously. "We are The Brotherhood, and while I cannot claim innocence for my brother, I will say it would not be right for you to have two pieces of Father's stone. We are equal in our places, each with a single piece. Warren's ring should be placed in a sealed box, left where all eyes can keep watch over it. What say you, brothers?" Turning to the remaining three, he stood erect and oddly patriarchal, despite his being fourth in line. His slow turn received nods, recognizing that he was, after all, trained as a cleric and knew justice, whether he lived it or not. They also knew that any one of them having two rings would unbalance the unstable existence they had, causing incalculable danger to the rest.

"Fine," Jared admitted ruefully. "I hear the justice. I was merely attempting a quick resolution to the problem. The ring is here. Is there a box to hold it?"

"I have several reliquaries. I'm certain one will work," Byron answered, grateful that it hadn't come to additional blows.

"Then be quick about it. We don't have all day. We have a fugitive to find."

Lev was exhausted by the time she returned to the citadel, but found Blue grazing calmly on the short grass of the same sparse meadow she'd used before. How he'd gotten there didn't matter. If

Blue was here, then Rhone was too. The thought was either reassuring—or very bad.

The ride had been long and tiring, each mile grinding her down. Now she crouched in a rocky notch overlooking the grounds and settled into her vantage point. The stillness and fatigue stretched endlessly, monotony dulling her focus—until a sudden commotion caught her attention. Her first instinct was to run, but she forced herself to stay, needing to understand what was happening before she moved. Flattening herself against the hillside, she slowed her breathing, becoming just another shard of stone in the broken terrain.

Men poured from the citadel like wasps from a disturbed nest. They were searching—of that she was certain, but whether they hunted Rhone or her, she couldn't tell. Either way, she was in the wrong place. It was time to leave.

Relinquishing her position, Lev backed away and followed the route she'd rehearsed, slipping back through the stiff brush. She knew the terrain worked for her as much as it worked against them. They would face the same obstacles, but they hadn't combed the area as she had and didn't know the small game trails and cuts that let her approach unseen. Even so, she watched her step. She wouldn't be helping anyone if she twisted an ankle.

By the time she completed her circuitous route, the men had already given up and returned empty-handed. Her route may have been time-consuming but now granted a bit more leniency.

With days of surveillance behind her, she had narrowed her options to a single viable approach. Without the cover of darkness to hide in, she chose a line that allowed the least exposure to the citadel's windows as possible. It was, after all, broad daylight—something she wouldn't have advised anyone to attempt. But waiting wasn't an option.

Testing each handhold before trusting it, she hauled herself up, rock scraping softly beneath her boots as she carefully kept her sword from clattering against the wall. Once at the top, she rolled onto the narrow surface and flattened, sliding the blade aside with practiced precision.

Lying still, she counted breaths, listening for any sign of her intrusion.

This was her opening. There wouldn't be another.

CHAPTER 23

Desperation

Their guest had made a clean getaway.

Tired of the mindless running about, Byron walked slowly toward the short wall that surrounded the citadel's seaward courtyard and stood staring over the cliff's edge to the sea far below. His many decades had taught him when to pay attention to his 'intuition', and whether it was intuition, God, or the ring, he had learned to follow where it led. He was about to turn around when his ring gave a soft throb and began to glow dimly, pulsing to the slow beat of his heart.

"I hear you," he whispered. "I don't understand, but I hear you." A few more steps brought him up against the short wall, and still not understanding, he sat, using the broad wall as it had been designed. "I am here," he whispered again, settling himself as his training dictated. Understanding would come as it would. It could not be forced.

Rhone almost choked at hearing the words, but held his position, his knuckles beginning to cramp as they gripped at the rough rock. While his position was stable, he was already tiring from crouching for so long. Now, someone was sitting just above his head, saying the very words that were so dear to him, the first words Stone had ever spoken. The unfairness was almost too much to bear. He couldn't even talk to Stone with the possibility of other We overhearing, so he clung to the rocks, frustration driving him nearly mad. Then, a thought crossed his mind that he must look like a starfish, splayed out as he was on the rocky cliff face, fingers and toes gripping at the rock as though they had suction cups. He nearly laughed, but quickly stopped himself, fearing he'd be overheard. There was nothing else he could do unless he wanted to give up and drop into the ocean far below. Even then he would probably bounce off the cliff face before he reached it.

The man seated above hadn't moved for a quarter-hour. He seemed to have gone into a trance, his occasional mumbles sounding as though he was talking to himself. Beyond that, all was quiet.

The buffeting winds had stopped, which should have made Rhone feel better, but instead, he groaned quietly, exhaustion making his legs shiver, tired muscles shifting restlessly as they weakened from holding their position for so long. Then, his left leg began to bounce uncontrollably, its movement enough to dislodge the rock it rested on.

As the clattering stone slid down the near-vertical cliff, it picked up others, creating a minor cascade of debris that followed suit, falling away to the foaming waves far below. Rhone tried desperately to hold himself in place, but the effort only caused more gravel to loosen around him. Suddenly, he too was sliding, fingers digging futilely into the rocky surface.

With a soundless scream, he fell, eyes closed so he wouldn't see his coming end.

But his slide had hardly begun before it halted, a hand clutching his shoulder in a painful grip that pinned him to the wall as effectively as a bug on a display board.

"What have we here?" asked an interested voice.

Rhone's rush of thanks dropped into the heartbreak of defeat, as assisted by the hand, he managed to scramble up the rocky face before flopping bonelessly onto the stone bench.

"So this is where you went," the voice commented. "I must say, I doubt I would have done the same. I have far too much regard for my own life to attempt such a hare-brained scheme."

The words sounded friendly enough, but Rhone knew better than to believe them. This was The Brotherhood, not some lay brother from a lonely priory tucked away on a distant cliffside retreat.

Raising his head, Rhone saw a middle-aged man with shoulder-length silver-blond hair blowing gently in the cliff's breeze. His smile held a hard yet quizzical stare, somehow carrying the look of a beneficent savior that was altogether hard to define.

"And who would you be, wandering the yards of the citadel as if you owned them?" But when Rhone didn't answer, the man only gave an altruistic shrug at the refusal. "Cat got your tongue, does it? Well, I doubt I would answer either. Yes, best you stay silent, not that speaking would help your case." He seemed to consider his statement but ended up shaking his head ruefully. "I'm afraid you will remain forever young, as growing older does not seem to be in your future."

His soft chuckle sent a shiver down Rhone's spine, and too tired to move, he lay draped along the stone bench, head throbbing, not only from his recent contact with the door but his previous fall through the trapdoor. Resigned to his fate, he stretched his aching neck and shoulders, the move unfortunately giving his captor a glimpse of Stone's collar.

"And what have we here?" the man repeated, intrigued enough to echo his first sentence. He was reaching for Stone's collar when his ring suddenly blazed, its blinding light sending the man staggering back in amazement. With a groan, the man dropped to his knees, grabbing his head as he shuddered in pain.

Rhone's eyes had closed as he awaited his doom, but the brilliant flash instantly brought them wide again. Blinking to clear his still hazy vision, Rhone saw the man groveling on the ground and his opportunity for freedom. But to where? There was no way he was going over the wall again, and the cobbled courtyard gave nowhere to hide. With the gardens too far on the other side of the compound to be a quick option, he took the best option left. He followed Stone's directions.

To the citadel! Quickly! Stone commanded, his voice sending shockwaves through Rhone's still aching head. *The others will have felt the ring's call and will undoubtedly arrive shortly.*

He had barely rounded the corner when the image flickered, the glowing lines scattering, then vanishing altogether.

With his vision still blurred, he never saw the man until he slammed headlong into a broad chest.

"Ooof!"

The cry burst from them both as the collision sent them reeling, then they crashed to the ground in a tangled heap.

Rhone lay gasping like a fish out of water, lungs refusing to suck in air as he attempted to clear his jumbled thoughts.

Oh my. That was very bad timing, Stone said apologetically.

"You think?" Rhone shot back, kicking blindly at the man now clawing for his legs. There was no time to argue as the man's fingers clamped around his calf.

Twisting violently, Rhone tried to wrench himself free. Then his training took over, and the panic vanished.

With sudden clarity, he drove a fist down squarely into the man's nose, its sickening crunch bringing a grunt of surprise from his assailant, his grip loosening enough for Rhone's next move. Without hesitation, Rhone's boot whipped around in a wide arc, connecting solidly with the man's more tender parts. Instantly, the man doubled over in pain, releasing Rhone's calf.

Free at last, Rhone scrambled away like a crab across a hot beach, thankful no one was around to witness his undignified retreat.

Is this your fastest method of transportation? Stone complained, his voice strangely hollow. *Perhaps you should attempt to run.*

"Hey, I'm trying," Rhone groaned, as he staggered to his feet, lurching toward the door less than ten feet away.

He came within arm's reach before his battered legs simply gave out, driving him shoulder-first into the heavy wooden door. Pain exploded through the same shoulder he'd abused all day, and he slid helplessly to the floor, whimpering in pain.

"I'm done in," he wheezed, but giving up wasn't an option.

With a resigned sigh, he reached for the latch and used it to haul himself upright once more, every muscle protesting the effort.

"Stone, how can we get away when there are people everywhere?" he panted.

Get away? But we cannot leave. We must go back inside, Stone demanded. *Now hurry. Your previous opponent is regaining his feet.*

Sure enough, a glance showed the big man was indeed climbing to his feet. Nor did he look happy as he wiped blood from his dripping nose.

"Ahhh... We've got to go!" Rhone sputtered, panic lending him enough strength to wrench the heavy door open.

Interestingly, it flew much more easily than expected, but his surprise lasted only an instant as a man toppled through, one hand still outstretched where he had been pushing from the other side.

"How many brothers are there?" Rhone blurted, and acting on instinct, stomped his foot against the edge of the door, stopping it mid-swing.

Thunk!

The man's forehead struck the solid wood with a satisfying crack, followed immediately by a colorful curse as he rebounded back into the building.

Not waiting to admire his handiwork, Rhone slammed the door shut and threw his weight against it, chest heaving with ragged breaths. A heartbeat later, the man hurled himself into the door, his greater weight beginning to win as it slowly forced Rhone back inch by inch against his enthusiastic, yet ineffective strength.

Rhone braced himself for the worst when Stone's voice rang through his head like a battlefield command. *Ready... NOW!*

"Aaahhhgg!" Rhone jerked backward as a jolt of electricity crackled through his hand, the sparking handle sliding from his grip.

Instantly, the door flew open, smashing into the stone wall hard enough to chip rock. Behind followed the man, shoulder down as he charged through. But finding nothing left to push against, he lurched forward, stumbling over his own feet, dropping to the ground like a sack of potatoes.

Done playing defense, Rhone drove his boot into the man's chin, snapping his head back into the stone wall with a hollow *thunk.*

"That should hold him," Rhone growled, a hint of pride in his voice. But his moment was shattered by an orange warning flashing across his mind.

Behind you*!* Stone shouted, his voice thin and wavering, sounding much like fingernails on the slate chalkboard Mom had used to help him learn his letters.

Rhone grimaced, but prepared for action. Spinning on the ball of his foot, he dropped into a fighter's crouch. Just five feet away, the big man from earlier closed in, his sword steady in his grip as blood spilled from his nose, tracing a dark line down his chin.

One look told Rhone there'd be no talking his way out of this one, and with no weapon, there was nothing he could do.

Stone? he asked silently, his voice filled with desperation.

I am sorry, *my friend. My energy is depleted,* Stone answered, his voice raspy and low, sounding more like an eddy of windblown sand than his normal sharp critique.

It's okay. We did good, Rhone thought to his friend.

They had lost. There was nothing more he could do.

He flinched as the big man's muscles tightened for the killing blow, but the strike never came. Instead, the man's expression turned to puzzled surprise, then stiffened, slowly looking down at the arrowhead protruding from his chest. He was still staring at the arrow when a thin ribbon of blood dripped from the corner of his mouth, mingling with the crimson streak still dripping from his battered nose.

For a long heartbeat, he simply stared. Then his knees buckled and he collapsed forward, the question still frozen on his face.

"But . . . Who?" Rhone mumbled in confusion, his tired mind refusing to recognize what was happening.

Wake up. We have things to do, Stone ordered, dragging his attention back to the present.

Starting a slow turn, Rhone searched for his unknown ally, continuing his turn until it reached the low outer wall.

There, just beyond the low stone wall hung The *Lady Luna*, suspended in place with Aundrea standing on the prow, bow in hand as she searched for additional targets.

Stunned, Rhone swept his gaze up to the quarterdeck where Captain Belle called orders to her crew.

He may not have expected a rescue, but he was more than ready to accept it. Turning to run for the airship, he had barely taken a step when Stone's voice broke into his thoughts.

What are you doing? You cannot leave yet. We must free those of my kind, Stone ordered. *Quickly now. Get the rings!*

Rhone didn't bother to reply. He had been through it before. With a resigned sigh, he raised a hand to the airship, then turned to the prostrate form at his feet and began prying the ring from the finger.

The moment it was in his hand, he limped to the unconscious form at the door, and once again worked to remove the ring. It was more difficult than the previous, but he finally managed, taking it along with some of the skin. With the two rings in hand, he glanced wistfully at Luna fighting to maintain her position in the blustery wind. But even as he watched, he saw her lose ground, turning away to the safety of the sea.

Knowing there was nothing he could do for them, Rhone turned back to the door he had so recently exited.

It was an agonizingly slow run down the hall, making Rhone wish he had never left his warehouse. "Are we there yet?" he wheezed, barely managing to keep to his feet.

That is not very funny. Why do you not put more of your energy into running instead of simply running off at the mouth? Stone replied, sounding as worn out as Rhone.

"I'm doing the best I can," Rhone grumbled, his stumbling gait not elegant, but he was getting there, if slowly.

Yes, I suppose you are, Stone admitted. *Luckily, our objective is just ahead.*

Rhone was more than thankful when he limped around the next corner and saw the mother-of-pearl inlay set in the dark wood of the door. "Hey, I recognize that door."

As you should. Unfortunately, I cannot tell if the ring is still there, Stone apologized. *The We in this place seem to have an output signature so low, it makes them difficult to find or follow, especially with my depleted energy level.*

"Or maybe they're doing it on purpose. You know, so no one can find them," Rhone said thoughtfully.

Hmmm. I can follow your reasoning, but I think not, Stone answered. *The energy fluctuations are far too random to be a controlled pattern. Regardless, we must enter. Are you prepared?*

"I'd prefer a nap," Rhone mumbled, pushing on the door, too tired to even consider another option.

The room hadn't changed much, except for the addition of a small table and the solitary figure seated in one of the grand chairs. Rhone was already turning to run when Stone stopped him.

What are you doing?

But . . . Rhone thought in panic, knowing he wouldn't be able to outrun anyone, even with a good head start.

But nothing. This man is not going to attack you. Look at him.

Reluctantly, Rhone turned, noting the man's dejection as he sat rocking, hands covering his weeping eyes.

Ahh...What's going on? he asked in silence.

He is blind, at least temporarily, Stone advised.

Rhone's own red haze had become more of a light fog than a solid wall, but he understood the pain and depression the man must be going through and almost felt sorry for him.

Then his thoughts were interrupted by Stone's excited voice. *Rhone. We are not alone. The ring! Do hurry,* please.

What? Of course we're not alone. The guy's sitting right there, Rhone thought with annoyance.

No. Not him. He has no ring, but there is another *nearby. Now, are you going to stand there* gawking, *or can we get moving?*

Alright already, Rhone responded, his gripe more tired than grumpy. *What do you want me to do?*

Do? Get the box, of course. There is a ring inside.

"There's a ring in a box, but he doesn't have one?" Rhone asked in confusion, his voice echoing dully through the open room. Realizing his error, Rhone stiffened, eyes rolling toward the man rocking in misery. Oddly, he seemed indifferent to their presence, so with a shrug, Rhone hurried to the small table with its wooden box. *Never mind. I've got it,* he advised, snatching up the ornately carved box with glass inserts set into its sides. A quick glance showed a ring tucked neatly into the box's padding, its small chip of gemstone glinting brightly in the candlelight. Smiling at the find, Rhone spun towards the door, box tucked neatly under his arm. *What now?*

Do you require my directions for everything? Stone replied sarcastically. *You know the way out. I suggest you use it. There are more rings to gather after all.*

"More? How many are there?" Rhone asked in dismay, barely pausing as he shoved his way through the door and back into the hallway. "There was a whole room full of guys, but we don't know if they all had rings."

We do. Or at least I do. If you had not been so distracted by the little things, you could have used your senses and felt their presence too.

"But I was . . ."

Hiding, Stone answered for him, his accusation mild but undeniably there. *That is no excuse for a lack of thinking. Now think. How many are there?*

The sudden accusation surprised Rhone, but he knew better than to try evading. Scrunching his brows, he tried to work his way through the mental maze as he stumbled tiredly down the hall. "Let's see. I remember the guy's voice from our cell. I think they called him Mathias."

Correct. And . . .

"Ahh . . ." Rhone thought foggily. "There was a really deep voice that must have been the leader. And there was a quiet one that might have been the guy that saved me from the fall." Things were coming to his memory now, and he settled his mind to constructive thought. "Let's see. Then there was someone named Byron, and of course, the guy we just left in the room."

Very good. You are starting to think, Stone said approvingly. *While you were hiding, I was listening. There were five different voices, and five different We signatures, although I recognize that you do not have the expertise to have recognized that. So, as I was saying, with the three in hand, how many does that leave? See? It does not take a mathematician to develop an understanding. Just a bit of thinking.*

"Yeah. I get it. I should have figured it out for myself," Rhone said apologetically, actually upset at having missed something so simple.

But a moment later his grumps were forgotten as a dull electric pulse shot through his limbs, and Stone's panicked voice urged, *RUN!*

He hardly needed the stimulus—the urgency in that single word had already sent him into a stumbling run. His lungs burned with the effort, and his legs felt like lead, but somewhere in the mind-numbing haze his tired brain caught the irony of being at a *dead run*. The snort that escaped almost cost him dearly, as he slipped, barely managing to save himself from another head-banging. With a quick hand to the wall, he managed to stay upright, and relieved, took a deep breath, searching for his next move.

Ahead, a doorway seemed almost to glow, its edges lined in a golden gilt as daylight seeped through. With freedom at hand, Rhone pushed his way forward, throwing open the door with one hand, his other thrown up to shield his eyes from the sudden blaze of light. Too late, he noticed the body sprawled at his feet. With no energy left to jump, he went down hard, his toe catching on the body, sending the delicate box jolting from his grasp.

Rhone watched in disbelief as the intricately carved box spun crazily out of reach, the glass in its sides shattering into a thousand tiny fragments as it tumbled and spun across the flagstone courtyard. Even in his exhaustion, he was already scrambling to rise, just as his unsteady legs suddenly cramped from abuse.

But it wasn't his legs that suddenly doubled him over in pain. It was the boot planted squarely in his ribs. Helpless and beaten, he retched violently onto the cobbled paving.

"I believe I underestimated you," came a humorless baritone, as the man peered down at Rhone's prostrate form wallowing in his own vomit. "I must say, I would never have connected you with the OPR, although I cannot see who else would be putting in the effort. Regardless, I'm afraid I will have to put an end to this. We simply cannot have intruders lurking behind every wall."

Rhone flinched as the man in black leather drew his thin-bladed sword, but there was nothing he could do. He was too tired to put up a fight.

Are you simply going to lie there? Stone asked in dismay.

"But I don't even have a weapon," Rhone groaned, trying to explain, and speaking to Stone without thinking.

Surprisingly, the man looked aggrieved by Rhone's statement. "I would hate to have someone consider me unsportsmanlike for simply piercing an unarmed opponent, so I'll grant you a boon, though little good it will do you."

Taking a step to his unconscious brother lying piled against the wall, he gave a snort of disgust, then slid the sword from its scabbard. With a smirk, he turned smoothly, tossing it blade first toward Rhone.

Move! Stone ordered, a small static current rippling through Rhone's battered body.

It was a small jolt, far smaller than some Rhone had received, but it was enough to get him back into action. With a spasmodic jerk of muscles, he was moving, though barely enough to evade the sword's point casually lobbed in his direction.

Continuing his move, he reached out, snatching the sword's hilt like it was a thrown knife. Scrabbling crab-like on three appendages, he scuttled further away, giving some distance.

"Since I would have expected more from an agent, you must be a simple gutter-wretch who lost his way from the big city. If so, it is simply bad timing, but I'm afraid that fact won't save you."

The man's sneer scarred his otherwise handsome face, but Rhone barely registered it, his now sharpened awareness noting the tightening shoulders and weight shift the moment before the lunge.

Even as Stone's warning flashed in his mind, more pink than red, he was already moving, obeying before his body could argue. He twisted aside, the man's blade whispering past his ribs close enough to tug at his jacket.

Then, muscle memory took over. Flicking the blade aside, he brought his own around, steel humming as he swung. The strike was clean, well placed, but far too slow, his leather-clad opponent merely sidestepping the cut before returning the effort with a cut of his own. Again, Rhone's muscles reacted, feeling the stroke more than seeing it, the air parting where his flesh had been a heartbeat earlier.

Working on something like intuition, he struggled, far too weary to out-think his adversary.

Again and again, steel rang, sparks leaping at each exchange, jolting up his arms and draining what little strength he had left. Sweat stung his eyes, and his lungs burned.

Another thrust, another parry, and suddenly Rhone was tripping over his own feet, too exhausted to keep them under him.

One more, he told himself. *Please, just one.* Dragging himself back to his feet, he again raised his sword, every muscle screaming in protest.

Feinting left, slow and obvious, fatigue giving credence to the slow move, he played his last card.

Taking the bait, the man drove in with a thrust meant to finish him.

Now, Stone whispered, his voice barely heard amidst the furious action.

Rhone twisted his body around the blade, so close he felt the heat of it, his own sword sliding toward its mark.

But the blade never reached its target. Knees buckling, Rhone's legs betrayed him, crashing to the ground with an impact that knocked the air from his lungs. Gasping in defeat, eyes bleary with pain, he stared up at the sky, knowing he had failed.

"A good attempt, my young friend," the man said, grudging respect roughening his tone. And giving Rhone an eloquent nod, he whipped his sword up in a final salute.

"Are you so afraid of me that you can't even let me get to my feet?" Rhone asked, his complaint distracting the man a moment longer.

"It won't change the outcome," the man answered, tipping his head with a shrug. "I figured, the quicker the better. You have simply extended the pain of knowing you are going to lose, and die. That can't be easy for someone your age."

Rhone had taken the moment to force himself upright, dragging his weary body back into a fighter's stance. With legs trembling and arms aching with fatigue, he locked his grip on the sword.

He wasn't going down without a fight.

Stone was there—quiet now, coiled tight in the back of his mind, not warning, not guiding. Watching.

Lunging unexpectedly, Rhone double-stepped his thrust, aiming for the man's chest.

But as fast as it was, the man's sword was faster, snapping out to slap Rhone's blade aside with effortless precision. Steel rang against steel, the impact screaming up Rhone's arms and into his skull.

The man's eyebrows rose appraisingly, giving a head-tip of approval. "That too was well done. Now you can die knowing you gave good effort."

With blinding speed, the man's sneer widened as his sword whipped around, the arc of the blade already cutting toward Rhone in a final, merciless strike.

But the sword never reached Rhone.

A perfect parry deflected the blade, followed by a flashing riposte, burying itself deep into the man's chest.

"Not today you won't," Lev spat, her words as vicious as her blade.

Disbelieving hatred flared across the leather-clad man's face as his lifetime of sword-work instinctively corrected his own blade's path.

Far less than a heartbeat later, his arching thrust had buried its length into the center of Lev's stomach.

Lev's eyes widened as the man staggered forward, dropping to his knees, his forward motion burying his sword even deeper as he gasped for a breath that wouldn't come. Then he fell face-first to the ground, the sword's heavy hilt dragging the blade through Lev's entrails.

With a sharp, broken gasp, Lev clutched at the sword, her fingers slipping uselessly along the slick metal as her strength gave out. She sank in slow motion toward the ground, her face caught between pain and disbelief—but beneath it all, the fierce, instinctive love of a mother who had finally found her child.

"Lev... what are you doing here?" Rhone whispered, the words tearing from him as his mind struggled to catch up.

Lifting her gaze to his, Lev managed the faintest smile. "I made it," she said softly. "I wasn't sure I would—but I got here."

Rhone barely heard her, his attention trapped by the dark blood and glistening ruin spilling from her middle.

Rhone! Help her! Stone shouted, his voice a thunder inside Rhone's head.

"But—I don't know what to do!"

Then Lev drew a breath to speak, forcing the words past her clenched pain. "Rhone... I've been looking for you for days."

Her voice faltered as a wet, choking cough seized her before she could continue. When it passed, she swallowed and tried again. "I'm sorry it took so long. But I made it."

"I don't understand," Rhone pleaded, shaking his head as if denial alone might undo the damage. "But don't worry about that—just hold on. The Luna is here. I saw her. She can take you to the Stronghold where they can fix you up."

Lev shook her head sadly as sparkling tears filled her eyes. "Not today. We both know it." Her eyes locked on the young man she had so recently adopted, and she actually smiled, a thing that lit her face. "It's okay, honestly. I did what needed doing, and now I can go to my husband." Tears filled her eyes as she gazed at Rhone, glistening as one slid down her face. "Thank you for bringing me back to the fold. This is far better than dying alone."

Rhone tried not to see the blood or the sword still embedded in her body, so he just nodded, not knowing what else to do.

"One last thing," she added, sudden pain causing her to stifle a groan through gritted teeth. "Remember the little dragon around my neck? I want you to take it. Give it to Bella. It should go to loving hands, and I know how you feel about her, even if you aren't sure yourself. It deserves that much."

Rhone was about to answer when the sound of running feet made him spin in panic, his blade coming up instinctively. *How many attackers are there?* he asked Stone, but his panicked eyes found Aundrea running hell-bent toward him. Behind her followed several of Luna's deckhands, swords, handguns, and weapons of all kinds held threateningly in their grips.

Aundrea took one look as she slid to a stop and saw all she needed. With a quick command to the men, she dropped to a knee and laid a gentle hand on Lev's arm.

"A good agent to the very end," she said approvingly. "I never doubted you, not after Rhone's support of you. I want to thank you for your service, both now and before. You were given a bad deal, but you finished with a win. I also want to thank you for saving our young man here. For that, I can't thank you enough."

Lev's eyes were large as she worked to swallow, her sparkling eyes and smile holding firm as blood ran slowly from her body. Then her hand went limp, her eyes losing their luster as they stared at nothing.

Rhone gasped a tortured breath and turned away, trying to hold back tears that might be considered unmanly, but were there, nonetheless. Even the loss of his real mother hadn't been like this. That had taken months, oddly preparing him for the outcome. But this had been so sudden, almost instantaneous, and she was gone. He hadn't even known she was there until it was over. Lev, his onetime assailant, his protector, mother, and now his debt. He owed her his very life, and he knew it.

"Thank you, Lev," he whispered, his voice catching, hoping she heard from wherever she was.

Dragging an arm across his damp eyes, Rhone turned to Aundrea still kneeling beside him. "She told me to take her little dragon," he said, unsure how to go about it. "I'm supposed to give it to Bella. She told me to."

Aundrea blinked away her own tears and stooped to cup Lev's dusky cheek in her palm. "I believe she understood something I never realized before, but now that I've met Captain Belle, I understand." Then, knowing Rhone might be sensitive to digging through a woman's clothing, tasked herself to remove the little mechanical dragon from around Lev's neck. "It is gorgeous," she breathed, again noting the fine detailing of the tiny metal figure. "It's a perfect gift for Bella." Rising, she handed the beautiful necklace to Rhone. "I'll have the men gather Lev as soon as the ship is securely tied off. She'll get a true funeral as an honored agent of the OPR."

Signaling the men, she gave them a few words before turning back to Rhone. "She'll be fine resting here for the moment, but I believe you have someone else you need to speak to," and with a sad smile, Aundrea turned to follow the men and the other details of her job.

Rhone knew when to follow orders, and climbed unsteadily to his feet before laying out Lev's still body on the flagstone-paved courtyard. His face an emotional wreck as he drew the long blade from her blood-soaked abdomen. Once she was settled, he moved to the man's body and removed Lev's blade, then pried the ring from the dead man's finger. He was sorely tempted to kick him, but refrained, almost seeing Lev's look of disappointment at the ungentlemanly display.

With one last look at Lev, he walked slowly around the corner of the citadel and stopped, taking in the scene of The Lady Luna floating proudly in place. The man he had left near the short wall was still there, now held by two crewmen as he moaned loudly, rolling on the ground in misery.

With a grim frown, Rhone made his way to the man's side.

"Sorry, friend. This is not how I planned things," Rhone said apologetically, remembering only too well how the man had saved him from his fall. "I'm afraid I have to take your ring, but if you allow me, these men won't have to take the finger with it." The announcement at least gave the man the option that he wouldn't have given Rhone.

When the man's eyes flashed a painful acknowledgment, Rhone nodded and took the man's hand. A few moments later the ring was freed, tucked securely in his pocket.

That done, Rhone walked resolutely toward the airship's massive form, its ballooning envelope shivering as if in anticipation, as men struggled with the hawsers, fighting to hold her in place against the jostling wind.

CHAPTER 24

Turmoil

The airship's vast hull swallowed most of the evening sun, with only a few narrow spears of golden light slipping past its edges, rimming the Luna in fire.

She was the most beautiful sight Rhone had ever known—graceful and powerful in a way no human form could ever match, yet stirring something just as deep. But that place, that particular pull of his heart, belonged to Bella, standing patiently on the quarterdeck, waiting.

Maybe patiently wasn't the best description—as patience had never truly been her strength. Still, she was his Bella.

Captain Belle, he corrected, the thought landing with unexpected weight.

Then a worrisome fear rose in him. Was she still his? Would she understand that he'd had no choice? Whatever the reason, she was captain now, and he was the one who had vanished.

You will not know until you try, Stone murmured in encouragement.

Thanks, Stone, Rhone said silently, knowing her eyes would tell him all he needed to know.

Catching the dangling rope-and-rung ladder, he started up, his legs protesting from their recent abuse. Still, he climbed—until his steps began to falter.

It wasn't the pain that slowed him. It was the knowledge that Bella was waiting above.

At last he hauled himself onto the deck and crossed toward the stairs. His limp made him move more slowly now, wondering, not for the first time, why he'd ever thought so many steps were a good idea.

When his head finally cleared the railing, he saw Bella at her station, intent on holding the airship steady. For a moment, the world narrowed to that single sight, his throat closing as his words tangled.

"Bella... ah—Captain Belle," he corrected, forcing the title into place and giving due respect to the woman she had become.

"I wondered how long it would take you," she answered, deigning a quick glance his way. "In trouble again, I see. Nothing new about that, now is there?" Her eyes were already back to her task, signaling her approval to the men on the hawsers.

Finally lashing the wheel in place, she turned to face him, eyes hard and brittle, not at all the eyes he remembered so vividly.

Rhone was shocked by both her words and her eyes, and had to take a breath before he could continue. "Hey, I didn't ask for this. I'm not even sure how everyone got here. I mean, nobody knew where I went. I made sure."

"Which doesn't excuse the fact that they had to come rescue your worthless hide, now does it?"

Captain Belle's eyes flashed with what might as well have been fire, her new position having developed their strength until Rhone could barely look at her. She had the upper hand and knew it, but she didn't need her captaincy for that. Even when she had thought him one of the gentry, and she just a lowly serving maid, she had marched right over him. Nor had she lost her touch.

"I didn't know they were searching for me," Rhone tried again, but knew it wouldn't make a difference. His heart dropped in despair as he remembered Lev's sacrifice, which truly had saved his life. "I know it doesn't mean much, but I am sorry."

With a deep sigh, and knowing he had lost this battle, he tried a different approach. "Hey, I tried to get leave time to come see you, but the project had to be finished before I could go. It was important."

Which was also worthless. He could have walked out, and maybe been fired, but he hadn't tried. Somehow, it hadn't seemed quite as important as his projects at the time. And Bella would always be there. Wouldn't she? They were a team . . . or had been. They had built all the projects together, including The Lady Luna. Which was now hers. Even that seemed tiny next to his want of her.

The memories flashed by in a moment, leaving him to cover for his loss.

"Thanks for coming," he blustered. "I'm not sure how it all came about, but I wouldn't be here if you hadn't." His voice stalled as he tried to find his way through the mess and express his true feelings. But she had been right. He did seem to be in trouble a lot, if not most of the time. Then Lev's necklace came to mind. "Oh . . . I have something for you," he mumbled, fumbling at his pocket.

"And why would I want something from you?" Bella demanded. "Trying to buy your way back on board my ship?"

Her tone held an edge that gave Rhone goosebumps, and he realized how effective it would be with the crew. "No. Nothing like that. It was Lev's. She told me to give it to you." He couldn't help the slow turn of his head as he glanced at her still body lying on the cobblestone courtyard. The very sight blocked his ability to speak.

"Lev?" Bella asked, her eyes following his glance. "She must have been something special to gain your favor." With a sigh, her anger fell away like leaves from a tree, and her eyes softened. "Did you love her?"

The words were so bizarre that Rhone stood there, mouth partly open, a look of surprise on his face. "Did I love her? You mean like—?" Finally, he understood and stammered, "What? No! Nothing like that. She was my friend—Head of Security for the new division, and basically my guard. She must have followed me, because I took off without telling her where I was going. Actually, I'm surprised she figured it out." Then his face froze in grief, realizing Lev was dead because of him. He had led her here, to a place she never wanted to return to.

I am here, Stone murmured in silence, repeating the phrase of their first meeting.

Bella understood the look and stepped forward, placing a hand on Rhone's shoulder. "Stone, I've missed you," she whispered to the collar around Rhone's neck.

With sudden decision, she wrapped her arms around a stunned Rhone and buried her head against his chest. "You, too, I suppose, although we really do need to talk."

This was a far cry from the woman he had seen a moment before, and having no words for the situation, he wisely chose to keep his mouth shut, merely wrapping his free arm uncertainly around her waist.

They stood that way, braced against the ship's wheel as The Lady Luna rocked gently in the buffeting breeze.

⚜

Once Lev's body had been carried on board and laid respectfully in the hold, The Lady Luna's nose rose, fan-sails spinning at full. Like a stallion released from his harness, she turned seaward and within minutes was far out from shore, rapidly climbing to cruising altitude.

The puff and wheeze of her boiler mixing smoothly with the impeller's whine made music to Rhone's ears, but the melancholy memory of Lev's body being carried below shattered his joy of the moment. Despondent and alone, he stood by the railing, watching as the crew did their duties, keeping the sails taut while Captain Belle kept the airship's nose pointed where she wished to go.

He, unfortunately, was totally out of place.

Once safely away, Rhone made his way below deck to where Aundrea knelt beside Lev's covered body. With a sigh of despair, he sank down beside her.

"I'm sorry. It wasn't supposed to go like that," he mumbled in desolation. "I had no idea you were coming, not that it would have made a difference. I thought I could take care of it."

Aundrea reached out and took his arm, her grip gentle and steady in the way only a mother's could be. "Lev made her own choice," she said softly. "She came to me when you were gone and told me what she intended to do. She cared deeply for you, and she decided it was her responsibility to find you." She paused, contemplating him before continuing. "Lev believed she knew where you had gone, and I allowed her to go. That was when Jewel and I went through your tinkerings. Once we figured out what you were doing, we made our way to Corgy with a plan."

"Corgy," Rhone said with a wistful chuckle. "So that's how you found The Luna."

"Yes, although I found Captain Black first. He is quite the man, not at all what I expected," she said, the admission adding an almost invisible sparkle to her smile. "He made an excellent choice for someone to train under. It was through him that I reached Captain Belle and The Lady Luna. She really is a beauty, by the way."

Rhone was about to agree, then wondered if she was speaking of the airship or the girl. "Bella?" he asked, looking as dumbfounded as a young man could.

"Perhaps you should call her Captain Belle," Aundrea said reprovingly. "At least while on board. I believe she deserves the title."

"Yeah. Of course," he agreed. "And you're right. We talked, some, but there's just so much . . ." He didn't finish, ending up with a shrug, feeling stupid. Rising to leave, he hesitated, speaking to the blank wall rather than to Aundrea. "Thanks for coming. I'm sorry I caused such a problem," and without another word, slowly climbed the stairs to the deck.

After pacing the length of the airship several times, he turned toward yet another flight of stairs, cursing his lack of foresight—and wondering, not for the first time, where he stood in Bella's eyes.

He had come a long way since Corgy. The journey hadn't been wasted, but it had cost him both the skies he loved and the woman who had shared them. At least the memory of all it had taken to get

Luna into the air brought a thoughtful chuckle, lessening the frown lines on his face.

Unfortunately, it also betrayed him.

Bella turned at hearing the unexpected humor, her quizzical glance taking in Rhone's worried face. "A penny for your thoughts?" she asked. "I'm good for the coin."

Rhone smiled, remembering the line she had used once, so long ago. "Oh, nothing. I was just remembering all the trouble we had trying to figure out what we were doing." Instantly, he chastised himself for thinking about the airship instead of her. She was the treasure, after all, although in reality, they both were.

"We did have problems," she agreed. "I thought you'd gotten yourself killed on more than one occasion."

"Me? If I remember, you were the one who got hurt," he laughed, but quickly covered his humor as he remembered the reality of her burns." Gently reaching for her hand, he turned it over, smoothing its palm as he had done when she had been so afraid. "I wasn't sure you'd ever be able to use your hands again, but it's healed well. I would never have known they were burned so badly."

Bella's eyes took on a wary look, but she didn't remove her hand.

"I thought you knew what you were doing?" she said. "I had faith in you."

"I did, sort of. My mom treated my burns the same way, so I figured it would work on you too."

Bella nodded with a thoughtful look. "I guess it did," she had to admit, "and I'm glad you were there. The doc in town would probably have bled me for weeks, or something just as dumb. Then if I survived, he'd have gone around strutting like a rooster, saying how good he was. Dad never trusted him much."

Rhone diverted his eyes, not wanting her to see how much that meant to him.

The airship was making good speed, and the crew were keeping their distance as they worked, undoubtedly wondering at having two captains on board. They had all heard the stories, even if they hadn't been hired until Bella had been given captaincy. No, Rhone was an oddity to be looked at but not worried about. Captain Belle was at the helm now and had successfully protected Corgy from the pirate horde. They were proud of both their Lady Captain and their airship, and with the addition of Captain Black and his Backwater Mistress watching their backside, they had no complaints.

"Land at three o'clock," came a cry from the bow watch.

"Received. Land at three o'clock," Captain Belle shouted in reply, her feminine voice effectively cutting through the quick breeze as easily as Captain Black's bellow had. A moment later she called, "Two points to windward, please. We'll take her into the river's mouth as soon as it comes into view. Another few hours and you should get your first glimpse of the Capital Stronghold."

"Aye, Captain. Two points to windward," came the reply.

Rhone was impressed with her knowledge of ship matters. His own captaincy had been a dicey thing, figuring things out as they went. Things had gotten done, but with only the two of them, it hadn't been the efficiency he now saw. More a case of running from one task to another before it got out of control.

A hollowness grew in his chest as he felt the ship, his ship, holding her course, the great beast surging relentlessly against the coastal wind as she worked her way to her destination.

But he wasn't captain. He wasn't even crew. He was nobody.

"I'm nobody," he whispered, the words caught by the wind, only to be thrown back in his face.

Lonely, desolate, and unable to watch, he moved to the forward rail and huddled deeper into his coat.

He was deep into his personal doldrums when Stone, his closest friend and collar-mate, slipped past his guarded mind. *Not true, my friend. You are the designer of this magnificent airship, and it was your ideas that brought it into being. It was also you that brought about the downfall of The Brotherhood, something that should go into the history books, though I doubt it will. To my understanding, there are few who even believed in their existence, which does not lessen the fact that it happened.*

"Thanks, Stone. I appreciate your support, but I'm not sure this is something you could understand," Rhone mumbled, his voice low and barely controlled.

Low in spirit, he shut off their contact, watching the distant line of waves breaching against the approaching cliffs.

He was well into his depression when Stone's irritated buzz forced its way through the simple block. *Listen to me, young man. I have been around humans long enough to know of their attachments. Love is of the mind, as well as the heart, and I too have a mind. Are you and I not connected similarly?*

It was similar, yet totally different, as so many things seemed to be. But the very thought of loving a rock brought a light chuckle from Rhone.

As I suspected, Stone said appreciatively. *We are similarly connected, whether it is called love or not.*

"Yeah. I guess we are," Rhone admitted. "But what does that have to do with Bella? She's a captain now, not a waitress at The Common House. It's just not the same."

But she was not a waitress when she became your lieutenant, now was she? *Things change. Even I am not as I once was, nor as hard-headed as some.*

Rhone appreciated the jest and scanned the horizon again, feeling slightly less like wanting to jump overboard.

Now, if you are feeling better, I would like to change topics.

"Of course. I'm sorry. Are you okay? I haven't taken time for you for days, but like I told Aundrea, it wasn't supposed to turn out like this, and there you were, right in the middle of it all."

Yes, we were, Stone reminded him. *And now you have the rings.*

Rhone had totally forgotten that small matter. First, Aundrea's appearance, then Bella and The Lady Luna showing up, and Lev's death. There just hadn't been time to think about the rings. Even the simple mention of them brought the feel of their weight in his pocket. How could so much happen in such a short amount of time, and how was he supposed to process it all?

Let us take one thing at a time, Stone offered. *Captain Belle is dealing with the flight, and Aundrea is writing a report on our recent situation and Lev's death, that leaves time for you and me to systematically deal with our own recent events.*

"But what about the rings?" Rhone blurted, then looked around warily to see if anyone had heard his outburst. Speaking in a calmer tone, he asked, "And what happened back there? It was weird. I mean, people went stiff. The door zapped me. Then Lev showed up to save me, and The Lady Luna arrival—it was unreal." He was mentally running through the events when he asked, "Stone, did you know your map was blinking out?"

Ahh, yesss . . . well. It was quite a show, was it not? Stone commented, totally evading the real issues.

"Stone . . ." Rhone growled.

Oh, all right. You do not have to be such a fuddy-duddy, Stone grumped. *I was tired. Exhausted, actually. I had used far too much of my energy, and things just . . . ran out. Then there was the small bit of confusion as we began our assault.*

"Confusion? What confusion?" Rhone said in surprise. "You're never confused. You know everything."

A rumbling chuckle rolled through Rhone's mind, finally becoming words. *Thank you, my friend. I appreciate your trust in me. But no, I do not know everything. Undoubtedly, more than you, but certainly not everything. Now, as to the confusion. It was not I who was confused. As we suspected, The Brotherhood's rings do indeed contain We, though they are somewhat damaged. Much as Jewel was when we found her in the commissioner's vault.*

"Is that bad? I mean, it is, sure, but how bad?" *Rhone asked in concern.*

Let us say, our communication was less straightforward than I had anticipated. Their years of servitude to The Brotherhood—men with no understanding, or even social graces towards those of my kind, have left these poor We unknowing of their past or even who they are. They barely knew how to communicate within themselves. Consequently, because of translation inconsistencies, *some information was lost during our initial contact. There is more to the story, of course, but let us leave it for a future time. For now, let us say, once communication was initiated, and translation codified, they were quite willing to assist us for the chance to be free. Even rocks do not like being slaves, you know.*

Rhone's eyes widened as the information took hold. "Wait. You worked with them? But why didn't you say something?"

You, my friend, were in no position to be distracted. I dealt with it as best I could, and I hope that does not create problems, Stone explained.

Rhone thought it over before answering. "I'm pretty sure there won't be a problem with your making terms. I mean, nobody but Aundrea would even know. I can also understand why they want to be free. What I'm a little worried about is. . . what does that even mean? We can't send them back into space, so what does being free mean to a rock . . . ah, crystalline being? Do they want dumped into the ocean, or maybe the desert?"

That is a very good question, Stone rumbled. *Unfortunately, I was quite busy at the time and did not ask.*

"But you already gave them your word," Rhone reminded him.

That I did. I did what I thought was best, but if it becomes a problem, please advise me, for as you say, I am not human, so I cannot fully understand your human reasoning.

Rhone released a long breath as he considered how to proceed. "Alright, I get it, but maybe you'd better tell me their whole story. If we can figure out what they really want, or need, then maybe we can find a way to give it to them."

That is good thinking, Rhone. Now, as to the problem. It is the ring stones. Those of my kind. By my understanding, they are all part of a more original piece. Do you remember our discussion of the original We collective?

Maybe, Rhone said with a thought. *We had lots of discussions, but I remember you were part of a big cluster or something.*

We were, but I am speaking specifically about the amount of time it took for me to understand your energy patterns. It was not the same for these We. Prior to The Brotherhood, the man who possessed the original We stone fought it for dominance *and ended up thrusting the poor creature into an inferior position, one of servitude not of cooperation.* These smaller pieces are mere fragments of that original. Their long slavery and separation have caused them to forget their We-ness.

"I think I'm missing something," Rhone said apologetically.

Yes, of course. Did I mention the original stone was broken by its master? The broken pieces were then taken by his sons and placed in rings. The result is, these pieces have very little memory of their original togetherness, much as I did of mine.

"Got it," Rhone said as the information clicked. "So, the ring stones are pieces of a more original We, but not as far back as you and the . . . collective, group thing, or something like that." Squinting as he tried to piece together the happenings.

There. I knew you would understand, Stone said graciously. *In a way, the ring stones are much like a magnet, drawn to each other, yet at odds, pushing and pulling as the brothers apparently did, each attempting to keep its distance so as not to make connections, yet they are connected.*

"I thought I had it. Now I'm not sure," Rhone said, shaking his head as he tried to keep up.

You must understand, I had very little time to communicate with them. Enough for them to know that I was one of their kind and wished to help, but little else. To put it quickly, they joined our battle for freedom, using their limited skills to manipulate their masters.

"Okay. That makes sense," Rhone said in relief. "If nothing else, please thank them for me. I'm pretty sure we wouldn't have made it without their help."

I have done so already, but back to your question. What to do with them. You do realize you cannot simply leave them in your pocket. Nor does that fulfill my obligation regarding their request for freedom.

"Of course not. Besides, they're making my skin itch," Rhone said, distractedly scratching his thigh. "Are you in connection with them now?"

We are not, but only because I have placed a barrier, much as when I block you, Stone said almost wistfully. *Unlike you, however, they are quite disorganized, having never run things on their own.*

"Hey. Was that a compliment?" Rhone asked with a grin.

Do not let it go to your head, Stone grumbled. *I was merely trying to assist with your understanding of things.*

Rhone chuckled, but let it go. "Whatever, but will you be able to work with them like you did Jewel? You know, like, fix them, or are they actually crazy?"

No, they *are not crazy, as you say, merely traumatized,* Stone said, his hollow laughter turning thoughtful as he began rummaging through Rhone's thoughts. *Hmmm, that is a fair question. Let me see what I can do,* he offered, then changed subjects yet again. *Now, what are your plans with Bella?*

Rhone winced, hating these changes in topic. "I don't know. I miss her, but you already knew that, and I'm still an agent with the OPR. I miss being on The Lady Luna too. I'd forgotten how great it was to fly, pushing through the clouds, the sound of the steam boiler huffing away, and the creaks of the ship. I miss it, and . . . yeah. . . her too."

He stood staring into the distance, the feeling of loss almost overwhelming.

He had lost Lev, Luna, and now Bella. What good was he if everything he loved was taken away? Dragging in a heavy breath, the weight of despair seeming to squeeze his insides. What else might he lose—his job, Aundrea, maybe Stone?

Rhone, you are not alone, Stone whispered in support. *You have spoken with Captain Belle, and there will be time to figure things out. Not much, mind you, but there is some. Spend some time with our girl. You have made a start, but unless it goes somewhere, it will only go down in flames.*

"Wow. That's a great way to support a guy," Rhone muttered, his glance taking in Bella standing at the wheel.

With a deep breath, he whispered, "Thanks, Stone. It's good to know you're there."

CHAPTER 25

Returning Isn't Easy

Rhone felt like a fish out of water as he again approached Bella, grimacing inwardly at his lack of preparation. "Hey, I missed you," he announced, his words almost shy and unsure. "I know you're busy right now, but perhaps when we land . . ." He let the sentence hang, hoping she would pick it up.

She did, but not the way he'd hoped.

"Not good enough," Bella stated, knowing he was there but not turning to look. "So are you planning to slink away again, or just turn tail and run? Both work, I hear."

Neither her frown nor her words bode well for Rhone, and he took the hit as she'd intended.

"Well, I don't plan on jumping ship, if that's what you mean," he said, faking a grin as he tipped his head to the waves far below.

She turned, staring at him with a deadpan glare and a shrug of acceptance.

"Or we can talk now. I just didn't want to take you from your job," Rhone added, his wry smile doing its best to make up for his loss. "You're doing awesome, by the way, at least from what I can see. Far better than I did when we first started flying."

"Thanks. It is going well," she granted, relaxing slightly now that the initial salvo had been fired. "And now is fine, if you're up to it. The quarterdeck is sort of sacred ground on board, so the men don't come up here unless I call them."

Sacred? That's an interesting choice of words, and Rhone wondered what he was missing. "Okay, yeah, now's good, as long as it's okay with you. She's your ship, after all. I'm just a passenger."

The word 'passenger' brought a caustic smile to Bella's wind-burned face, making Rhone's stomach curdle. He grimaced unconsciously, but she must have noticed as her tone changed and she looked away.

"I don't know what you want, Rhone. I'm captain of The Lady Luna, and I have a crew to run and jobs to do. When your boss told me you needed rescuing, I came. You deserved that much."

The awkward moment held until Rhone's snort of acknowledgement broke the tension. "Yeah, we did. Stone and I wouldn't be here if you hadn't shown up, so thank you, again. But come to think of it, Luna wouldn't even have been made without your constant hounding to get her built."

"Hounding?" Bella sputtered in surprise. "I didn't hound you! I had to fly, and you found every excuse to do anything rather than build."

"That's not true. I was designing, then redesigning the design," Rhone reminded her, feeling both defensive and hurt. "Things aren't right until they're right. Remember the failures we had? What would have happened if we'd been in the air when that blowout came? As it was, I was knocked, top for keister, and lucky to survive."

The remembered scene brought light laughter from Bella, the sound like tinkling crystals to Rhone's ears.

It also broke the stalemate as Bella retold the vivid scene. "You did bounce pretty good. I thought you might have given up the ghost, just like poor BoToo. Those were good days." They stood quietly, remembering the moment before Bella spoke again. "Do you remember my first flight on Bo? It changed my life, you know."

"How could I forget, you dancing with the wind," Rhone mumbled softly. His memory of her floating like an angel, bare legs dancing in rhythm as she drifted through the air. It had changed both their lives.

"I haven't been the same since," she acknowledged. "I'm sorry the way things have turned out. Aundrea and I had quite the conversation on our way here, and I know it wasn't your fault. She thinks the world of you, by the way."

Rhone almost blushed, but held himself to a mere shrug. "Me too," he admitted. "She found me in the badlands and brought me out to the Capital Stronghold. Then she put me through the academy. With nothing for me back home, I couldn't think of a better thing to do with my life than be an agent."

Bella smiled knowingly. She had heard the story before, or at least most of it.

When Stone gave his approval, by gently warming in his collar, Rhone let Bella know. "By the way, Stone says, hi."

"Hello, Stone. I'm sorry I didn't acknowledge you sooner," Bella said, suddenly missing their old friendship.

"I would never have made it out if it hadn't been for him. Then he forced me to come talk to you. I was too scared."

Bella winced at the comment and quickly tried to smooth things over. "Thank you, Stone. It's just that your friend here has a way of getting my hackles up, and it makes me crazy."

Tell her I do indeed understand, Stone agreed.

Rhone groaned but dutifully relayed the message. "Stone says he has no idea what you mean."

A sharp static pulse zipped across Rhone's neck and he threw up his hands in surrender. "Alright, already," he grumbled, rubbing at the tender spot. "But that hardly seems fair."

"What did he do?" Bella laughed. "I'd almost forgotten how much fun it was being with you two. We did have some good times, didn't we?"

I told you I liked her, Stone whispered appreciatively.

Rhone knew better than to make comment as he worked to maintain his expression, but Bella also knew Stone.

"So, what did he really say?" she demanded flirtingly. "Come on. I know you two." Then, with a dangerous look in her eye, she teased, "Zap him again, Stone. It's good for him."

Rhone strangled a curse as he croaked, "Captain Belle! Is harassing your passengers any way to run a ship?"

Shrugging innocently, Bella's cherubic smile played across her windburned face. "I have no idea what you mean. I take perfectly good care of my passengers."

As her distractingly gorgeous eyebrows raised alluringly, Rhone ground his teeth in frustration.

Perhaps if I give just a tiny zap, you could groan loudly enough to show her how brave you truly are? Stone offered.

Rhone actually considered it, until Stone's muffled chuckle made him reconsider.

"Alright, you two. Enough is enough," but it only gave Bella the opening she was more than happy to fill.

"Thank you again, Stone. You are a true gentleman," she cooed. "Your partner, however, seems to be in a snit. He doesn't even want to talk to me. Now why would that be? Maybe because I'm right?"

"Now hold on," Rhone griped, tired of being blindsided by the two of them. "Are you two working in cahoots?" His eyebrows drew together as he considered it, but he knew it couldn't be. She didn't have a We to connect with.

He was still thinking about it when Stone's excited vibrations ricocheted through his skull like church bells in the town's steeple. *Rhone! There is the answer,* Stone shouted. *If I can repair one of the ring stones, perhaps you can give it to Bella. Then you two could communicate no matter where you are.*

Bella squinted at Rhone's startled expression, her curiosity demanding an explanation. *"What's going on in there? If you two are cooking up something, I want in. Come on. What gives?"*

"Listen, Bel . . . Captain," Rhone corrected. "Stone just brought up a possibility, but it's a long way from being viable. You know how he . . . eoowww!" Rhone shrieked, gritting his teeth at the unexpected shock. "Dad-gummit, Stone. You don't have to zap me every time I open my mouth."

I would not need to if you would speak honestly, Stone replied.

Rhone took a deep breath and tried to gain some control. *Listen, Stone. It's more complicated than that,* he said silently, not ready to explain it to Bella. *I simply don't have the authority to do what you're suggesting. Not yet anyway.*

Bella pursed her lips before thrusting out her hand. "Deal," she said gravely.

"Deal? What deal? I haven't said anything," Rhone complained.

"You said plenty—and I'm in." Bella said, her voice carrying more passion than he'd heard since their days in Corgy. "I know you, and I know Stone. I even know Aundrea now. And for the record, I see why you think so highly of her. She's pretty amazing. She'd have to be to talk me into this joyride. Shoot, I even broke my contract to do it," she went on, unapologetic. "She promised she'd make it right, even said she'd set up a deal with the OPR if that's what it took. So how's that, big shot?"

"Really? She said that" Rhone asked in amazement, though it did make sense. Luna would be a perfect tool for the OPR.

A sudden tug of emotion brought Rhone back to his days as captain of The Lady Luna, and what he might have done with the commission. But he'd been recalled, forced to give his airship to Bella while he returned to the Capital Stronghold and his life as an agent. He may be head of his own department now, but it was still subject to the demands of the job—which she didn't know about.

"By the way. I got a promotion," he said quietly, not sure how she would take it. "I'm head of my own department now. They haven't settled on a name yet, but we deal with new technology. Stuff like that."

"Stuff like Luna?" she asked, surprised at actually wanting to know.

"Yeah, though not much yet. Just some little bug things that run around."

"I know. I saw one," she said, grinning at his startled look.

"You saw one? But how? They're in my workshop."

Bella's sparkling eyes glinted mischievously as she said, "Not any-more. Aundrea used them to find you."

"Wait. You know about my tinkerings?"

"She had to find you, and thought it was the best way since I already knew about Stone,"Bella answered, raising a shoulder as though it was nothing.

"I guess it makes sense," he agreed. "She did find me, though I still don't know how." But guilt followed, the memory of Lev and how he had used her to find The Brotherhood. It was his fault.

He didn't notice Bella's concerned look as his mind replayed the moment, not until she spoke.

"So what's the secret?" she asked gently. "What was Stone so excited about?"

Still off-balance by his thoughts, Rhone answered more sharply than he meant to.

"Bella, it's OPR business. You know I can't tell you. At least not yet."

"Well, like I said, I want in," she stated, her fists on hips as she stood her ground. "And Stone, you'll keep him to our deal, won't you?"

Rhone groaned aloud when he felt the vibrating chortle from Stone. "

"That's no fair," he griped, knowing he'd already lost the hand.

But Bella's brilliant smile made him change his mind.

Losing a hand wasn't so bad if he ended up winning the game.

The courtyard fell into stunned silence as *The Lady Luna* drifted down from the sky, her shadow sliding across stone and steel while the great balloon eased between the towers of the Capital Stronghold.

Soldiers shouted as they drove the gathering gawkers back, clearing the landing area while lines were dropped and anchored to turrets and ironbound gates.

Once the ship settled with patient grace, Aundrea and Rhone stepped down, the last echoes of the landing still humming through the courtyard.

At Captain Belle's command, the lines were loosened, allowing *The Lady Luna* to rise just enough to hover above the walls—safe from hopeful hands willing to put themselves at risk just to touch her.

It felt like home as Rhone slumped comfortably in Aundrea's softly upholstered office chair, waiting as she wrote orders for a security team to deal with Lev's body, then longer as she filtered through the stack of documents Bran hadn't managed to finish.

"Okay, I've got to know," he stated, breaking the silence.

Aundrea looked up, eyebrows raised in question. "What's on your mind, and does it have anything to do with a fine young lady, or the monstrous balloon thing dominating the skies of the Capital Stronghold? Things will never be the same around here, you know. You have people worried about what the world is coming to."

Her words were lightly chastising, but her smile denied any real problem.

"Neither. I want to know how you found me. It wasn't just luck. Even I didn't know where I'd end up, so how'd you do it?"

Aundrea bobbed her eyebrows, letting him know she was the one in power. But relenting, she gave a light shrug. "First, it was Lev. She came to say you were gone and had an idea where you went. After that, Jewel and I simply took your data and applied it, using your bugs to triangulate your whereabouts. Good work, by the way. They did their job."

"Yeah, about that. Bella said you'd snatched my bugs, but she didn't say why."

"Well of course not. It was OPR business. What I needed from her was transportation, which she willingly gave."

Rhone chewed his lip as that, before saying, "Okay, but she also mentioned she had to break a contract to do it."

"She did," Aundrea agreed. "With the mayor of Corgy, which I thought you might find interesting. Unfortunately, her acceptance of our situation made it a requirement. He wasn't in favor, of course, but apparently, a veiled threat from our young captain made him change his mind."

Now it was Rhone's turn to raise his eyebrows, wondering how much leverage it had it taken?

"I do not believe there will be a problem," Aundrea said, seeing his concern, "and if there is, I told her I would see it corrected. If not, I am sure the OPR could use her services in lieu of what she lost in service to us. We might even consider using The Luna for a full-time contract. It's hard to say at this point, and we'll just have to see."

She looked to Rhone as though expecting approval, but his frowned concentration made him unaware of her scrutiny.

"Would that be a problem?" she asked.

"It doesn't tell me how you found me," he replied.

Aundrea surveyed her protégé thoughtfully. "Jewel warned me you might be jealous, but I didn't believe it. I told her, my men wouldn't stoop so low as to be jealous of their womenfolk, especially when they are just doing their duty. Was I wrong?"

Rhone scowled in frustration, but knew it was far too close to the truth. Luckily, Stone came to his rescue.

Tell them thank you. If they were able to use our technology, especially in our own defense, then what could be better? She was correct after all.

Rhone nodded in embarrassment, then turned to his boss. "Stone told me to say thank you, although he shouldn't have had to. If it hadn't been for you and Lev, I'm pretty sure we wouldn't be here. I would be dead, and Stone would be lost." He paused a moment, reviewing his actions. "We went looking for trouble, and we found it. But even knowing there were other We didn't prepare us for what we found." He shrugged uncomfortably, hands in his pockets. "As to how? I'm sure Stone and Jewel will discuss it, and he'll let me know what I need to know."

Her scrutiny made him fidgety, his fingers brushing against the tangled lump in his pocket. "Oh, I forgot to tell you, I have The Brotherhood's rings. I'm kind of surprised they're still here."

"Their rings?" Aundrea echoed, a flicker of conflicting emotions crossing her face as she weighed what that might mean.

"Stone and I have a possible solution for what to do with them," Rhone offered. "But you're the boss here, so it's really up to you."

Aundrea nodded, smiling warmly at her favorite young man. "Let me start with a thank you. You, too, Stone. It's because of your service, and Lev's sacrifice, that The Brotherhood are no more. The entire incident is almost unbelievable, and most people will never know. But it did happen. There will undoubtedly be changes occurring in the Council, and hopefully, it will be good, but only time will tell.

Now, as to the rings," she said, making a nose-wrinkling expression before continuing. "Obviously, you two have thought about it, so before I give judgment on something I know little about, why don't you explain what you two are thinking? Why waste time if it's already worked out?"

"Sure, if you want," Rhone replied, suddenly not so sure. "I know Stone will give Jewel a more detailed account, but the basics come down to two things." Now that he was talking, he became excited, inching forward to the front of his chair. "First off, The Brotherhood's We have been traumatized, much like Jewel was when we first found her. The difference is, these pieces were all part of a bigger stone that had been shattered. The broken pieces were then used to make the rings we have. I figure, that would be enough to twist anybody's mind, but it also severed most of the contact between the pieces."

Aundrea looked worried, "Can Stone help them?" remembering Stone's work with Jewel, and how it had taken time for Jewel to come to terms with the human partnership they now enjoyed.

"Possibly, but there's more," Rhone said carefully. "Stone also offered them their freedom if they helped us."

That made Aundrea sit back, brows gathering as she absorbed the information. "Okay—go on. I'll wait until you're done before I ask questions."

Rhone's brow creased as he considered how to explain. "We were just thinking, if Stone can get one of the pieces healthy again, maybe it would be willing to connect with Bel . . . Captain Belle," he corrected himself, determined to get it right from here on. "Anyway, we thought that with her having her own We, you could make contact whenever you needed."

"I was thinking much the same," Aundrea said thoughtfully. "I've come to think a lot of our Captain Belle. She has a head on her shoulders, and it's more than just her captaining. She has the smarts to go with it."

"I know. She's probably better at it than I was," Rhone agreed, his eyes taking on a faraway look as he remembered he and Bella working side by side, creating an airship from nothing but a whale's bladder.

Aundrea noted his mental drift, and her eyes softened. She knew her young man, and his willingness to take lumps that weren't always necessary.

"Maybe so," she said softly, "but by my understanding, it was you and Stone who came up with the concept and the plans."

Rhone gave a half-hearted smile, lifting his shoulders slightly in acknowledgment. "We did, but honestly, we didn't know what we were doing, even if it worked."

"Which it did," she reminded him. "And now it's Bella's." Her gaze held his, knowing the hit her words brought.

When Rhone finally gave an embarrassed grin, she continued. "It is, and I think she deserves one of the pieces. If Stone finds one acceptable, and it agrees," she added. "I'll not do to them what The Brotherhood did. We owe them that much." Then a gleam came to her eyes. "Can I see them?"

Tell her yes, but not to touch them, Stone cautioned. *I also requested Jewel to refrain from contact. The poor creatures are being blocked at the moment and will need additional instruction before they will be ready for any outside connections.*

When Rhone saw Aundrea receive the go-ahead from Jewel, he pulled his pocket inside-out, dumping the rings onto her desktop.

"They're so beautiful," she cooed, breathing out a long breath as the lamplight sent tiny glints of color scattering across the room.

From my analysis, the smallest one has sustained the least damage, Stone informed both Rhone and Jewel. *It would therefore be my suggestion as a partner for Bella. That, however, would be entirely up to the We.*

Aundrea nodded as Jewel passed her the information, then bent to look closely at the ring.

It is even smaller than I am, Jewel commented happily.

"It is, my beauty. Perhaps it will be a new friend," Aundrea said lovingly."

But not until I have fully assessed its functionality, Stone warned, his comment going to Rhone and Jewel simultaneously.

At least Stone's directive made Rhone feel better, less worried that Bella would have a damaged We to contend with.

"When will we know? Or is there any way to determine that yet?" Aundrea asked, eager for the exchange.

"We'll just have to wait and see," Rhone replied, not waiting for Stone's input. "But just as importantly, we have another idea for the others."

He was feeling smug at holding important information, until Aundrea whispered, "A brain bank? That's an amazing idea. In fact, it might be the most positive concept of the ages," she said in amazement.

Leaning back in her chair, she stared at the coffered ceiling, considering what it might mean. "I have just the place," she whispered, sitting up and turning her attention back to Rhone. "I have a place in mind where they would be free of most human interference, yet collectively in association with each other." Jewel has explained much of the We's history, so it makes sense that they might desire something like it again. What could be better?"

"Unless someone finds them," Rhone commented dryly.

"And even more reason to keep it secret," she commented. "Very few would have admittance, and even then, only those with a We would have the ability to make contact. If they were discovered, they would appear as nothing more than a treasure of gems."

The gleam in her eye said she was well on the way to developing a full action plan.

I could help, too, Jewel said hopefully. *I am very good at keeping lists.*

With the plan all but accomplished, Aundrea rose from her chair. "Now all we need is for Stone to do his magic. And Rhone, you are relieved of active duty until Stone has completed his."

"But . . ."

"I'm sorry, but after what you've been through, I think it's a good thing. Take some time off and let Stone do his work. I'm also quite certain Captain Belle would appreciate a tour around the Capitol Stronghold," she said, giving him a gentle, almost motherly look.

"Yes ma'am, I'll see to it," Rhone said, blushing that he hadn't already considered it.

Taking it as the end of the discussion, Rhone used his shirttail to scoop the rings back into his pocket, but as he turned to leave, Aundrea spoke again.

"Rhone, please give Bella my thanks. Without her, you may well have been . . . stranded."

Or worse, Jewel sent, a pointed thought Stone was more than happy to pass on.

Gee, thanks, Stone. Like I needed that, Rhone sighed.

With a resigned breath, he headed to where The Lady Luna floated at her tether.

CHAPTER 26

Capitalized

Maynard, the old Keeper of Histories, removed the giant key, latching the massive lock into its equally massive hasp. "Well, that should keep out all but the most determined," he said cheerfully. "Remember, locks only keep honest people honest."

"That may be true, but I feel better already," Aundrea replied, laying a hand on her old mentor's arm. "I couldn't think of a better place for these."

"I believe it is as secure an option as you will find," he replied, his rusty voice announcing his advanced years. "No one ever comes to this area of the depository. The information here is so old it's not even remembered, just filed away in the darkness to be forgotten."

He sounded almost wistful, his mind running through the old documents in his care. No one knew how old Maynard truly was, but he was here long before anyone else now employed had been with the OPR. Back then, he had been an agent, but with his mind's almost perfect memory, he had chosen the Halls of Histories as his love. Now, Keeper of Histories, he could find almost any document requested, knowing how and where to find it, as well as most of the information it contained. He was perfect for the job, and Aundrea had used his vast knowledge on more than one occasion.

"Thank you, Maynard. You know how much I enjoy my time with you."

Maynard gave an appreciative grin. "Likewise, my girl, and I'm glad I could be of assistance. I do feel left out of most of the happenings in the world. Now, before I forget, I would like to thank you for the information on The Brotherhood. It has bothered me ever since our conversation about the badlands."

Aundrea graced him with a warm smile, knowing he seldom forgot anything. "Our young man has turned out to be quite a find. It was he who finally turned the tide on The Brotherhood. It may take time, but good does tend to prevail."

"Only if they are extremely careful, and lucky," Maynard said with a chuckle. "Too many are lost, but they go knowing they did right. It is only when the weight of that right finally balances the scale that there is a period of peace, and I, for one, thank you and our young man for your continued service."

"Service I learned from you," she reminded him.

Shrugging in embarrassment, Maynard turned to light the way down the cabinet-lined hallway. He spoke as they walked, arm outstretched, carrying the not-so-negligible weight of The History's lantern. "Do not expect an instant change," he warned. "Those at the top will simply change positions, shifting their power into slightly different locations. Remember, energy never dies. It simply changes form, and power is energy, in its own way."

She could only agree. The thought of the We's stored energy, now sealed safely in the vault, brought a sense of relief. It had been their choice—once she suggested it—but they had been adamant. To the We, it was freedom. A chance to rebuild their connection with one another.

It might take years, but with a lifespan like theirs, years were insignificant. Damaged as they were—emotionally, mentally, and socially—healing would take time. With Stone's help, and his transfer of knowledge about their separation and the full history of the We—they finally had a firm foundation on which to rebuild.

Now it was up to them. Perhaps someday they would be whole enough to seek reconnection with humanity. If and when that day came, they would let Stone know. He would reach out from time to time, just to check on them.

Until then, they were safe.

But safe from whom? Aundrea thought, the chill running down her spine forewarning that her job would always be needed.

"Perhaps we will have a small respite as things shuffle into their new positions," she said hopefully, her attention returning to Maynard and his guiding lantern. With a wistful look, she reached out to her old friend and mentor, touching his wrinkled hand. "I would love to spend more time with you, but I'm afraid I'm needed back at the office. Would you care for dinner later this week? I can make time, as long as I get it in the schedule." She grimaced at the recognition of her position's requirements.

"That sounds lovely, my dear," Maynard replied. "I would love nothing better. My schedule is not much more than blank spaces, so just send a missive as to when and where."

"It's a deal. I'll have Bran set it up," she said. "He knows my schedule better than I do."

They had reached the newer rooms of the basement storage where other clerks were now busily filing and searching documents when Aundrea gripped Maynard's hand.

Thank you, she mouthed, sending her caring love to the man she owed so much.

R hone had spent the day working in his now well-stocked workshop, though it felt strangely empty without Lev's quiet presence somewhere in the background.

Stone had devoted the same hours to the newest We, and had finally given his approval. The tiny crystal had not only endured his exacting tests, it had willingly agreed to attempt a connection.

"That's awesome!" Rhone announced, instantly energized into action. "I know exactly what I'm going to do with it."

Scooping up the dragon necklace, he placed it on his workbench and began the painstaking process of installing the tiny We into its new setting. Even with Stone's guidance, it had taken hours, working to adjust the placement until the crystal's fractured back was all but concealed, giving the intact facets the greatest possible freedom of vision.

Finally, blinking weary eyes, Rhone allowed himself to relax.

"What do you think?" he asked tiredly.

But before Stone could respond, the necklace seemed to take on a life of its own, the golden-pink eye sparkling its pleasure at seeing itself through Stone's vision.

Ah. Very good, little one, but it will take time before you are ready to make the connection, Stone warned, sending the announcement to both the tiny We and to Rhone. Then, in a conspiratorial tone, he addressed Rhone separately. *It looks as though the little one has accepted its* position *and is ready to begin training.*

"That's great!" Rhone said happily. "Bella's going to love it." Then he paused abruptly. "You're sure it's not . . . ahh, you know, got problems?" he asked carefully, not wanting to start on the wrong foot with the little We creature . . . thing.

No, not at all, Stone verified. *I did a thorough examination, including a mental test. Unlike the others,* this piece *was held almost in reverence by its previous owner, and though willing to assist us for its freedom, it does not wish ill on its previous owner. I was happy to let it know he was doing well, though I was careful not to mention, he is now incarcerated for his actions.*

Both parties wanted the partnering to go well, but it would take actual contact before they could tell. It would either work, or it wouldn't. There was no way to tell until it happened. With Stone's training, the little crystal had a great head start and the background information necessary to understand humans, at least better than its previous owner had.

Now, if you will leave us to our training, we shall get on with it, Stone informed his friend.

"Hey, no problem. I need to talk to Bella anyway. I'll let her know you're almost ready."

That is a good plan. Now go. I have work to do.

Smiling at his friend's fervor, Rhone unclasped the collar and laid the two stones together, knowing that physical contact would help the transfer of knowledge. Like the We's original crystalline community, each We was a unique individual, yet connected, granting the ability for a nearly seamless transfer of data.

"Good luck. I'll check back on you in a while," Rhone called.

Once outside, he slid the doors closed, latching the new lock. "Make sure no one enters," he ordered the equally new guard, feeling oddly comfortable in his new role as a boss.

"Will do, sir, and will you be needing an escort? I'm not sure of all the protocols yet, but according to Bran, if I goof up, I'm done for," stammered the obviously concerned guard.

Rhone almost chuckled but knew it was his job to ease the man's entry into the new position. "Thanks, but I'm fine. Besides, this is a personal break, not quite business." But even as he said it, he realized that wasn't entirely true. Bella. . . Captain Belle, would now be part of the OPR's operative community. While not exactly an agent, she would be partnering with a We, a much closer-knit association than any other OPR employee.

Smiling to himself, Rhone made his way to where The Lady Luna hung suspended over the big city. His chest filled with pride as he noticed others' eyes on the gigantic balloon, fingers pointing upward in awe. It really was impressive, even if the bulk of the Capital Stronghold dwarfed it many times over.

"When will she be grounding?" Rhone asked the officer on duty.

"Twenty minutes, sir," the man replied automatically, then snapped to attention as he noticed who was speaking. "She'll be right on time, sir. Don't you worry."

Nodding his understanding, he again addressed the officer. "Please let Captain Belle know that I will be awaiting her arrival at the coffee shop on the corner."

"Will do, sir. Enjoy. I hear it's the best around."

Rhone accepted the comment with a smile and headed for the shop. Twenty minutes. "Just enough time," Rhone said to himself.

He had nearly finished his cup and was absorbed in the newspaper he'd bought from a street lad when a hand touched his shoulder, the feminine voice bringing a smile to his face.

"Too engrossed in the news to even notice me?" Bella asked, studying the headline he'd been reading.

"Not at all," Rhone said, quickly folding the paper as he rose. "Sorry—I was waiting and got caught up in the story. Here, allow me." He was pulling back her chair when he froze, appreciative eyes wide as he caught her outfit.

"Wow. You look great, Bell... ah, Captain," he stammered.

With a calculating grin, she accepted his help and sat, signaling a hovering waiter as Rhone took his own seat.

"A cup of tea, please."

Still awed, and barely able to contain himself, Rhone fidgeted, refolding the paper and glancing around the café as if seeing it for the first time. It wasn't until the tea finally made its arrival and the waiter had turned away that he leaned forward, eager to give his news.

"It's ready," he said, unable to keep the excitement from his voice. "I worked on it all night."

Bella clapped her hands with a very girlish squeal, almost shivering in anticipation. "I was hoping so. I couldn't think of any other reason you would want to meet so early in the morning."

Rhone cringed inwardly at the comment, but her very animation made him catch his breath, remembering other times. But those were long past, before she was a captain. This Captain Belle was anything but the picture one might expect an airship captain to be, if they even considered the issue. Her clip-fronted skirt caught many an eye, legs barely covered, showing her brightly colored stockings above the calf-high boots. Rhone, at least, was somewhat used to the look, but to the other customers, it was purely roguish, even beyond the colorful and odd accoutrements the city folk often wore.

"Finish your tea, and we'll head to the lab," he said, his face coloring at his thoughts. "Stone wanted some time to finish preparing, but really, I think he's just nervous. You know how he loves perfection," he said, grinning conspiratorially.

"Oh, I do miss him. We had such good times," Bella said, her lips forming a tight line of regret.

Rhone nodded in agreement. "We did. Maybe this will make things better."

"Let's go then. I can't wait any longer," and leaving her tea, she scooted her chair back without waiting for Rhone.

Understanding her need, Rhone dropped a banknote on the table, signaling it to the worried-looking waiter who had noted their quick departure. After offering his arm, he led her the few blocks to his warehouse lab.

Waving off the guard who was stepping forward to get the door, Rhone said, "I've got it, but thanks," as he unlatched the shiny new lock.

"Ahh, yes, sir," the guard stammered, eyes going round at Bella's appearance.

Covering a smile, Rhone ushered Bella into the large space, then closed the door. A window had recently been installed in the roof, making the space far lighter and friendlier than its original appearance, and with the floor swept and shelves filled, it was almost homey—which may have been a stretch, but it was his.

"What do you think?" he asked as Bella took in the details.

Bella paced slowly around the space, her eyes taking in every detail. "Looks just like you," she said, then snorted lightly at his confused look. "And where are the toys?"

"Toys?" Rhone said, bobbing his eyebrows enticingly. "Oh, those toys. I've got them hidden. Apparently, you guys got into my stuff while I was gone, so I changed a few things, and hid the rest."

"That wasn't me. I didn't go digging around in your baggage," Bella said, raising her hands in defense. "I was on Luna."

"Alright. I get it. Anyway, I did a little reconstruction since I got back and added a wall."

Reaching for a shelf bracket, he pulled, and the entire wall swung back like a door.

"I designed it after the hidden stairwell I found in the commissioner's vault in Skragmoore."

"And as I remember, that was when you fell down the entire set of stone stairs," Bella reminded him sarcastically.

"Yeah," Rhone grimaced, remembering the painful tumble.

"Hey. I think it's awesome," Bella said, genuinely impressed by his idea.

The door opened onto shelves upon shelves of components—an astounding assortment of gears, shafts, and pulleys and parts.

"So, what are you building?" she asked, reaching, but choosing not to touch anything.

"Oh, it's just stuff," but his lips quirked into a smile as he turned to the back wall.

Bella's eyes grew round seeing the safe built neatly into the wall's framing, then to Rhone as he stood beaming with pride.

"Nothing as beautiful as your necklace," he said happily, "but I'm trying." Then, stepping to the safe, he spun the dial, first one way then the other, before opening the heavy door and drawing out a tray. Inside lay the dragon necklace, its brilliant eye blazing with the light from the sun shining through the window above. "What do you think?" he asked again, setting the tray on the workbench.

"Ohhh . . . It's beautiful," Bella breathed, reaching out with questing fingers. But once again she stopped, looking to him for permission.

Rhone nodded happily. "It's okay. Stone already gave his go-ahead."

Bella glanced from him to the necklace, and back, before slowly reaching out. "Hello. I'm Bella," she said quietly, her caressing finger hovering over the tiny mechanical figure. "I hope we can be friends." But again she stopped, not quite touching the glint of stone set as the little dragon's eye. She heard no words, but a flash of golden-pink flickered brightly in the room, its light shining on the walls in dancing glints and glimmers.

It didn't hold for long, but it was enough. A flow of soft warmth flooded through Bella's mind like the warm caress of a hot bath, soothing her body and her worries. She stood in open-mouthed awe as the unique warmth radiated through her.

I believe she has been accepted, Stone whispered in silence. *I have not trained our little one the tricks, as I did with Jewel. This she has done on her own.*

"It's a girl then?" Rhone asked in surprise, forgetting to think his words during this eventful moment.

Bella responded instantly. "Of course she is. She may not be big like Stone, but she is a perfect lady," her words a chastisement that he would even consider otherwise.

"Ah, yeah. Of course. I just wasn't sure," Rhone said in apology.

"Well, you should have. Why do you think she endured the mis-handling of her former owner as well as she did? We women have always had to put up with the fumbling efforts of men."

Then cuddling the little dragon to her neck, she cooed soft words of love. "We will do just fine, won't we, my little gem? In fact, would you mind if I called you Gem?"

A soft golden glow flared briefly in the dragon's eye before dimming once more to a gentle sparkle.

And she now has a name as well, Stone observed, as though he had made the decision.

But Rhone wasn't so sure. "Jim? But isn't that a boy's name?"

"Oh my gosh," Bella responded in disbelief. "I said, Gem, not Jim. Are you deaf?"

"Well, okay. Gim, or . . . Gem? Never mind. It's good," Rhone mumbled, knowing he'd hear more about it later. Besides, it had always been like that. Bella would name something, and unique or not, it was up to him to agree. Bo, BoToo, and even The Lady Luna, all had been Bella's naming. Gem was just another in what he hoped would be a long line of wondrous creations.

"Be patient, Gem. He's not really so bad. It just takes him a while," Bella explained. "And wait until you see Luna. She flies!" Her excitement bubbled over as she intuitively understood the need to share, well...everything, with her new partner.

Cuddling the little dragon in her hands, she continued whispering soft endearments to the necklace—her friend, her partner, now part of her life.

Knowing it would be useless to try to interrupt, Rhone shrugged, reaching up to rub Stone's collar. *Thanks, Stone. You did a great job,* he said silently.

We did, did we not? It will take time, but with a bit of guidance, she will indeed be a rare gem.

Hey, was that a pun? Rhone asked in surprise. *I didn't know you had it in you.*

Oh, ye of little faith. Stone replied, his purr of satisfaction rippling through Rhone like a flowing stream.

Rhone smiled softly as he watched Bella talk sweet nothings to her new friend and partner. He remembered what it had been like, learning to connect with Stone, and how difficult it had been to see things through an entirely new perspective.

But it had also been exhilarating.

The crystalline We were thinking entities, understanding through thought and connection, while humans learned by action and experience. Not the same things at all. But with Bella happy, he was happy, and with his new position in the agency, and the ability to put his creative thinking to work, life was good.

What happened next would be the future. His, or theirs, time would tell. But for now, that was enough.

The End

Author bio

A multi award-winning author, Strider began his writing after a twenty-five-year career as a firefighter/EMT. The emotions and experiences of those calls carry themselves through every story, bringing true 'been-there' reality to the scenes.

With additional years as a general contractor, designer, big game guide, ski instructor, backpacker, and sword fighter, his wide range of knowledge is intricately woven throughout his stories.

To date, Strider has written YA (young adult), NA (New adult), and general fiction in the realm of: sci-fi westerns, light steampunk, dystopian (post-apocalyptic), gaslamp fantasy (early mechanised era), and just fun reading.

Contact Strider at: DuramenPublishing.com or: <u>DuramenPub lishing@gmail.com</u>

Duramen
Publishing